ADVANCE PRAISE FOR
THE WHISPERS OF WAR

"War is never simple, and its toll is vast and varied. *The Whispers of War* deftly captures the easily overlooked world of a family left behind, and the complexities of their sacrifice, guilt, and love. Bravery, Peachey proves in this timeless narrative, is not just crucial on the battlefield, but at home."

—Gian Sardar, *USA Today* best-selling author of *When the World Goes Quiet* and *Take What You Can Carry*

"*In The Whispers of War*, Anna Pechman navigates life as the daughter and sister of soldiers, but also as her indelible self: an intelligent young woman whose thoughts and actions may be shaped by wartime but not wholly defined by it. Peachey writes Anna and her family with the attunedness and care of someone who knows military life, and who, luckily for us, has the added gifts of insight, empathy, and talent to share it. *The Whispers of War* is a moving, intelligent, beautifully written book. I could not stop reading."

—Andria Williams, author of *The Longest Night* and *The Waiting World*

"Sarah Peachey's debut, *The Whispers of War*, draws a searing line between the September 11, 2001, attacks on American soil to the US pullout from Afghanistan in 2021. Peachey's novel details the growing division and splintering within an active-duty Army family as they wrestle with the impact of America's post-9/11 wars. These struggles not only reflect issues faced by the military community, but those of the entire nation during US combat operations in Afghanistan and Iraq.

The Whispers of War asks, at what point does America demand too much from its small volunteer military, and how many simultaneous wars can our armed forces fight before breaking under the weight of absence, grief, guilt, and injury?"

—Siobhan Fallon, author of *You Know When the Men Are Gone* and *The Confusion of Languages*

"*The Whispers of War* is a beautifully crafted punch to the gut. Sarah Peachey has brought to life the raw emotions of our generation's forever war through a very human lens. It is a powerful novel that speaks with refreshing honesty about the sacrifices our military and their families have endured over the past two decades."

—Julie Tully, award-winning author of *Dispatches from the Cowgirl: Through the Looking Glass with a Navy Diplomat's Wife*

THE WHISPERS OF WAR

PART I OF *THE SCARS OF WAR* SERIES

SARAH L. PEACHEY

MILFORD
HOUSE

an imprint of Sunbury Press, Inc.
Mechanicsburg, PA USA

MILFORD HOUSE

an imprint of Sunbury Press, Inc.
Mechanicsburg, PA USA

For information about special discounts for bulk purchases, please contact Sunbury Press Orders Dept. at (855) 338-8359 or orders@sunburypress.com.

To request one of our authors for speaking engagements or book signings, please contact Sunbury Press Publicity Dept. at publicity@sunburypress.com.

FIRST MILFORD HOUSE PRESS EDITION: January 2025

Set in Adobe Garamond Pro | Interior design by Crystal Devine | Cover by Caitlin Audrey Design | Edited by Gabrielle Kirk.

Publisher's Cataloging-in-Publication Data
Names: Peachey, Sarah L., author.
Title: The whispers of war / Sarah L. Peachey.
Description: First trade paperback edition. | Mechanicsburg, PA : Milford House Press, 2025.
Summary: Anna is an anti-war military child who longs for freedom. Robert is her career-Army father who can't imagine being anything else. Afghanistan is the long war bound to change them once Robert is gravely injured, forcing Anna to place her hopes and dreams on hold. As she learns that more than physical recovery is at stake, Anna must decide if family bonds are enough to heal the wounds of war, or if it's time to walk away alone.
Identifiers: ISBN : 979-8-88819-265-8 (paperback).
Subjects: FICTION / Coming of Age | FICTION / Family Saga | FICTION / War and Military.

Designed in the USA
0 1 1 2 3 5 8 13 21 34 55

For the Love of Books!

For the members of the silent ranks,
who make a whole lot of noise.

And to my children,
who should always follow their dreams.

‖ CONTENTS ‖

‖ AUTHOR'S NOTE ‖

While the stories and people in this book are fictional, the troubles they face and their experiences are real. In the course of my research, I spoke with medically retired service members and their caregivers about injury, interviewed service members who were serving on 9/11, interviewed the 10th Mountain Division's historian for details about the actions of Fort Drum soldiers in Afghanistan, and researched oral histories through the Combat Studies Institute out of Fort Leavenworth's Operational Leadership Experience. These characters' stories are rooted in real experiences of the post-9/11 world. The locations of the specific battalions or where companies deployed are real and match the particular unit's timelines. While the names, narrative, and dialogue are manufactured, the stories are verified.

I chose to root the story in actual events because I wanted limitations on my creativity. I didn't want my imagination to concoct stories that fall too far outside the lines of what combat is, what would be possible, and how it would unfold in a single day. Many combat stories don't include units being pinned down or fighting for their lives daily, though those stories exist (check out the stories of COP Keating and OP Restrepo). Those stories also make for block-buster hits, but they can warp the concept of what combat is for the average service member.

Because of the reliance on real stories to craft my fictionalized narratives, I've included a list of sources at the end of this book. I encourage you to review them to learn more about those who have lived these experiences.

If any historical errors exist in this book, they are my own, either unintentional errors or shifts made to further the story.

For content warnings, please see page 273. For a glossary of terms, see page 268.

‖ EPIGRAPH ‖

To fight aloud, is very brave –
But *gallanter*, I know
Who charge within the bosom
The Cavalry of Wo –

Who win, and nations do not see –
Who fall – and none observe –
Whose dying eyes, no Country
Regards with patriot love –

We trust, in plumed procession
For such, the Angels go –
Rank after Rank, with even feet –
And Uniforms of snow.

—Emily Dickinson, 1890

2021

CHAPTER ONE

WHAT WAS IT ALL FOR?

AUGUST 30, 2021

For the past twenty years, Annaliese Pechman had known a country at war. Today, that war was ending.

Anna was a woman of words, but at the moment, she couldn't find a single one. Strings of consonants and vowels fought to form inside her head, but the sentences failed to encapsulate the moment before her as her lunch grew cold in its Styrofoam container.

She paused at the entrance to the bullpen, the open area in the Fort Polk Public Affairs Office where she'd spent twelve years as a reporter. Four of her fellow journalists formed a horseshoe in front of the TV as phones pinged throughout the building.

"*The last American plane has now flown out after two decades of war. The United States government has not officially confirmed, but I can tell you this. Hamid Karzai International Airport—this is from air traffic control there and this is an official notification sent out and I'm quoting. Effective immediately as of three minutes ago, Hamid Karzai International Airport, or OAKB, is now uncontrolled. No air traffic control or airport services are available. Aircraft operating into or out of Kabul, or landing at the place should use extreme caution. Aircraft should adhere to standard reporting procedures. In other words, according to the reporting of the Associated Press and to air traffic control, all planes from the United States have now left Kabul.*"

They were bearing witness to the first draft of history.

Despite knowing it was coming, the news slammed into Anna, almost knocking her off her feet. The deadline for troops to leave was scheduled for tomorrow, just before midnight, but it had already happened.

It was finally over.

The reporter on screen read off a flurry of three-letter agencies. Split screens with the Pentagon appeared. Scrolls on the bottom of the screen raced to repeat the information. And through it all, the room in Louisiana was silent except for the drone of the television and the echoes of high heels and dress shoes tapping against the tiled floors.

On a darkened airstrip half a world away, Anna knew that American troops had finally stepped onto a dimly lit plane on their way out of Afghanistan. They were the last ones left, and each footstep along the ramp was one step closer to home. Once aboard, they'd shed their gear, get as comfortable as possible in the belly of the giant aircraft, and await their arrival at home.

Soon they would follow that same ramp to waiting buses that would take them to their spouses, to their children, to their families.

More coworkers filed into the room, finding a vacant chair, sitting on the counter beside the printer and copy paper, perching on the corner of a desk or table, or leaning against the walls and doorframes.

"It's been two decades of military deployments. 2,461 Americans killed. 1,144 NATO allies killed. More than 48,000 Afghans killed. 300,000 Afghan soldiers trained, only to collapse when confronted. About a trillion dollars spent, and more to come, to care for the wounded. Afghanistan handed back to the very same Islamic fundamentalists the United States drove from power just weeks after 9/11. A generation of Afghans raised with expectations of freedom and fundamental rights under an umbrella of American protection. It all ended today. A war once called Operation Enduring Freedom, proving to be neither enduring, nor leaving a legacy of freedom."

"Holy shit, it finally happened."

Years of war had created a pressure that formed her thoughts and opinions into diamonds, honed them to crisp edges, and buffed them to a shine. The last few weeks had crushed them to dust, ultimately swept away by the winds of change. The right sentiment, platitude, statement simply didn't exist to define the level of grief, trauma, and sadness her community experienced over the last twenty years of war that almost destroyed her family, her life, and herself.

She could picture tomorrow's headlines emblazoned on the front pages. A few days ago, a newspaper wrote, "All For Nothing" after thirteen service members were killed at the Abbey Gate Bombing. Other outlets began using words like "failure" or comparing the moment to Vietnam.

But this wasn't like Vietnam. It was twenty years of combat operations, even though the government had started using the term "support" during the final decade. This war began with mothers and fathers and ended while deploying their sons and daughters.

"I can't even watch," a gruff voice said beside her.

Gary Greene, her editor and a former Army Ranger, turned toward his black computer screen, dummy pages spread out in front of him. The newspaper plan was the last thing on anyone's mind.

Most days, he'd be in exercise clothes by now to take his daily run around the golf course during his lunch break. But today wasn't a normal day.

Anna's purse had slid off her shoulder, and she readjusted it as she approached her desk, muttering "Excuse me" as she wove through her coworkers. Yet as she stored her purse in the bottom drawer and sat her lunch beside her computer screen, she couldn't find a reason to do anything. She stared at her reflection in the darkened screen, remembering the wounds that changed her forever, the ones that bled for years before finally scabbing over. Left behind was bright pink scar tissue, a lasting reminder of the memories she wished she could forget. But for people like her, the skin threatened to reopen.

She listened as clips that had been running for two weeks replayed. A plane lifting into the sky, loaded shoulder-to-shoulder with Afghan evacuees, barely any room to stretch their legs, departing in hopes of a better life, or something more, of a chance to be who they were in a land that would hopefully accept them.

Unsure of how long she stared at the screen, she rose from her chair and walked down the tiled hallway, lined with front pages and awards for the weekly newspaper, *The Fort Polk Guardian*. Turning the corner into her father's space as the installation's public affairs officer, she found him seated behind his large desk, eyes locked on his own television, his body rigid.

Many times over the last two decades, Anna's family reached this same level of stillness, this exact moment of holding their breaths, unsure of the future, afraid that the tiniest movement would set off a wave of chain reactions, the butterfly's wings that cause a tidal wave across the earth.

She eased herself onto the chair beside him and placed a hand on his shoulder as they processed the scene before them, watching recycled footage of the longest war her father and brother had been sent to fight. Not always in the best way—not always in the "right" way for the people there—but in the way service members knew how, with little guidance from the powerful people who sent them.

Acid burned in Anna's stomach. Each focused inhale and exhale failed to ease her anxiety, and her breathing remained shallow and unsteady. Worry clawed at the back of her throat, but there was nothing she could say that he wasn't already feeling.

A moment of "what's next?" caught them like a mouse in a trap, a quick snap, then held fast. They knew that their experiences with "the next" had tested their determination, *their* hearts and minds, putting them through the wringer, and leaving them to put themselves back into shape the best way they knew how. Perhaps none of them were even back in shape yet—that process might take years longer, sorting through the heavy load of pain, sacrifice, and sorrow.

Tomorrow morning, they would wake up for the first day in twenty years that the United States of America wasn't at war—with anyone—yet they were as shocked as the day it all started.

"It's the end of an era," she murmured, squeezing her father's shoulder.

"An era that lasted too fucking long," he whispered, rubbing his fingers roughly against his knee. "Twenty damn years, and for what?"

"Don't say that. It mattered, Dad, no matter the sacrifice. We may not see it right away, but it mattered."

Over the past few weeks, she and Dad watched as Gardez, Khost, Bagram, and finally Kabul fell, places that knew sacrifice and loss, where their feet had touched the soil, where American blood had spilled. And yet, mixed in with the grief and trauma of decades past, Anna couldn't ignore the sheer relief.

It was over.

It was finally over.

No more would the next generation of service members be left to bear the burden. No more would the current generation shoulder the weight of the conflict. No more would the former generation have to question where they went wrong, whether they could have done more, or if they had done their best.

The war that started when she was fourteen finally ended two months after she turned thirty-four.

This moment should have been one of celebration, and yet the events during the final weeks nagged at her. Many wondered, *what was it all for?*

"Who would have thought the greatest military on the planet would fail?" Dad asked.

"It's the graveyard of empires. The odds were stacked against us."

The newscasters switched to the next story of the day, and Anna lifted the remote from Dad's desk and turned the volume down. Even after all her years as a reporter, it still surprised her how quickly broadcast news could switch from one story to the next, vanishing in an instant while Anna couldn't throw off the weight.

"It's hard to believe that one day created a war that lasted twenty years," Dad sighed.

Anna tilted her head as she remembered the attacks on the Twin Towers and the Pentagon, the plane that had been forced down in a western Pennsylvania field. "No one knew it would happen like this. I remember sitting outside for the candlelight vigils. Do you remember that? The president had asked people to step outside and light a candle. I remember standing on our front porch alone."

He turned in his chair, one eyebrow cocked. "That's what you remember most from that day?"

She twisted her wedding ring around her finger. "I wanted to know we were all in it together, that our town would do everything it could to support us. But it didn't happen that way. People wanted to be angry and demand retribution, to punish people, but they couldn't be bothered to step outside and have a moment of community. Who would have thought that would be the summary of the war? It was like we were invisible."

Dad reached out and placed his hand on top of hers. "I know you felt like that a lot." He patted her hand a few times, punctuating the silence with an ellipsis, more to come, more words to make sense of the sudden end. "The war played out more like—"

"Please don't call this my generation's Vietnam."

"I'm not," he said, raising his hands to hold off her lecture. "But this war didn't affect people like the others. It wasn't the Greatest Generation fighting back after Pearl Harbor. It wasn't young men drafted into a war that shocked people with the death toll."

Anna nodded reluctantly. "And even though the broadcasts out of Vietnam spurred people to protest, I don't think that happened with Afghanistan. Iraq, yes, as you well know." She forced a smile to soften the blow, but he stared into the distance. Her voice grew softer as the stab of humor faded to a grimace. "Our taxes didn't even go up."

"While the military went to war, America went to the mall," Dad said, echoing the slogan passed around service members over the past twenty years.

"What was it all for?" Dad whispered. Anna glanced at him, unsure if he was working it out for himself or interested in more conversation. She waited, but he didn't speak again. He sat hunched in his chair.

For those two decades, American media would write that the country was "war-weary," and it made her grit her teeth. The nation may have been tired of *hearing* about the war, but the war certainly wasn't exhausting their bodies, testing their tolerance, draining them after too many sleepless nights, aging them prematurely, or breaking them down. "Thank you for your service" was uttered as carelessly as "thoughts and prayers" after a tragedy. Yellow ribbons faded in the sunlight, the magnets flaked and peeled off cars, and American flags slowly disappeared.

The American public was now tuning in, realizing the country had been at war the whole time.

As the news showed old pictures of a plane flying over the Afghan mountains, the landscape was firmly imprinted on her mind, mapped out in ridges and valleys, where the people she loved lost bits of themselves. Someone had to tell their stories, to share the tales of woe and heartache, of death and sacrifice, of loss and despair, of a generation left to carry a war that began when they were young and carried on far too long until it was forgotten.

The attacks on 9/11 altered the trajectory of her life.

When her father went to fight.

When her brother deployed in support of the second war.

When she met a soldier, married him, and vowed to follow him in his call to serve.

When she found herself involved as a reporter, reading, editing, and processing the horrific accounts of IED explosions, civilian casualties, and the pain of those at home.

When separation, death, injury, medical retirement, communications blackouts, substance abuse, suicide, PTSD, TBI, and divorce became words whispered throughout her community.

That's when everything changed.

PART I
2001

I measure every Grief I meet
With narrow, probing, eyes –
I wonder if It weighs like Mine –
Or has an Easier size –

I wonder if They bore it long –
Or did it just begin –
I could not tell the Date of Mine –
It feels so old a pain –

I wonder if it hurts to live –
And if They have to try –
And whether – could They choose between –
It would not be – to die –

I note that Some – gone patient long –
At length, renew their smile –
An imitation of a Light
That has so little Oil –

I wonder if when Years have piled –
Some Thousands – on the Harm –
That hurt them Early – such a lapse
Could give them any Balm –

Or would They go on aching still
Through Centuries of Nerve –
Enlightened to a larger Pain –
In Contrast with the Love –

—Emily Dickinson, 1896

CHAPTER TWO

DREAMS FOR THE FUTURE

SEPTEMBER 11, 2001

As the pipes rattled in the walls, Anna rolled over in her bed, the sky still dark, the birds silent. After fourteen years of moving from place to place, there was one thing she knew for sure. Before signing a rental agreement or buying a house, she'd turn on the faucets and wander the apartment, hoping for quiet or, at the bare minimum, only the sound of rushing water. Then, she'd wander the halls and rooms, testing out the floors, listening for any creaks. If she found even one, she'd move on to the next place.

After seven homes, she wanted one that was peaceful, restful, and comfortable.

Her alarm clock flicked over to six as she heard the hallway floors groan under Dad's weight as he headed for the door, starting his morning run without delay.

That was another thing she'd nix from her future—the military. Dad had been serving in the Army her entire life, and with all the coming, going, unknowns, restarts, and separations, one thing was certain: This life wasn't meant for her.

Yet again awake at an hour she'd rather ignore, she tossed the thick covers back from her bed, pulling a fleece blanket from her chair and wrapping herself in its warm embrace. She flicked on the desk lamp in the corner, shuffling textbooks and school folders to the side, straightening her Emily Dickinson bobblehead, and making room to open her leather-bound journal. After sliding the satin ribbon from its prison between the pages, she eyed the crisp lines, unmarked with her latest thoughts.

While she'd typically light a candle—a nod to Emily's time—Mom had taken the matches and hidden the candle stash last month after Anna left one burning when she went to school. Instead of her favorite lavender candle, Anna inhaled the scent of her journal.

This was the time she craved. It was when she dreamed about the future, the years she'd spend as a best-selling author, or saving endangered animals in China or India or Tanzania, or urging people to save the rainforest, or volunteering with the Peace Corps.

What a word—*dream*. An action word or a describing word, with numerous definitions attached to each. Her favorite, though, was *something that fully satisfies a wish*.

Sure, Mom often told her she could use her time before school more wisely. Why not pick up the dirty clothes all over the floor? Why not straighten the books on her shelves or make room for the ones stacked in the corner? And, for the love of God, couldn't she manage her closet?

But who wanted to bury themselves in chores when there was quiet time to *dream*? Dad understood it—but he'd only recently gotten back from Kosovo, so he was too busy absorbing his time at home to care what precisely that home looked like.

She shook the thoughts from her head and ran her tongue against the roughness of her braces. Now was not the time to fret about anything but filling the empty pages.

She twisted her gel pen between her fingers, a small glob of ink on her thumb, wondering where to start today. Right now, on a September morning with the sun just beginning to brighten the sky, the day felt rife with opportunity, with *possibility*.

Birds chirping filtered through the crack in her window, and she smiled. *Hope is the thing with feathers* . . .

And so, with birdsong as her symphony, she charted out her possibilities with the hope that she could—no, *would*—make it come true.

||

Robert Pechman's morning started as it always did, following his usual routine, rain or shine, whether in frigid winters or muggy summers. He woke at 0530, grabbed his first cup of coffee, and then started his five-mile run at 0600 on the nose through the small community of Watertown. Headlights snaked down the road beside him as blue-collar workers headed out for the long day ahead. He swept through the town as it slowly rose with the sun, past the First Presbyterian Church, its steeple standing sharp and straight, down to the public square along Arsenal Street, around the Soldiers and Sailors Monument, erected in memory of those who fought in the Civil War, to South Massey Street, veering onto Holcomb, before finishing back up Washington, carving out a large rectangle in the slowly brightening morning as the stars dimmed in the light.

He lived for those quiet mornings, the chance to have the town mostly to himself as his feet pounded a steady staccato on the pavement. It was him, his breath, and his muscles racing against the clock to see how quickly he could finish his five miles.

As he approached his apartment building, reminiscent of the Flatiron Building of New York City, he slowed his pace, then walked a circle around the parking lot as his heart steadied. He lifted the hem of his shirt to wipe the sweat from his face as the sun crested the surrounding hills, lighting up the buildings as the rays cascaded over the surface.

He let himself in the main entrance, following the stairs to the third floor, and opened the unlocked door. Once inside, he gently twisted the deadbolt and slipped off his running shoes before walking to the kitchen.

"Morning, Dad," his son—his oldest—said over a bowl of Cheerios.

"Hey, mornin', Garrett. Your sister still sleeping?" Robert lifted the hot coffeepot, scheduled to brew while on his run, and filled two mugs, splashing creamer into one.

Garrett shrugged. "Haven't seen her." He twisted his wrist to check his watch. "She's gonna be late if she doesn't hurry it up."

"I'll get her." Robert slipped a finger into each ear of the mugs and carried them into his dark bedroom, placing the lighter one on the bedside table, where Katherine was still dozing with an arm tossed across her face. The scent of coffee would wake her before he could.

In the weeks since he'd been home, he got the kids out the door when his schedule allowed. This let his wife catch up on precious sleep after burning the midnight oil surrounded by textbooks.

He approached his daughter's room, where the bed was empty, a sheet half hanging from the footboard, a pillow prostrate on the floor, while the desk chair held a lump coiled tightly in a blanket.

Robert knocked softly on the doorframe. "Hey, get a move on, kiddo— you're gonna be late."

A groan sounded as a hand emerged from its fabric, index finger raised. Robert stood, tapping his foot against the floor, silently urging her to *move already*. On three separate days last week, she only made it on the bus because they ran.

Anna finally sat down her pen and spun in her chair to face him. Papers and books coated the surface of her desk, and more books were on shelves throughout the room. "Be out in a minute."

Robert tried to sweeten the deal. "I'll grab a quick shower and then get some breakfast going for you. Sound good?"

She stared at him for a moment, the only movement a raised eyebrow. "Breakfast sandwich?"

"Will that help you get dressed and ready faster?" He checked his watch. "Because if so, it's a deal."

She threw off the blanket, racing to her drawers and digging past layers of black clothing.

Robert chuckled as he turned toward his bathroom to get ready for another day of work.

He showered and shaved, pulled on the green, black, and brown Battle Dress Uniform he wore as part of Charlie Company, 1st Battalion, 87th Infantry Regiment at Fort Drum, then kissed Katherine's forehead. She paused mid-sip to squeeze his hand before he headed to the small kitchen to prepare a quick breakfast for Anna, who, he was pleased to see, was brushing her hair, dressed and otherwise ready.

The kids were only a few years apart and couldn't be more different. Garrett was fair-haired; Anna was dark. Garrett preferred a light breakfast, while Anna was happiest with a full stack of pancakes, or eggs, meat, and hash browns filling every square inch of her plate. (He still wondered how a girl her size could put away as much food as a soldier after a week in the field.) While Anna enjoyed her alone time and only had a handful of friends, Garrett was a social butterfly who surrounded himself with friends. Anna had an organizational system all her own and perpetually ran late, but Garrett was neat as a pin and early to everything. Anna was a creative free spirit; Garrett was logically inclined and regimented.

To Robert, they were perfect: the light of being home, the thing he missed whenever he was gone. Whenever he had a slow morning, he made the most of it with his kids, to Garrett's despair and Anna's delight.

"What's on the docket today?" Robert asked as Garrett put his bowl in the dishwasher.

"I have soccer practice after school and a paper to finish up. Mom said she'd mark it up today so I can make the final changes tonight."

"Good, good. She'll enjoy that." Katherine was currently attending night classes toward her bachelor's and, eventually, a law degree. "What's the paper on?"

Anna rounded the corner and didn't miss a beat. "Is it about how a control freak can learn to loosen his hold?"

Garrett leaned against the counter, crossing one neatly tied tennis shoe in front of the other. "No, actually it's a process analysis paper covering how you can go from the messy slob you are to learning how to put things away for once."

Remembering Katherine's scolding to *not* laugh at the snark between their children, Robert swallowed his building chuckle. "All right, you two."

"Maybe it should be about how to remove the panties up your—"

Robert placed a hand over her mouth. "Not another word."

Garrett snickered, shaking his head, and Robert glared before returning his attention to the stove. The eggs were a little more done than he'd wanted, but it sure beat the powdered kind he'd had plenty of. He lifted the fried eggs from the pan onto the waiting toast before topping it all with shredded cheddar. Anna squeezed herself between the boys and poured a small glass of orange juice.

"We should head out if we want to be on time," Robert said, after yet another time check, before wrapping the sandwich with parchment paper.

Anna gave him a mock salute, a sloppy one at that, while she chugged the last of the juice, some dribbling onto her shirt.

"Gross," Garrett muttered with a shake of his head, slipping a backpack onto his shoulders.

Anna swiped at it with the back of her hand and wiped it on her pants as she walked into the living room to retrieve the hoodie she'd thrown over the couch the day before. Robert resisted tapping his foot or checking his watch as she searched for her Converse high tops under the armchair by the door.

"They're in the closet, Anna," Katherine's tired voice said from the darkness of the hallway. She entered the living room, wrapped tightly in her terrycloth bathrobe.

"Why were they in there?" Anna asked, finally shoving her feet in her shoes, then sitting to tie them.

"Because that's where shoes go, baby. Not right in front of the door where we all have to trip over them."

Anna's eyes drifted to the side in the beginning of an eye roll before focusing on her shoes.

That was a close one, Robert thought as the corners of his mouth quirked up. He slipped an arm around his wife's waist and kissed her cheek. "I'll be back in a bit."

"You aren't heading straight in?" she asked him.

"Late call because of the range time last week. What, you don't want to share a cup of coffee with me?" he joked.

That earned him a smile. "I'd love to. All right, kids, give me hugs before you go," she called.

Anna kissed her mother on the cheek after a brief hug, while Garrett sighed, bending slightly to place a kiss on her other cheek. Katherine opened the door to let them out and called, "Do good and be good!"

Anna rolled her eyes in full this time, fortunately waiting until she was facing away from her mother, while Garrett strutted ahead to lead the way.

"You best never let her catch you doing that," Robert said as they headed down the stairs. He handed Anna her sandwich, which she gratefully accepted.

"She's been telling us that since kindergarten."

Robert shrugged. "You follow orders every day, though."

"What does she think I'll do at school?" she asked around a mouthful, a string of cheese caught on her lip. "I go to my classes, take a break for lunch, then head home. When is there time to do bad and be bad?"

"One day, kiddo, you'll see that bad people will always find time to do bad things."

Anna shook her head. "You don't have to talk to me like a little kid. I know there are bad people out there. You didn't go to Bosnia or Haiti or Kosovo for nothing."

"You know I always go to help the good guys, right?"

As they stepped out into the September morning, Anna settled a trucker hat on her head. "Yeah, yeah, I know."

"We should be home until next year at least. That'll be a nice change."

Anna shrugged. "You're almost done, though."

Robert adjusted his patrol cap. "Something like that."

For him, military service was in his blood, and he often wondered which side of the military equation he would fall on—the one that grew from it or the one it destroyed.

His great-grandfather served with the 3rd Infantry Division—the Rock of the Marne—the storied division that fought the Germans back from the Marne River and held the line, allowing Allied forces to manage an offensive and turn the war around. He came home, had a gaggle of kids, embarked on adventures, and discovered new hobbies until he died at the ripe old age of ninety-three. Robert only had a handful of memories of him and his pale blue eyes, unfocused once blindness struck him late in life. Robert always sat across the table from PapPap, and somehow, the old man's eyes struck straight to his core. Perhaps the old man saw more than anyone thought.

His paternal grandfather served during World War II, parachuting into Sicily with the 505th Regiment. He never spoke much about his service as a devil in baggy pants, but he lived with vigor for the rest of his life. He poured his energy into his grandchildren, never sharing war stories but always willing to create a tale at bedtime before tucking them in and promising pancakes or eggs in the morning.

On the flip side, Robert's father served early in Vietnam as American involvement was growing, and he came home with shell shock and a habit of heavy drinking, which put him in an early grave. Robert remembers him as withdrawn, sometimes mean, and a victim of his service.

Robert shook off the memories of long ago, grateful that things had been different for his own children. When Katherine first found out she was pregnant as a senior in high school, Robert knew he'd be there. They'd eloped, he'd enlisted, and together, they swore that family would be everything. And even though Robert was called away time and time again, he always returned and made his wife and children his focus.

Anna finished her sandwich, folding the paper in half and shoving it into a side pocket on her Jansport backpack, then brushing off her hands on her jeans.

"I'm thinking of signing up to write for the school paper. The deadline's today, and I think I'd have fun doing it."

"You'd be good at that. You're always scribbling away in that journal. You could do that for the Army after you graduate."

She eyed him in that way that said *are you serious?* "Dad, no."

He held up his hands. "I'm just saying."

"I've been doing the military thing my whole life. A break might be nice," she said with a shrug.

"You could always come back to it after a few years. Get your degree, commission . . ."

She raised an eyebrow. "Dad, seriously, no. Not for me."

Robert crossed his arms and checked if the bus was coming down the street. "Never know, you might find some handsome soldier who sweeps you off your feet."

She rolled her eyes—one day they'd roll right out of her head—then shoved her hands into her back pockets. "No thanks, Dad. But you can try talking to Garrett. He might be more interested."

They leaned forward to peek at Garrett as he propped himself against a light pole, talking to his friends. Then they caught each other's eye and laughed. While Robert loved the thought of Garrett carrying on the family tradition, the boy was destined for different things. He had his life planned out, year by year, probably including when he would get married and when his first child would be born. He would never fall into service with its unpredictability, constantly changing plans, and endless lists of shortcuts to doing the right thing the right way.

Robert rubbed his hand over Anna's hat, twisting the cap and pulling her hair across her face. "Don't make fun of your brother."

"You started it!" She gave him a not-so-gentle shove as she straightened herself up.

As they waited for the bus, Anna talked more about the newspaper and how she'd like to write about improving lunch quality, canceling standardized testing, and diversifying after-school activities beyond sports.

"So Op-Eds, huh?"

"Op-whats?"

"Op-Eds. Opposite the editorials. People write about the things they feel passionate about with a bunch of evidence to back it up. It's like an opinion piece, but the authors usually either know a lot about what they're talking about or have a unique perspective on the issue. You'd be good at that with all the schools you've attended."

"I guess moving has been good for something then, huh?"

Before Robert could respond, the bright yellow of the school bus appeared around the corner. Garrett's eyes met Robert's, and he gave a simple head nod.

Anna wrapped her arms tightly around Robert's waist.

"Good luck today, Anna. I'm sure you'll do great."

She waved at him and made her way to the line of kids waiting to board the bus. Robert smiled as he remembered how, when he saw them off for their first-ever day of school, the kids practically climbed those big steps. Now they could walk up them, almost fully grown. Robert rubbed at the tightness in his chest as the bus door closed, catching Anna's still-smiling face through the tinted window as the bus puffed down the street toward their school.

Robert made the brief walk home in silence, soaking up the cloudless morning and the quiet he knew he couldn't enjoy once he got to work.

He climbed the last few stairs of the apartment complex and was immediately hit by the blare of *The Today Show* from the living room television. Katherine was finishing her breakfast, ready to sink into the morning's segments, before spending the rest of her day studying in preparation for her night classes. She gave Robert a finger wave from the couch as Matt Lauer introduced an author talking about his book on Howard Hughes.

"I love you, baby, but that's loud as hell. Wanna turn it down?"

"Language, Robert!" she scolded, grasping the remote and turning the television to an acceptable level. Time overseas or in the field too long can turn any soldier's mouth foul, and Katherine made it her duty to civilize him whenever he returned. When Robert came home from Bosnia a few years ago, she introduced a swear jar. A quarter per cuss word. Once it reached ten dollars, she got to plan her ideal date, and Robert had to sweep her off her feet. She still didn't know he often threw in double or triple the fee so he could surprise her.

He kissed her cheek now that he could hear properly.

"This book sounds interesting," she said, rubbing a hand against his arm. "It would make a great movie. CIA plots, defense contracts, all the famous women he dated."

"Oh, yeah? Sounds like a busy guy." Robert entered the kitchen, only half listening as Katherine continued talking about the book. He pulled the coffeepot from its warmer, poured a dark stream into his mug, then leaned against the counter to take a sip.

"Huh, that's odd," Katherine said, joining Robert in the kitchen to refill her cup.

"What is?"

"They cut away from the interview, saying there was breaking news at the World Trade Center, then went to a commercial. Do you think it's another bomb?"

‖ CHAPTER THREE ‖

THE NEXT GENERATION'S WAR

SEPTEMBER 11, 2001

"We have a breaking news story to tell you about. Apparently, a plane has just crashed into the World Trade Center in New York City. It happened just a few moments ago."

Robert leaned an ear toward the living room, half listening to the television and half hearing Katherine as she shifted into thinking aloud. Now he wished he hadn't asked her to turn it down.

He held up his hand. "Hold on a second." He walked back into the living room and paused before the TV, one hand on his hip.

"Can you please tell me what you saw, and can you give me any information about what's going on there?"

As the caller spoke to Katie Couric, Robert saw thick black smoke pouring out one side of a tower, debris floating through the air like confetti, and his throat tightened. He swallowed against it as he listened. *How does a plane crash into buildings like that?*

"Katherine, come in here."

She came around the corner, and her eyes caught on the television screen. Her free hand flew to her chest. "Oh my God—was it an explosion?"

"They think a plane crashed into it."

"What? How? No pilot can be that bad."

They'd visited the city with the kids over the summer, and he pictured the layout in his mind: the harbor only a short distance away and the towers standing tall above the surrounding buildings. How would a pilot hit something like that? Had they lost control of an airliner? Was it a tourist plane?

"We're getting reports that an airplane hit the building."

"Oh, I didn't even know that."

Robert pulled his eyes from the screen, staring into the depths of his mug. He heard Katherine's heavy sigh as she leaned against the back of the couch. He glanced at her as she rubbed her hands against her cheeks, her eyes focused on the television.

"There's so much smoke. How will they get everyone out of there?"

"I don't know, hon."

Lines of strain appeared on her face as the news consumed her.

"We are looking at the north side, and that is where the largest hole is."

"How does a plane leave that large of a hole?" Katherine asked, eyes wide.

Robert shrugged. "Maybe it wasn't a plane."

"But people are saying it was."

"Early reports can be wrong."

"Could a tourist plane do that much damage?"

Robert could only shake his head slowly, eyebrows raised, as they watched the lick of flames reaching toward the higher floors of the building.

They stared in silence for long minutes as the news hosts and the person on the phone—a different one now—referenced the bombings of the World Trade Center in the early nineties. Then Robert watched a speck move in from the right corner of the screen.

"What the hell is that?" Robert whispered to himself as he lowered onto the arm of the couch.

It was a small black triangle, like a fly on the TV, but it was moving diagonally toward the center of the screen.

"That's a fucking plane," he said louder, horrified.

It faded from view for only a few seconds when someone on the TV said, *"Oh my God,"* followed by a lull, then *"Oh, another one just hit,"* and a puff of smoke rose from the lower-left corner of the screen in the other tower.

Cameras that were zoomed in on the first hole abruptly pulled back in time to catch a fireball exploding from the second tower.

"Oh my God, Robert." Her hand flew up to cover her mouth.

"That looked more like a 747."

"This isn't a fucking accident," Robert said. He swallowed against the panic.

"I wonder if there are air traffic control problems," someone on-screen questioned.

Over the years, he had learned that when the unthinkable happens, people will grasp any explanation to avoid the truth. They're happy to bury their heads in the sand, make excuses, turn the blame in other directions, but they often can't see what's right in front of them. But military people were different. They didn't have the choice to hide from it—they were trained to respond to it.

While the reporters speculated, while Katherine questioned, while the images played out on the screen, Robert sat back, sipping from his mug, and knew what it all would mean.

"They must be terrified, being so close like that, watching it from their window." The corners of her mouth tilted down. They were safe three hundred miles northwest of the site.

"There won't be a soul out there not watching this by now."

Then the cameras cut to a previous recording from another angle, showing a full-sized airliner—a passenger plane. Robert's gut twisted.

Katherine inhaled sharply, and her hand squeezed his.

Robert's voice shook as he spoke. "You know what this means, right?"

She stared at him. "We don't know anything yet."

"Kay, it's a 747, for God's sake. It wasn't an accident. Tell me you know what this means."

She shook her head as she stared at the ceiling, tears rising in her eyes. "You're going to war."

He gently squeezed her hand. "I should head in." He kissed her cheek, and when he tried to turn away, she reached for him and pulled him back, wrapping her arms around his waist and cradling her head against the divot of his chest. They held each other that way for a long moment, the television droning in the background, delivering the news that would be difficult to process in the coming days. But at that moment, for a brief blot of time, it was the two of them, their love forming a barrier against the horror of what was ahead. They froze themselves in an etching of the present so they didn't have to consider the next. If they held onto one another, they wouldn't have to think about the unknown. They could simply bask in the scent and feel of the other, the comfort that comes from familiarity in a life of uncertainty, the calm that comes from the nearness when they would spend months apart, the confidence that comes from a love that is nurtured for decades to carry through the difficult times.

He slipped from her arms, kissing her firmly on the mouth, and she held onto his hand as long as she could, not ready to surrender him for others to use as the Army had trained him in the past. His fingertips slipped from hers like a heavy rope, leaving her frantic to pull it back.

He watched as tears rose in her eyes, a drop sliding down the curve of her cheek, and he knew it was for the pain on the horizon, her worry for him, and for the separation from their children. How many times had they done this already? The winds were changing, swirling together to form a hurricane, and his family was defenseless in its path.

By the time Robert arrived at his platoon's building, another plane had crashed into the Pentagon, and he stepped into his role, taking a headcount and talking them through the uncertainty.

The south tower collapsed as leadership was called into a meeting, and Robert's eyes skirted over the faces of the young soldiers in his platoon, some only a few years older than his son. Those soldiers had never seen war, only accustomed to training and pretending. There was the specialist with a baby on the way, the sergeant who got married the previous month, the private who had only graduated high school a few months before, and the corporal applying to college. They would be the ones to fight the battle in a country they had never heard of, against a people they were unfamiliar with, who spoke a language few were fluent in, with customs they didn't know, to complete an unclear mission.

It was up to him to prepare and lead them.

II

The bell rang as Anna shoved her binder into her backpack, ready to head to the next class of the day—chemistry. Kids jostled each other in the hallways, students trying to squeeze between walls and people, backpacks making them wider than usual. Some students were grouped in the hallways, a few crying.

Anna turned the corner to enter the classroom where a usually blank television was alive. An icy line followed her spine, raising the hair on her neck. The Twin Towers were on fire, thick black smoke pouring out of them and stretching across the sky. She remembered seeing them over the summer, but they were barely recognizable from her view inside her classroom.

The high-pitched voices suggested panic, and the long pauses signified fear. Even her beloved Emily Dickinson didn't have the words to describe this level of tragedy.

A girl in the front row had a hand over her mouth and tears in her eyes.

A boy pleaded in front of the teacher's desk, asking to go to the office to call his dad, who lived in the city near the site.

James, Anna's best friend, leaned against the front row of desks, close to the TV, listening intently.

Anna's mouth dropped open as she timidly stepped closer, as if the nightmare before them would somehow spill into the classroom. "What happened?!"

"Planes crashed into the towers," he answered, his eyes never leaving the screen.

"Both of them?"

"No one knows why, but they think it was on purpose."

A reporter interrupted to say a plane had also crashed somewhere in Pennsylvania when the image vanished as the screen went black.

"That's enough now. Please go to your seats and open your textbooks to page forty-six."

"Are you serious, Mrs. Stewart? With all that's happening?" Anna responded, pointing at the television.

Their teacher frowned and observed all of her students before shaking her head. "I'm sorry, kids. The school wants the TVs off. They want us to keep things normal."

"How the hell is this normal?" James asked, gesturing to the screen.

"I'm sorry. I have to follow the rules sometimes, too. Come on now. We'll make it a fun lesson."

The class was supposed to spend the day experimenting on pennies, turning them gold, green, and some as shiny and bright as if freshly made. Anna couldn't focus. James kept muttering things about the motions, the steps, the chemical reactions, but Anna was certain she wasn't the only one who wouldn't remember the lesson.

The bell finally rang, sending the students to their next class, and James followed along.

"It's crazy, isn't it? I mean, how did this happen? Who would do something like this?"

"None of it makes sense."

To think she started her morning pondering the prospect of hopes and dreams.

James stared at his shoes as they moved toward the classroom door. Now they were in a rush, too. The hallways were quiet, students whispering, more crying. Where kids would usually linger against the lockers or have hurried conversations walking down the same hallway, everyone walked with purpose, intent on getting to the next class, hoping a teacher would break the rules.

Anna's classmates were lucky enough to find a reprieve in their European History class. Mr. Reinhart strode to the front of the room, arms crossed, a reporter's voice booming, as Anna and other students quickly filed in and sat at their desks. Backpacks flopped to the floor, some sliding into the aisle, ignored as eyes focused on the screen. Multiple images were showing now: the Twin Towers in worse shape than before, and now the Pentagon on fire.

"This is horrifying," Anna whispered.

"This is history in the making, and your generation will be the one to deal with the fallout," Mr. Reinhart said, gesturing with the remote control. "I have only one thing for you to do this class period." He walked to his desk and picked up a pile of lined paper, handing a few sheets to the students in the front row to pass backward before lifting a box of envelopes and passing them out, too.

"What do we do with these?" James asked as he smoothed the paper on his desk.

"Watch and reflect," Mr. Reinhart responded, pacing before the blackboard. "When historical events happen, we think we'll remember them forever. Unfortunately, we don't—bits and pieces fade over time. I want you to write yourself a letter. I want you to remember what happened and how you felt today, something you can share with your children when you have them, something you can reread in twenty years and revisit. Seal it up, and put it somewhere you'll stumble across it occasionally."

Anna held her pencil loosely between her fingers. How could she possibly put together all that this might mean? She was fourteen, for God's sake. What did *she* know about international relations or war? That was for people in suits to figure out. If the rumors on the news were true—if this was intentional— would it lead to war?

I measure every Grief I meet with narrow probing eyes . . .

While she scratched her pencil across the paper, writing about how her life might forever change and how others' challenges would be of "easier size," the news kept its constant updates until a student shouted, "Oh my God!"

Mr. Reinhart gasped from behind his desk in the corner.

Dozens of students stared at the screen, mouths agape.

A heavy silence hung thick in the air, settling on their shoulders.

It was like a movie's special effects at work. Hot metal bent and twisted as it fell. Great plumes of smoke released into the air. People raced to escape the growing cloud that nipped at their heels.

But this was real.

A crack sounded near Anna, and when she inspected the noise, her pencil's point was broken.

▮▮

An announcement eventually came over the school's loudspeakers, dismissing the students to board buses that would take them home after only a few hours spent at school. Anna picked up her backpack and made her way to the door. It was as if, the whole day, voices droned on, making noise but without words.

Shortly after that, the last tower fell.

She and James stepped out of the classroom, descending into the mass of students, hundreds of them filing out the handful of doors that led to the buses.

He slipped his arm through hers as they often did, but neither spoke. They overheard their peers planning to hang out after school or sharing their worries that more planes would crash, that the day's attacks weren't yet over.

Anna wasn't scared of *that*, wasn't *connected* to that—she had no reason to be—but everything felt wrong. How long would it stay that way? Were they shifting into a new reality, a clear delineation between the before and after? A place they would wander, running their fingertips over the things they knew yet didn't fully understand.

"This is crazy," James said quietly.

She pushed a lock of hair behind her ears as the wave of people carried them forward. "I don't understand what's going on. It's weird to see teachers scared, you know? How are *we* supposed to feel?"

He squinted at her and tilted his head to the side. "Are you okay?"

All she could feel was the twisting of her stomach, the rise of it like driving over a hill too quickly, that tingling of unease. "It's a weird feeling, I guess."

"Maybe it's what our parents felt after the *Challenger* explosion or what our grandparents felt after the Kennedy assassination."

She nodded but remained quiet as they boarded the bus. How could she explain that this felt like something even more significant? It was like waking in the middle of the night, remembering she had a paper due or a test the next day. It was that feeling of her stomach dropping, unease and tension veering through the thoughts as they ricocheted in her head.

Years later, she would remember this moment, the dread she felt then, the depth of unease that didn't make sense. It was as if she saw it through a mirror, the pain that would rip through her body as the glass blew apart, the grief that would consume her soul in its aftermath, the worry that would steal her sleep, the restlessness of the waiting, and the loss that would leave a hole she could never fill.

"You want to hang out at my house?"

"Nah, I should probably get home." She glanced back at Garrett, who was still at the bus stop talking to his friends.

James walked her home, then cut between the yards to Nana Mackey's place, while Anna climbed the stairs in her building, slipped her key in the door, and bent to remove her shoes when Garrett came in behind her.

She waved to him as she hung her backpack on the hook and shoved her shoes into the closet. They sat on the torn leather sofa, and Garrett propped his feet up on the coffee table and turned on the television.

Things hadn't improved. Rescue efforts had started in New York and Washington. Crews were on-site in Pennsylvania, but everyone figured there wouldn't be survivors. The news was saying the passengers may have forced it down. She frowned as she watched and listened, unable to shake the feeling in her gut.

From the corner of her eye, she kept seeing Garrett glance at her, then back to the TV, as if she were playing ping-pong with the screen. She bit the inside of her cheek so she wouldn't snap at him, silently scolding herself with the Pechman motto: *Family over everything.*

"Hey, you wanna play chess? I can dig out Pop's set."

She hated when he did this, acting as the never-rattled, nonchalant, I-can-handle-any-chaos big brother. Yes, she was rattled from the day, but did he always have to step in to make things better? Emily would be hunched over her desk in dim candlelight, quill in hand, recording her feelings as they flitted through her mind, not playing chess and tuning everything out.

And yet, she found herself nodding. Anna would be mature, seize Emily's wisdom, and process the difficult information. While she waited for him to return with the set, she watched the ticker scroll along the bottom of the screen until she saw a name.

"Who's Osama bin Laden?" she asked.

She botched the pronunciation—oh-SAM-uh bin LAY-din—unsure how to string the various syllables together, emphasizing the wrong parts of each name. She'd never heard it before.

Garrett returned to the room, frowning, a Styrofoam box in his hands. He corrected her pronunciation, then explained as he opened the box and pulled out the crystal board. "He's the head of a terrorist organization called al-Qaeda." He held one chess piece of each color. "You want to be white or black?"

It wasn't so much black or white as frosted or clear, each piece made of heavy crystal. She tapped the clear piece. "The news said they're who attacked us. I never heard of him before. Where'd you hear about it?"

"Dad and I have talked about them," he said with a shrug as he set up the board. "Bin Laden supposedly helped set up truck bombs outside of some American embassies a few years ago, and he killed a lot of people. The building in Kenya was there one minute, the whole damn thing gone the next. They bombed an American destroyer last year, too."

"I don't remember any of that."

He finished setting up his frosted pieces, then set up the clear ones for her. "We'll learn more about al-Qaeda in the coming days if it was them."

"What'll happen?"

His hand slowed as he set a rook in the corner. "Probably a war, Anna. I mean, look at that." He gestured toward the TV. "You don't think people will want to get back at whoever did it?"

"Maybe. But war, Garrett? The last one was the Gulf War."

"I don't know. Al-Qaeda isn't a country—it's a group of people spread throughout a region."

"Where would the military go?"

"I don't know. Once we know who did it, we'll send people straight to them. It won't take long to find out."

Their conversation halted while Garrett discussed the rules. While Pop could spend days playing with Garrett, Anna struggled to sit still and think five moves ahead. She listened to her brother review the rules anyway, trying to ignore the thoughts rolling through her head. The Army would send the infantry first, as they always did, which meant Dad could go. And at that moment, the knife she felt in her gut twisted, and the dread and unease she'd tried to hold in finally flowed out.

Dad would be leaving again, and soon. This time, though, it would be for war, not peacekeeping missions or to help in humanitarian crises.

He'd be sent to kill people.

A chill rippled down her spine as she watched Garrett shuffle pieces, demonstrating how each one moved, but no sound escaped his mouth. Her ears were stuffed with cotton. At that moment, she realized how little she understood when she was small, how she had never considered what her father did. She saw the crossed rifles on his uniform. She knew he carried a gun. But somehow, she failed to string together that it meant he would be tasked with taking another person's life.

Garrett picked up the remote and lowered the volume on the TV, watching her out of the corner of his eye. "Ready to play a round?"

She nodded and cleared her throat, forcing her eyes to bring the pieces into focus, and they began. She asked questions, like how many spaces a pawn could move at a time, whether or not bishops could jump over her pieces as knights could, and which specific directions a queen could move.

He quickly defeated her.

"Let's play again, but tell me the rules one more time," she said, moving her pieces back to their starting positions. "Best out of three."

She'd do anything now to stay focused on the game.

Garrett sat with one leg under the other, and his foot on the floor wiggled up and down, rattling the couch and making a few pieces dance in their squares on the board. All movement ceased, then he met her eyes. "I think I'm gonna enlist after graduation."

Anna dropped her pawn, and it hit the board with a crack before rolling across the open space and onto the floor.

As if the first declaration about Dad going to war wasn't enough, the knife had now been yanked out, leaving her bleeding across the couch.

"*Why*, Garrett?" she asked sharply.

He bent down to pick up the stray piece. "We're going to war whether people want to or not."

"Why do you have to go, though? This is the one we were supposed to sit out."

"Dad will get it. I mean, Dad, Grandpa, Grandpa Pechman, and then his dad? What will I do after graduation anyway?"

"Literally anything. Come on, Garrett, you're smart. You could do anything you wanted: finance, law, hell, go to medical school. You have all this potential—you don't need to pass it off to the military. You can do it for *yourself*."

He stared at her. "I don't want to do any of those things. The thought of endless school sounds like hell. The men in our family have always stepped up—"

"Oh, shut up. Even if it's what the men have always done, it doesn't mean you have to. You can break the cycle."

"What if I want to be a part of that legacy, huh?" He left the game unfinished and walked back the short hallway to his room.

The door clicked shut quietly, and then Anna was left alone, the news cycling replay after replay of such a tragic day.

She held her face in her hands. Every nerve in her body begged to fire, to activate the muscles to swipe her hand across the board, to knock every piece to the floor, to watch the glass shatter, and maybe chip the crowns off the queens or an ear from the knights. Instead, she carefully picked up the pawn that had fallen to the floor and nestled it gently inside its space in the Styrofoam. She continued with every piece, then wrapped the board in a cloth and pressed it into its square in the packaging before closing it all up. She held it in her lap for a moment, the quiet of the apartment buzzing in her ears, then left the couch in favor of the comfort of her own space. She walked past Garrett's door, where music was kicking on, then closed her own, leaning the chess set against her dresser. She fell onto her bed and wrapped her arms around the teddy bear that James had won her at a fair during her first fall in New York.

The memory of that day from three years ago chased the chill from her body, and the corners of her mouth pulled up. They'd been seated next to each other in their sixth-grade classroom and instantly bonded over the new Harry Potter book he was reading. She couldn't wait to ask him what else he enjoyed, and before she knew it, they were chatting at recess, over lunch, and on the way to the bus. He'd been delighted that she was only a short walk from his house.

As the weather cooled, the trees turned beautiful colors—golds, umbers, and rusts—coating entire hillsides. It was the first time she'd seen anything like it in person, only experiencing the southern autumns that were a blip and gone, only a few trees changing color rather than an entire hill. James showed her around the local fair, saying it was something she *had* to do, something a local couldn't get enough of, so she went. They gorged themselves on sweet funnel cakes, crispy French fries that burned their tongues, and cotton candy that left their fingertips and mouths sticky. James had thrown a few softballs into a milk jug and let her choose the prize. The brown teddy bear was soft and large enough to tuck under her pillow. She didn't sleep with it at night (she wasn't a baby, after all), but the smooth fur was a comfort.

For the last three years, James had become a refuge. She frequently sought him out, longing for his perspective that wasn't tainted by the military, to know she could be a typical teenager with him. It might not have been what Emily would have done, but it was okay for her to be wrong about *something*, right?

James and Anna had spent many evenings at Nana Mackey's house, the two of them chasing lightning bugs in the summer, attending every festival they could find in the fall, braving feet upon feet of snow in the winter (after he helped her find the appropriate warm clothing), and welcoming the first hint of spring as the frost melted away.

Music boomed in Garrett's room, interrupting her reflection. Everything was about to change, and it was a freeze-in-place, suck-the-breath-from-your-lungs fear. She squeezed the bear more tightly to her chest before releasing a long exhale and leaving her room.

She knocked hard on Garrett's door and cracked it open as Led Zeppelin's "Immigrant Song" poured from the room.

"Can we talk for a sec?"

Garrett let her in, then sat back on the bed and lifted the needle from the spinning vinyl, giving her the freedom to take control of the conversation. She held the bear in front of her, shielding herself from the potential explosion.

She rubbed her toe across the carpet, avoiding his eyes. "I don't want you to be mad at me."

Garrett nodded stiffly. "What do you want me to do about it?"

As much as she wanted to scream, *don't enlist, you could die, I can't lose you*, she knew she couldn't. "There's so much happening right now, I can't keep up."

Garrett swiped his hand down his face. "That makes two of us. I don't know how I'm gonna tell Mom."

Anna's head spun so quickly that her hair swung and hit her in the face. "What do you mean you don't know yet? You always have a plan." This wouldn't be the first time Dad left, and Garrett had always powered through it. He was responsible. He was dependable. He was level-headed and calm, even in tough situations. That's what their family was all about—they'd pivot when needed, intent on supporting each other.

"Today, I don't want to be in charge. If you don't want to be treated like a kid, don't walk in here squeezing a teddy bear and looking like someone kicked your dog."

As he spat daggers, Anna backed away. Would he leave her floating in the ocean without a life vest or raft, nothing to help her feel secure in all the uncertainty ahead? That's what family was for, wasn't it? She didn't want him to think of her as his bratty little sister, so she gathered some strength, settling her heart, her brain, and the pumping of her blood.

He sighed heavily, swiping the back of his hand against his forehead. "I just . . . I want to sit here, listen to some music, and tune out the bad news. I want to be angry like you, but there's enough of that going around, so I'm gonna be quiet. At least until I can think."

He paused for a long while, and Anna understood what he wasn't saying. Things might get bad in the coming days, and once Dad left, it would get worse. Once again, Dad's voice would be missing from home. It would be back to emails, broken phone calls, and brief communication like when he was in Bosnia and Haiti and Iraq.

"There's still a chance Dad might not go," Anna said, holding on to her last sliver of hope.

He laughed humorlessly. "You don't get it, do you? Dad's unit's been all over the place the last few years. He'll probably be one of the first to go."

She crossed her arms. "You don't know that."

He tsked, turning the dial on the stereo and sitting back against his pillows as the music—quieter this time—drowned out the silences between their phrases.

"For all we know, it might not even last that long."

Anna scoffed. "You have no way to know."

"Anna, it just happened today! Nobody knows *anything*."

"Then shouldn't you take time to think this through?" She stared at him, but her vision grew blurry as tears rose in her eyes and her voice flattened under the weight of emotion. "I don't want to go through the next few years without you *or* Dad. I want us to be a team—like we've always been."

Garrett let out a long exhale, and his voice softened. "I already told you I'll think this through."

Anna pulled the strings of her hoodie back and forth. Once again, he was trying to reassure her. Her concerns were valid and she had a point in all this bickering, that Mom would struggle if Dad and Garrett were both gone. But he'd never tell her so.

Now who's acting like a child?

She pulled the hood up over her hair, and her shoulders slumped. "I'm not ready for Dad to leave again."

Garrett stared at the floor. "I know. We'll get through it, though. We always do."

"Yeah, we're straight-up pros."

Garrett gently punched Anna on the shoulder. "Hey, we'll make it," he said with more feeling.

"Dad hasn't been in combat in a long time. Almost all his soldiers have *never* been in combat. No one's ready for this."

"The military will send the best people while training everyone else. Then, they'll start sending the other people."

Anna shook her head. "I'm not ready for this."

This time, Garrett stayed silent as the opening strains of Staind poured out softly enough to keep conversation open. Then, he lay back on his bed to listen, closing his eyes.

Anna watched him, unsure whether she should stay or leave. Of course, he would be adult about it, even if it meant faking his way through, never letting on to his concern, but in that small apartment, she saw the first few cracks in his facade. Would he slowly crumble if she left? She folded herself into a ball on the bean bag chair in the corner, still clutching the teddy bear to her chest and leaning her face against its soft fur. The two sat with their thoughts of the future, soothed that at least they would be together for a little while before any difficult decisions had to be made.

That Friday, the president called for a vigil, asking communities to light a candle on their front porches or sidewalks or driveways or balconies and observe a moment of silence. Anna watched the clock count down to the right time, a small candle in her hands and a long lighter—one Mom didn't hide—at the ready. When the clock chimed, she carried her candle outside, sat on the stoop of the apartment building, and carefully lit it.

Dad was still at work, Mom was at her night class, Garrett was out with friends, and she sat alone with her candle, watching for her neighbors to step outside, too, to observe that sense of community and togetherness everyone was talking about on the news when they weren't showing the pictures of the faces still missing.

Only James joined her, appearing from between the tall pine trees across the street, his hands tucked in his pockets. He sat beside her and put an arm around her shoulders.

"You good?" he asked her.

She blinked rapidly and tried to catch her breath. "I'm scared."

He studied her for a moment. "I know."

She tucked her face into his shoulder and cried.

|| CHAPTER FOUR ||

GOODBYE IS THE HARDEST THING

OCTOBER 1, 2001

For the coming weeks in the Pechman apartment, deployment loomed, a dark cloud overhead, impossible to ignore. It filtered into every corner of every room, growing more prominent as the days passed.

War was imminent.

It had been a month since the attacks, and Anna couldn't escape the media coverage of Al-Qaeda, bin Laden, terrorism, or Afghanistan circulating on news networks. Newspapers were still piecing together every aspect of the day, creating timelines and infographics to help readers understand how everything happened right under America's nose. Anna had diligently cut out the timelines, placing the cuttings into a manila folder. Special operations units were already arriving in Afghanistan, and rescue operations were still underway at Ground Zero, where the towers had stood.

While some of her classmates ignored the coming war and how closely it was converging on their home, while Mom ducked her head and tried to distract her children, Anna was bearing witness. Last week, she'd checked out a book from the eighties on Afghanistan's war with the USSR and learned how the United States had armed the Mujahideen to fight a common enemy—the Soviets.

The enemy of our enemy wasn't our friend after all.

She'd received a book about the various sects of Islam from an interlibrary loan, trying to understand the differences between the Sunnis and Shia. The information was confusing, and there wasn't much on Afghanistan in the nineties, when the Taliban gained control of the government. Her searches on Al-Qaeda turned up complicated academic books she struggled to understand.

Closer to home, planes landed on the airfield at Fort Drum and lined up on the tarmac, drawing the attention of local media, who kept questioning when those planes would move troops to the Middle East. Soldiers stood watch on CQ duty, guarding the exterior of the barracks. The installation gates closed to the public, and security increased. Word spread among the 1st Brigade Combat Team that 1st Battalion, 87th Infantry Regiment would be the "lucky" unit flying to Uzbekistan and landing at the Karshi-Khanabad Airfield, known as K2.

Soon after the special operations forces deployed, Dad came home with a packing list and handed it to Mom without saying a word.

Anna walked down the narrow hallway made narrower with piles of olive drab bags, footlockers, and gear—vests, belts, gas masks, uniforms in various colors, extra boots—and peeked into her parents' room. Mom had flipped over a basket full of laundry, picking up pieces one by one and folding them just so before adding them to neat piles at the end of the bed. Her movements were slow and measured with a grace Anna lacked. If not for Mom's careful clothing origami, Anna would shove her clothes into a drawer only to come out wrinkled and creased. But Anna caught a change in Mom: heavy sighs and shoulders pulled a bit too high. When was the last time Mom had said goodbye because of *war*? More than a decade ago.

The cloud loomed, thick and heavy.

"Want some help?" Anna asked.

Mom glanced over her shoulder, shaking a T-shirt out before lining up the bottom hem to fold. "If you want to. Go ahead and grab from the messy pile. If it's black, it's probably yours."

Anna smiled at Mom's soft voice, the hint of southern drawl that was always so soothing during bedtime stories and nighttime lullabies. Despite numerous shopping trips and guiding Anna to shades of teal, periwinkle, or even navy, a close friend of black, Katherine Pechman couldn't get her daughter to wear anything except the absence of color. Emily wore all white most of her life, so why couldn't accident-prone Anna choose black? It suited her.

Spotting some socks near the top of the pile, Anna dug through to find a match, pinching the waistband of Garrett's underwear between her fingers and tossing it closer to Mom.

"Annaliese Marie, those are clean! It's not like you need to worry about cooties." A hint of a smile quirked up the corner of her mouth, but it didn't reach her eyes.

"Still gross, Mom."

"I've got the shirts if you want to focus on the socks."

"Thanks for the confidence in my folding."

"It's just easier, sweet pea."

Anna finally found the matching sock, aligned the two neatly, then twisted them into a ball. *Not too shabby.*

"How was school today?"

Anna shrugged. "It was fine. I think it's mostly back to normal now."

"It's so much at this age, watching your world change. You're just kids." Mom shook her head sadly.

Anna dug through the pile of clothes. "I guess so."

"I remember the end of the Vietnam War and the start of the Iran hostage crisis. It was like the ocean evaporated, and countries I'd never heard of were suddenly right next door."

Mom's experience was also compounded by the installation near her hometown of DeRidder, Louisiana. Fort Polk was the key location that trained soldiers in Tigerland before sending them to the jungles of Vietnam, and the post still trained soldiers today.

Anna stayed quiet, so Mom kept going. "I saw the books in your room."

"I want to understand where Dad's going."

Mom balled up the underwear in her hand, dropping her arms to the bed. "You don't have to do that. You'll understand more than all your classmates even without that. The war comes home, too."

Anna frowned. "I'm only getting the lowdown." *Maybe then this will all make sense.*

"That isn't always a benefit."

"I can't ignore it."

"I'm not asking you to, but you don't need to dig into it either. Sometimes ignorance is bliss. If I focused on everything he's doing and asked myself all the same questions, I'd never leave my bed."

Anna tossed the clothes aside. "But it's war, Mom. It's different than other deployments Dad's had."

"I know that, sweetie, but I've been doing this a long time. If you focus on it too much, you see nothing else."

"I don't get it. Whenever you see your friends, you talk like it's no big deal."

Mom sighed and smoothed the comforter before sitting on the edge of the bed. "I have a responsibility to those women, just like your dad has to his men. But I worry about your father every time he leaves. Everyone else is worried, too, so there's no sense adding to it. The newer, younger spouses need to see our strength right now. But I can tell you that I'll cry when he leaves and I'll worry about him every second he's gone."

Anna watched as Mom inspected the room. Dad's decreasing presence was unmistakable. Gone were the family photos he kept on the mirror—only stray pieces of used tape showed anything ever hung there—a few gummy outlines to guide their replacement next year. Dust surrounded a clean rectangle on his nicked bedside table, marking where his Bible always sat. Even the laundry on the bed was missing his military socks and uniform shirts.

They spent yesterday evening toting gear upstairs from the storage area in the basement. The Army had swapped out the BDUs for Desert Combat Uniforms, a muted, smudged mixture of beige, light green, and dark brown, a sharp contrast compared to the darker shades of before.

But Anna's stomach twisted as she remembered that the hazards in the hallway that attracted her big toe would soon be gone.

"When will he go, Mom?"

She swiped a hand across her forehead before standing and folding again. "The date keeps changing, but we think it'll be about two weeks from now. That can always change again, though, so we have to be ready in case it does."

"I wish they couldn't move things around."

Mom's eyebrows scrunched up as she tried to smile. "Me too. But you know the saying about the Army . . ."

"If the Army wanted you to have a family, they'd issue you one," Anna quoted. "That's dumb."

"It's the world we live in, baby. We have to make the most of it."

Anna sighed as she dropped onto the bed. "I get that, but there's no time for it. Dad's always at work, and when he's home, he's packing."

"We document the little things."

Anna rolled her eyes. "It gets old always having to make memories."

"But you don't want to look back and realize you wasted the time."

Anna picked a clump of lint off a brown sock. "What was it like when Dad was in the Gulf?"

Mom thought for a moment. "It's been ten years, but I remember it was challenging. Garrett would have been about . . . six, and you were only three. Fort Bragg was far from Grams and Pop, but they visited all the time. They'd plan all sorts of things for you and Garrett, and I'd sit in the quiet of the house. It was still a combat deployment, but Haiti and Bosnia were harder for me. You and Garrett were older, and you needed more of me."

Anna curled a thread from a T-shirt around her finger. "It never seemed hard for you."

Mom pressed down a neat stack of underwear. "We do what we have to to get by."

"I guess so."

After folding a black T-shirt, Mom handed it to Anna. "Dad got you this to wear when he leaves."

Anna didn't need to open it to know what it was. "I don't know, Mom . . ." Yet another unit T-shirt. She never wore them; the bottom drawer of her bureau was stuffed with shirts from toddler size on up.

"It's black . . ." Mom said as if that would be enough to convince Anna to take it into the light of day. "I think it'd mean a lot if you wore it to say good-bye." Mom picked up a stack of laundry and held it out to Anna. "Think about it while you put these away."

"Yes, ma'am," Anna mumbled. She balled up the shirt and stuck it under her arm to take the clean clothes to her room. She was probably one of the few military kids who tried to hide her connection. As she set the clean items on her bed, she let the shirt fall open. There was the mountain in the background, the ice pick and ski pole, the long tradition of the 10th Mountain represented in twelve square inches of a cotton shirt. The inverted crimson horseshoe mocked her. Didn't everyone know the horseshoe should be open at the top so all the luck stayed inside? Nothing like mocking the universe.

Anna crumpled the shirt into a ball, shoved it in the back of the drawer (where she hoped to forget it), and slammed it closed. Her gaze then settled on her journal. While the leather cover housed her hopes and dreams for the future, it also reminded her of those that were dashed as her life veered off course—again. The dream of being an artist went up in smoke when she left Fort Bragg at five, and the community painting classes were left behind. The dream of being a poet like Emily faded to nothing after leaving Fort Polk at eight and the writing camp that filled her soul. The dream of being a marine biologist was dashed when she left Schofield Barracks at eleven, sea animals hours away now rather than a short walk. The lid was slammed closed on the dream of being a concert pianist when the only piano teacher near Fort Drum insisted that students only play on a real piano, not a keyboard. The full-sized instrument wouldn't fit in their apartment, let alone make it up the narrow stairwell.

She'd been thrown into this life, and no one else was flipping through that journal to see all she'd aspired to and still wanted to be. The Army always came knocking, and it was her duty to make do. But a small part of her cursed it, and refusing to wear the unit T-shirt was her small act of defiance, of not letting the Army bleed into her wardrobe and claim that as it had marked her furniture with scuffs and scratches.

But still, deployment nagged at Anna like a splinter under the skin. Whether she liked the Army or not, her father would leave in two weeks.

II

In the weeks following the attacks, Robert learned that everything was urgent: training exercises to prepare service members for combat, weapons proficiencies not to check a box but to ensure a barely adult person could shoot another human being from a distance, relying on muscle memory to do the work rather than a thought process. It was about controlling the second-guessing, the humanizing, the morality struggle. One slip-up could make the difference between killing the enemy and sending you or your buddies home in a box. They needed to shoot without hesitation.

Every hour was filled with meetings, and if there weren't meetings, there was training, and if there wasn't training, they were packing too many items into too few containers. Those moments were essential to a platoon, where every soldier needed to understand their role and their duty. Robert handled most of the details involving the soldiers, while the lieutenant handled most of the elements coming from the company commander. The section sergeants ensured their sections were squared away, leaving the squad leaders to watch some of the younger soldiers more closely. The younger soldiers did their best not to disappoint anyone, and prove they could manage themselves and their responsibilities. No fuck-ups this close to the real deal.

Despite it all, the young Joes' eyes were fresh, filled with the excitement of finally getting to do something. At that point, combat wasn't something to be afraid of but to prepare for, a way of cementing bonds that would outlast their time in-country.

Lieutenant Mike Conlin entered the shared makeshift office, dropping his green book onto his desk. The slim journal was filled with notes from his morning meeting. He rubbed his strained eyes roughly, then dropped into his chair. "You wanna sync up, Sergeant?"

Robert sat back in his seat, crossing his fingers over his stomach. "Sure thing, sir."

These syncs were a daily occurrence, happening at the start of the day and then again at the end. Both Robert and Lieutenant Conlin connected the information they received from their various areas of responsibility to ensure they had everything in order.

"Everyone needs to get to medical and dental today to make sure they're squared away. They'll get shuffled through quickly, but if anyone needs anything, the offices can get 'em rolling."

Robert nodded his head and let Conlin keep talking. The LT was a kid, twenty-three years old, only a year post-college, four months into his time with the platoon. To civilians, it would be odd to have someone so much younger and inexperienced leading the platoon, but it was the norm in the military. The noncommissioned officers had the experience and used it to guide their platoon leaders, though the LTs made the final calls. A good LT usually understood that he needed to sit down and shut up, but some would walk into the office that first day and give all the instructions while ignoring the guidance. Conlin was a mix of the two. He knew what he didn't know—an admirable trait—but he also had his own way of doing things, clinically seeing the big picture rather than recognizing the real-life scenarios.

It worried Robert and some of the squad leaders, all men with at least ten years of experience compared to Conlin's one. And while the young man had plenty of training in tactics and decision-making, it was all in planned scenarios that often made it obvious which choice he should make. There was no "fog of war," no chaos around him to stir up his thought process, no real sense of urgency of being shot at or having to shoot back, no shouting over the sounds of fighting.

"We also have ACS coming by to go through deployment paperwork. They'll cover wills, powers of attorney, and financial information and answer any questions. We want to get all those papers turned in today."

"We'll get it done. Sergeant Rodriguez was in finance before the Army, so he's been explaining some things to the guys."

Conlin's head jerked up from his book, and he frowned. "Oh, good." There was a momentary pause. "Which one is Sergeant Rodriguez again?"

Robert schooled his features when he'd rather pound his fist on the desk. "The weapons squad leader, sir." There were fewer than thirty people in the platoon; shouldn't he have known all of them and their positions by now?

Conlin nodded his head absently. "Right, right. Well, Sergeant, I'll leave you to it. We'll sync up again at seventeen hundred."

"Roger, sir." Robert scratched at his cheek and let out a heavy breath. He had hoped there would be more time to get Conlin settled in with his soldiers—it had already been four months, after all—but now time was something they didn't have unless it was time waiting. There was plenty of that.

Robert left the office and walked to the open area inside the company's headquarters. "All right, listen up. Squad leaders, take your soldiers down to medical and dental for any incomplete paperwork. Once those are signed, bring 'em back, and we'll hand 'em over. This afternoon, you'll sit in a briefing by ACS, and we'll do some more paperwork to get your finances and things in order. If you have a spouse, you'll need to decide what powers of attorney you need and get those signed. JAG will be here to help with that, too. Any questions?"

Private Jack Kowalski raised his hand, and Sergeant Rodriguez immediately shook his head. "Don't do it, Ski. Don't you do it."

"No, it's all right. I asked. Go ahead, Ski."

"Uh, Sergeant, when do we actually get to start doing things?"

Robert chuckled despite his better judgment, and Sergeant Rodriguez rolled his eyes. "Ski, have you ever heard the saying 'hurry up and wait?'"

Kowalski peered at the people closest to him, who shrugged. "No, Sergeant, but I think I can figure out what it means."

"Welcome to it. Now get moving. Y'all know where you should be."

They stood, and Robert watched as Sergeant Rodriguez caught up to the young private, then leaned in and likely scolded; Robert couldn't hear it, but he knew it well enough.

Even if the LT was an uncertainty, Robert at least knew the soldiers would be ready to go. That mattered most of all. Two weeks would feel slow to them but the blink of an eye to their families.

October 5, 2001

For Robert, the days had scrolled by like a time-lapse, quick glimpses of emotions and events, most a flurry of undefinable experiences and deep feelings. Duffel bags, footlockers, and backpacks no longer littered hallways or bedroom floors. Headquarters buildings across the battalion were quiet and empty except for the rear detachment that would remain behind. Vehicles were safely stowed or already on their way to Afghanistan. The planes were readied for flight on the airfield. Cars and people were everywhere in the parking lot across from the hangar, spilling along the roadways and into the overflow area across the street. Children were decked out in red, white, and blue, hugging their parents' legs, sucking thumbs, or clinging to stuffed animals. Couples held each other with heads tilted closely, lips meeting in soft, slow kisses. Some young soldiers simply held their wives as they cried.

A light fog cloaked the airfield in the dim light, and the rising sun glinted off the numerous planes lined up on the tarmac, a beacon for their departure. Colorful leaves demanded the sun's attention, glowing in yellows, oranges, and reds, and the cool morning was as crisp as the leaves that now cloaked the ground.

Robert and his family had arrived early. There would be soldiers who didn't have family in the area, who instead said their goodbyes to parents or girlfriends earlier in the morning over a telephone, sharing one last conversation and a litany of assurances as they prepared to board a plane and eventually go to war. Robert would shuffle them away from the displays of families as they waited for the others to finish their farewells.

But he had to say his first.

II

Anna watched Mom climb shakily out of the car once Dad was out of eyesight, but she wasn't yet ready to move. Her seatbelt was still on as she listened to the muffled conversation outside the car. Garrett, always the helper, always the one with his shit squared away, was already shouldering some of Dad's bags, helping to carry them to the drop-off area across the street near the hangar access. And still, Anna sat.

The door beside her popped open. "C'mon, sweet pea. Time to get out. Let's put on a brave face, okay?"

The two weeks passed in a blink, and Anna couldn't remember a single special thing they'd done. Mom had tried to be supportive, always searching for the bright side with her positivity that bordered on toxic. While Anna had accepted it as a child, it no longer worked.

Mom glanced over her shoulder. "Anna, your dad'll be back over in a minute. Let's do this right, honey."

As she leaned against the car, Anna could make out Dad's head—always the tallest one in the room—returning to them. She pressed the seatbelt's release button, then finally pulled herself from the vehicle. Her elbow bumped Mom's hands, and that's when Anna noticed how dark her unpainted nailbeds were, the line of white that extended halfway, how pale her knuckles were. Garrett's face was a mask, void of emotion, as he walked back with Dad, but her brother's hands were clenched in tight fists at his sides. Anna did her best to contort her features into nothingness, what would be expected of her, rather than frustration, sadness, worry, and even anger.

How could she say goodbye to the one person in her family who so easily understood her? The one happy to treat her as an adult and entrust her with information. Mom and Garrett had always relied on distraction.

Let's play a game together!

How about we watch a movie?

Dinner out sounds good tonight, don't you think?

Come hang out at the park with me!

It made her wish James were here.

She breathed deeply, trying to release the tension that had settled in her shoulders, forcing them closer and closer to her ears. They wouldn't budge.

Worry—to harass by tearing, biting, or snapping, especially at the throat.

That definition suited best of all.

She pulled her jacket tighter around her body as Dad approached. It was as if he were a mirage, a figment created out of smoke, and as soon as she touched him, the wisps would separate, and his face, his body, his presence, would disintegrate, evaporate, disappear. Dad put a hand on her shoulder, guiding her and Garrett to the edge of the parking lot, farther from their mother.

"I want you both to know how much I appreciate you helping your mom over the last few weeks. Make sure you keep stepping up while I'm gone. Help her around the house, don't give her any lip, and if she asks you to do something, you handle it." His gaze rested heavily on Anna.

Garrett's chest puffed out a little while Anna cowered from the responsibility. It wasn't as if she didn't help Mom or step up in the day-to-day. Why couldn't he say how much he wanted to stay with them, how he hated to leave them? Anna was sure he felt those things, too, but would it kill him to say it now when she needed it most?

All around them, fathers crouched to hug toddlers, their arms almost wrapping around the children twice, and Anna was jealous. Jealous of their innocence. Jealous of how easily they could cope without a parent. Jealous of how little responsibility they'd need to take. Jealous of how many people would support that tiny child who had no idea what was happening in the world or what their father's job meant.

"All right. I need to make some time for your mother. Give your old man a hug." As one, Garrett and Anna stepped into his embrace, their bodies filling the circle of his arms. Tears rose in Anna's eyes as she focused on how much she would miss his warm embrace, how much her father's comfort would leave a hole no one else could fill. Dad kissed her head, and Anna clung to him a few seconds longer, his uniform blouse caught in her hands.

She felt Garrett back away, but Anna squeezed Dad one more time.

"It's okay, kiddo. I'll be hanging out somewhere far from the action."

He meant the words to be soothing, but it was more than the danger, more than the war itself.

"I'm going to miss you." Her voice broke on the last word, and Dad pressed another kiss to her head.

"It'll be over before you know it. Start writing some letters and send them all to me at once when you get my address. I'll read them slowly." He ran a hand along the back of her head as it rested against his chest, her hair catching around his fingers. "It'll all be okay."

Anna sniffed, then stepped back from him, nodding in response to what he said, but already the tears had broken the floodgates. No amount of willpower could hold them back. Dad grabbed her hand, holding it between his larger ones.

"No fear, sweetheart. I love you."

"I love you too, Dad." Then she stepped back, giving him space as Mom approached.

When Anna reached Garrett, he was leaning against the hood of the tan sedan, his hands twisted together behind his back, staring at the asphalt beneath his feet. "It's gonna be fine," he proclaimed.

Sucking in deep breaths, Anna tried to stop the tears that blurred her vision. She settled her weight on the bumper. "I wish everyone would stop saying that."

Garrett tapped his foot against hers. "We're all saying it because it's true."

Yeah, until it isn't.

She refused to meet his eyes, staring off toward the distant hillsides, allowing the tears to evaporate in the autumn breeze. The cool air cut between her fleece jacket and her neck, making her shiver. She pulled the zipper up higher, tucked her hands into her pockets, and slouched into her safe haven of warmth while she watched her parents say goodbye. Dad opened his arms wide as Mom walked into them, and she watched their bodies fit together cleanly.

Anna knew Mom was crying when Dad touched her face with his thumb, likely wiping away a tear.

Anna pretended not to see, but she was engrossed by the display. Hadn't everyone been saying it would all be okay? Hadn't Mom said being strong was most important? Despite all those confident words, Mom was slowly breaking apart.

When her parents kissed, Anna finally turned away, giving them peace in their moment, but no matter where she focused her attention, she was invading someone else's private goodbye.

Children cried as fathers walked away, the men doing their best not to show their sadness, tension in their shoulders as they refused to turn back as toddlers yelled "Daddy!" with the hope that their dads would simply turn around and return to them. Wives held each other as husbands gave one final wave and moved toward the tarmac. Mothers forced themselves to release their sons, their faces taut as their little boys walked away, slowly morphing into men.

Garrett scooted closer beside Anna until his shoulder touched hers, and she leaned more against him, each of them a crutch to hold up the other.

"This sucks," he whispered.

Anna could only nod as she watched Mom's shoulders shake. Her hand slipped from Dad's grasp, but she remained in place until Dad was out of sight. Then her back slowly straightened, she wiped her eyes, and she turned back toward her children.

"Is my makeup running?" she asked when she was beside them.

Anna's eyes moved over Mom's face, amazed at the mask she'd skillfully put in place. "You're good. Go do your thing."

Mom offered a half-smile before approaching a small group of wives a few feet away. One had a toddler on her hip, while another had an infant seat at her feet. Two other women wrapped their arms around each other, and all four watched the uniformed bodies grow smaller and smaller until they disappeared.

Anna couldn't remember any of their names, but judging by Mom's stopping to chat, they were married to men within Dad's platoon.

"The day finally came," one said.

Mom offered the woman a side hug. "If there's anything you need, Amber, let me know. That goes for all of you." She rubbed a hand up and down the toddler's arm. "Anna was about this sweetheart's age when Robert deployed for the first time."

"How are you so calm about this?" one of the childless wives asked. Her mascara had run down her cheeks, and her eyes were bloodshot as she sniffed.

Mom dug in her purse for a pack of tissues, pulling one out and handing it to the crying woman. "That's the million-dollar question, isn't it? It doesn't get any easier, saying goodbyes, but you get better at dealing with it. Take your time for the first few weeks—God knows the rest of us will. We're all in this together."

While the words may have soothed the young wife, Anna only hoped they were true.

2002

For each extatic instant
We must an anguish pay
In keen and quivering ratio
To the extasy –

For each beloved hour
Sharp pittances of Years –
Bitter contested farthings –
And Coffers heaped with tears!

—Emily Dickinson, 1891

|| CHAPTER FIVE ||

OPERATION ANACONDA

MARCH 1 AND 2, 2002

"You will never forget this," Colonel Frank Wiercinski said after climbing atop a Humvee in the glare of floodlights on the night before the largest combat operation ever conducted in Afghanistan. "You will never forget that man or woman on your right or left. You will never forget the fact that you stood here in Afghanistan."

It was either late in the night or early in the morning, but Robert knew better than to check his watch for confirmation. For the last five months, Robert and his fellow soldiers of 1-87 Infantry did nothing but wait and feel useless. Still, as they waited in formation outside the hangar with the rest of the soldiers, readied for their mission that was about to begin, they found their purpose. It had been wet and cold and exciting and frightening—it depended on who you asked.

In a few hours, the rest of Task Force Rakkasan would board three Chinooks, escorted by six Apaches, that would drop him and his company at the top of a mountain on the southern edge of the Shah-i-Khot Valley.

"A lot of us have two questions always going through our minds," the colonel continued. "You may be asking yourself, 'Why?' and, 'How will I do?' As for each why, each and every one of you has to answer that for yourself."

They were dressed in their DCUs with rain gear as the colonel shouted from the dry protection of the hangar over the tattoo of precipitation hitting the thick GORE-TEX. Robert's breath rose in front of his face with each exhale.

"For me, it's 9/11: For those families that watched as their loved ones never came home. For those firefighters, emergency workers, and police officers who charged up rather than came down. It's for them. We do this for them."

In a matter of hours, the 10th Mountain Division hoped to climb to glory in partnership with the Rakkasans out of Fort Campbell, and anticipation bubbled in Robert's chest. He couldn't wait for the rumble and vibration of the Chinook as they lifted from Bagram and headed to the high ground of the Hindu Kush. It would be colder than now, but adrenaline can come in handy sometimes.

"As for how you'll do in combat . . . You're probably thinking, you've never been in combat, but you will be good in combat because of who you are. You volunteered. It started in your heart. You will do it for each other."

Damn right, they would. It wasn't the success of the mission that depended on it but the chance for all of them to get home. If they didn't fight for each other in addition to fighting for their country, casualty rates would be worse than they could ever imagine. Because 1-87 didn't conquer mountains but also power. And after months of living in less-than-desirable conditions, months of "hurry up and wait," they would gladly give it all for each other and the bonds they had forged.

⫚

Anna stuffed her hands deep into her coat pockets. The northeastern wind cut through every little crevice at her neck that her scarf didn't cover as she and Mom raced toward their sedan. Mom quickly unlocked the doors, then Anna dropped onto the bitter-cold seat while Mom started the car. Roughly rubbing her hands together, urging the friction to warm them, Anna impatiently waited for the car to heat even the slightest bit so she could remove her gloves.

"So what did you think?" Mom asked as she waited for the engine to warm enough to begin the drive from Fort Drum to their apartment in Watertown.

Anna shrugged, though her heavy winter coat hid the motion. Mom had brought her along to the commander's house to forge bonds with new friends whose dads were also deployed. "It was okay."

"Could you have given me a more teenage response?" Mom huffed.

"Sorry," Anna said sarcastically. "I don't know them well, that's all."

"But that's why we were here."

"I don't know, it was awkward. We read magazines, talked here and there, and listened to music to drown you guys out."

The event was a wives' coffee hosted by the commander's wife, but Anna spent the gathering in the commander's daughter's room with a few other girls. Anna knew the coffees were a long-held tradition in the Army, dating back to Martha Washington. The wives would talk business (fundraising, supporting the soldiers overseas, ensuring that families within the unit were taken care of) and enjoy their time together. But over the centuries, the get-togethers had modernized. The days of white gloves and coffee served in china cups in the afternoon were long gone. Now, the women met for tacos and margaritas, pizza and beer, brunch with mimosas, or wine and a charcuterie plate, talking about their days, their kids, and their jobs. If teens were around, they'd sneak in to fill plates of their own. Anna loved watching Mom laugh without care, living in the moment rather than holding back.

"You enjoyed yourself," Anna said. She couldn't recall seeing Mom so happy over the last few months.

Finally, the air from the vents warmed the interior enough to loosen scarves, pull off gloves, and unzip the tops of coats. Mom flexed her bare fingers in the air stream. "Events like this are good for us. We need the camaraderie as much as they do."

As more women filtered out the front door, Anna watched them. "I guess so."

Mom hesitated with her hand on the gear shift. "What's going on with you?"

"It's nothing."

"It's obviously something."

"It's something you said tonight."

"And what was that?" Mom put the car in gear to begin the long ride home, and Anna paused before speaking.

Robert's journey to that airfield in Afghanistan had been long—indirect and exhausting. One of the worst parts of the military is the waiting: waiting to deploy, waiting to arrive, waiting for that first mission, waiting for the next one, waiting for a day to end, waiting for a day to start, waiting to go home, waiting to feel useful, waiting to call home, waiting to hear from home, waiting to finally shower or eat hot food again. And Robert and his soldiers waited a long time for a real mission to reach them.

The first stop was K2 in Uzbekistan, near the border with Tajikistan, where it felt like the waiting would never end. Camp Stronghold Freedom sounded like a cool name to some of the younger soldiers, named after a place fortified to protect against attack. Still, the fighting—the *action*—was to the south, and everyone itched to join it. They'd had enough sitting around an airfield, holding the same trainings week after week. The tent city, standing in long, neat rows, was bare-bones. A strange, terrible smell permeated the air from a long trench nearby, curling inside Robert's nose along with whatever particles floated through the air. That was one part he'd never forget—the sheer amount of dust that got into *everything*: tents, beds, gear, eyes, noses, throats.

By November, it was revealed that the odor constantly plaguing everyone at K2 was from jet fuel vapors under the ground (likely leaking from some sort of fuel storage the Soviets used), and asbestos and low-level radiation in the soil scattered around the airfield (likely from the destruction of Soviet missiles back in the day). Leadership filled the trench and contaminated areas with clean soil and placed dull yellow signs around the base, warning of chemical agents and unexploded ordnance.

"Did you see this?" Sergeant Rodriguez asked, pointing to the sign. "I'm used to the possibility of being blown up or shot, but now I gotta worry about growing another arm?"

"That's some fucked-up shit, man," Specialist David Owens remarked.

"Yeah, but think of all the things you could do with that extra arm!" Private Kowalski added, which led to some imaginative dirty jokes and lewd gestures.

Naturally, the soldiers posed in front of the signs for pictures to send home to loved ones. Kowalski asked Owens, who was about the same height and build, to stand behind him, holding a canteen up in the air while Kowalski held a cigarette in one hand and grasped his crotch with the other.

In the waiting, the soldiers found as many things to occupy their time as possible, including sitting down for a game of cards, playing practical jokes, or hosting fitness competitions (there was plenty of time for exercise). Some wrote letters home to family, keeping them updated on how they were since phone calls were rare, brief, and often difficult to hear, combined with extended delays.

Finally, in late November, the order came for 1-87 to head to Bagram Airfield in northeastern Afghanistan for "regional security and support." Like many things in Afghanistan and their current home at K2, the Soviets had built the airstrip in the 1950s. The Soviets had abandoned it in 1989, so the living arrangements hadn't improved.

The Northern Alliance and the Taliban fought over Bagram Airfield for a decade. Now that the Taliban was forced south and British forces secured the area in October, the Americans would follow in the footsteps of the Soviets, making it one of the primary air bases in the country. Hopefully to a better end.

"Thanks for the memories, K2," Kowalski said as the Chinook lifted them off to join the war.

As they lowered down into the small area that was Bagram, the mountains stretched for miles. Whereas Iraq had been a series of warm colors—oranges and yellows—Afghanistan was all pale blues and lavenders, reminding Robert of the colors of his children's first bedrooms. He'd spent an afternoon with his face inches from the wall, carefully edging his paintbrush along the baseboards, wanting everything to be perfect for Katherine.

As the mountain range shot up higher, snow coated the tops like icing on a cake, sparkling as the sunlight danced over the surface. If not for the sharpness of the peaks, they could have been white clouds low in the sky. And just for a moment, it took him back to his wedding day, and how the little sparkle on Katherine's dress glittered and cast reflections on the ceiling of her parents' living room.

Once on the ground, a tent city awaited them. An American flag had been raised atop the old Russian control tower, which was painted in a strange camouflage pattern of orange, tan, and blue. The roof had holes; many windows were smashed or missing glass entirely. Security patrol routes led soldiers past destroyed Russian jets, red stars still clearly displayed on the tail fins, along with other rusted-out equipment that might fall apart if the wind blew too hard.

The first major combat operation of the war in Afghanistan happened in December with the Battle of Tora Bora. The U.S. believed that Al-Qaeda was headquartered there, along with bin Laden. Forces were inserted, bombs dropped, and fighting occurred off and on, but despite weeks of searching, bin Laden wasn't found, and many believed he had escaped to Pakistan. Forces did, however, find small training camps and bunkers.

In the aftermath of Tora Bora, though, the insurgency grew in Paktika Province, which led to the second and largest combat operation in the war in Afghanistan—Operation Anaconda.

▌▌

Anna couldn't stop the thoughts flowing through her head at a rapid clip as the dark pine trees on the sides of the road rushed past the car. She opened and closed her gloved hands, her knuckles flexing and loosening, the tension going in and out. The distraction of the evening, while not a ton of fun, dissipated like morning fog. It lifted, revealing all the concerns and fears it had concealed for a few peaceful hours.

"What did I say that bothered you?" Mom asked again.

"There was a woman who started crying—"

"Amber Kowalski."

"Sure. Anyway, she was crying and talking about how hard things have been and how much she misses her husband, and a couple of the ladies kind of got on her about it. I heard someone say how she had to be strong."

"Well, they aren't wrong. She *does* need to be strong. That's a big group of women, and we don't all know each other well. You don't want to put it out there that you aren't squared away. People gossip, baby. And sometimes, the wife is a reflection of her husband."

"We aren't in the fifties anymore."

"No, but we have to be careful. If her husband is distracted by problems at home, he can't do his job over there. He can't keep himself or anyone else safe."

"Are there things you don't tell Dad?"

"When he isn't here, he can't help me. I have to do things on my own. I spent a night in the emergency room with your brother when he had the flu. You were just a tiny thing. I slept there with you in my lap, Garrett hooked up to an IV, and your dad never knew about it until he came home."

"You didn't call Grams and Pop?"

"It was the middle of the night. But that's why we do things like this. We come together and commiserate, but the big stuff should go to the people we're closest to."

"But everyone made it sound like a problem. 'You have to be strong for your husband.' You're all going through the same thing. If she can't go to you—her people—then who else does she have?"

"Anna, being strong is often the only choice we have. We're stuck with what we've been dealt, and we have to find our way."

"But deployment *is* hard, Mom, even for you. I see the strain on your face. You don't smile as much."

Mom sighed. "This time is different."

"How?"

Mom's eyes flicked from the glowing dashboard to the world rushing past the windshield as her hand reached to turn back the heater. "It's hard sometimes to go home to the quiet. Home to the darkness. Home to an empty bed. You guys wave hello after school, kiss me on the cheek, then beeline down the hallway for your rooms or hustle off to sports. I get you for dinner until you're finished and then you go back to your rooms. I don't blame you, but things are different for me, too."

"We still need you, Mom. But half the time you're hiding behind being strong like it'll help me. It doesn't. I need to know you and Garrett worry as much as I do."

"Maybe it's different now, then—harder for me to see. Before, it was snuggles in front of the TV, extra kisses at bedtime, and more songs to soothe you to sleep. You needed comfort then."

"You don't think I need comfort now?"

"You're older—"

"I don't mean snuggles, Mom."

But Mom was right about one thing—deployment had sucked Dad's warmth from the house. None of his laughter boomed off the yellowed apartment walls, none of his constant singing as he folded laundry or prepared a meal, none of his ribbing after school or roughhousing with Garrett on the living room floor, forcing the neighbors below to hit the ceiling with a broom handle to make them pipe down.

These moments amplified the emptiness in her chest as homecoming inched closer but still too far away.

"Your dad's unit is on a mission right now. He called last night to say it would be a bit until he could call again. Before you ask, I don't have any other information."

Anna sucked in her questions—*How long? Where to? What for?* When he said that, it meant it was a big mission, encapsulating all the risk and worry and horror humans know as war.

As flurries caught the headlights on the road ahead, Anna knew that Dad could be walking through the Afghan darkness right now, and she dreaded what he'd find there.

‖

In the mostly dark belly of the Chinook, Robert kissed the picture of Katherine, Anna, and Garrett, their faces lit by the eerie red glow of the interior of the helo, before tucking it back into the pocket on his chest. He patted it for a second as a rush of sensations flowed through his memory. He paused for a minute, only the one, to remember how much his children had grown, how Garrett was becoming a good man, and how Anna was finding her voice.

Then he thought of Katherine, letting the vanilla smell of her hair drive away the tang of sweat. He imagined the softness of her skin in the palm of his hand that final night before he left. How her dark eyes sparkled with humor at his lousy jokes or glazed over with overwhelming pleasure in bed. Slowly, the images in his head faded, the memory dissolving into wisps of fog swept away by the rotors above. It was time to let the thoughts of his wife and children dissipate. No distractions. He tucked the memories into the recesses of his mind that he would access once the battle was over and his men were safely back at Bagram.

He buckled the chin strap of his helmet, tightening the lines of his flak jacket and his heavy rucksack, slipping his hands into a pair of gloves, his M4 carbine clipped to his utility vest, the barrel tilted toward the floor of the bird. It was 0625, and soon the Chinook would drop them on the flattest mountain the operation planners had found before making their way to higher ground at

Objective Ginger to cover one of the primary escape routes leading to Pakistan. At the same time, other forces entered different areas of the valley on foot.

Robert stood, grasping a bar running along the ceiling of the Chinook to maintain his balance. "All right, men, five minutes until we land. Make sure you're ready to roll."

Many believed that the Al-Qaeda fighters who escaped from Tora Bora were holed up in the valley, and American soldiers were ready for a fight. This time, though, enemy escape wouldn't be easy. Blocking positions would be set up throughout the valley, covering the major escape routes, using the combined strength of the United States, Australia, Canada, Denmark, Germany, France, Norway, New Zealand, and Afghanistan. Afghan and special ops forces would be positioned in the northern escape routes while the U.S. forces (and Robert's platoon) landed in the south. Then, like an anaconda itself, the numerous groups would tighten their grip on the enemy, choking them out before swallowing them whole.

Robert's eyes bounced from Conlin, to Masters, to Owens, to Rodriguez, to Becker, to Wilson, and on and on down the line of thirty-odd men. This would be their first test, and many things could go wrong, as often happened in any firefight. Everyone was still learning how to move in a combat environment, work together, and fire efficiently—they hadn't yet practiced in such a hectic moment. It would be up to Robert to guide his platoon leader and the rest of his men. He had resigned himself to that long ago, but they were now lowering into their first battle, and the situation was becoming real.

In the dim lighting of the belly of the bird, he saw the pinched faces of some of the younger soldiers, the jittery legs of those who'd been in for a while but never saw combat, the ones staring at photographs and still harboring the fear of not coming home, and the heads of a few bowed in prayer. He recalled his first time in a helicopter and how he had about shit his pants during the rough flight. Hell, he hadn't even been to war then. Robert clapped Kowalski on the back and smiled at him. "Ready for your first taste, Ski?"

He watched the young man swallow hard. "Yes, Sergeant," he commented weakly.

"It'll be fine, son. Remember your training and follow Taylor's orders. It should be mostly uneventful."

Kowalski simply nodded his head in response.

What would come would come, and they would meet it when it did. Robert was battle-tested and an experienced leader—if nothing else, he'd be ready.

The Chinook finally hit the ground with a thump, and the ramp slowly lowered for the soldiers to disembark.

Anna jumped as a tire caught the pothole no one could miss when turning into the small lot behind their apartment building. While Mom pulled into the parking space, Anna stared into the darkness. "Why didn't you say anything before now?"

Mom turned off the lights, but her hand hesitated by the keys in the ignition. She sat back in her seat. "Would it have made a difference if I did?"

Anna huffed. "I know you miss us being little, but I'm fourteen now. I don't need you to hide the hard stuff from me."

Mom rubbed her eyes. "Oh, Anna . . . Every teenager thinks they're ready to hear it, but it's hard when it's someone you love. With you reading all those books about Afghanistan, clipping all the news articles about the war . . . I'm worried about you. You're so close with your dad and you don't remember going through something like this before."

"But I'm willing to talk about it," Anna said, and her voice shook. "You and Garrett act like it's no big deal—you lock it up and tuck it away. Like it's some bad word we can't say out loud. I'd rather talk about it, cry about it, yell about it!"

"You don't think I want to cry and yell, too? Your dad isn't here. I sleep in my bed alone. I have to run our house alone. I had a great night with good friends, but I don't even want to go home and be reminded that he isn't here." She swiped her thumb under her eye before continuing. "In all the news coverage of troops deploying and working overseas, no one talks about *us*. Sometimes I don't want to sleep at night because all my worries come out in nightmares. I dread leaving the house in case I miss a two-minute phone call, even though I'll barely hear him on the other end."

Anna sat speechless in the silence of the car as the threads that held Mom together slowly frayed and unraveled.

"The problem is, Anna, I don't have the privilege to sit in those feelings. Regardless of how I feel, it's my job to fill as much of Dad's absence as I can. And even if you and Garrett don't need me as much as you did when you were younger, it's still my job to be a parent, which means sheltering my kids when the world is too much. And like Grams does with me, you'll never be so old that I stop doing that. So yes, I tuck my feelings away until I'm alone because I have to be ready to support you and your brother. I also have to be there for the spouses of the company. Some are newly married. Most of them have never experienced a deployment. More troops will deploy in the coming months, and more war brides will start a battle of their own—coping with the separation in a world that doesn't understand them, one that doesn't always welcome them."

For the first time, Anna understood sacrifice. As a child, she always understood that Dad had signed a blank check to the United States government,
which could make as many demands as it wanted. For a long time, that was all
she knew as sacrifice. But now, it was different. She saw sacrifice on the home
front. She saw it in her friends who had also said goodbye to a parent. It was in
Mom's voice. Anna felt it all the way to her bones: the empty recliner with its
worn arms and cushion, the vacant seat at the dinner table, the quiet without
his booming voice as he laughed or told a story or joke.

Anna didn't know what to say, so she reached across the center console and
patted Mom's shoulder, sitting in the quiet of the night.

Mom wiped a tear that had just begun to fall before it could leave a trail. "I
don't do things the way you do, Anna. Crying and yelling never solves anything.
It might help you process what you feel, but if I do that, there's judgment.
Those women from tonight? They're going through the same thing as us, but
they don't have the years of experience to guide them. I *do*."

Anna placed her hand in her lap, biting at a piece of skin on her lip. "I
just . . . I need my mom to be there as my mom. I don't want you to smooth
it over and think distraction will fix it. I want you to go through it with me."

Mom smiled sadly. "Sweet pea, it's okay to feel what we feel, but we also
need to get past it. I did it the wrong way when Dad left for the first time. He
packed his bags, was out the door, and I basically sat on the couch for a week.
I didn't shower. I barely ate. I just cried. Once I got myself together, I swore I'd
never do that again. I'm trying to show you another way."

The tightness in Anna's chest finally ebbed, the stabbing sensation eased,
and her breaths slowed.

Mom sighed, her head falling back against the seat. "All I can ever think
about when I cry is how your dad could be getting shot at, and I'm sitting safe
at home, crying over missing him. It's never made sense to me."

Anna's voice was soft and steady. "But you're allowed to, Mom. It's scary
and no one knows what'll happen next. So when you're sad . . . come get me,
okay?"

Mom faced her then, her eyes roaming across the planes of Anna's face. She
reached over and smoothed Anna's ponytail. "You're not so little anymore, you
know that?" Mom sniffed, then flipped the interior light on as she checked her
eyes in the rearview mirror. "I don't want your brother worrying."

Anna rolled her eyes. "You two are too much alike."

The corner of Mom's mouth rose. "We balance you and your dad. C'mon,
let's go inside."

The silence in the vehicle was marred by the rasp of zippers and rustling
fabric as they bundled up for the walk to the door. All warmth drained away

quickly as Mom turned off the ignition and removed her keys. The passenger door creaked as it opened, and the slam could have woken the dead in the quiet of the night. Anna walked around the back of the vehicle toward the sidewalk that led to the front door, but Mom had paused on the driver's side, tilting her head back to stare at the clear sky.

"It sure is cold out here, but I love how clear the sky is during winter. Maybe it's because there aren't any leaves, but there's nothing like a winter night sky."

Anna tucked her hand in her pockets as she raised her eyes. "I never really thought about it. James and I always say a summer sky is better. Lightning bugs and all that."

Mom hummed in thought. "I guess there's no bad time for a clear night. Your dad always talked about how he'd be the first to see the moon at night, wherever he was. So I'd wait for it to come to me later. I found comfort in knowing it would circle its way back around to him. It was like a continuous love note between us. Every night, it was the two of us and the sky."

Anna furrowed her brows. "Dad said that?"

"Mmm hmm."

"It's grossly romantic to come from him."

Mom swatted her arm gently. "Maybe you don't know your dad so well after all."

"Not true. I'm his favorite."

Mom laughed deeply, and it warmed Anna to her toes. Maybe she could help Mom find her footing in the darkness to chase it away, much like Dad's nighttime sky chased away Mom's fears each night.

All was quiet as the men trailed off the Chinooks, fanning out to take up their security positions as the rest filed off the chopper. The only thought in Robert's mind was all he'd learned through years of service: where his men moved, any potential threats, how he held his rifle, each careful step on the rocky ground.

But as the bird lifted away, dust rising as the rotors spun faster, the valley exploded with small arms fire.

Robert dropped low and pulled his rifle to his shoulder, searching for the muzzle flashes ahead and firing in that direction. A few soldiers around him whooped with excitement, the adrenaline feeding into their systems and ratcheting up the thrill of the battle. They rhythmically dropped spent magazines, reached for new ones, slapped them into their rifles, then racked the bolts back into place to fire, all without lowering their weapons too far, speeding up the process of fire, reload, fire, reload. All the training they'd conducted stateside, at K2, and in Bagram paid off as the soldiers relied on muscle memory to carry them through the battle, their eyes focused ahead, aware of the location of each element of their firing system from beginning to end.

That was how he wanted them to perform, and Robert felt the corner of his mouth quirk up. Even for himself, a firefight had a certain level of thrill. His job was to shoot the enemy, and he was good at it. The smell of sulfur seeped into his nose, his eyes focused, and he squeezed the trigger, popping off a few rounds at a time, the recoil easily absorbed by his shoulder in a comforting push/pull.

Loud explosions and the following shockwaves rocked his body, quaking straight through his chest, leaving his ears ringing and muddling his thoughts in a world underwater. And still, the mountaintop rattled as mortars and RPGs bombarded the ground around him, startlingly accurate. Robert shook off the surprise, and his mind instantly developed contingencies, countermeasures, movement, and fire suppression. His eyes flipped from boulders on the rocky terrain, to wide shrubbery shredded by bullets, to piles of snow in the dips of the ground, and the objective that was well beyond sight. They needed to go up, but how?

More shells pulverized the ground near their position, kicking up dirt and debris that stung sections of exposed skin and sucked the air from around them. Agonized groans and urgent screams for a medic blared in his ears when his hearing returned. The mortar fire was too close, and the thought twisted Robert's gut.

The enemy had already zeroed in their weapons on the battalion's location. It meant that the enemy not only knew where to hit, but they'd had the time to prepare in advance.

He frantically sought familiar faces, counting them up in his head—four, five, six—scouting his men, their situation, and whether they had taken any casualties within their platoon. There was Kowalski, hunkered down behind a wall of boulders. Not far from him was Rodriguez, his face tight, gaze focused. But where was Conlin?

Finally, the situation became clear—they might not reach their objective. Less than five minutes on the ground and they were already going off book, a literal clusterfuck. He crawled through thick, snowy patches closer to the edge of the ridge to see if there was a line of sight from their current location to the path they were supposed to cover. But the jagged Afghan mountains blocked his view, and a few rounds near his head had him ducking back down. Someone had to climb high enough to see over, which meant the peak of Taku Ghar.

There was a dip, a sort of depression, lower down the mountain, hidden by some larger rocks, and already a platoon was making its way there. It was a good plan for cover, but they needed to draw the fire while the special operations forces got into position, helping to deplete the enemy's strength and all of their ammunition so incoming units could clean it up. They needed to wrap their tails around the terrorists and pull tight.

The soldiers were thousands of feet up, the air was thinner, and their packs were heavy. Snow-covered peaks awaited them if they went up; below, it was rocky dirt with only scattered patches of snow that caught the light of the rising sun as its rays streaked across the sky, chasing away the chill of the night but not the battle. Everywhere around them, the earth exploded. Already, the forward observer was on the radio calling in for air support to drop bombs on the rocky ridge that cut the battlefield in half.

They'd been calling it "The Whale" in briefings. The mountain lazily sloped upward before easing back down on the other end, an orca or a humpback rising above the surface. But right now, it was where vast amounts of small arms fire were coming from, and maybe even the mortars.

"We need to get to cover. There's a creek bed ahead that we can lie low in. Drop your rucks and take only what you need. We can move faster that way," Conlin shouted, shrugging off his pack quickly while interrupting Robert's forming plan.

A line of soldiers immediately moved into formation to follow him.

Robert grabbed Conlin's sleeve, intent on protecting his men. "Sir, we need—"

"We need to get to cover until we can get in air support. Let's move, Sergeant."

Conlin low-crawled down the slope and into the creek bed, but it only offered a modicum of protection. The men that already followed were pressed as flat as they could go but barely covered, and now, an entire platoon, maybe even more, were huddled close together. Mortars were already dropping around them. It would only be a matter of time before those shells were walked in as the enemy made corrections, eventually wiping out the entire formation.

The same feeling as his first time in a helicopter stirred in Robert's gut.

"Sergeant, do we follow them?" Kowalski asked as a mortar exploded, clouding the line of sight to Conlin.

"Keep your pack on, and let's move."

They low-crawled away from the other platoon in their company, following their LT down the rocky surface as grit and grime fell into the crevices of their gloves and tangled in their sleeves. And all the while, the mortars shook the ground, kicking up soil and debris on the mass of DCUs ahead. All it would take is one mortar to land in the middle of them to blow them all to pieces. Robert hesitated to join them, but where else would he take cover?

A whistle sounded overhead, more mortars incoming, when one landed amid the platoon still seeking cover near the landing zone. No one waited for an order, no one asked permission, no one even discussed their next actions, but immediately Robert and others moved out of their slight depression of protection, pulling wounded soldiers they hadn't known and getting them under some sort of cover as the medic moved from one to the next.

The rattle of Apaches echoed overhead as the birds finally swooped in, the sounds of guns and mortars growing silent as the helicopters strafed the positions called in earlier by the forward observer. The helos provided a respite from the fighting and allowed the soldiers to regroup. Robert wiped his brow.

Someone finally spotted a dip in the terrain, with two sides partially protected from the incoming fire that had stopped—for the moment. The distance was far, and Robert didn't know how they would get there, including taking the wounded with them. Most of the men were ambulatory, though if the gritted teeth and breathless groans were any indication, not without pain.

Conlin had fallen silent. His eyes were wide, mouth agape, as he stared at the bleeding men, already bandaged or grimacing. When his eyes caught Robert, they were unfocused. He was shaking, the helmet on his head jostling a little with the motion, and Conlin's features shifted in Robert's mind, taking on that of the son he'd left behind. At the moment, while bombs from American air support pounded into the ground, the boy couldn't piece together a plan of action to move the five hundred yards they had to go.

Five hundred fucking yards, under fire, with wounded men who couldn't maneuver themselves. If they moved, they'd have slightly more protection; if they stayed put, the enemy would wipe them out.

The echo of the helicopters in the valley softened, and when the men thought the pilots had handled the issue, the fire roared to life again, hot and relentless, eating up the terrain around them.

"These fuckers are crawling into their caves when they hear the birds, then coming out when they leave. We need something bigger!" someone shouted.

"Rodriguez, take your section and make your way up the ridgeline. Get those mortars set up. Take the FO with you to keep the birds comin'. We need to get the wounded to that depression ahead, and we'll try to move when the birds are here. We'll need to lay down suppressive fire to keep them from getting a good look at where we're going. Once you're there, dig some hasties."

Some of the older soldiers exchanged glances.

"Hasties, Sergeant?"

"We need to dig in, fellas. This could take a while."

No one wanted to think about the Ranger Graves, hand-dug foxholes meant to offer protection to a soldier when there wasn't enough around to hide behind. They weren't deep, it wasn't much protection, but it was their best option.

It was a flurry of coordinated movement as soldiers stayed put, firing to keep the enemy down. A small group moved up the ridge while others made the long, slow forward progress toward their new position, moving as fast as they could when the Apaches moved in and waiting impatiently for the next strafe.

Anna and Mom climbed the stairs of the apartment building, the fatigue of the day catching up to them. "Well, kiddo, it's five months down at least."

"Yeah, but the last month is like eight hundred days, so maybe not such a fun countdown."

Mom chuckled. "Those last thirty days are stubborn little bastards."

Anna paused with her foot hovering over the next step. "Wait, does that mean you have to put a quarter in the swear jar?"

Mom shrugged as she unlocked the apartment door. "Can you think of a better word?"

Anna followed her into the dark living room and slipped off her shoes. "No, 'bastards' sounds about right.'"

A haze of light flowed toward the beginning of the hallway. Mom freed herself from layers of fabric. "Your brother must still be up."

"I'll go see what he's up to." Anna closed the closet and turned down the hall, knocking softly on her brother's door.

"Come in."

She peeked through the crack at first—big brothers and all that—before opening the door fully to see Garrett lounging on the bed, flipping through a CD binder. The stickers covering every surface told Anna it was hers. She glanced pointedly at it, leaning against the frame of the entrance. "Did you *ask* if you could borrow that?"

"Excuse me, but it was in the living room because *someone* never puts any-thing away. Fair game."

Anna rolled her eyes, dropping onto the bean bag chair near the foot of the bed. "You better not scratch them."

"Oh, please. You're more likely to scratch a CD than I am."

"Nope. Radiohead. *Amnesiac*. You dropped it between the seats when we went to New York City. You still owe me a new copy."

"I'll get you a new one after practice tomorrow. I wanted something different to listen to on my drive." He stopped at the "N" section of her binder, pulling a disc from its protective plastic.

The iridescent blue back told her it was yet another one of her burned copies from James. It could only be one genre. "Ooh, a little punk rock in the morning?" He sat the CD on her bed, and she paused to read the title scrawled in permanent marker.

"New Found Glory. That okay?"

"Don't scratch this one. It's one of my favorites."

He zipped the binder closed. "Don't worry—Lover Boy can easily make you a new copy." Anna snatched her CDs from his hand as Mom peeked in the door.

"How was the coffee?" he asked her.

"It was nice. I got to catch up with some friends, laugh a little. It's cold out there, though. That car does not warm up as quickly as I'd like."

"Makes you wish for home, huh?"

Anna inwardly cringed at the word. Whose home was that?

Mom smiled. "It sure does." She stared at the floor for a few seconds, turned partway, then stopped. "I think I might need to warm up from the inside out. You guys want some hot chocolate? I think I have some of the little marshmallows."

Garret opened his mouth, and Anna internally panicked, predicting her brother's no, so she kicked his foot.

Anna smiled at Mom. "Sure, we'll be right out."

They watched Mom walk away, then Anna turned back to her brother. "Just go with it tonight, okay?"

Garrett stared, then leaned over to turn off his music. "What's with you two?"

Anna shrugged. "I think she needs us more."

"I'll be out in a minute then."

"Thanks. And don't forget that you owe me a new CD."

He rolled his eyes on her way out the door.

"I saw that!"

"You were meant to!"

From the hallway, Anna heard the clink of heavy ceramic mugs, and she knew it had to be the Santa ones that hadn't been out in years yet were still toted from place to place. But with only her second wintery location in her fourteen years of life, there was something special about Santa during a season of snow. Grams had bought the set when Anna was little, and for years, every drink had to come from that cup, no matter the season. But for some reason—maybe the mug's shape?—cocoa never tasted right out of anything else. The recipe had been passed down with the mugs, and Anna couldn't remember the last time they'd used either.

The scraping of a spoon against a saucepan caught her attention, and she leaned against the wall at the kitchen's entrance, watching and listening to Mom humming as she added bits of things to the pot. Milk. Cocoa powder. Sugar. Chocolate chips. Vanilla. Peppermint. Anna's nose tingled, and she could already picture the thick puddle of melted chocolate.

Anna stepped into the kitchen. "That smells so good."

"Just like Grams always made it."

Anna turned the mugs so all the handles faced the counter's edge, then Mom poured enough liquid in each to almost reach the brim, leaving enough room to fill to the brim with the little marshmallows that made it special.

"Those are the best part," Mom said, gesturing with her head. "Go ahead— pick one."

"That was fast," Garrett called as he entered the kitchen. He snatched a mug before Anna could choose one, then left the room.

Anna accepted one and followed her brother out, finding a spot on the floor, stretching her legs in front of her and taking her first piping-hot sip. Silky chocolate coated her tongue before it slid down her throat, and she leaned against the couch, savoring the warmth of the drink in her belly and the comfort of the soft furniture against her back.

"Mom, you coming out or what?" Garrett shouted, then he lowered his voice. "What's she doing out there?"

Anna shrugged, taking another sip, rubbing her stockinged feet together to warm her still-chilled toes. When Mom finally entered the living room, she paused, glancing from Garrett to Anna and back.

Garrett gestured to the empty cushion beside him. "Sit down already."

"This isn't what I was expecting. You're both in the living room, no books or headphones in sight!"

As Katherine found a spot on the couch near Garrett, they talked about minor things: the coffee, Garrett's marathon study session for midterms, Anna's week at school.

No one discussed the missing family member, not wanting to draw attention to the unmistakable, palpable absence. Once or twice Anna's eyes flicked to the worn recliner out of her line of sight, and she couldn't help but notice how Garrett angled his body away from the empty seat.

II

By midday, it had grown hot, the small patches of snow melted, leaving mud in their wake. As Robert lifted his arm to wipe sweat from his brow, he hissed as a round snapped by his ear and another grazed his bicep. It was like a bee sting, maybe worse, but the adrenaline was pumping, so it was hard to tell. He glanced at it but couldn't see his skin flayed open, so he kept shooting.

Everyone had finally made it into the safety of the depression, what Kowalski later dubbed Hell's Halfpipe, as rounds continued to cut through, gunfire coming from practically every angle, kicking up dirt and debris, ricocheting off the rocks behind them. Everyone was dangerously low on supplies—water, medical kits, ammunition—the rucksacks abandoned somewhere too far away to even think about, but the day wore on.

The enemy fire hadn't lessened, which meant something must have gone wrong with the special forces groups at the northern end of the valley. The reinforcements that should have landed on the ridge behind them also never arrived.

"Why are they still shooting, Sergeant?" Conlin asked, his voice shaking.

"Nothin' we can do about it, sir. We keep watch, we stay put, and we figure it out."

One thing they'd finally figured out was how to get mortars up. Rodriguez's team boomed from somewhere out of sight, and eventually, they'd eliminate the enemy mortars that had Charlie Company at greatest risk.

The men craved the arrival of anything in the air—bombers, helicopters, hell, it could be a UFO—because it paused the fighting long enough to take a break. A moment to wipe away the sweat, rest a forehead against the ground, or change position. And as the sun set lower in the sky, Robert prayed the firing would subside.

The Americans huddled in Hell's Halfpipe had one advantage—they could move under cover of darkness, using night vision to find their way safely out of the valley, then await transport to return to Bagram.

That's finally what they did, almost eighteen hours after Robert and his soldiers first stepped off the Chinook when the sun had still been below the horizon and the morning chill had been strong, when the men were anxious or excited to get the operation underway. But after the trial of the day, jaws were slack, eyes were bloodshot, and the men were bone tired. Despite the darkness, they couldn't all swoop out at once. They had to start with the company's twenty-eight wounded men. In the still-dark hours of the next day, all eighty-six members of Charlie Company would be lifted out to safety, not one death or one person left behind.

Exhausted, Robert sat in the helo as it rose in the sky. He wanted the platoon's first combat experience to be one to celebrate, some sort of victory worth talking about at home, creating the first of a long list of war stories to come. Instead, they hunkered down for the entire day. Sure, they'd kicked some Al-Qaeda ass, but not nearly enough. Despite it all, Robert was proud of his platoon. A series of boys became men that day, getting that first taste of combat on their tongues. Not one hid from the fight.

Everyone shuffled to their feet as the bird touched down back at Bagram. Some of the Joes had nodded off on the flight back, spent from the adrenaline that had flowed through their veins and drained their systems. They were unsteady as they stepped off the Chinook, but they'd crash hard in their tents.

Kowalski hovered near the edge of the airfield, helmet off his head, the chin strap hanging from his fingers. Robert paused to watch him, knowing he was walking back through every step of the day. He was just a kid, thrown into a war and put into a tense situation. Robert had done the same thing after his first firefight. After giving the young private a few moments, Robert approached Kowalski, resting a hand on his shoulder.

"C'mon, son. Let's get settled."

Kowalski nodded, but his eyes didn't focus on anything as he stared into the distance.

As they walked past the hangar, the floodlights turned off, the vast space dark. There was no fanfare this time, no colonel offering a speech.

"So, that's it, Sergeant? That's what it's like? Combat?"

Robert unclipped his helmet, letting the cool night air reach his sweaty head, and rubbed a hand over the top. "Not always exactly like that, but you get the general idea."

"How were you so calm?"

"I've had years of practice in these situations, Ski. A little bit here, a little more there. You were baptized with mortars. I wouldn't say it happened the same for me."

"I guess I always thought we'd run some Hajis down, take control of a building, or do something big, you know? We spent half the day hiding."

"Well, Ski, we received a mission and followed it. Everyone plans the best they can, but once our boots hit the ground, we have to wing it."

"Most of us didn't have our packs and people got hurt and—"

Robert bit his cheek but patted the young soldier on the shoulder. "In the end, we all made it out of there, and that matters most."

"We did good, Sergeant?"

"We did good, son. And we'll get better."

Kowalski gave him a half smile, his chin lifting a little higher, but the seed was planted in Robert's mind now, leaving him wondering. Was it a success? A failure?

Later, Robert would learn that the original estimate of two hundred enemy fighters was closer to eight hundred to one thousand, leaving TF Rakkasan severely outnumbered from the get-go. The battle unfolded badly with the special forces unit that was supposed to be the tail of the snake. Their Afghan counterparts fled when their convoy came under heavy fire. At least one portion of the Special Forces unit made it to the right place, and they assisted in calling in targeted airstrikes—the same ones that allowed Robert's company to move into a more secure position.

While Charlie Company's mission was over, Operation Anaconda was not. It would unfold over almost three weeks. A disastrous joint special ops mission consisting of Navy SEALS, Army Rangers, and airmen left seven dead and twelve injured. Fresh troops from the 10th Mountain Division arrived by March 12, and finally, the operation ended on March 18. It would be called a success, but those sent to fight were already learning how badly it went.

Two weeks after Operation Anaconda ended, 1-87 packed yet again. Their deployment was over, and it was time to go home.

At least until next time.

CHAPTER SIX

WELCOME HOME

APRIL 5, 2002

"You see those blue flashing lights?" the division commander asked in the late-night glow of spotlights on the parade field. "That's the MPs. And behind those MPs are the buses. And on those buses are each of your soldiers, ready to walk into your arms and finally be home."

Anna bounced on her toes and scratched the inside of her coat pockets as she released a cloudy huff of breath in the chilly night. People around her clapped and cheered, the noise a surge of electricity that knocked out his voice.

Such is the Force of Happiness—The Least—can lift a Ton . . .

Not to be perturbed by the noise, the commander raised his voice and held up a hand. "It might take a few minutes for them all to get off the buses, but I promise you, they're eager to get off."

"That's what she said," Amber Kowalski said from Anna's left, her fingers tightly gripping a small cardboard sign.

Anna snickered, feeling her cheeks go warm as Mom elbowed her side.

"You aren't supposed to know anything about that!"

"C'mon, Katherine—six months is a long time and she's almost fifteen," Amber defended.

In the meantime, until the dreaming could start, Dad, her biggest fan, would be home. While Mom had managed the past six months well, even springing for some fun after a long day of classes every Friday, everything was better when they were together. It didn't matter if it was a move across the country or a broken-down car or a leaky pipe. They could conquer anything when they were together.

Anna had skipped school, joining Mom for a manicure, then preparing for Dad's late arrival, spending hours on her simple sign. She'd left the unit T-shirt in her drawer, choosing fleece-lined leggings, boots, and a heavy black sweater under her coat. With all the warmth flooding her body, the excitement bubbling from every pore, Anna could have left her jacket behind.

"I'm glad it's over. Now we get the Hollywood kiss after all this time," Amber continued. She opened her mouth to say more, but the cheers drowned out her voice as the first soldiers made their way onto the field, rucksacks on their backs. Anna jumped to her feet, trying to peek between signs and people.

"Do you see him yet?" she shouted, stretching up on tiptoe to peer over the shoulders in front of her.

"No, not yet," Mom yelled back, her voice barely rising above the din around them. Families clapped and cheered as two more lines of soldiers marched across the grass, falling into formation. Mothers, fathers, and spouses stretched six deep around one side of the field, signs waving in the air, toddlers holding American flags, children jumping excitedly.

It was a sea of camouflage—patrol caps, blouses, pants, rucksacks—transforming every man into a carbon copy of those around him. The only way to distinguish one person from another at this distance was by skin tone, height, or the occasional mustache. All too short to be Dad.

"Your dad will be a good head taller than everyone around him and tends to tilt his chin up as he walks."

If only he wore glasses to catch the light, a beacon signaling, "Here I am!"

"I see him," Garrett finally called, pointing a finger over the shoulders of the woman in front of him. "Right there. He just stepped onto the field."

"Ugh, I can't see him. Keep your eye on him so we know where to go," Mom said.

Anna lifted her sign above her head, hoping the neon pink background would catch his eyes immediately. She'd carefully painted, "We can't wait to give you a Pech, man!" so he'd know exactly who was holding the sign. The wind picked up, but Anna gripped the posterboard tightly.

The men continued disembarking from the buses and crossing the field. "Seriously, how many more of them will there be?" Amber asked.

"An entire battalion is a lot of people," Mom answered.

Anna had a clear view of the last bus as it inched forward, gaining speed.

"You still see your dad?" Mom asked as the last soldier approached the field. Garrett nodded once. "Yeah, I got him."

"I still can't find him—where is he?" Anna complained. She bobbed and weaved between shoulders and the tops of heads, but all she saw were glimpses of half a face or a boot stepping forward. She wanted to push to the front like the little kids but forced herself to act like an adult.

Finally, *finally*, everyone was assembled on the field.

The division commander stepped up to the microphone. "All right, I know everyone is antsy to grab their soldiers and go home, so let's get this moving. If you aren't already standing, please rise for the National Anthem."

Ah, the anthem. A mark of pride any time Anna heard it. While she placed her hand over her heart, the experience this time was different. Dad had seen the rockets' red glare and the bombs bursting in air, but today, the song dragged on. And through every note and every line, Anna wanted to speed past the reminders of war to have that moment of goosebumps that came with how the flag would always still be waving, a sign of light after the storm. And at the end of this long storm of deployment, the waiting, the *missing*, was over. They'd pluck Dad from the field and bring him home to board game nights, laughter, and their own form of peace.

The song ended, the crowd remained silent, and every muscle in Anna's legs twitched, waiting to hear those few words that would have her racing across the field. The division commander picked up the microphone. "I'm going to keep this short. Your loved one on this field was one of the first conventional forces in Afghanistan, going to that country to break up a terrorist organization that committed atrocities not only in this nation but in our home state here. You should be proud of what they did. They made a difference, and their success will be seen for months to come. Now go get your loved one. Soldiers, you are dismissed."

A wave of people spilled across the field in an explosion of noise. Garrett led the Pechman family charge, Anna falling in behind him, zig-zagging around kissing couples and embracing families, before running toward Dad. Garrett charged into a tall, camouflaged figure, and Anna paused as she finally caught sight of her father's unmistakable size as he patted Garrett's back. A grin bloomed across her face, and she bounded ahead, the sign falling from her fingers so she could jump into his arms and squeeze him tightly.

There it was—the familiarity, the warmth, the feeling that everything was just as it should be, everyone safely together in the same place for the first time in six months. It would be back to the breakfasts together in the morning, the walks to the bus stop, the laughter at the dinner table, and the hugs before bed.

Dad kissed her cheek before setting her down. "God, you're heavy! I swear you've grown another two inches. I didn't think you could grow anymore, but you somehow did!"

"Welcome home, Dad!" Anna shouted.

"It's good to see you, kiddo," he said, ruffling her hair. Then, Dad's eyes found Mom's, and he slowly lowered Anna to the ground. He slipped the rucksack off his back, dropped it in front of Garrett, then walked toward Mom.

The bright field lights highlighted the tears in her eyes. After years of welcome homes, Anna and Garrett knew to grab their moment first and then allow their parents the same private moment as when Dad left, but Anna still couldn't turn away. To see Mom's face light up and Dad's soft smile as they slowly approached each other as if they were teens themselves. In that moment, everything else ceased to exist, so Anna stepped back as the story about the moon made sense. There was hesitation when Dad reached for Mom, but she stepped into his embrace, and the puzzle pieces fit seamlessly. Her shoulders softened and her chin lowered, and Anna was confident that the peace of the moment was a balm for the last six months of pain.

They whispered things Anna couldn't hear but which Mom undoubtedly savored as a tear slid down Dad's cheek and Mom wiped it away. They had come full circle. They'd sent him off with brief tears of sorrow as they watched him walk away to war, and now they welcomed him home with tears of happiness and relief as his feet landed on American soil.

Each that we lose takes part of us; a crescent still abides, which like the moon, some turbid night, is summoned by the tides.

Anna smiled as her parents laughed over a quiet joke or a happy thought. "It's nice to see them like this."

Garrett tucked his hands into his pockets. "It's hard to think he'll be leaving again so soon."

Her stomach plummeted. "What do you mean?"

He tilted his head in that annoying way he did when he knew something she didn't. "He's gonna go again. And again and again until either he retires or the war ends."

As the beauty of homecoming curled at the edges, Anna could only stare at her brother.

"Probably next year."

Anna shook her head. "You're such an ass. Can't you let us enjoy it?"

He shrugged. "I thought you'd want to know."

"Not *that*! Gar—" She stopped as her parents approached.

"Let's get my bags and go," Dad said, gesturing toward the cluster of olive drab littering the parking lot. Mom put an arm around Garrett's shoulders while Dad reached for Anna. He asked about school and friends, attempting to fill in the blanks while the family wound their way through the crowd.

Instead of the homecoming being a happiness that lifted a ton, it became a rock weighing her down.

It was all temporary.

The crowd dissipated as families peeled off to collect gear, load up, and go home, while others were still embracing on the field. The day had started with a rush to get ready and arrive, finally in a quick forward motion after months of inching along, then everything halted for the reunion.

Anna watched as soldiers held their children close, kissing full cheeks they hadn't touched in months, smelling downy hair, and holding dimpled hands. Couples simply stared at each other, unsure whether to trust that it was, in fact, real, and not something they'd conjured in a dream. Despite the happiness, a chill cut through her coat alongside Garrett's words.

Another deployment. More time apart. More time trying to be seen as independent and capable.

As they walked toward the bags, Dad stepped away to help a soldier load another duffel onto his shoulders. "Where are you headed, Rodriguez?"

"I'm going to see if there's an open barracks room, Sergeant. I'm . . . not ready to go home. You know how it is."

Anna focused on helping Mom heft a heavy duffel onto Garrett's back, but she couldn't help overhearing.

"Need a ride there?"

"A bus is driving everyone over. I'll be good, Sergeant. You go enjoy your family."

"Take care of yourself. You need something, you call me. Roger?"

"Roger, Sergeant. Have a good evening."

Mom regarded Dad as he came back over, and he paused to kiss her on the lips again before grabbing another bag.

"Anita didn't come?"

"Unfortunately, not everyone thinks their partner is worth waiting for."

"I saw her at the coffee last—"

He interrupted her with a kiss. "I'm fine. You're fine. The kids are fine. That's all I want to think about right now. Tonight, I want to enjoy being with you and the kids."

He turned his attention to Garrett and Anna. "All right, who's ready to go home and have a sundae before bed?"

"Dad, we aren't twelve anymore," Anna replied, fighting with herself about the proximity to the one person she couldn't get enough of while readying herself to be without him again.

"I'm sorry, I didn't know midnight sundaes had an age limit. I haven't had one in a while, and I think it's the first thing I'd like to have. More for me and your mom then, I guess."

Together, they made their way to the car, ready to embark on the next chapter and all the twists and turns ahead.

⚎

Early the next morning, when the sky was just turning from black to gray, before the birds began their songs, Robert and Katherine were wrapped around each other, the sheets in a tangle at their feet as the candles burned low. Their breathing matched as they lay in the relaxed aftermath of reunion.

Katherine gripped Robert's hand against her chest, and he felt the steady beat of her heart against it. Her hair was spread across the pillow, tickling his nose as he inhaled, but he refused to move even an inch as he stroked the smooth skin of her arm.

This was what he'd missed, what he hadn't allowed himself to think about while he was gone other than the quiet few moments in his bunk before falling asleep to dream of her. Oh, how a separation could lead to teenage hormones and fantasies! But he'd missed her, even when he forced her image out of his head.

All the waiting left time for thinking, but when the mortars dropped around his unit, when they were pinned in Hell's Halfpipe, that was the first time he'd worried he might not see her or their children again. To pull her close, feel her warmth against him, smell her skin, even feel her heartbeat, was the soothing reminder he needed that not only was she still here, but so was he.

Katherine kissed his hand. "Remember when the kids were too little to come along, and we didn't wait until we got home?"

Sweaty times in the backseat of the car, pulled off the side of the road at a rest stop or at a trail that led into the woods, as if they were teenagers, which, in hindsight, they weren't far away from being.

"How things have changed," he replied. "But at least we know the kids can occupy themselves. No tucking them back into bed because they're so excited to see me. No nighttime feedings. No soothing after a bad dream."

She chuckled and he delighted in feeling her reaction.

"So how was it?" she asked softly, turning to face him.

He inhaled deeply, letting the breath out slowly. "Different from anything I've done before."

Her eyes flicked to the pale pink gash on his bicep, his souvenir that matched the peaks of the Hindu Kush where he'd earned it. She ran a finger over the shiny patch of skin. "Good different or bad different?"

He hesitated but refused to lie. What was the point? She was staring at the evidence of how close he had been to the danger. "A little bit of both. How was it for you?"

"Hard. Harder than I imagined."

His chest squeezed tightly. "A whole new experience for both of us then."

"I didn't know what to do with myself, but I guess you didn't either."

He chuckled. "I can't tell which of us deployed and which stayed home."

A laugh stuttered out of her.

"I'm serious," he murmured as he slid her hand away from his arm to kiss her palm. "Now that I think about what this must have been like for you, I realize it might have been harder for you than me. Everyone asks about me, but you had a lot to deal with, too."

She sat up in bed, her hair settling around her shoulders. "I wasn't getting shot at."

He shrugged. "For the most part, neither was I."

Her eyes flicked back to his still-healing skin. "You don't have to do this. You don't have to compare our experiences."

He squeezed her hand tighter. "I want you to know I appreciate all you've done. Being here, finding your way with the kids, being the strength of our family. It's important to me. I can focus on what I do because I know I don't have to worry about home. You have it under control."

She sighed wearily, her chin dropping. "Not always."

He gently caught her chin and turned her head toward him. "You won't always, baby. But you had it under control in all the ways that matter."

She lay back down and let her cheek rest against his chest. "You make it easier."

"You're the glue that holds this family together. You're the reason we keep moving forward." He ran his fingers through her hair. "Every time we PCS, every time I leave, you manage everything, and I'm proud of you for that."

Her hand grazed his chest in a repetitive back and forth. "How did your soldiers do?"

He swallowed back the memories of Hell's Halfpipe and the incoming mortars that hit far too close. Reaching toward the end of the bed, he pulled the sheet up over them. "They did the best they could under the circumstances."

She lifted her head. "Were there problems?"

"I don't know about this war, Kay. I know what our mission was, but all we did was sit around for months. When we finally got some action, it didn't make sense, and it was a blip and over. We eliminated some of the enemy but didn't secure any new ground or anything. We spent the day on a mountain, flew out while other people flew in, and for what? What was it all for?"

"But all of your soldiers came home, Robert. You've always said that if you came back with everyone, you'd call it a success."

He stared at the flicker of light on the wall. "Yeah, but I hoped we'd do more there. I guess it takes time."

Katherine fell silent then, and as her breath slowly evened out and slowed, he watched the first sign of dawn lighten the walls. He thought of Rodriguez spending his first night home in the barracks after separating from his wife (as if an entire ocean between them hadn't been enough). He thought about Kowalski and his transition to being back home and falling in step with the wife he'd barely ever lived with as they both processed their first combat separation. He thought about the problems that would be on the horizon: DUIs, domestic abuse, substance abuse. If soldiers would experience all those things, shouldn't the war at least count for something?

CHAPTER SEVEN

DON'T GET USED TO IT

APRIL 15, 2002

Robert sighed as he leaned against the shower wall. Hot water flowed from the top of his head, along the front of his face, and trickled down his back. He breathed in the humid air, relishing every thick inhale. He'd already washed his hair and thoroughly scrubbed his body, grateful for the soft washcloth against his skin, but he couldn't yet bring himself to twist off the faucet. The pressure of the shower eased his sore back, the drain kept him from standing in stagnant water, and there was something special about knowing only his wife and he used this particular bathroom. His fingers wrinkled into raisins, but he was determined to remain in the shower until the water ran cold.

Robert had finally planted his boots back on American soil, but the transplanting would take time as his roots adjusted. The silence too loud, the budding hillsides too bright, and the soft fibers around the house jarring. Right now, it was the little things—the give of the mattress when he lay down, the thick support of a pillow, the gloriously rich, hot meals. He could turn on a fan if he were too hot or grab an extra blanket if he were too cold, and sometimes, he flipped on the air conditioner or cranked the heat just because he could. Everything he wanted was right at his fingertips, no waiting for it to be flown in or shipped from the States, if it even could be.

The Army granted him two weeks of leave to use as he pleased. Many of the Joes made trips to their families, especially the single ones, while the married ones found ways to stay closer. Already, a few had been drinking too much, a couple even getting behind the wheel. And everyone struggled to find their footing in a world that didn't recognize they'd been gone.

Even in Robert's own home, he struggled to fit himself back into the puzzle he'd always been a part of. It was as if his piece got wet, and while it mostly appeared the same, the cardboard had swelled with water and no longer fit quite right. Same piece, slightly different shape.

Now, on the morning of his tenth day of leave, his family had returned to their routines. Anna and Garrett had two days left of Spring Break, and Katherine was now taking her classes during the day, opening up her evenings to share with him. Everyone fit neatly back into the world they were used to, and yet Robert lagged behind.

Finally, he forced himself to turn off the water and step out of the shower, drying off with a clean towel washed only a few days ago, luxuriously thick compared to the thin, frayed, dirty-brown towel he'd used the entire time in Afghanistan. He slipped his dog tags over his head out of habit rather than necessity, the cold feel of the metal against his chest familiar, welcome. As he pulled on a sweater and jeans, he was grateful to go without the rasp of Velcro, the many buttons, or the lacing of boots, but he found himself wanting the solid rifle in his hand and the male energy of war.

After getting dressed, Robert opened the bathroom door. The haze of humidity snaked into the cooler bedroom. He'd taken to sleeping late—well, seven o'clock was late for him—reluctant to get out of the warm comfort of his mattress before the sun's rays seeped through the blinds. He tucked in the flat sheet tightly and straightened the pillows and bedspread. The green duffel in the corner caught his eye, but he tried to ignore it. He'd kept it packed in case Uncle Sam called again. Conlin had told him there were whispers of leaving again in a year, but Robert had assumed as much. The LT, however, would soon be on his way out and new, younger butterbars brought in to take his place.

Robert walked down the hallway. Katherine was in the kitchen scanning the newspaper, already dressed in jeans and a long-sleeved shirt.

"Good morning, babe," he said, planting a kiss on her cheek.

Katherine refolded the paper, setting it aside. "Good morning. I was about to check on you. You were in there a while."

"Still haven't gotten over having water pressure. I didn't realize how much I missed it."

She smiled warmly. "Take all the time you need."

"I thought I'd take everyone for breakfast since the kids are off school."

Her lips turned down. "I'm sorry to miss it."

"I take it you're headed in for the day?"

"I have a morning class, then plan to catch up on reading at the library before my afternoon classes."

Robert pulled a mug from the cupboard and filled it to the brim with coffee that wasn't overly watered down or burnt or cold. His first sip warmed the parts of his body the shower couldn't reach. "Dinner afterward?"

Katherine rose from her chair and kissed him on the mouth, her lips sticky with the gloss she often wore. "I can pick it up on my way home." She gathered her tote bag and began to walk away, but he reached for her before she got too far.

Gently, he turned her around and grasped the bag, taking it from her and setting it on the floor. He opened his arms, and she walked into them, resting her head against his chest. Immediately, he felt her shoulders relax. "I love you, baby."

She gave him a slow kiss before stepping back and lifting her bag. "I love you too. I'll see you later today." Then she left, leaving disappointment welling in his chest.

He should be happy. He and Katherine had resumed sharing space and returning to some level of normalcy without much trouble. He was proud to see her filling her time toward a pre-law degree, working toward a dream she thought had faded away when she was eighteen and pregnant. They hadn't been fighting, they spent time together in the evenings, sharing a glass of wine or watching the news. But something still felt off.

When he woke in the mornings, her side of the bed was empty. The dress she always reached for on date nights wasn't in the center of the closet anymore. The empty swear jar was cast into a dusty corner on the counter, partially hidden by cookbooks they rarely used. The couch was now pushed flush with the wall rather than perpendicular to it, and his recliner was in the corner of the room rather than in the middle.

Robert leaned against the counter, sipping his coffee, relishing its lack of bitterness. He was happy to be home, grateful even. Every homecoming had an adjustment period—for everyone. It wasn't always easy and certainly not instantaneous. After Iraq, he had post-combat jitters, uneasy about being out of the Iraqi desert. It had been odd to walk outside the door and not feel the rush of heat or cover his face to protect against the dust. He'd had to remind himself he didn't need the mask he often wore. After Haiti, he had to force himself to stop inspecting the pedestrians on the sidewalks or the windows of buildings.

This time, he wasn't pulling away; he wanted to hold her closer more often. Everything in the apartment showed how much they'd changed in six months, everyone else moving forward while Robert's feet were caught in the muck and mire of absence, of reaching back to the past, to the familiar.

Footsteps shuffled down the hallway before Anna entered the kitchen, her hair wet from a shower.

"How are you the first one up this morning?" Robert asked.

She stopped rubbing her eyes long enough to focus on her father. "I'm not. Garrett's in the shower."

"You were in before him?"

She raised her eyebrows. "Yeah. Is that a problem?"

He held up his hands in surrender. "No, just getting the lay of the land."

Anna pulled a mug from the cabinet and reached for the coffee pot, and Robert stared in surprise. *Up before her brother and drinking coffee?*

Shaking the cobwebs loose, he focused on Anna. "Did he eat breakfast yet?"

She shrugged her shoulders, taking a sip. "Check the dishwasher. If it's empty of everything other than a bowl and spoon, he's eaten."

Robert frowned, then reached for the handle. The dishwasher was full of clean dishes. "Looks like he hasn't. How about breakfast at that little place around the corner."

Anna's mug slowly lowered as her eyes widened. "We haven't been there in a while."

Robert lifted an eyebrow. "I bet they still do the breakfast platter."

She slammed her cup down, a little bit of liquid sloshing over the side, then raced to her room.

"What's she in such a hurry for?" Garrett asked as he turned the corner.

"Two magic words: breakfast platter."

Garrett rolled his eyes but couldn't stop the smile creeping across his face as he grabbed a bowl from the cabinet. "You gonna roll her home once she eats her weight in protein and pancakes?"

"Gladly! You wanna join us?"

Garrett glanced at the bowl in his hands. "I, uh—" He paused to clear his throat. "I don't want to cramp your thing." He reached for the silverware drawer, but Robert put his hand in front of it.

"You aren't cramping anything. There's nothing I want more than to enjoy breakfast with my kids. Your schedule is already so full. I'll take whatever time you can spare."

Garrett's fingers tapped against the bowl a few times before he placed it on the counter. "All right. I'll go." He stepped out of the kitchen briefly before returning back to Robert. "But you're carrying her back by yourself."

Robert laughed from deep in his belly, and the vibration flooded his system with euphoria.

II

Within ten minutes of meeting the kids in the kitchen, Robert was walking the short distance down the street to the local breakfast diner, Anna's hair in a wet ponytail, Garrett's hands tucked in his pockets. The restaurant was inside a narrow, squat building in red and white, not unlike a trailer. It was one of those old-school places that cooked the food behind the counter, with vinyl-covered barstools in a line where the singles or couples could sit. There were only about ten or so booths along the row of windows that faced the parking lot. With a smile, Anna claimed one near a family of four, pulling the menus from behind the napkin holder and handing them to Robert, who slid in beside her, and Garrett across from them.

Robert smiled as Anna settled into her seat and perused the menu even though he knew exactly what she would order: the breakfast platter with apple juice. Garrett would choose something more sensible—oatmeal with fruit and orange juice. As Robert read the menu from front to back, he counted out four things he'd happily take in front of him but reeled it back to a single item.

A waitress wearing a black tee and jeans approached the table with a carbon copy notepad. "Morning, folks. What'll it be?"

Anna went first. "I'd like the breakfast platter with coffee and a water, please."

Garrett was next. "I'll do the ham and cheese omelet with orange juice."

Robert stared at the menu despite the waitress's expectant gaze. "Um . . . I'll do the potato scramble. With a coffee."

The waitress tapped the pen against the pad. "Be back with your drinks."

"I forgot how much I love this place," Anna commented as she turned toward the television mounted above the griddle.

Robert fumbled with the paper seal around his silverware. "The food is good," he said with a nod.

Garrett shook his head as he reached for a straw from a tall glass in the center of the table. "I don't know how you guys can eat like that so early in the morning."

Anna's eyes widened. "Oh, please. You at least got an omelet. But seriously, you can't go wrong with eggs and hashbrowns and bacon and sausage and pan—"

He blew the paper off his straw, hitting her in the face. "All right, I get it. You like breakfast."

Anna spread out her silverware on a napkin. "All I'm saying is that maybe there's something wrong with people like you who usually choose oatmeal. You're seventeen, not seventy."

"All right, you two." It was an order, but one given with good humor as the sibling bickering began. *Some things never change.* "Let's agree that you each like your own things and move on from it. Tell me about how school's been going."

As Garrett talked about his final few months before graduation, Robert's eyes settled on the table behind his son. A girl of about four, with dark hair braided into pigtails, sat beside her mother, happily using a red crayon to color on a paper placemat with a barnyard scene. Her tongue poked out as she concentrated on keeping each crayon stroke within the lines. Robert could only see the backs of the father and son, but the two played a game of tic-tac-toe in bright blue on the back of another placemat.

How much time had passed? When Robert and Katherine brought their first child home from the hospital, everyone told him how fast the time would go. *Cherish every moment*, they said. And before he knew it, Garrett was walking, then talking, then starting school. Then Anna came along, and they swore they'd slow down. And again, the time passed too quickly, and one day, she morphed into a teenager.

At the crux of it was his time away. Every moment he stepped away to follow the profession he loved—that brought him *life*—he turned away from the *people* he loved and who brought him life. Every month away was changed hobbies—photography classes, soccer, lacrosse. Every year added up to a new character trait: the children creeping toward adulthood, the teenage attitude and backtalk, the growing up and growing more confident.

Anna's pigtails disappeared long ago. Garrett stopped wearing ball caps in middle school. The Velcro shoes had been replaced by laces, the dimpled hands lengthening to elegant fingers, maturity in both of their faces.

Where had the time gone? How much had Robert missed?

"Yay!" the little boy shouted as he defeated his dad with a row of three O's, putting a line through them.

"Dad?" Garrett waved a hand in front of his father's face.

"Sorry, buddy. Keep going. I'm listening." Robert wrapped his arm around Anna's shoulder, pulling her close and kissing the top of her head as Garrett continued.

Time runs away from everyone; there's no way to stop it, no way to control it. Six months had passed for Robert, many years of watching his children grow flew by, but if this stint in Afghanistan had taught him anything, it was that he would cherish the little moments, not knowing how many he had left before he was gone again.

⊔

Anna zipped her fleece jacket as they stepped outside after breakfast.

"So what's next?" Dad asked.

"I should probably get my paper finished," Garrett answered.

"Okay, that's one gone. What about you?" Dad turned his attention to Anna. "We still on for chess? You keep getting better every time we play."

Anna shoved her hands into her pockets. "I'm gonna see if James is home."

Lines formed between Dad's eyebrows, but what was there to say? Sometimes you need your best friend.

"Well, don't stay out too late, kiddo. Mom's picking up dinner on her way home tonight."

"We might head to the park. I'll be home before then."

She gave him a quick side hug, then walked in the opposite direction of Dad and Garrett, who were already talking sports.

It was an early spring day in New York, that time of year when the ground thawed enough for things to soften, for mud to stick to shoes and feet to sink a fraction of an inch when walking across the grass.

The sun shone, and Anna was pleased to wear a fleece jacket and hat rather than her thick winter coat. She even skipped the boots for once. While it was a beautiful day now, it could turn into a late-season snowstorm tomorrow. It was too soon to plant flowers or watch crocuses poke their pointed leaves through the ground, but those days grew closer. Soon, the trees would leaf, and the flowers would bloom.

She inhaled the crisp air as she walked along, and her shoes crunched over old pieces of salt and cinders from the winter months. She craved the quiet, for the sounds of nature and the town versus conversation and questions.

Having Dad home, knowing he was safe after all he went through in Afghanistan, was comforting, like coming inside to the warmth after being out in the cold. She'd missed him and the fun and reassurance he brought to their family, but he wanted to spend every moment together since he got back. And somehow, the pressure was mounting. She'd found ways to give in here and there—heading to the park for a game of "horse," a hike and picnic last weekend, breakfast today, chess in the evenings—but she appreciated the time to breathe.

How did I get here?

Anna paused at the corner, turning back to see Garrett and Dad almost out of sight. Should she stay, or should she go?

Maybe this was why Emily liked her seclusion. If you aren't intertwining your life with others, you only have yourself to worry about. But even Emily needed family; after all, she still communicated with friends via letters.

Friends.

Anna turned left at the end of the road.

Something had changed since Afghanistan. Not at the level of the grandfather she'd always heard about but never met, the alcoholic who forgot his son.

Not the great-grandfather who couldn't forget the war when he came home. Instead, it was almost like Dad was trying to make up for the years of separations all at once.

She finally reached James's house and walked up the uneven sidewalk to the front porch. Footsteps pounded on the stairs after she knocked, then he opened the door, a smile blooming across his face as he greeted her.

"I wanted to see what you were up to. I was out for breakfast with Dad and Garrett, and I thought I'd stop by before heading back."

"You wanna come in?"

"I thought we could hit the park. It's too nice to be inside."

"Let me get my jacket and shoes. I'll be right out."

Anna sat on the porch swing, coasting it back and forth with a toe while he gathered his things. James was her closest friend, and she sometimes wondered how it all happened. Most of her school-age years were a blur of faces and names and towns and moving boxes, always leaving as soon as she felt at home. But she'd met James on her first day of school after bonding over the copy of *Harry Potter* he'd left sitting on his desk. She'd fallen in love with the cast of characters (close to her age!) over the summer, impatiently waiting for the next book. She hadn't been able to wait to ask who his favorite character was (Ron), what house they'd be sorted into (Ravenclaw for her), or what adventures Harry's next trip to Hogwarts would entail (ones that would keep them on the edge of their seats). They'd been inseparable ever since. On movie nights, he'd bring a Blockbuster rental, popcorn, SnoCaps for her, and gummy worms for himself. They biked in the spring, hiked in the summer, played basketball in the fall, and wrapped themselves in blankets during long winters.

Perhaps they were simply birds of a feather, both accustomed to having loved ones far away, whether in distance or in emotions. His mom had died when he was young, and his dad had retreated into grief afterward, sitting alone, unable to engage with his young son who needed him. Nana Mackey took James in one day, and he'd been there ever since.

"I'm going to the park with Anna," James shouted as he opened the door.

"Tell her she's been gone too long. She should come for dinner," Nana Mackey's muffled voice called in return.

James stared at Anna for a moment.

"I'll come next Friday, Nana!" she called.

"You better," Nana said back.

James locked up. "What do you want to do?"

"We can walk down to the park and shoot some baskets? I thought about kicking a soccer ball, but I don't want to ruin my shoes in the mud."

He led the way to the driveway and the detached garage in the back. After James opened a side door and stepped inside, an orange basketball rolled toward Anna's feet. She picked it up, bouncing it a few times while he closed everything back up.

Once finished, he pulled the zipper to his chin and stuffed his hands in his pockets. "Hopefully it's warmer in the sun."

"Are you kidding? If you can't see your breath, it isn't cold."

"Well, I didn't have a half-mile walk to warm up. I was tucked in my nice warm house." He thrust out a hand and smacked the basketball from her control. "Didn't you say you were out with your family this morning?"

As she listened to the hollow bounce of the ball, she kicked a pebble ahead of her. It rolled along the sidewalk while thoughts did the same in her head. She nudged it along again when it halted in a crack. "I needed some air."

James passed the ball between his hands. "I'm sure it's weird. He was gone a while."

"Yeah, but he's always gone a while. This isn't any different."

"It's a little different, though, isn't it?"

"He's been gone plenty of times."

He turned toward her and tucked the ball under his arm as his eyes narrowed. "But last year, you had a list forever long of all the things you'd do. This time, you're here instead of there. Talk to me."

Oh, the list . . . It was as long as some kids' Christmas lists, each item carefully considered, all things they'd miss, a way to make up for lost time. And together, she and Dad had crossed off every single one.

A gust of wind blew from the side, and it scattered her thoughts like sheets of paper in front of an open window. She considered snatching some from the disruption while waiting for others to settle. As much as she wanted to share, it was better to tuck them under a boulder.

James and Anna entered the park to see children on the playground, like a slew of ants covering the crumbs from a leftover picnic. Kids of all ages pumped their legs on swings, raced down slides with arms in the air, and jumped on the rickety bridge that spanned the two playground structures. They ran and screamed without abandon, keen on the thrill of connection and fun. A dark-haired girl cut between Anna and James as she raced away from a red-haired boy in a game of tag. A smile pulled at the corner of Anna's mouth.

Oh, to be like them.

James nudged her with his elbow. "Seriously, are you good?"

She watched the children play as she put together her feelings. "I'm kind of jealous of them."

While she was still a kid, the ones on the playground didn't have to pay attention to the bigger things happening in the world. These children, if even aware of a war, were too young to understand it. Afghanistan was a foreign word to them, a place no different than Agrabah in *Aladdin*. Soldiers in uniform were exciting, reminding them of the green plastic Army men in *Toy Story*.

"I could be like them, playing with toys or reading or playing video games when my parents watch the news. But I don't get to. Everything that's happening . . . I *have* to face it." She was too young to remember Dad's deployment time in Iraq. Haiti and Bosnia were faraway places with weird names, where Daddy was the good guy, there to help people and hand out aid packages. Now, she knew he carried a rifle and might repeatedly go to war over the coming years.

James stared across the playground. "Ignoring wouldn't be easier, though, would it?" He stepped onto the basketball court, bouncing the ball on the foul line and passing it between his legs before launching it into the basket with a clean, soft swish. "If I had a dollar for every time I've heard, 'You'll understand when you're older,' I could send myself to college." He passed her the ball.

She bounced it a few times. "I want to understand it because I don't have any other choice. Knowing is easier than not knowing, right?" She tossed the ball half-heartedly at the basket, missing.

James grabbed it, then dribbled back to the foul line, lining his toes up with the white mark on the court and bending his knees in preparation to shoot again. "I think it depends on who you ask."

"What about for you? Would it help to know all the details?"

"I don't know. Maybe. But no one gave me a choice." He paused mid-shoot and glanced at her. "Huh. That might be the worst part." He released the ball, rolling it across his fingertips as it sailed to the basket, pounding off the backboard and missing the hoop.

Anna ran toward it and took possession. "That's what I'm saying. I don't have a choice either. Dad's gonna go whether I want him to or not." She stopped dribbling in the paint and tossed the ball easily into the basket, passing it to James to follow.

He twisted it in his hands. "Maybe the grass isn't always greener then. Getting to ignore it compared to not." Swish. Pass. "But for me, it would have been nice not to be treated like a little kid."

Anna groaned as she approached the foul line. "I *want* to be trusted with big information. Mom says we have to be strong, so she rarely talks about it. And now, she and Dad are all clingy, so it's like she doesn't even worry about it. Garrett talks to me like I'm stupid, but I've checked out the library books, and I'm reading the newspaper articles. We don't have the option to ignore it, you know? But they treat me like I'm going to break." Miss. Pass.

James lined his toes up behind the three-point arc near the bounds line, doing a series of bounces and spins in his hands. "Maybe you *won't* break. Maybe you're just cracking a little. You know, like the bridges we made last year? The frame stretched across fine, and the weight would break them. But if you put supports inside, like that triangle pattern we both did, it could hold a bunch of weight."

Anna leaned against the metal pole under the basket. "Maybe. My family's good at being the support. It's practically our motto. I just—I never stopped worrying while he was gone, and then once he's here it . . ."

James tucked the ball under his arm and walked toward her. "C'mon, Anna. Say it."

She sighed heavily. "It makes me sound like a bad person."

"Who else is gonna know? It's you and me."

She stared at the children on the playground again and watched as a father put his daughter on his shoulders, helping her reach the monkey bars and then supporting her from underneath. The security of having him close so she wouldn't fall was enough to propel the child forward all on her own.

"Dad asked me to go back and play chess."

James shrugged. "But you guys have always done stuff like that. And you enjoyed it."

"Yeah, but it's different now."

"How so?"

She groaned and tilted her head back before focusing on him again. "I don't want to spend time with him like that. Honestly, I can't wait to go back to school on Monday so I don't have to." She covered her face with her hands. "It sounds so bad when I say it out loud."

James let the ball fall, then he gently pulled her wrists down. "I would've thought you'd want all that time. You don't know when he'll leave again."

"But that's just it. I *know* he'll leave again. People are saying next summer. I'm afraid to get used to it—to expect him to always be gone—but I also want that so I can deal with it when he leaves. So it won't be so hard."

His face scrunched up in a way that suggested he didn't know what to say, and it was enough for her to wish she'd remained silent.

"I won't pretend to understand how it feels. I don't. But I'm here." He spread his arms wide, and she walked into them. "I hate that I can't do anything, but I'm here."

"I'm at least glad to have you. With Garrett off to college next year and Mom graduating from college and starting a job . . . I'm gonna feel so alone."

He squeezed her a little tighter. "You always have me."

‖ CHAPTER EIGHT ‖

YOU KNEW WHAT YOU WERE GETTING YOURSELF INTO

APRIL 17, 2002

Robert sat on the couch, watching the news, biding his time until the chicken finished roasting in the oven and he'd call the whole family to dinner. Sometimes there were perks with light duty, and this was one. He could take care of the family while they all returned to normal.

One thing that hadn't returned to normal was Anna's interest in the ongoing war. Every evening when he watched the news, she'd join him, sitting on the couch, her elbows on her knees, tuned in to every battle update or new firefight that broke out somewhere.

She'd asked Robert to tell her when the news replayed President Bush's speech at the Virginia Military Institute. And there they were, listening to the voice that soothed them in the aftermath of 9/11 as they all learned how much longer the war could drag out.

"And today, we are called to defend freedom against ruthless enemies. And once again, we need steadfastness, courage, and hope. The war against terror will be long . . . It will not be enough to make the world safer—we must also work to make the world better."

Anna huffed. "Whatever happened to no nation-building?"

"It's a soundbite, Anna. Take it with a grain of salt."

She shook her head then focused back on the TV.

"We know that true peace will only be achieved when we give the Afghan people the means to achieve their own aspirations. Peace will be achieved by helping Afghanistan develop its own stable government. Peace will be achieved by helping

Afghanistan train and develop its own national army. And peace will be achieved through an education system for boys and girls which works."

"Can't argue with those aims," Robert commented. "What did Emily Dickinson say? *There's something in their attitude that taunts her bayonet?*"

Anna rolled her eyes, a big sweeping gesture that accounted for the floor, ceiling, and every wall. "She did *not* mean Iraq, Dad."

"Seeing as she died in the nineteenth century, I'd imagine not." He lowered the volume as the correspondent segued to Afghan news.

"She was talking about American pride and patriotism," Anna corrected, flopping back on the couch.

"Yes, during its struggle for freedom. We can't take that to other countries? Show them what it's like?"

She stared at him in that frustrating way teenagers had that suggested they knew so much more than their parents. "Like we're the only country with freedom?"

"Saddam is a dictator. If he has WMDs, we can help protect people within the region. Not every person in Iraq has a voice he's willing to listen to. I already went there once because of it, and the U.S. didn't go alone."

That earned him another massive eye roll. "Hmm . . . What's the saying, Dad?" She gazed at the ceiling and tapped a finger against her chin, and Robert wanted to roll his own eyes at the sarcasm that oozed from every gesture. "*With great power comes great responsibility?* Maybe it isn't for us to get involved."

"The UN got involved for almost a decade. Maybe we should take responsibility when a threat like this still exists after all that time and no one else in the region is willing or able to take responsibility."

"Or maybe we shouldn't. And I don't think Emily would support it either."

"She seemed to believe America was pretty damn perfect."

"I'm telling Mom you swore. And anyway, Emily probably wrote that *before* the Civil War."

"She probably would have sided with the Union anyway."

Anne huffed. "She refused to take a side."

Robert shrugged, reaching for the remote. "Well, sometimes you have to take a side." Proud of his victory discussing literary criticism and current events, Robert's finger hovered above the power button.

"Wait, not yet."

He turned it off anyway. "Sorry, kiddo. Mom'll be home soon, and I'd like her to have a nice hot meal."

Anna groaned, pulling herself from the recess of the cushions. "I'll check in the paper tomorrow, then. Let me know when dinner's ready." She disappeared down the hall.

Robert chuckled as he walked into the kitchen to check on dinner. Should he encourage her fascination or try to cull it? Parenting books probably never covered something like that, so perhaps he should base the decision on harm. Would the information she read harm her, or would it help her learn? If history truly repeated itself, eventually the news reports would slacken and there would be little information for her consumption anyway.

The scrape of keys in the lock caught Robert's attention, and he smiled as his bride walked in. Being in school gave her purpose that added color to her cheeks, and Robert enjoyed listening to her talk about fellow students and the readings and lessons. "Hey there, baby. How was your day?"

She kicked off her shoes in the corner by the door before joining Robert in the kitchen, kissing him on the cheek. "It was good, but I wouldn't say no to a stiff drink. Where are the kids?"

Robert pulled a chardonnay from the fridge and poured her a glass. "Two guesses where." He slid the goblet across the butcher block counter. "What brings on the drink?"

She stared at the counter, her mouth slightly open, the words on the tip of her tongue but not yet ready to be uttered. It was in these moments that Robert readied himself.

"I heard parts of the president's speech on the way home." She gulped her wine.

"Ah, Anna and I watched the highlights a few minutes ago." He opened the oven door, checking that the roast was browning before letting it close again.

"Nation-building, reports of WMDs in Iraq, whispers of us going there next. What is *happening*?"

Robert tucked his hands in his pockets, leaning a hip against the counter. The worry in her dark eyes was unmistakable, and no words would help her because no explanation would soothe her. The war was like smoke suspended in the air. It had been present in their lives for so long that it clung to the walls of their memories, where nothing could remove it. The odor was a constant reminder, curling into their noses, inescapable. There would be no forgetting that this war was far from over. The president had admitted it.

She caught what he wasn't saying and sipped from her glass. "So what's next?"

"Leaders have already suggested Saddam needs to go, but fighting two wars could make Afghanistan harder to win. *But* . . . if there's a connection between Saddam and 9/11 or Afghanistan that could help us fight, then maybe it's the right thing to do."

Katherine inhaled deeply. "I meant what's next for us—this family."

Robert's chest twisted, so he turned his attention to the oven, switching it off, letting the residual heat keep the food warm and give him time to think.

"Maybe we should talk about where we go from here," she continued. "You only have two years until retirement—"

Robert turned then. "I never planned on retiring unless I couldn't do my job anymore, Kay."

"Well, you said we'd talk about it once you hit twenty."

"I'm not there yet."

"But you're almost there. And you're getting older, Robert. The heavy packs, the riding in helicopters or bumpy Humvees . . . How long can you do that without long-term issues?"

Anna came around the corner then, skidding to a halt. Her widened eyes flicked back and forth between Katherine and Robert. He forced himself to relax his face.

"Sorry, just . . . grabbing a drink." She slipped between her parents, pulling a water bottle from the fridge as silence rang in the air. "I'll be in my room until dinner."

Robert recovered first. "Go ahead, kiddo. We'll get you when it's time to eat."

Anna nodded and disappeared from the doorway.

After pulling a beer from the fridge, allowing the cool air to ease his temper, he gestured to the table. Once he rounded the counter, he pulled out a chair for Katherine. "This deployment showed me I'm still fit enough, strong enough, and prepared enough to stay in."

His wife settled stiffly in a chair. "But it's more than that, Robert. A second war now . . ."

He shrugged, taking a seat beside her. "We always knew there would be another deployment, another mission that pulls me away."

Katherine traced the wood, grazing it with a finger, avoiding his gaze. "But what if I don't want you to leave anymore?"

He huffed out a breath. "This is what our life is, baby. Always has been."

She tilted her head to the side and her brows pulled down. "But it isn't only about you. For the past eighteen years, we made decisions primarily for your job, but that can't be it anymore." Her eyes fell to the table. "Couples are already falling apart. Amber Kowalski called me today. She and her husband are having a hard time."

"I know it's hard to see, but that has nothing to do with us."

"This time." Katherine twisted the wine glass between her fingers before abandoning it on the table. "But what about next time? What if the war—or wars—starts affecting *our* relationship?" Her voice slowly rose with each word, and she paused, clearing her throat. "You'll be gone in another year or two, and what if the next deployment is a year, fifteen months, longer?"

"Babe, we've done this before." He tried to smile.

"Mail was a rarity this time. We barely spoke while you were gone. I get things could have been worse, but what if they *are* worse next time?"

He narrowed his eyes and spoke tersely. "What are you asking, Katherine?"

She leaned her forearms on the table and stared at the floor. "Maybe . . . it's time . . . to talk about getting out."

The sentence wasn't even fully out of her mouth before he shook his head repeatedly, cutting in and overlapping as if it would erase what she said. "I can't leave before twenty. To give up that boost in retirement would be stupid."

"Well, damn the money, Robert!" she exploded, flying out of the chair as the fight surged into her. "There could be two wars next year. Two!"

He slid his chair back, still shaking his head. It was one thing to ask him to leave before retirement; it was another to ask him to leave his company high and dry in the lead-up to a deployment. After all these years, didn't she know how that looked?

But instead, he said, "You can't ask me to walk away this close. Besides, Anna only has a few years of school left. We need to stay in one place and let her do high school like Garrett."

"We could stay here until she finishes school—"

"What would I even do here?"

Katherine's eyes searched the room for a place to settle, fumbling for an answer. "There are civilian jobs, things you could do on the installation, still working around soldiers."

"That isn't what I want to do."

"Is that more important than holding on to our last few years as a family?"

"How would you feel if I asked you to quit school, Katherine?"

Her back pulled tight. "Don't go there. I've given up plenty of things. When I wasn't working, I was raising babies while you were God-knows-where. Once the kids hit school, I started working, and I quit every job when you got orders. And how many schools did I drop out of when it was time for you to move on? You aren't the only one who's sacrificed in this family."

"You knew this when you married me. We talked about this before then—"

"What would I have done back then? I was already pregnant with Garrett, you were already signed up, and I loved you. What was I supposed to do? The obvious choice was to follow you."

He rose from the chair, frustration forcing him into movement. "You've never raised a fuss before."

She averted her eyes, picking at her cuticles. "Your job has never weighed on me so much before."

||

Anna leaned against the wall around the corner from the kitchen, careful not to move a muscle and make the floor creak or a toe crack.

Her parents had fought at times throughout her life. They'd always believed that insulating their children from marital issues made it harder for the kids to see how to apologize or make things better. Granted, no one swore at the other. No one name-called. It was constructive, even if they yelled.

Listening to Mom's pleading made Anna proud, for sharing how much it sucked moving around, separating, deploying, and all the other "ings" military life brought. Mom was stepping into the crossfire that had haunted Anna. How many other kids had to deal with those things? How many couples had to say goodbye so often?

"I'm asking for two years," Dad's voice said. "Two years, then we'll talk about it again. That will get me to retirement. Can you at least give me that?"

"Two *years*? You'll ask me to wait that long before we talk about it again?"

"I'll have hit twenty by then—"

"Two years, Robert! How many times will you deploy? Twice, at least? And for how long?"

"I don't know!" he shouted. A loud pound against the table sounded—his fist?—and it left the glasses in the cabinets ringing.

Anna wanted to roll her eyes at his frustration. Didn't he know how hard it was for all of them? To have Dad's employer calling all the shots in their lives? Sure, someone needed to fight the war, to find bin Laden, to change the tides of war, but did it have to be Dad?

Anna wrapped a lock of hair around her finger, winding tightly, then reversing the direction.

"So much can happen between now and then. So many things with consequences for this family," Mom responded. "They're already saying you'll go again, and we aren't even in the second war people are already considering. Think about this!"

"I always think about this!" he snapped. "Don't you think I've considered all I've missed? Hell, I just got back—it's fresh in my mind."

"All I'm saying is maybe this next one should be your last one. The worry I felt when you were gone . . . I never had to feel that before." Mom's voice shook. "The other places you've been were dangerous, yes—nowhere is entirely safe—but this is something I've never had to get through before. The worry is sometimes *paralyzing*."

Anna's heart broke a little at Mom's admission. They'd talked about feelings, but Anna didn't know they went this deep. *Paralyzing: to make powerless or ineffective*. Mom never showed that, but the emotion in her voice said more than words ever could. It was enough to squeeze Anna's heart, to make her want to run into the dining room and hug Mom and tell her it would all be okay.

"You knew all of this could happen someday," Dad replied.

Poor Mom, baring her heart only to have Dad throw it in her face.

His comment was a knife in the gut, one of those deep cuts that leaves a person's insides spilling out, but Dad couldn't see it that way. The twist of pain, the bright red of anger, the burn of sorrow because he simply wouldn't choose his family over his job. A tear slipped down Anna's cheek as she heard her mother shout.

"Stop saying that. I knew you'd be in the Army for the long haul, but I don't want it to go on too long. I want to know that you'll come home, that you'll come back to us, that you'll be a part of this family *with us*."

"You don't understand what you're asking."

"*You* don't understand what you're *saying*. Yes, I agreed to live this life with you, to follow you. But our kids didn't make that choice. They were thrown into this life and expected to deal with it. And while they've managed all this time, they're older now—at impressionable ages. They need their father. They need to know that *both* parents are here."

Anna heard the click of the heaters turning off, and in the resulting silence, she held her breath so they wouldn't know she was there.

"I'm asking you to choose your family," Mom begged, "the ones who have always been here waiting, the ones who have accepted your mission, your life, your ambition, and lived it *with* you. If you won't get out now, then one more deployment and done. Please, let this be the last one."

Footsteps echoed in the dining room, and before Anna could scurry away, Mom rounded the corner. Her face was tense as she paused beside Anna, but then Mom retreated to her bedroom.

|| CHAPTER NINE ||

ANOTHER ONE BITES THE DUST

JUNE 6, 2002

Anna walked across her school's parking lot, the last day of ninth grade finally complete. The warmth of the pavement seeped through her thin sandals, and the heated breeze drifted across her face. It was a constant reminder that one day, summer would act as the beginning of the rest of her life.

In celebration of the end of the school year, crowds of students filed out the doors hours before their usual dismissal. The excitement of all to come spilled into the parking lot as everyone around her tittered about upcoming activities, graduation, and a long break from the usual grind.

Garrett was kind enough to wait for his kid sister despite the opportunity to join his friends who were flocking to the local park. She spotted him leaning against his old, powder-blue Buick, the one Dad recently bought for him to take to college. His hands were tucked into his pockets, sunglasses covering his eyes, likely trying to spot his new girlfriend he wouldn't call a girlfriend—something about not wanting to be tied down before leaving. Stupid boys.

"You better not be checking out girls behind those glasses," she scolded.

He held his hands up in surrender. "Hey, I'm not tied down."

Anna laughed and punched his arm. "Whatever."

"Are we waiting on Lover Boy, or can we go now?"

Anna's stomach growled in preparation for their end-of-year tradition. It started in kindergarten. Mom and Dad or just Mom would pick up her and Garrett, then take them for the ice cream of their choice. Garrett and Anna enjoyed it so much after the first time that they pleaded with Mom and Dad to keep it going, no matter where they lived, choosing Dairy Queen or Suzy's or Frosty Freeze, or whatever new place they discovered.

Once Garrett was old enough to drive, he and Anna started going alone, that first step toward independence, borrowing a car, then sitting on the curb in front of the restaurant, scooping ice cream with a plastic spoon from a Styrofoam bowl or speedily licking it from a cone so it wouldn't melt all over their hands. For the last few years, they'd folded James in.

Anna leaned against the car beside her brother. "Do you *have* to call him that? We're friends."

"Mmmhmm . . ." He pointedly raised an eyebrow at her, and she wanted to smack the dark glasses off his face.

"Honestly, we're friends."

"Yeah, until the day he tries to hold your hand or kiss you."

Anna shoved her brother roughly, refusing to give him any satisfaction. "Would you quit it? He'll be here in a few minutes."

"Oh, wouldn't want him to overhear that you're in love with him, too."

"Garrett, I swear to God, if you don't shut up—"

He rifled her hair, sending dark strands in front of her eyes. "Chill, I'm messing with you."

Anna reached up to straighten her hair. "So, how does freedom feel, anyway? Last day of school, big things ahead at college." She nudged his shoulder with hers.

He glanced back toward the school. "It's gonna be a change, that's for sure."

A group of girls giggled as they climbed into a tiny sports car parked a row over. A couple held hands as they stopped to chat with some friends. Someone revved the engine of a giant pickup and peeled out of the parking lot, accompanied by a thumping bass.

"Do you think you'll miss this?" Anna asked.

Garrett shrugged. "Probably. Do you realize this is the longest we've been in one place? I got to do all of high school here. We all grew out of the awkward phases of braces and weird haircuts together."

Anna shuddered at the reminder. Her awkward phase lasted half her life. She finally lost the braces a month ago and was growing proficient at using a little eyeliner and mascara. "I bet your friends would love that you remember their ugly duckling periods."

"Eh, most people grew out of it."

She swiped her feet at the gravel. "Have you thought about what you're gonna do over the summer?"

"I might travel."

Anna's eyes lit up. "Ooh, where—"

"*Not* with you, little sis. Alone."

Anna waited for more, but Garrett wasn't giving it up. "The reason for that being . . ."

His head jerked up and he smiled at something behind Anna. "What's up, man? About time you showed up."

James gave a crooked grin as he drew closer. "Sorry. I don't know who designed this school, but if it had been me, I would have built it differently. Not only is the tech wing in the worst location, but it connects to the narrowest set of stairs that are also the busiest. How is that not a fire hazard? Half the time, I stand there waiting for people to move."

Anna chuckled. Of course the future architect would focus on the design flaws of the building on the last day of school.

"Okay, Frank Lloyd Wright, you can bore us with your observations while getting in the car." Garrett waved a hand to help guide James's way.

"Yeah, yeah, I get it. We're on a mission." He opened the back door and tossed his backpack along the wide seats before folding his tall body inside.

Anna opened her door and was immediately stalled by the mess of the front seat. Empty water bottles were heaped on the floor, almost covering two shoes—not of a pair—along with a hoodie rolled into a tight ball. Papers, folders, and a backpack obscured the seat.

Anna stared. "Geez, Garrett, your car's a pigsty. Is this what happens when you're a neat freak in every other aspect of your life?"

He quickly ducked his head inside the car, his eyes latching onto the mass of papers on the passenger seat. "Oh, sorry, let me help you move it."

They reached for the folder on top at the same time and spoke over each other as they pulled.

"It's fine. I can move it for you—"

"Here, I'll take that—"

It would have been fine had Garrett grasped the folder firmly. It would have been a non-issue had he tucked the folder under the driver's seat or into the back pocket. It would have gone unnoticed, unspoken, and unproblematic had one small brochure not dropped right in front of Anna. Garrett could have gone on like everything was the same, carrying the secret where no one could reach it.

But that didn't happen. Instead, the brochure fell into the middle of the seat, the yellow Army star standing brightly against the black background.

Anna's shaking hand jerked away from it. "Garrett, what the hell is this?"

He groaned loudly, crumbling the brochure into a ball and chucking it into the backseat, barely missing James's head. "You weren't supposed to see this. I wanted the right time to talk about it."

Anna backed away, fist to her mouth, the door still hanging wide open, only stopping when her back bumped into the car parked beside Garrett. She repeatedly shook her head as if it would stir up the events that occurred, like a snow globe, clouding the scene and maybe, for once, revealing a new picture. "What branch?"

He turned toward James as if waiting for his response first, and Anna wanted to scream at her brother to focus on her, to take in every detail of her face when his answer came.

Garrett sighed heavily as he dropped into the driver's seat. "Infantry."

Her back stiffened. She vacillated between wanting to hit something, wanting to run away, and wanting the pain stabbing her chest to disappear. She was dazed, demoralized, devastated. "When do you leave for basic."

"Anna, get in the car."

"You need to answer me first."

His hand smacked the steering wheel. "Let's not do this here. Get in, let's go get ice cream, and we can talk about it more while we drive."

"Garrett, tell me!" She didn't mean to shout it, but her voice echoed in the parking lot. No, she wouldn't give him an easy way out, an opportunity to focus elsewhere while he crushed her with the complex emotions of "missing," a word that should be a verb on its own.

He stared into his lap, wringing his hands. "In two weeks."

Anna slammed the door shut, raced through the parking lot, and hopped the curb onto the sidewalk. Tears ran down her cheeks, and she roughly swiped them away. What was wrong with him? Sure, he'd mentioned an *interest* in joining months ago, but then he buckled down, completed the college applications, received acceptance letters, and selected Syracuse University, a great school in the state. After that, Anna had let the worry leave her, finding solace in all of Garrett's careful planning, the dependable brother he always was, just a little bit away if she needed him.

But those plans included elaborate lies, and Anna couldn't stomach it.

She knew all about her grandfather's nightmares of his time in Vietnam, refusing anyone's help, pushing the rest of the family away, and finally ending it with a bullet one drunken night. Hadn't Mom always said the war comes home? Now it was Mom and Dad's turn, and they'd been fighting off and on for the last two months. While things were okay for now, he'd be leaving in a year. And then what?

Why would Garrett want this as his future? He had the grades and the athletic skills and freaking *scholarships* to take on a college that would set him on a path toward a stellar career. Why did he insist on throwing it away for the Army?

A car engine grew louder, and Anna turned her face away from the road.

"Anna, come on—please get in the car," James called.

She glanced at the car to see her brother white-knuckling the steering wheel, eyes focused on the road, lips held flat. She shook her head. "Count me out."

"C'mon, it's tradition. You can't skip out."

"I'm not in the mood, James."

Garrett gassed the car, jerking the wheel to the right, then slammed on the brakes. The park lights clicked before he wrenched the door open and stomped toward her. "I didn't do this to hurt you, but this isn't your choice."

The forcefulness with which he spoke threatened to knock Anna over, which made her push back all the harder. "Garrett, you lied! Not only to me but to Mom and Dad. We all thought we'd drop you off at school in the fall. Two weeks isn't enough time for Mom to process this."

"You mean you don't have enough time. For God's sake, Anna, I want to make a choice that means something. This does. I'm not doing it for you, or Mom, or Dad, or anyone else. This is something I want to do *for myself*. I don't care if you accept it or not, if you hate me for it or love me through it, but this is *my* choice." He paused, catching his breath. "Now, are you going to get in or not?"

Anna gritted her teeth because what was there to say? She walked away, continuing down the sidewalk on her journey home.

"All right, well, I'm not leaving you behind. You're choosing to walk, and I'm not sticking around."

Anna shot her middle finger into the air.

"Real mature, Anna!" he called after her.

During the long walk, Anna fumed. She thought of the news stories she'd seen on television and read in the newspaper. Was it only nine months ago that this all started? So much had happened since then, both at home and abroad. Sure, Afghanistan had a new government, but would it work? Plus, there were the major operations. They'd been called a success, but would they hold? What would happen with the reconstruction efforts? What about all the talk of Iraq and arms inspections? Everywhere she turned for answers led to more questions, and none of the responses soothed her. None gave her hope for her family's future. And now Garrett would be gone.

White-hot pain sliced through her chest at the thought of him joining the infantry. He would be shipped out shortly after completing his AIT and getting to his first duty station. Then he'd be another one in a crop of people showing up to be shot up.

Her hands curled into fists, and she cursed the war. Would it never stop knocking on her door? Now Garrett was a loaded gun and the owner was his country, using him as they saw fit. But he could die!

What a stupid decision, to go to war, to avenge deaths to start in one place before going to another. How far would it go? Hadn't Garrett said it could be quick? Sure, the Taliban wasn't in power anymore, but they weren't why Dad went there. Who was the United States fighting now? Who would they be fighting next year? How would things be a year from now? How much worse would it get? Her stomach twisted at the thought.

As she strode forward, she caught her loose shoelace and almost fell. She huffed out a breath as if everything were conspiring against her, before kneeling to retie it. She had finished looping it into a fresh knot when footsteps stopped beside her. When she rose from the ground, James stood waiting, his face tight.

"Oh, so you did get out after all," she said sarcastically, the fight bubbling in her belly and tingling in her fingertips.

James scooted a pebble around the sidewalk with his toe, staying silent.

She shook her head angrily. "I can't believe he did it. He mentioned it— *once*," she raged. "I thought I'd be packing his room in August, not shoving shit into duffel bags to put him on a plane to Georgia before he heads for the front lines."

James kicked the pebble away. "I know this isn't what you were expecting."

"He *lied* to me. There wasn't anything to expect."

James tossed his arms wide. "I'm not on anyone's side, Anna. I understand he hurt you."

"This isn't about me, though. It's a death sentence!"

He raised his eyebrows. "Could you stop yelling at me for a minute?"

She spun on her heel and walked toward home. "Don't talk to me right now."

A hand closed over her bicep, halting her progress. "I don't mean you should stop talking—just ease up on me a little. I'm here for you. Let's talk through it together."

"I hate it, James. I hate the Army. This war is stupid. It doesn't have a point except to drag the people fighting it deeper and deeper into trouble."

"I know it's put a lot of weight on you."

She paced the sidewalk: a few steps toward home, then quickly turned around. "You know how many houses I've lived in? How many states? I keep waiting for my dad to come home with orders, and if I'm not worried about that, I'm worried about sending him back to Afghanistan or now maybe to Iraq. You don't know how scary it is to send your dad to war or where he could get shot. You don't know what it's like to spend so much of your life without your dad."

As soon as the words left her mouth, she knew she'd taken it too far. She pictured herself grabbing the pronouns and accusations and verbs and shoving them back behind her teeth. He knew what it was like to live without parents. But once her mind had fixated on everything she hated about military life, she'd stopped thinking. Her shoulders pulled up to her ears as she watched James go from supportive best friend to straight-up angry, his mouth dropping into a flat line.

"Are you serious?" he asked. "I'm standing here trying to help you. You aren't being fair." He nudged past her and walked on, not turning around to see where he was. "You don't get to talk to me like that. If you decide to treat me like your friend, you can call me later."

Anna raised her eyes to the sky, shaking her head, finding her footing in the world that kept threatening to throw her off its surface. "I'm sorry. You're my friend, but I'm pissed—"

He spun around quickly. "There's no 'buts.' You want to talk about being friends? Then don't say things like that."

This time, when he walked away, he didn't slow.

Anna was frozen in place by a full-body cringe. James's back was rigid, and she saw him shake his head. She followed in his footprints for the long walk home, working through the problems the whole way. Ugh, why did it always have to be struggles with the people she loved most? Dad leaving, now Garrett leaving, and James mad at her because she railed on Garrett like an idiot . . .

But Garrett was the first issue to tackle. She could apologize for blowing up (was there anything worse than apologizing to a sibling?) without sacrificing her principles. And after that? The most immediate problem would be James, and she would need to have her head straight enough to give him the most heartfelt apology she'd ever muster. Did Emily have any guidance on that?

She mulled poetry through her head, searching for a line or two that would reassure her, but she kept coming up empty. Finally, she reached her building and trudged up the stairs, hearing the pounding bass of her brother's music long before she reached their floor. *Here we go . . .*

The sound assaulted her as she opened the door, rattling pictures on the walls. She followed the narrow hallway and banged on the door, knowing he'd never hear a civil knock. The door instantly opened, and the music was impossibly louder.

She squinted against the noise. "Mind turning that down?" she shouted. "The neighbors are gonna get pissed."

He pressed a button on the white remote in his hand before sitting atop the foot locker at the end of his bed. He stared at her expectantly.

She forced herself to think before speaking, and her words came out slower than usual. "I'm not gonna make excuses for what I said, but I'd like you to think for a minute about how I feel. You'll be gone this summer and for however many years. Dad will be gone again next year. Mom will be back at work. You're leaving me to face a lot on my own. We were always a team, Garrett."

He frowned. "I don't need to be the one to take care of everyone in this family. You want to be treated like an adult? Now you are."

The admission slapped her in the face, and she fumbled to respond. "I'm not asking you to take care of me. I want a partner through this. I'm already worried about Dad, and now I have to worry about you, too. I don't want something happening to you. Did you at least talk to Dad about it?"

"I don't need anyone's permission."

"I don't mean for that. Dad could help when it comes to telling Mom."

Garrett stared at the floor, his knee jostling up and down. "I haven't figured that out yet. I have no idea how to tell Mom."

Anna sat on the edge of the bed as the fight slowly seeped out of her. "I heard them arguing a couple months ago, after Dad got back."

Garrett paused, and the anger left his face except for the lines around his eyes and mouth, only hinting at the tension he still carried. "About what?"

"She wanted him to get out, but he's too close to retirement. He wasn't budging, so she gave him an ultimatum: one more deployment and then done."

He frowned. "What does that mean? What happens if he stays in longer?"

She shrugged. "I don't know."

"Did they mention divorce, or—"

"I didn't hear that, Garrett. I'm telling you what she said."

Garrett shuffled his foot along the rug, back and forth, a soft scuff the only sound in the room. "Well, that's good for you if he gets out. They'll stay here to let you finish school."

"I don't care about school." It shocked her. Hadn't she always been focused on what would be next for her? She plowed ahead anyway, shaking the thought from her mind. "Mom's taking all of this badly. And while you get to leave, I have to pick up the pieces."

He groaned in response. "Would you stop? Even if I went to college I'd still be leaving. Syracuse is close, but that wouldn't mean I'd be here every weekend. You'd be by yourself no matter what."

Her heart sank and the lion of anger reduced to a meek kitten. "But you'd be close if I needed you. When you're gone, you're gone. If you go overseas, it'll be a while until I hear from you. It's not like I can call you in the middle of the night."

"You don't even know how soon I'll deploy or if I'll ever get the chance."

She stared at the stained carpet. "If I assume you will, I'll be ready when it happens."

He huffed out a breath. "You and I both know it doesn't work like that."

"Why couldn't you have told me this before? It was like a bomb, Gar."

He leaned forward, placing his elbows on his knees and scratching the back of his neck. "I didn't want a repeat of September. The look on your face? It was like you hated me for suggesting it."

"So, you thought lying would be better?"

"No. But it wouldn't have been hanging over our heads for weeks."

She pushed quickly off the bed. "You mean you wouldn't have to be here to see it. You know what, Garrett? Do whatever you want. It's your life. You don't want to include me in it enough to be honest with me? I get it. Go sow your oats or whatever the hell it is. I don't want to hear any more about it."

She beelined for her room, slammed the door behind her, and locked it. There she stewed, leaning against the bedroom door, as the betrayal, the secrets, the announcement burrowed deeper under her skin. Is this what her future would be like? Running into her room and hiding from everyone when things got hard?

She pushed off her bed, scrawled a note on the kitchen counter, and left the apartment building, breathing in the summer air. If she cut through the yards to James's house and then a few more behind him, the trees gave way to an open field. There was a buffer of grass in between, a small pond a short distance away, but it was where Anna and James went when they wanted to be alone. They'd gather an old quilt to sit on, pack a bag of snacks, and head out to their tiny oasis.

It was their favorite in the summer. They'd sit out there for hours, watching the sun set behind the ridge miles away, surrounded by the scent of fresh-cut grass and the summer humidity. As the sun lazily slunk down behind the sky-line, the sheen of perspiration on their skin would cool as the steady drumbeat of cicadas hissed from tall trees, the leaves rustled in the gentle breeze, and the lightning bugs lit up the night with their steady staccato. That time of year was beginning. It was their escape, their haven, the one place where bad news ceased to exist.

She forced herself to ignore James's cheery yellow front door and keep walking straight, pushing roughly through tree branches that clawed at her clothes before reaching the clearing.

Where James was already sitting on a blanket.

She sighed loudly, kicking at a spiteful weed with her dirty Converse.

"Want to talk about it?" James asked, not turning to face her.

The sky was shifting from bright blue to orange and yellow, treating the grass, their skin, and the water to a beautiful golden glow.

*Bring me the sunset in a cup . . . tell me how far the morning leaps - tell me
what time the weaver sleeps who spun the breadths of blue!*

Tonight, the area was quiet except for the distant lows of cattle from over
the hill.

Anna twisted her fingers around each other, grasping for the words she
knew she needed to say. "I'm sorry I snapped at you. I know you were trying to
help and I was too angry to listen."

His head turned slowly toward her, and his dark brows pulled together as
he laughed humorlessly, scratching at his jaw. "You think I'm mad that you
yelled at me?"

"Well, yeah," she said uncomfortably. "You were trying to help."

He shook his head and turned away. "That isn't even close to why I'm mad."

After sitting on the blanket beside him and taking a deep breath, she pulled
the words from deep in her throat, and they hurt so much more coming out this
time. "I'm sorry for what I said about you not knowing what it feels like to be
without a parent. You know better than even I do."

"I know you're upset, and sometimes we say things we don't mean, but you
have to stop thinking it's you against the world."

Anna picked at a purple string on the quilt, stretching it as far as she could
so the fabric bunched before releasing it to settle. "I took it too far."

"Too far? You don't say those kinds of things to your friends."

She chewed on the inside of her cheek. "I really am sorry, James. I was livid
and I lost control."

James picked at a blade of grass and twisted it before tying it in a few knots.
She heard his long exhale as his shoulders finally sank lower. "I'll forgive you.
But I mean it—I'm here for you to talk to, but I won't be your target."

She scooted closer to him. "I understand, and I'm sorry."

"So . . . What are you gonna do? Do you want to send him off with this
between you? Have him leave, maybe deploy, and regret that you never made
it right?"

She stilled. "Um, are you completely missing his part in this?"

"No, I get it." He spoke slowly, his words still tense. "But I know you. Do
you want to send him away without having things good between you?"

She cringed and groaned.

He sighed heavily and placed an arm around her shoulders, closing the
distance between them. "You're upset and angry. I think any sister would be.
But Garrett's always been there for you. You're gonna feel bad about it later if
you push him away, but by then it'll be too late to do anything about it."

"Sometimes it's annoying how well you know me, you know that, right?"

He smirked and shrugged. "I get it's a lot, but it isn't Annaliese Pechman versus the world. You know Nana and I are always here."

"It's hard for me. It's either I'm at school with mostly kids who don't get it or I'm at military events where everyone is going through the exact same thing. I don't want to talk about it at school because people say such stupid things. And with other mil kids, they don't have it any easier. It sucks for all of us."

"So why not come to me?"

She rubbed her eyes. "I don't know how long I'll have you."

"Nana always says not to worry about the things you can't change. You can only control how you respond to it. I might not be perfect, but I can be there for you in ways that help."

Anna leaned toward James and set her head on his shoulder, the two of them watching the sky turn pink. "I'll try to do better."

"I'll always be here."

"I know."

Together, they sat in their oasis, but there was a tension in the air that hadn't existed before. There was much more to be said, but both of their hearts were fragile. Maybe it was their fight, but they'd had spats before—stupid ones they always resolved the same day. Perhaps it was the dark future that loomed. Possibly they were bearing the heavy weight of the day and all they would lose in the coming months. Whatever the cause, not once did they lay back on the blanket and gaze at the sky, oohing and aahing at the changing of the colors and the first star's appearance. Not once did they talk about their dreams or what the summer would hold for them, feeling the excitement building in their bellies, then shooting into the sky along with their voices, exploding like fireworks.

Anna knew why—the fear plagued her year after year after year. Once again, the wall she constructed would need to protect her from the hurt of inevitable goodbyes.

CHAPTER TEN

FROM BABY BOOTS TO COMBAT BOOTS

JUNE 20, 2002

The room was silent as Anna leaned against her closet door, legs stretched straight out. Absence was nothing new, but this time, it felt different. For everyone.

For Dad, it was pride. And when Garrett finally came clean, Dad's chin lifted a little higher, his chest puffed a little fuller. He grabbed two beers, sharing one with Garrett despite him being underage, telling him, "If you're old enough to go to war, you're old enough to have a beer. I'm proud of you."

Anna watched from the living room, a library book in her lap, as they shared their drink. They laughed and talked, their voices rising to crescendos then falling back to low rumbles. After realizing she was squeezing the paperback's cover, she loosened her grip, quickly smoothing out the bends and warps.

When was the last time he said he was proud of *her*? When was the last time he gave her credit for her opinions or goals? But here, Garrett got some pats on the back and a drink, all because he was following in Dad's footsteps.

How would Dad feel if Garrett died?

Mom, on the other hand . . . she'd expressed everything Anna wouldn't allow herself to. She screamed, cried. "Did you have something to do with this?" she'd asked Dad. "If you did, I swear I'll never speak to you again."

The two had stared at each other across the dining room table, tears casting a sheen in Mom's eyes, determination settling into Dad's. One was daring the other to take that first step off the cliff, knowing all that would tumble after them if they did.

Then Mom stormed off.

As for Anna, she'd been speechless since her initial blowup with Garrett. What was there to say now? Would pleading with her brother not to enlist change anything? It wouldn't make a difference. Garrett was still going, and it hurt.

Right now, he was in the next room, doing a final review of his bags in preparation for basic training. And all the while, Anna was seated on the floor of her room, processing their argument from weeks before and the stony silence ever since. At the moment, she was accomplishing nothing. She gathered all her ego and released it on an exhale. It's what Emily would have done.

She gathered herself from the floor, then peeked around the corner of the doorway, not wanting to intrude on his concentration. His head tilted forward as he read a paper. His eyes flicked back and forth across every word, checking and double-checking that he had all the right things. Typical Garrett.

They would all drive him to the airport tomorrow morning to catch his flight to Fort Benning, Georgia, for basic training. He'd stay for his AIT, then get orders to his unit unless they wanted him in Airborne school or elsewhere. The where and when would come when the Army felt it was best, as it had throughout their lives.

His small gym bag lay flat on the bed. Beside it was a stack of neatly folded clothes, with lines so crisp the creases would hold for days even after hanging up. A large bag of toiletries and gym shoes also waited to be neatly arranged. He paused as he looked around the room.

What must it feel like to follow your own path? She imagined the surge of excitement to take that first step toward *her* future. One day . . .

Finally, she knocked on the doorframe, announcing her presence outside the room. Garrett turned to face her then. Noticing who it was, he averted his eyes, attempting to flatten the bag stuffed with toiletries into a neat line: toothpaste, foot powder, deodorant, baby wipes.

She wished he would focus on her. The argument about his service was a wall between them. The entrance to his room was the line they'd drawn in the sand, the precipice of giving in or standing firm, of apology and forgiveness versus refusal and stubbornness, of love and care against disbelief and defiance. They hadn't spoken much since their argument, avoiding each other when they could, dancing around each other when they couldn't. She'd taken the brunt of Mom's anger about his enlistment but had never thrown him under the bus. He had to manage a little respect for that, at least, right?

The tension was a cloud of humidity in the room, sticking to their skin and thickening in their throats, but Anna knew she had to speak first.

"I came to talk to you, but I don't know what to say."

He didn't stop his movement, placing the toiletries to one side of the bag, but his head turned toward her slightly. "If you have anything to say about not liking my decision, you can get out now." He finally eyed her for the first time in what felt like weeks.

"Honestly, I'm kind of jealous of you right now, and I *hate* admitting that."

He huffed out a breath. "And why's that?"

She ran a finger over the dresser that a thin layer of dust would cover in his absence. "It must be nice to go your own way—Fleetwood Mac-style. Making your own decisions . . ."

He gave her that look that said, *you're saying something without thinking. Pause and start again.* And because he was right, she'd stayed silent.

"The Army will still tell me what to do, where I can go, and how long I can stay in."

"Yeah, but *you* chose to do that. It wasn't shoved on you by Mom or Dad. It wasn't a piece of paper handed to you that you weren't expecting. *You* made it happen."

He sighed heavily, needlessly arranging his clothing. Shorts on the bottom, shirts on top, then underwear and socks balanced just so. "Did you need something?"

A cold swept through her body, removing any of the humor she'd attempted when entering the room. She twisted her fingers together. "You're leaving in the morning, and I don't want you to go with this between us."

He scooped up half the pile of clothes, placing them gently in the bag, then folded his arms. "What do you want me to say."

She tugged at the bottom of her shirt. "You don't have to say anything. I don't know if I can say I support you through this, and I *hate* saying that to you, but I don't want to send you away as if everything's fine. You're my brother, and I love you. And I don't want you to go." Her voice cracked.

He lowered himself to the bed, rubbing a hand over the top of his head. "I've already signed the papers. I have to go, Anna."

"I know. I'm not trying to stop you. It's always been the two of us, you and me, no matter what was happening with Dad or where we lived or how often Mom was home because of work or other responsibilities—it was always you and me. Now I have to do it myself."

"James will always be here."

A line burrowed deep into her forehead. "No one can replace you. I feel like I'm losing half of me."

He pulled the desk chair toward the bed with his foot and gestured to it. "Can you sit instead of hovering?"

She followed his suggestion, twisting a string at the hem of her shirt.

"You won't be able to reach me on the phone, but you can write letters. God knows I'll need them."

"It isn't the same."

They both stared at the floor, and their bodies bowed with the heaviness of goodbye.

"I can't let you leave without making this right," she murmured.

He shrugged, powerless to resolve the situation. "I'd say 'It is what it is,' but you hate that saying."

"You know I love you, right? That I said what I did *because* you mean so much to me."

He smoothed a corner of the bedsheet. "Yeah, I get it."

"You could go over there and never come home, and that terrifies me." Her voice shook and tears blurred her vision. "It's scary enough knowing it could happen to Dad, but now I have to worry about you."

"There's only so much we can control. Dad had to go, but he came back all right. That's how it goes for most people. If you think about every possible thing that could go wrong, you'll exhaust yourself."

His response was so similar to Mom's.

Anna focused on a frame on his dresser. An identical one sat on a shelf in her bedroom. Funny—she couldn't remember the last time she actually focused on that photograph, held it in her hands, and reflected on the moment it was taken. She'd have to rub a layer of dust off it with her sleeve. Instead, his frame sat neatly in the back corner, shining in the sunlight thanks to his religious Saturday morning cleanings.

This particular photo had been taken when they first moved to Watertown. It was autumn, and they'd found their way up into the hills with a photographer, standing in front of a natural background of umbers, rusts, crimsons, and citrines, the colors of fall. Mom and Dad had bickered about the long walk (Mom thought it was too much for Anna), Dad insisted he made the right decision, Garrett twisted an ankle halfway up but vowed to trudge on, and Anna's hair caught on a few low-hanging tree branches she couldn't avoid, pulling her braid loose. But once they saw the overlook, hill upon hill upon hill of color stretching for miles, everyone knew Dad had made the right choice. They snapped the picture with Anna's hair still slightly askew, Mom and Dad holding each other tightly, and Garrett putting his arms around Mom and Anna.

Whenever she saw that picture, she'd cringed at herself, but now she saw the beauty of it. The memory of that day was still there, and it all added to the photo she rarely looked at. Garrett's eyes followed her gaze to the dresser, and he left the bed and snatched the frame, peeling back the metal pegs and lifting the cardboard backing to remove the picture.

"Remember how often we used to fight?" he asked as he slid the photo into his duffel bag.

A corner of her mouth tilted up. "So much that it drove Mom and Dad crazy."

"When the hell did that change? It's like I woke up one day, and you weren't as much of a bratty little sister."

"Don't worry—I eventually had a change of heart that you weren't always a jerk of a brother."

He chuckled and shoved the chair away with his foot, sending Anna rolling back a few inches.

"But seriously, Garrett. I'm glad we became friends."

"And you'll write to me?" he asked as he zipped up his bag.

"You don't have to worry about that." Anna stared at him for a long moment. "Last chance to back out," she said, raising an eyebrow.

He observed the room and the two small bags on his bed. "Nah, I'm making the right choice. You'll see."

||

JUNE 21, 2002

Anna sat on the floor in her brother's quiet room, leaning against his closet door. It was much the same—he'd only been gone for two hours. The record player and stereo sat silent. His dressers were freshly dusted, the lemon scent still clinging to the air. The desk was free of notebooks or stray papers, everything stowed in drawers for the foreseeable future. And all the while she sat there, she imagined hearing his footsteps coming down the hall, then seeing him walking in, turning on the latest Red Hot Chili Peppers album or spinning a The Who vinyl.

As she stared now at the perfectly centered pillow atop smooth blankets, she wished he were still here so she could try again to say things the right way, because last words never feel like enough. She'd have led by telling him how she didn't want him to go. While she wanted to be like Mom and ask that he only do his four years and get out, it hadn't felt right.

So she'd gone with honesty. And while Garrett left on fine terms, there had to be more she could have said.

She'd revealed more than she intended when saying she was jealous of him, of this chance to break free, to choose his own path. While she hated his choice—would never stop hating it, still believed he was influenced too much by Dad—she understood him needing to make it for himself. So she settled on being proud in a different way.

Her eyes flicked to the dresser where the empty frame stood. The optimists would say the vacant space would allow her to imagine starting fresh, filling the clear glass pane with whatever *she* wanted. But the pessimist in her saw it for what it was—another mark of his absence.

A knock sounded on the door, and Mom's face came around the corner. Her eyes were still red and swollen, her voice scratchy. "What are you doing in here?"

"Why did you knock?"

"Force of habit."

"Same." Anna shrugged. "I wasn't sure where else to be right now."

Mom slipped inside the room, sitting on Garrett's bed and rubbing her palms together. "I'm sorry I snapped at you at the airport."

Anna wanted to roll her eyes. It was a stupid disagreement, another example of not seeing eye-to-eye. No sweat—it would happen again in a few days. "You don't have to apologize, Mom."

"No, I do. You couldn't understand why I was so upset at the airport when it was only basic training. And I gave you the response I always hated when I was a teenager, that you'd understand when you were older or that it would all make sense when you had more life experience. Even if it's true, it isn't helpful to you. I'm sorry."

Anna picked at her raw cuticles. "I thought we could be more open with each other. We came so far while Dad was gone."

Mom lowered herself from the bed to the floor to be level with Anna and leaned back against the side of the mattress. "You're right. You want to know how I'm feeling?"

Anna nodded.

"When I was in the bathroom before he boarded his flight, I couldn't get myself together. After years of saying goodbye to your dad, dealing with that emptiness and worry, I couldn't get myself to grin and bear it. It was like cinder blocks held me in place."

"What's so different about it this time?"

"I'm sending my baby boy to prepare for war." Her voice broke, and she shrugged helplessly as the corners of her mouth turned down. "But my little boy is now a man. There was a day when I picked him up for the last time, and I never knew it would be the last time. If I had, I would have picked him up again and squeezed him tight." She sucked in her cheeks while staring at the ceiling, letting the waver in her voice settle to gentle rocking. "I swear, within sixty seconds, I thought of fifty careers that would better suit him, twenty reasons college was a necessary experience, ten reasons he should skip the Army, and a hundred reasons I love him so dearly. None of my pleas would change his mind. I know that."

Anna understood. Instead of choosing the road less traveled, Garrett had chosen the one with generations of footprints ground into the soil.

"I only had a week to process all that this means," Mom continued. "I can deal with him leaving home—every mother has to—but this isn't him leaving to follow his dreams or marry a good woman or take on the world. He's leaving to take on the war."

Mom's eyes slid out of focus, staring at the worn carpet, her fingers pulling at the pile. "I told myself I would get through it, but all I could see was the moment the doctor placed him in my arms, his body smaller than I expected. Did you know I spent that first night refusing to sleep after you both were born? I couldn't stop feeling your skin against my cheek. I wanted to look at you and hold you close."

Mom's gaze traced the lines on the walls to the shelf above his dresser, where he displayed a few old toys: a P-52 sat angled, its propeller facing out toward the room. A Sherman tank parked resolutely beside it, four green Army men in a line.

"When we said goodbye to him, I had to wrap my arms around myself so I wouldn't put them around him, so I wouldn't squeeze him to me and pull him away from where he needed to go. But then he was gone. Blurred into oblivion at first, then simply gone."

Anna scooted closer and grasped her mother's hand.

Mom squeezed Anna's fingers. "I know it's hard for you too, baby. I know it is. But my job as a mother has always been to keep you safe, to make you feel loved, to protect you. This is the first time I've had to forget all that. I have to let him go, and it's the hardest thing I've ever done."

"I'm sorry for getting frustrated with you."

Mom wiped her eyes with the back of her hand. "I understand."

The floor outside the door creaked, and Dad stepped into the room. "You doing okay?"

Anna couldn't control how quickly she leaned away from him, and she couldn't ignore how Mom glared, refusing to meet his eyes.

An uneasy silence filtered through the room, and Anna searched her brain for something—anything—to say. "Just . . . processing, Dad."

He sighed and leaned a shoulder against the doorframe. "Even once he's ready to go it doesn't mean he *will*."

Anna chomped on the inside of her cheek to keep herself from scolding him.

"Now isn't the time," Mom said as she left the room, brushing briskly past Dad.

He stared at the floor for a moment until his shoulders relaxed. He stepped farther into the room, and Anna rose to leave.

"She's right, Dad. Now isn't the time." She turned toward the doorway, but he stopped her.

"Why is everyone mad at me all of a sudden?"

Anna delivered the final cutting blow. "He left because of you."

"I had nothing to do with it—"

"But you did, Dad. You had everything to do with it."

2003

If I can stop one Heart from breaking
I shall not live in vain
If I can ease one Life the Aching
Or cool one Pain
Or help one fainting Robin
Unto his Nest again
I shall not live in vain.

—Emily Dickinson, 1890

|| CHAPTER ELEVEN ||

SIXTEEN WORDS CHANGED IT ALL

MARCH 20, 2003

The nation had already spent eighteen months in Afghanistan, but now the battle plan shifted to a country Americans knew. Dad's boots had sunk into the dust of that desert a decade prior, departing after Mom gave him one final kiss, leaving the rest up to fate. Anna had been only a toddler when she'd said goodbye, retaining few memories of Dad's first absence. But now she knew better, knew more.

Sixteen words convinced at least half of Americans that there was a reason to go to Iraq again: "*The British government has learned that Saddam Hussein recently sought significant quantities of uranium from Africa.*" No one knew how turning the attention to Iraq would affect the mostly uneventful battle in Afghanistan. By the Iraq invasion, there had been only twelve combat-related deaths in Afghanistan.

That was about to change.

||

While the airstrike on Iraq unfolded almost six thousand miles away, Anna and James drove the hour south to Syracuse. They'd left at their usual school hour, skipping the day for a little political action, and Anna had left a hastily scrawled note that she would be home later than expected. She originally planned to go alone, not wanting to ask anyone else to skip school, but James insisted he go along. At least then, if anything happened, they'd have each other.

When James arrived to pick her up in Nana's borrowed tan Plymouth sedan, Anna was waiting on the curb down the street, the front of her sign pressed against her body. She carefully nestled her poster behind the seat, ensuring the thick paper didn't bend or crease. Then, she pulled off her mittens, scarf, and hat and shoved them into the footwell alongside James's, unzipping her heavy winter coat to release some body heat. The spring thaw was still far from the long New York winters. Rain was in the forecast, and the sky was gray and ominous, leaving them unsure what they would get: an event without a hitch or a coming storm.

"Are you all set?" James asked.

"Yep, we can roll out."

"So where are we going exactly?"

"Clinton Square. Get on 81 until the Syracuse exit, and I'll guide you from there." She flattened the unfolded MapQuest directions across her lap.

"And the protest starts and ends there?"

"It starts there, but we'll have to walk about a mile back."

"Hopefully we stay dry," he said, leaning forward to gauge the weather. "What do you know about the group that organized it?"

"It's the Syracuse Peace Council. I saw something in the newspaper about them when the Iraq talks started. I signed up for their newsletter, and then they mentioned a protest today."

"You looked into them, right? They're legit?"

"Since when does a protest have to be legit?"

"I mean the permits."

Anna laughed. "They don't need permits, James."

He huffed. "Yes, they do. They can get arrested—"

"And likely released without charges if they aren't doing anything destructive."

"But they need a permit."

She rolled her eyes. "Kind of defeats the purpose of a protest, doesn't it? Asking for permission?"

"Better than going to a police station," he mumbled as he merged onto the interstate, glancing over his shoulder.

"It'll be fine, James," she said louder over the road noise in the old car.

"I don't want Nana to have to drive down to get us."

Anna placed her hand on his arm. "She won't. It'll be fine."

He changed lanes to pass a semi, glancing at her. "You at least seem excited."

"I guess I am," she said. "I've spent my whole life around people who firmly believe in using the military and standing behind their mission. I haven't always felt that way. This group isn't military-connected, and while they aren't against the military, they want peace over anything else, so they're against go-ing into Iraq."

"So, like Emily," he said with a lopsided smile.

She stared out the window. "Anything that keeps us from sending more people."

Probably sensing the shift in her mood, James changed the subject. "Put some music on. It'll be a good forty minutes on here."

Anna lifted the CD binder from the floor, paging through the plastic-covered pages until she spotted Anti-Flag's *Mobilize* album. It was the perfect anthem for the events of the day, for the message of the day, for the experience of the day. And it wouldn't hurt to drive home the ideas of resistance, freedom of speech, and fighting the system. She slid the CD from its pocket and inserted it into the head unit James installed last year, then she cranked the volume as the first riffs of "911 for Peace" poured out of the speakers. She sat back in the seat, drumming her fingers on her knees as James nodded along to the beat as they sailed down the highway toward their first anti-war protest.

As they rolled slowly down the streets of Syracuse, a mass of people gathered in Clinton Square. "So that's it, huh?" James asked.

"Must be. I see street parking on the other side."

Some carried American flags, while others held homemade signs for peace. A few groups carried wide banners gripped by multiple hands.

Drop Bush, Not Bombs.

No to war in Iraq.

This is What Democracy Looks Like.

She hadn't even joined them yet, but the thought of being surrounded by people who rallied for the same cause sent a rush coursing through her body. It was like the dampness of the day: permeating the air, slick on the skin, and felt by everyone. Anna happily inhaled as she hopped out of the truck, letting the thick air coat her throat like sticky-sweet honey.

She removed her handmade sign and brushed her fingers over the words. *One is Enough.*

One war is plenty, one life is enough, one voice can change the world, one sign can change minds and alter the tides of war, forcing them back out to sea. War would always be somewhere on the horizon—she knew that. While the average citizen could force it to stay far from the coast, she knew what happened when war impacted a person's life every day. She believed in her message, and it sent light into her bones, making her shine for others as she explained all it meant and how much it mattered.

People were angry, and they should be. What no one in her house talked about—the phrase that would increase Anna's distaste for war, the words that would make the veins in her father's neck pop and the lines in her mother's face deepen, the sentence that would make Anna shake with frustration and worry—was that Garrett was deploying to Iraq.

There was a real stake in that war now.

This was where she was meant to be. She knew that as surely as she could breathe.

James came around the car, pulling gloves on his hands. "You ready?"

Anna removed the packs of hand warmers, holding a pair out to James, then opened the others for herself. "You'll probably want these."

He slipped them into his gloves and reached for her sign. "Here goes nothing."

She chuckled. "It'll be fine."

They made their way toward the crowd, and Anna was in awe of the beauty of the square.

A stone bank sat on the corner, five stories high, with sharp, angled roofs. Next to it was an equally tall, impossibly narrow building with a clock tower. An American flag inside the square caught the breeze, fluttering softly. And in the center of the space stood the Soldiers and Sailors Monument, a large square column topped with a sphere, erected to honor those who fought in the Civil War and later rededicated in memory of all service members from that particular county.

One side showed the Call to Arms, a soldier with a bugle to his mouth, while another in the foreground repaired an American flag. The other side was the defense of a hill, guarding the flag and willing to take the final stand. Anna soaked up the symbolism of the art, breathing in the willingness to accept that tattered flag, the destroyed bits and pieces of a country two years into war, and repair it, make it whole again, heal it, then ensure any future calls to war are considered more deeply than this one.

A smile crept across her face as she gazed at the people around her, reading more of the signs.

"Glad we came?"

"I am." Goosebumps rose on her skin, creeping up her neck. She was in the right place.

"What's the plan?"

Anna adjusted the backpack on her shoulders, which held a few bottles of water and some snacks. "There will be a speech here, then we'll walk through the streets to the church for a service there."

He stared at her from the corners of his eyes but said nothing.

"What? It's for peace, James."

"Honestly, it's not the protestors that worry me." His eyes followed a few people gathering on the sidewalk across the street from them.

"There shouldn't be any trouble. It's all about peace. Who could have an issue with that?"

A woman held a megaphone to her mouth, saying something unintelligible as a series of shushing and quiet-downs passed through the crowd.

"We are here today because of an unjust war started by our president, an unjust war that will send American troops to the front lines, to be killed, injured, or forgotten. You are here today, joining us, because you agree that we should not be there. The problem with this war is that the United States—our country—is stepping in and trying to convince the rest of the world to join us. But we need to tell them no. The United States does not get to violate the will of the rest of the world by dragging everyone else in."

Cheers rang out around them, and Anna lowered her sign, leaning into the message.

"But listen, this war will be felt here at home by some of you organizing here today. If you have someone over there, it can be all-consuming. You will live it every day, worrying about someone you love every day, watching them change if they make it home. But if you don't have someone over there, then you can go about your life without ever even thinking of the fact that we're in Iraq. Don't let that happen."

Warmth spread from Anna's chest to her fingers and toes, and suddenly the chill of the day disappeared completely despite her breath coming out in a cloud with each exhale. Every inhale was filled with hope.

"That's why we organize here today. To remind people where we are and what's happening. It's why we carry the signs on this cold New York day. Sure, people will tell you that your protests won't change anything. That you taking to the streets as part of your constitutional right to assemble won't do any good. But they're wrong. You can never know how much impact you have and how much worse it would be if people weren't standing up and holding elected officials accountable for their actions. The Vietnam War would have never ended had people not stood up in the middle of it and asked for the bombing to stop."

More claps and hoots and cheers.

"Today, we're going to make sure everyone in Syracuse knows we're watching. We want our signs to show on the news so we can remind anyone watching. We want our elected officials to know we're watching. We're paying attention. And we aren't going to forget where we are."

James and Anna clapped hard as the woman stowed her megaphone and led the crowd in chanting, "This is what democracy looks like," beginning the march downtown.

"I didn't expect it to be like this!" James shouted so Anna could hear him.

She couldn't help but laugh. "You're such a worrywart sometimes."

As they passed a police officer on the corner, the skies opened up, and an icy rain fell onto their jackets, soaking into the top layer. Anna handed her sign to James for a moment, pulling her hood over her head. For now, the adrenaline was surging through her system, insulating her from the cold. Once he handed her sign back, the marchers passed through another intersection. A man on the corner stepped toward them and shouted, "This is unpatriotic."

James turned his head and shouted, "It's the First Amendment—doesn't get more patriotic than that."

Anna elbowed him. "Don't engage. They can say what they want—ignore it."

As they reached the end of the procession and filed into the church, Anna's throat was raw, her body was shivering, and her fingers were numb, but through it all, she'd grasped onto her principles, stepped out for the first time into a world that was new, finally cutting her way through the military cloak. Her heart was full, believing that there were good people out there who wanted to end the suffering, and she'd spent the day surrounded by them.

Later, James and Anna raced back to the car, their bodies shivering and fingers numbed by the cold. James cranked the heat as hot as possible, but they still struggled to get warm thirty minutes later. Their jeans clung to their legs, her hair dripped onto her sweater, and their bodies still shook in their wet clothes.

"I cannot wait to take a shower and get into dry clothes," Anna said through chattering teeth.

"This was your idea."

"I don't control the weather!"

James glanced at her before his gaze returned to the road, the wipers waving quickly across the windshield. "Was it all you hoped it would be?"

"Yes." She kept her answer simple because her reason for being there was more complex than James could understand.

This protest was the first flexing of her muscles to seek out something for *her*, finding a place where she naturally fit, like Garrett had.

James pulled up along the curb outside her apartment. "Thanks for the introduction to civic duty."

Anna laughed. "Thank you for going with me. Drive safe, okay?" She closed the door behind her and raced through the raindrops to the entrance to her building, letting herself inside and quickly climbing the stairs to the apartment. Her fingers were still stiff from the cold as she pulled out her key. She stepped into the warmth of home and shrugged off her coat and boots, tucking them into the closet, a smile on her face. The rain had rippled the posterboard, some of the marker running the length of the paper in drips, but she was thrilled with it. She'd hang it from her closet door later on but wanted to dry it off first.

She turned the corner to the kitchen to grab some paper towels and froze. At the table sat Mom and Dad, and the latter shouldn't have been home at that time of day. His work hours were long now as a first sergeant preparing a company to deploy in July. The telltale veins popped in his forehead, and Anna braced herself against the counter, letting the sign fall to the floor, out of sight.

Dad lifted the note she'd left this morning. "Care to explain this?"

"I told you I'd be home around dinner time."

His jaw tightened. "Where were you? And answer honestly, Anna, because I already know you weren't at school."

"If you already know, then why not say so."

He raised a finger, standing from his chair and stalking toward her. "Now, you watch it."

"Robert," Mom scolded, trying to capture the sparks before they ignited.

He took what might be considered a steadying breath, but the lines on his face deepened rather than softened. "Your mother was worried because she didn't know *where* you were. She called James's grandmother, and she said you had spent the day at a protest. Want to tell me what kind of protest it was?"

She willed herself not to glance at the sign on the floor, but the neon color had drawn his eyes as he approached.

"Please tell me that isn't what I think it is."

She pulled on every ounce of strength she felt that day and went with honesty. "I went to a protest against the invasion of Iraq." There was nothing that could make the situation worse at this point.

He folded his hands on the top of his head, pacing away from her before moving back toward her. "An anti-war protest. Where?"

"In Syracuse."

He made a series of noises as he gathered his thoughts before finally regaining the ability to speak. "You two drove all the way to Syracuse? What the hell is wrong with you, Anna? There are so many stupid decisions you made in the span of a single day, I don't even know where to start."

"It was fine, Dad. No one was arrested. There was no damage to anything in the city."

He glared. "My daughter was protesting the war her brother will fight in only a few months. What if things hadn't been calm? What if you had gotten arrested?"

She folded her arms, ready to go on the defense. "I researched everything. This organization doesn't cause trouble. No one got hurt. We were responsible, Dad."

"You call protesting the war responsible? Do you not understand your place in this family, Annaliese? You have a responsibility as my child. What if you were photographed? What if someone interviewed you?"

She scoffed. "No one's gonna read a Syracuse newspaper in Watertown."

"They do! What would it be like for my young soldiers to see you protesting the war they might be sent to fight? How can I look them in the eye? How can I lead them into the fight when they wonder what I'm preaching at home to lead my child to carry a sign like that?"

Anna yanked her sign off the floor and held it up. "Tell me what's wrong with this, Dad. One war *is* enough; it's more than we can handle, especially when they're separated by a whole other country. You said it yourself."

In the silence that followed, Anna wanted to suck the words back in, but she couldn't recall a single time when she'd challenged her parents like this. Not as a toddler stomping her feet or a child sassing after discovering her voice for the first time. It was as if her backbone had straightened and grown a few inches, allowing her to stand taller behind what she felt in her heart.

He snatched the sign from her hand and tore it in half, shoving it in the wastebasket beside him. "I can't believe you would do something like this."

Her mouth dropped open, but rather than surprise, outrage roared within her. "Why would it be so hard to believe? Why would I want you or Garrett sent there? Or any of your soldiers or anyone else? I know the cost of all of that. Our family doesn't escape war unscathed, Dad. I don't want that happening to other families." Tears rose in her eyes, and she swallowed hard. "I don't want kids to wake up at night wanting their dad and not having him. I don't want them to wonder if their father will remember them while he's gone, to wonder if he's thinking about them when he can't call. I don't want them waking up on Christmas morning to manufactured cheer or watching their exhausted mom try to keep a handle on 'normal' things when it's anything but. This was my chance to do something for me, something the Army can't touch. Something you can't take away from me."

His eyes widened as if she'd slapped him, and she watched as he bit the inside of his cheek. "Well, I'm glad to know that you've hated every part of this."

"That's not what I meant—"

He tilted his wrist to check his watch. "I need to get back to work, but you're grounded. I'll figure out any other punishments while I'm gone."

He walked away, slipping his uniform blouse on and buttoning it in silence before stepping through the door and slamming it behind him.

The quiet that followed was jarring, and the explosion left Anna's body tense and shaking. She leaned against the counter, putting her head in her hands.

"Your dad's right that you should have told us in advance."

Anna jumped, forgetting that Mom had witnessed the entire argument. She had a mug of tea cupped in her hands, the string of the bag hanging over the rim.

"I had it figured out," Anna replied. Hoarseness had settled in her throat, and all the strength she had gathered to fight Dad evaporated.

Mom gestured with her head. "Come sit with me."

Anna swiped her hands down her face. "I can't do any more lectures, okay? I'm tired. I'm upset. I'm still freezing. I don't want to talk anymore. I want to get a shower and lay in bed."

Mom nodded slowly. "Okay."

Anna frowned. "That's it? Okay?"

Mom shrugged. "Yep."

Anna glanced at the exit from the kitchen, then back at Mom, then back to the exit, her feet frozen in place. It was a trap. The second she walked away, Mom would throw a grenade, and then the roof would blow off the top of the building from the heat of their argument. "Come on, if you want to say something, then say it."

"Is that what you want?"

Anna nodded and stayed quiet.

Mom turned sideways to face her daughter. "You should have been honest with us about where you were going, simply for safety reasons. I'm glad James went with you, but you're still teenagers. I know things didn't go badly, but if they had, we wouldn't have known where you were. We would have been blindsided with a phone call from the police department."

Anna waited for Mom to say more, but she simply lifted her cup and sipped quietly.

"Is that all, Mom?"

She nodded in response. "Yep, that's it." She tilted her mug and drained the last of her tea, then pushed her chair back.

Anna backed toward the doorway, still uncertain if Mom was being truthful. The conversation couldn't possibly go this smoothly. As she turned the corner, sure enough, Mom spoke.

"Oh, there is one more thing."

Anna groaned as she turned back around. "Of course there is."

"I'm proud of you."

Anna startled. "What?"

Mom placed her teacup in the sink, then wrapped her arms around Anna. "I'm proud of you for doing what you believe in, for following your principles and putting yourself out there, both at the protest today *and* here. I know it's hard to say those things to him. He believes in what he does, but he has to remember that not all of us do." Mom pulled back and placed her hands on Anna's cheeks, tilting her chin up. "Keep fighting for what you believe in because God knows someone has to." She patted Anna on the arm, then walked down the hallway to her room, closing the door behind her.

Anna leaned against the wall and forced her mouth closed. Mom was fighting in *her* corner. And for the first time, Anna *wanted* Mom's support, her guiding hand, her focus on what Anna felt, her goals, her dreams. In the span of calm and a few words, Mom had spoken volumes.

The next morning, Anna found her protest sign at the foot of her bed, neatly taped back together, a sticky note attached. *Next time, take me with you.*

CHAPTER TWELVE

ZERO MILES TO HELL

JULY 8, 2003

Anna calculated all the things Dad would miss in the coming ten months: another school homecoming, another Thanksgiving, another Christmas, another round of fireworks counting down each hour to the new year, more bonding time they desperately needed in their shaky relationship since the protest. While Mom would always be there, Anna wanted his perspective on life—whatever that would be—and applying to college. A long-distance phone call wasn't the same.

The deployment had come before they were ready, as it often did. At first, the days inched by, slowly evolving into the next, before they blurred together at warp speed, launching her family into the anxiety of the fate ahead. No matter how many times they'd done it, no matter how many times they'd tried to prepare themselves, no matter how "used to it" they should be, it never got easier, never happened as they wanted, never passed by without the gutting of absence and the stab of worry.

Before she knew it, Dad was gone.

She'd known it was coming for more than a year; ever since the last one ended, they were preparing themselves for the next. Waiting with that cloud hovering above them was the worst, and it clogged the gears in the passage of time, slowing it to an unbearable pace.

She still remembered Mom's stories of when Anna was a toddler and Dad was in Iraq. Anna assumed Daddy lived inside the telephone, so she would pick it up, thinking he would always answer. It was a simple concept, and even as a teenager closing in on seventeen, Anna wished it were true.

Twas a long parting, but the time for interview had come, good old Emily had said. Sure, she'd meant the rapture and all sorts of religious stuff Anna didn't care so much about, but the sentiment was the same.

Time is a fickle thing, and a deployment showed that most of all. Throughout her life, Anna wanted to speed it up to reach the good parts, slow it down to savor the moments, or freeze it in place to remain caught in those most special. Yet, no matter what, time passed, all the same: one hour, one minute, one second at a time.

If only there were a dial she could twist once Dad left, to ratchet up the speed, blurring the surroundings until it was all over. No need to experience it, no need to watch Mom's hands shake while watching the news or listen to her crying in the bathroom with the shower on, hoping Anna wouldn't hear. But Anna was too old for that now, and Mom's sobs and fears broke through the wall and sliced into her chest with every shaking breath.

Dad's absence kept that open wound from healing, and it stretched wider every time Anna thought about how she'd only given him a brief hug, muttering "I love you" before he re-entered the war.

And there would be no hope of ignoring that pain in the time to come.

⫼

SEPTEMBER 28, 2003

While Robert was familiar with the waiting, time was something he knew he'd always have far too much of. As he stood in the watchtower overlooking the mountainsides around Firebase Shkin, the sun sank behind the peaks, the light slowly leaving the valley, the faint golds darkening to gray and then navy. In the peaceful moment, one of the few in his days, he took his first deep breath, letting the strain and the uneasiness weave through his lungs to depart on the wave of long sighs. The stars would be out soon, and in the skies here, there were more stars than he'd ever seen. Each night, he came to the same place, staring at the sky and hoping Katherine would do the same even as he worried she wouldn't.

In the Afghanistan evenings, the world was silent. Out in the remote locations, no harsh light competed with what came from the heavens above. No ambient noises drowned out the sound of the wind weaving through the brush. But the quiet was simultaneously reassuring and unwelcome. Unwelcome because it gave him too much time to think: of what he left behind, of everything he hated about Afghanistan, of those who were no longer there, lost due to injury or simply gone forever.

He was thankful for the days they spent up and down the surrounding mountainsides on patrols, rolling out in Humvees or taking them on foot. It was him, his men, and the wide-open skies, steadily scaling the rocky and sometimes snowy terrain despite the weight he carried.

After the last Afghanistan stint, the unit had done its usual post-deployment reshuffling. Recently promoted soldiers moved to new jobs in new locations. Officers headed to their next school before taking commands or moving into staff positions. Robert had been promoted to master sergeant, then offered the first sergeant position. No longer was he working with green lieutenants, like foals trying to get their legs under themselves—he'd finally be working with experienced soldiers, and Captain Gaines, the company commander, was one of them.

Gaines had been there in the mountains of Afghanistan in 2002 during Operation Anaconda with the 101st Airborne Division, the Rakkasans, landing on a different ridge on the northern edge of the valley with a much easier move to his objective. That experience alone was invaluable—Gaines knew what he was up against and could balance his approach with Robert.

Before the company deployed, they'd increased their PT, rucking long, hilly distances, increasing their pace whenever they stopped huffing. Whenever Robert's foot skidded over a mostly buried stone, he fell back into Hell's Halfpipe. His chest twisted as he remembered the rounds flying from every direction. The hair on his neck rose at the memory of reaching for another magazine, only to realize he had two left. The fear that locked into place with each memory reinforced how he'd never again make a similar mistake. Never again would he feel that he couldn't get enough air or that even moving down the ridge to safety was treacherous. No, Robert wanted his company ready to take on the steep inclines, but nothing could prepare them for the high elevation. The locals, however, could race up the mountainsides three times faster than even the quickest American soldier and barely out of breath.

1-87 returned to the mountains in a remote area of Afghanistan, nestled into the arms of Pakistan, only six kilometers from the border. Shakin Naryab, as the locals knew it, consisted of tribes who lacked technology and connection to the rest of modern society. Most of them didn't know Afghanistan had a new government, and when Robert and his men arrived, the locals thought the American soldiers were Russians. Robert had grimaced at that, especially since the Americans had taken over many previous Soviet locations.

This time, instead of being a support force, his company performed combat operations, rotating between various locations. They'd cross from Gardez, surrounded this time of year by mountains dusted with snow, southeast to the greenery of Khost, then farther south to the hell that was Shkin, and eventually as far as FOB Orgun-E, one of the largest Forward Operating Bases in the country. It wasn't much. HESCO barriers—wire cubes lined with thick fabric and filled with rocks—and sandbags stacked in layers, but it had hot food, even hotter showers, and a connection to home.

Shkin was a remote firebase that housed three hundred-some men behind thick mud walls. An American flag waved to the enemy from its pole above the watchtower. Coils upon coils of razor wire formed a perimeter, while artillery and armored Humvees could become additional battle stations if needed. They slept in windowless hooches, a bunch of men bunking together in a mostly open space, unless someone strung up privacy with some 550-cord and hundred-mile-an-hour tape, and some did that, too.

Welcome to the infantry. No Fobbits here.

They had television and hot prepared food, so it wasn't all bad. It had been two months and felt like home, but soon a replacement unit would move in, and the companies would shuffle to other locations.

There was no denying that the area was a challenge, and if a person was going to Shkin, they knew what they were facing. So much so, that a soldier had created a crossroads—so many miles to Fort Drum, so many miles to a tropical location, crude pieces of wood attached to represent the other units' homes—and pointed an arrow at their worn boots in the dusty soil. It didn't say Shkin, or Afghanistan, or Middle East—it simply said "hell."

They often took fire, and a rumor was getting around that this was the place to get into contact with the enemy, get your introduction to combat, and earn your CIB. America was noticing that, yes, the Afghanistan war was, in fact, still going on, and reporters were flocking to the area, asking if they could join the combat missions. A magazine reporter was here now; cable news folks were coming next month.

Robert gritted his teeth as he leaned against the watchtower wall, the last of the light fizzling out as the mountains faded into the darkness, the same ones where they'd take the most fire during daylight hours. Some reporters were still cutting their teeth on being in combat zones. They'd come here, ratchet up the drama in front of the cameras, wearing their flak vests and helmets, sometimes cowering when there wasn't even any danger. Then, they'd do live reports and line the soldiers up in the background. Robert fumed in the background every time and clenched his jaw through the dog-and-pony show.

When Iraq started, Americans forgot about Afghanistan, but now the service members here were intriguing again because reporters could make a name for themselves.

The company lost two soldiers back in August during a gun battle—Private Ian L. Wallace was twenty-one, and Specialist Michael A. Hawthorne was twenty-four—and news broadcasts barely mentioned their names. It was like the deaths in Afghanistan didn't count for anything; the war wasn't there. They were the company's first loss this deployment, and in the months ahead, they wouldn't come close to being the last.

Robert carried the loss of Wallace and Hawthorne every day, a load as heavy as the pack that acted as his lifeline.

ⅠⅠ

That afternoon, the phone rang, and the area code was enough to tell Anna that it was Garrett calling from some payphone somewhere.

"Hello?"

"Hey, Anna. How's it going?" There was noise in the background, other people grumbling as they waited in the long line for their fellow AIT soldiers to hurry up already.

"I'm doing all right. How's it feel to be somewhere new with a little more freedom?" She twirled the phone cord around her finger, pulling it so she could sit at the table.

"Well, I don't have a bunch of drill sergeants yelling at me to do things faster, so it's something, I guess. How are things at home since Dad left?"

"We're doing okay. I think Mom and I are finding a middle ground finally. It's been . . . nice."

Garrett laughed. "Ever since the protest?"

"Shut up."

"No, I'm not making fun of you. I think it's funny that, of all the things you could bond over, it's civil disobedience."

Anna smiled. "Mom has a shockingly high level of excitement for things like that. I never knew."

His deep breath echoed over the line. "Well, I hate to change the subject so quickly, but I don't have much time to chat. There's a big line behind me. I wanted to make sure you and Mom have a plan in case anything happens. We sat in a class about it today, and I wanted to check that you two have talked."

"Do you think I have a plan, Gar?"

"That's why I'm asking."

"If Mom has one, she hasn't shared it with me."

"Get a pen and a piece of paper and let me give you a quick rundown."

She heaved a sigh and walked over to the junk drawer, searching for a pen. After digging past never-used cookie cutters, restaurant menus from two duty stations ago, and batteries that were probably expired, she finally found something to write with. She flipped over a piece of junk mail on the counter. "All right, shoot, oh, master."

"This is serious, okay? If anything happens, Dad's unit will call and let you know. Take some notes if you can. After Mom gets off the phone, I want you to call Grams. She can at least come as support. You know she'll hop on a plane any time we ask. Then you'll want to follow whatever directions they give you."

Anna scribbled quickly, the scratching of the pen the only sound. "Okay. Let Mom answer, then call Grams."

"And that's if they call you. If someone knocks on the door—"

"Don't even say it," Anna scolded, dropping the pen. "I'll do the same thing. Let Mom answer, then call Grams."

She heard him swallow over the line. "Yeah, you've got it. Look at you having a plan after all."

"It'll be fine, though, right, Garrett?"

"Yeah, it'll be fine."

|| CHAPTER THIRTEEN ||

THERE'S NO DIGNITY IN AFGHANISTAN

SEPTEMBER 29, 2003

It was only an hour or so past dawn, the sun already rising as Robert left the TOC on his way for some chow. It was eggs and grits today, all from the best Army powders. He grabbed a tray, filled a plate, and sat at a table with some of his soldiers. A TV droned on from the mess hall wall, sharing the postgame details of the Women's World Cup match between the U.S. and North Korea.

First Platoon had earned a day off, and most of them would use it to exercise, play video games, or connect with family back home. Second Platoon was on patrol today, taking the armored Humvees to the ridges or dismounting and wandering along the dry streambeds.

Robert listened to the conversations happening around him.

"All I'm saying is there's no reason we should miss out on that USO entertainment because we aren't in Iraq. We can get cheerleaders here, man. *Cheerleaders*," Specialist Swanson commented.

"Are you kidding? They ain't gonna come here," Private First Class Olsen responded, shoving a spoonful of food into his mouth.

Swanson leaned across the table toward Olsen. "Picture it: Dallas Cowboys cheerleaders in their tiny skirts, dancing out there." He jutted his thumb over his shoulder out the mess hall door. "Tits all full and perky. Asses swaying."

Olsen grabbed Swanson's head and shoved him backward. "Yeah, and you smelling like a donkey's ass."

"A man can dream, Olsen. Christ, you're a buzzkill."

Olsen winked in response.

"First Sergeant, I heard we're getting some more reporters soon," Sergeant Morton commented from the end of the table.

Robert nodded as he chewed the rest of the flavorless grits. "You heard right. I don't know when they're coming, but they'll have cameras this time. Video."

"Shit . . . It makes me feel like a monkey in a cage. Some chump's entertainment. Some dude who's gonna say, 'I thought about enlisting, but . . .' Yeah, bull*shit*. Those motherfuckers piss me off."

Robert fought back a smile.

"It's why it's all the better when you get back, get all fancy in your uniform, and go steal their girl right from under their nose," Swanson commented. "I bet she calls you a hero and drops to her knees right there in the bar and—"

"All right, that's enough."

"C'mon, First Sergeant, I bet—"

"A female reporter will be here in a month. Try to hold back a little, okay?"

Swanson's jaw dropped. "Aw, man . . . Not again."

"Be respectful around her. Don't make her feel uncomfortable."

"But they gotta know we haven't even seen a woman in a few months, unless you count the few we run into on patrols."

Robert raised an eyebrow. "Guess you'll have to control yourself."

A lieutenant entered the mess hall, and everyone turned to face him. "We have a problem, First Sergeant. Grab your gear and meet the CO in the TOC."

Robert rose quickly from his seat to throw away his trash. As he exited the mess hall, a few First Platoon soldiers followed him. He beelined toward his hooch to grab his vest and helmet, his assault pack and rifle, but before he could get there, a Humvee came screaming into the compound. The platoon medic jumped out, dark stains soaking into his uniform. Robert immediately opened the door nearest him to see Sergeant Wilson, blood coating his hands, his neck, and the top portion of his uniform. The soldier's hands shook, and his fingers curled in agony as he reached toward his face, where bits of metal, silt, and other debris had embedded into his skin.

"It was a fucking mortar," the medic shouted, still feeling the effects of the battle that was far from finished. His hands shook a little, and his eyes were open so wide that Robert could see the whites around his irises.

"Help me get him to the aid station," Robert said to the nearest person, not noting who it was or what rank, or which platoon he belonged to.

The medic helped them carry Wilson, who struggled to talk, thick blood coating the inside of his mouth.

"Fucking Houser got hit in the arm with shrapnel, but the motherfucker used his leatherman and pulled it straight out." Houser was their company's sniper—and a good one. "He wouldn't let me bring him back to make sure he's good. He thinks he spotted the smoke from the tubes."

"First Platoon! Mount up!" Captain Gaines's voice boomed throughout the base.

Robert and the members of First Platoon raced toward their hooches, hefting body armor and helmets from hooks, taking their packs, the Humvees already loaded with what they'd need to take the fight to the enemy today.

Not a single person complained about losing out on a day off. Those who had been at the gym lifted body armor over sweaty heads, cinching it tight at their sides. Those who had been playing video games in PTs tossed their uniform pants and tops over their clothes, heads already shifting from shooting in virtual reality to taking on the real thing. The ones who planned to call family or had been mid-phone call now strapped in with determination, stowing the thoughts of home to focus on the battle ahead.

They filed out and across the vast dirt expanse in the middle of the compound, then climbed into Humvees headed toward the hilltop. Robert placed his rifle between his legs with the barrel pointed at the floor as he stared out the windshield of his truck. They raced along the path to Second Platoon's location, dust rising in their wake. Their gunner was above them, scanning the ridges as they moved into position, ready to unleash hell on any muzzle flashes he saw. The engine's roar was the only sound in the bouncing vehicle.

Robert's mind cleared as he focused on the task at hand, listening to the SITREP over the net.

Second Platoon had been moving on patrol when mortars landed nearby, throwing shrapnel at a few of them; some, like Houser, were able to pull it out, while Wilson had to be carried out. Houser was currently trying to reach a better vantage point to identify the enemy mortars and take them out. No deaths. Everyone that was still there continued to shoot back.

As they reached the summit, Robert opened his door before the Humvee stopped moving, heading straight for Captain Gaines. Already, the officer was in command, ordering the men of First and Second Platoons in different directions to seek out where the enemy might be. One would continue along the streambeds, another would move through the brush, and the third would take up firing positions and hold there.

Sergeant Morton gathered his team and followed the rocky decline toward the streambed. At the same time, Gaines and Robert remained on the hilltop, listening over the net as their soldiers moved into position, eyes scanning the hillsides around them.

Tension squeezed Robert's chest as his men faded into their surroundings, their uniforms blending into the browns and beiges of the environment. *The battle can't be over yet.* It couldn't be a few mortars and done. It didn't work that way there. Every engagement was a chance to take a few more Americans out of the fight. What was the endgame here? Why would they be shooting mortars that could easily be taken out by American air support or artillery, two things Shkin always had at its disposal? There had to be more to it, something they were missing.

"We got some wounded here, First Sergeant."

Immediately, Robert let the concerns of the battle die, entrusting the fight to Gaines. He reached into the side of his rucksack and removed the VS-17 panel, unrolling it and placing it on the ground as the casualties either walked or were helped to it.

Morton's voice came over the net. "Eagle Six, we have some footprints and the remains of a fire near our position. Must have put it out in a hurry. We're gonna fan out a bit more and get out of the wadi. Give some distance and follow 'em."

"Roger that, Red Seven," Gaines responded.

"Fucking ambush," Robert commented as he wrote down the nine-line MEDEVAC request.

"They've got it."

"I don't doubt it, but this still doesn't make sense."

"Does *anything* in this fucking place make sense, First Sergeant?" a soldier said from behind him, but Robert didn't respond.

"Eagle Six, be advised, there's a wire running underground, headed in your direction. It looks like one of the mortars cut it, but there's UXO near your position. Griffin is taking a team to see where it starts."

Gaines and Robert locked eyes and didn't say a word. What could they do? There was nowhere to run to other than off the edges of the hilltop, and they couldn't give up their location without increasing the risk to the teams on a hunt-and-kill mission and the four casualties awaiting evacuation.

For many, this would be the moment they pictured all the things back home, that moment where time freezes, leaving them to see the clichéd "life flashing before their eyes." Some might have suggested that Robert and the others pull back, go down the slope to the right that Morton had taken, and find some cover. Clamber back into vehicles and race around the way they came.

But they wouldn't cede the high ground. They were there to conquer the mountains, to take out the enemy that terrorized people from around the world, not to mention the people right outside the firebase in the village. It was their duty to provide safety in the mountains of Afghanistan, even if the threat was coming from Pakistan.

And so they stayed, some of the soldiers around them growing tense, maybe even holding their breaths as the realization of their mortality snapped into their backs like a bullet. Sure, Morton found one wire, but was there another?

"Easy there, boys."

What no one could know at the time was that five anti-tank mines were buried in the ground beneath the hilltop, under the company commander, under the company first sergeant, under the three Humvees that raced their QRF to this hilltop, under their radios, their overwatch. The "why" became clear—this was an opportunity to take out most of a company—but it was foiled by the enemy's own mortars.

Griffin's team knew what to do. They would follow the wire away from the hilltop, knowing that the blasting cap would be somewhere over there, triggered by a cell phone or a push-button or some other detonation device. The company trusted that Griffin's trigger fingers would be faster than the enemy's.

Suddenly, the rattle of an M-16 echoed for only a few short seconds, but to Robert, they stretched a minute each, with long pauses in between.

"That's three Haji's down."

Robert could have celebrated Griffin's quick response, but there was no time.

To the north, the same damn ridge that plagued them with gunfire from Pakistan day after day after day, that hillside was nothing but a series of muzzle flashes. Then, from the south, where Pakistani militia were stationed, RPGs flew toward the American position.

Gaines shouted through the radio, calling for Morton and Griffin and their men to take cover as five rockets headed straight for them.

"What the fuck?!" Robert shouted, eyes following the ridgelines around them, to the north, south, and east.

Gaines got on the radio, calling in that they were friendlies, hoping the information could get to that remote militia outpost quickly but likely not fast enough.

Spotters were already calling out targets based on the muzzle flashes they saw.

Twenty from the north. Thirty from the east.

A sniper from somewhere.

Machine guns.

Endless rocket and small arms fire.

The platoon's medic stumbled up the hillside along with another soldier, ducking as rounds flew over their heads and landed at their feet. Robert saw it was Olsen and stepped forward to pull the boy up. He wasn't moving, and Doc did as much as he could, packing a gaping hole underneath his vest, trying to stop the river of blood that wouldn't ebb.

"A sniper hit him. We tried to move him out of the line of fire behind a tree, but he got hit a third time," a soldier said shakily.

Robert was already on the radio, calling in a medevac, waiting for the Black Hawk to swoop in and get Olsen out as quickly as possible. Everyone could see his time was limited. He needed serious care, far beyond what Shkin's aid station could offer.

The wait was long, almost endless. Time could have stopped for all they knew if it weren't for the rounds smacking into boulders, shrubbery, the rocks under their feet, and the sides of their Humvees. Gaines had even dropped behind a boulder, narrowly missing another sniper shot that burrowed into the side of the vehicle rather than his shoulder.

The Black Hawk finally arrived, but it circled overhead, stirring up the dirt, trying to figure out a landing, only to be driven away by gunfire.

And at that moment, Olsen's body could hold out no longer. He fell into a coma from blood loss and died on that hilltop while Doc sat with him and held his hand.

Gaines was back on his radio, ready to end the shitstorm they were in, calling in everything they had: Apache attack helicopters and A-10 Warthogs. They would tear up those hillsides until there was nothing left, holes that obliterated the terrain, blowing bodies apart, leaving no chance of survival.

Once again, time froze, the bombs and rounds doing what the company needed, the shaking ground and noise a comfort to the Americans, and then the area went startlingly quiet as the sound of the rotors softened to silence.

Everyone assessed the vehicles, wounded men, and supplies. The bomb squad was already on its way. Somehow, it was over—the anticipation, the stress, the tension, the focus. It all evaporated in an instant, though the shakiness in their limbs and the far-off look in their eyes told a different story.

"How's Olsen?" Swanson asked as the platoon returned from their positions, showing every sign of battle weariness and worry of losing a teammate.

Doc swallowed hard as a muscle in his jaw ticked. "He didn't make it, man."

"Wh-what?"

A poncho liner already covered his body, offering him the dignity that Afghanistan couldn't.

"You're kidding me, Doc. Let me see him. Prove to me that it's really him."

Doc put his hands on Swanson's chest. "You don't want to do that."

"It can't be Olsen, man. We were shooting the shit a little bit ago. He can't be gone. Let me see him."

Doc sighed, wrapping his arm around Swanson's shoulders and steering him toward Olsen, and Robert followed.

They knelt beside Olsen, and Doc carefully pulled back the poncho. Swanson let out a cry, and Robert turned his face away to offer privacy but kept an arm around his shoulder, letting it rest there while Doc talked. Swanson's shoulders shook as restrained cries escaped from his mouth. Slowly, Swanson pulled the poncho back over Olsen, resting a hand on his chest.

Griffin walked over with Olsen's helmet and vest and held them out to Swanson. "You can do the honors when we get back."

Swanson accepted both, draping them carefully over his arms as he walked toward the Humvee where they were loading Olsen. They would mount the gear on the plywood wall with Hawthorne's and Wallace's. He wouldn't be alone there or in Valhalla.

Both platoons loaded up quietly after almost twelve hours of battle, the adrenaline wearing off and sapping their energy. If only Robert could say this was the first time or the last time, but it always hit the same. There would be another empty bunk until replacements were sent in to fill the space. Another name would be added to the board they'd hung outside the TOC. There would be another battlefield cross, another memorial ceremony, another moment of silence, and another body shipped home, welcomed with tears of sorrow rather than those of joy.

And there would be more to come.

Robert and Gaines met in the TOC once they returned. "We did everything right today, but so did the enemy."

"They're definitely clued into our actions. They knew how we'd respond to fire, where we'd set up, that, if they were lucky, a Black Hawk would show up."

Gaines leaned heavily onto the makeshift desk behind him, dropping his helmet. "If they couldn't blow the Black Hawk out of the sky, they'd have blown whatever was planted underneath us."

"Why the fuck did the militias fire at us?"

Gaines swiped a hand from his forehead to his chin. "We probably won't ever get an answer for that."

And so it went, with the focus on Iraq instead of Afghanistan, a war that was already forgotten while good men still died.

ⅠⅠ

OCTOBER 21, 2003

Anna closed the magazine in her lap and stared out the window. She'd received it from a person named Jen Jones, with a letter enclosed:

Dear Anna,

You don't know me, but I'm a reporter embedded with your father's company at Shkin Firebase. I arrived just after a battle there, and I

*wanted to tell their story. Your dad gave me most of this story, and so
I thought you'd like to have it.*

*I hope you know your dad speaks fondly of you and misses you
terribly. He told me about your stacks of newspapers in the aftermath
of 9/11 and how you checked out library books to learn more about
Afghanistan and Iraq. I hope this article gives you some more
information for your repository. If you like it, you can email me at
the address below and I'll be sure to send you more, even once I leave
Shkin.*

All the best,
Jen Jones

Anna finished the article in tears, her shoulders stooped with regret. Dad
had lost multiple soldiers already and faced a terrifying battle if Jen's reporting
were honest. And there Anna sat, safely on her bed in her home in the U.S., war
far from her front door. She couldn't even be bothered to write.

Huffing out a breath, Anna swore she'd write to him soon, no matter how
angry she still was.

CHAPTER FOURTEEN

AFGHANISTAN BITES BACK

NOVEMBER 24, 2003

With all the fighting in Shkin, reporters had flocked to the firebase in the fall. The primetime hitters were still in Iraq, but the green ones were cutting their teeth in Afghanistan. They'd come to see what all the fuss was about, take some pictures, maybe a little video, do one live broadcast in their war get-ups, then move on. At the end of each day, Robert's jaw was sore from clenching his teeth in response to the litany of insensitive questions.

Everyone wanted to know about morale. But what was the fascination with it?

You've taken some hits over the past month. What happens to morale then?

Robert wanted to ask, *What the fuck do you think happens?* The last thing he needed was media training, so he endured it.

The other day, Captain Gaines lined up the company men in front of some Humvees while crews fired up big spotlights, shining them in the soldiers' faces, practically blinding them. Then, the company created the backdrop to a reporter who overstated the danger in the area. Robert mostly stared at the rocky ground because his eyes were rolling so much. As he'd scolded his daughter for so many years, soon his own eyes would fall right out of his head, bouncing along on the gravel. A cameraman walked within a few feet of the gathering, the lens pointed at their faces, the young ones smiling, the experienced ones staring, waiting for it to end.

Robert would happily walk toward mortars, small arms fire, or the threat of mines over that shitshow. Finally, the reporter wrapped up after a litany of hero talk, then the soldiers were free to walk away.

Of the group sent to Shkin in the last month, one was at least tolerable. Jen Jones was young, a shaking fawn when she had first arrived, clutching her helmet to her head and ducking no matter how far away the fire was. One day, Robert took pity on her.

"It's when you hear a snap that you should be worried," he said.

"A snap?"

"Yep, like snapping your fingers beside your ear. Same sound. It means a round went right by your head, so best get down in case Ahmed wants to try again."

From then on, Jen sought him out to ask questions, and he forced himself to be patient with her. But after a few days, their conversations grew natural. Her vest was large on her small frame, and she reminded him of Anna with her dark hair and constant questions.

"How old are you?" he asked her one day.

"Twenty-four."

"What the hell are you doing here two years into the job?"

"It's actually six years in. I was hired at a news station right after high school and worked my way up. I asked for an Iraq assignment, but they sent me here instead."

"Well, you're lucky," he replied. "Iraq is a shitshow."

She smiled a little. "You think everything is a shitshow. But you have two months down, headed to Orgun-E next week."

"It's the closest thing we'll have to paradise here. Nice break for the men before we're back in a remote place. Y'all always want to know about morale. This is the morale boost they need. Get some mail, have some time to recoup."

"It's good timing after last month."

Robert's mouth tightened. "In this place, any boost is good."

A few days after their conversation, the command team asked Robert's company to perform another dog-and-pony show for the reporters.

"Where are we headed?" Jen asked, stepping close to his right. Any time they left the firebase, she insisted on riding with him, and he was happy to be the daddy goose leading the way.

"Out to Lazano Ridge. Some of your folks want to record themselves reacting to gunfire too far away to hit 'em. Then we'll bring y'all back here. Easy and done."

She rolled her eyes at him, so much like his daughter. "Give them some time to adjust. Not all of them have been in this situation before. I wasn't much better."

He pointed at her. "*You* wanted to learn. *They* only want people to call them brave."

Jen shrugged. "It isn't about bravery—it's about showing the people at home what you're doing here."

"What else is there to show them? We go out, get shot at, come back here, then do it all again tomorrow."

"Some people say it helps understand the war."

He thought of Anna and her protest sign. "No one understands a damn thing until they're part of it."

"We're doing what we can to help show it. I believe in that. I'm not much older than some of the guys serving here."

"What does that matter?"

"Well, did *they* know what they were getting themselves into? Sure, everyone was patriotic after the attacks, but did they truly know what they were signing up for?"

"Hell, Jen, I'm gonna be honest with you, and don't you print my name with what I'm saying. This is off the record." She nodded once, then clicked off her recorder. While he shouldn't have trusted her, he chose to anyway. "None of us knew what we were getting with this war, even the people who've been in for a while. This is nothing like the Gulf War. This isn't a formal army. We've had a lot of learning to do."

She raised an eyebrow. "I feel like you're setting me up for something."

He focused on the open area in front of them. "No, I'm serious. It's something my daughter constantly said to me." He shook his head. "Her and those fucking books—she studied the hell out of the Russian invasion and read everything she could find to understand what fighting here would be like. But we don't have any idea what the hell we're doing."

"Captain Gaines said events in the area have quieted down a little."

"The villagers have made peace with us, yes, but that doesn't matter to an insurgency. The Hajis can easily come down from the mountains, go into those villages, and slit throats to get people back on their side. The question becomes, how long does this go on?"

Jen stared at him, waiting for him to say more, but Robert glanced at his watch.

"Time to mount up," he said, then walked toward the Humvee.

Six other soldiers and three American reporters waited around the trucks, going through the motions. He overheard one speaking into a small tape recorder, talking about "renewed fire at the border."

Instantly he wanted to roll his eyes but fought against it. It was as if everywhere he turned, he was surrounded by idiocy. They didn't understand that the fighting wasn't renewed—it just was what it was.

It hadn't stopped.

With helmet in hand, a cameraman lifted a foot to climb into the Humvee, and Robert put out an arm. "Sir, you need that on your head before you get in, then keep it on until we get back here."

"But it's an armored Humvee."

"It isn't armored, sir. In this puppy, it's like riding around in a cardboard box. The flak jacket is for the gunfire. You need the helmet in case of a rollover. Put it on or stay here. Those are your choices. Sir."

The man grimaced but acquiesced, fastening the strap under his chin before getting into the back seat. Robert closed the door before settling into the front passenger seat with Swanson behind the wheel.

There would be eight vehicles in the convoy, and while a few led, including Robert, who was in the second truck, others would dismount, walking in between, giving reporters a chance to film, while more vehicles followed behind.

The sky was a beautiful clear blue, not a single cloud covered the sun, and the light reflected off the rocks, making some sparkle before a veil of dirt obscured it, kicked up from the vehicle ahead.

Jen rode in the same truck, behind Robert. Her voice shook with the bumps in the road as she asked her questions.

"You've been in for almost twenty years now. What makes you want to stay?"

"I've dedicated my life to service, and I'm happy to do my duty for as long as they let me," Robert responded with his scripted answer.

"But it must be hard on your family. You have a wife and daughter back home, and a son preparing for Iraq."

"Yes, ma'am, but when I'm here, it's all—"

And then the world went black.

All Robert knew was that he was in unbelievable pain. There was pressure throughout his body, but his leg hurt the most, and he couldn't understand why. Thick black smoke mixed with dust burned in his throat and clouded his vision. The pressure was on his left side, his right. He tried to breathe, but the agony rose beyond what he could bear, and he released a scream. Dizziness set in as the pressure on his left side ceased, more shouting surrounded him, he heard the sounds of gunfire, and all the while, the pain continued to mount.

Early in the morning in New York, the phone rang from the kitchen, high-pitched and endless. Anna, the only one who slept light enough to hear its shrill ring, answered the call.

"I'm calling to speak with Mrs. Katherine Pechman. Is she available?" a man's voice asked.

"Can I tell her who's calling?"

"This is Captain Walker. I'm the rear detachment commander for First Battalion."

Instantly, Anna's hand slackened on the phone, almost slipping from her grip, and tingles spread through her limbs. She opened her mouth to speak, to ask the caller to wait a moment, but the sound lodged in her throat. She finally cleared it and rested the receiver atop the counter.

She raced back to Mom's room, skipping the knocking and shoving it open roughly. "Mom, you need to get up. Someone's calling about Dad."

The woman who always needed five minutes to sit in bed, allowing herself to rise slowly with the day, jumped awake. Her eyes snapped open in a way Anna had never seen before, and she threw the covers off, kicking her legs over the side of the bed and hurrying to the phone, her nightgown flowing behind her. Anna followed, sliding on the kitchen's tile floor in her stockinged feet as she tried to listen to both sides of the conversation.

"Hello?" Mom croaked.

The lines on her mother's face deepened as she listened to the phone, her chest barely moving. Her lips parted, and she froze in place. Her eyes darted around the room as the low murmur of the voice floated to Anna's ears. It wasn't enough to make out the words, only the timbre changing, indistinct syllables accompanied by breaks between sentences.

"Oh my God. What happened?"

Worry rose in Anna's stomach, curling itself up her esophagus and scratching at the back of her throat. "What's going on?"

Mom leaned heavily against the wall then, her shoulders sagging. One shaking hand wound tightly into the coiled phone cord, turning her knuckles white.

"What do we do now?" Mom asked.

Anna stepped closer, leaning her ear toward the receiver, needing to hear what was going on for herself rather than waiting for a replay.

"C'mon, big man, let me get in here," a distorted voice said. It was like Robert was underwater. Words were coming out but not as clear as they should be. Someone pushed against his shoulder and moved his leg, and black spots peppered his vision. Someone messed with something on his vest as he faded in and out.

When he came to again, at first all he saw was that bright blue sky above, then Doc's and Gaines's faces came into focus, their mouths moving without any sound, sweat sliding down the slopes of their faces. Gaines's gloved hand was stained a dark red, and Robert thought of all he would say to rib the company commander. Something blocked the words from leaving his mouth, and Robert tried to shake his head, but his body felt weak—unbelievably weak—so he closed his eyes, letting the darkness take him.

॥

Anna still couldn't make out what the caller was saying. Something about a Walter Reed, getting a flight to D.C., packing for an extended stay.

"Thank you, sir," Mom said with a shaky voice. "I'll get down there in the next few days. I appreciate your call." She rested the phone on its hanger, placed her hands on her thighs, and bent over to suck in deep breaths. "Your dad's truck hit a mine."

Unease crept up Anna's spine as her stomach dropped. "But he's okay?" She knew he wasn't dead. Had that happened, someone would be knocking on the door instead of calling on the phone. It was the horror story of the military community—open the door, and there's an officer and a chaplain in dress uniform. What she really wanted to know was just how badly Dad was injured, and too many possibilities raced through her mind.

Mom said nothing. Anna wanted to shake her, find some way to snap her out of it. Mom didn't move except for the rise and fall of her shoulders as she breathed. Her gaze froze on the chipped tile floor.

"What do we do now?" Anna asked

"How did this happen?" Mom whispered, lines forming between her eyebrows.

Anna raised her voice. "Do we need to pack?"

Mom didn't even flinch. She swiped a hand down her face and slowly slid to the floor, staring straight ahead. Her eyes glistened, but no tears fell. "I said from the beginning that this would get worse."

Anna knelt on the floor beside her, gently shaking her shoulder. "Should I call someone?" She gripped Mom's hand, but it remained limp, her head tilted to one side, staring at nothing.

॥

Robert came to while a voice yelled over the thrum of a helicopter as something soft slid over his skin, and still, the pain would not relent. A needle slipped into a port on his arm—*when had that been put in?*—and all sound, sensation, and light were gone.

॥

Anna released Mom's hand. *Garrett said I would need to take control. But what am I supposed to do first?*

As she stared at her mother on the floor, she knew she had to do something to take care of her first. But what? Anna had never comforted her before. "C'mon, Mom. Can you stand up?"

Mom stood, her eyes still staring off at nothing, all processing shut down to hold onto whatever single thread that kept her conscious. Anna pulled her to her feet and looped an arm around her shoulders as she helped Mom shuffle to the living room, one slow, unsteady step at a time.

"Okay, you're at the couch. Go ahead and sit." Anna slid the blanket off the back of the couch and wrapped it over Mom's shoulders, tucking the ends around her. "I'll be right back."

Anna left her then, racing to the kitchen for Mom's school bag. She shoved past binders and textbooks to find the leather address book Mom dutifully updated with every move, flipping through pages until she found Grams's phone number.

Thoughts of Dad fluttered into her mind—Where was he now? How badly was he hurt? What would happen next? *Keep it together, Anna!*

She placed her hands flat against the counter, running her fingertips along the wood grain, noticing how cool the surface was, how loud the kitchen clock ticked, how soothing the hum of the fridge could be. Taking slow, deep breaths, she willed her hands to be still, her heart to slow. She couldn't lose herself like her mother.

Anna thought of Garrett and instantly wished he were there with her. A tear slid down her cheek, and she roughly wiped it away. *Focus on the now.* She dug through the junk drawer in search of paper but found none, so she turned to Mom's school bag. After flipping past pages of notes in her mother's steady hand, Anna reached an unblemished page.

First, she copied over Grams's phone number. Grabbing the phone from the wall behind her, Anna dialed a number she knew by heart. She peeked around the corner to see Mom was still on the couch, awake, staring. It would have to do for now.

As the phone line rang, Anna added tasks to her list.

1. *Figure out how to contact Garrett.*
2. *Pack bags.*
3. *Book plane tickets.*

No, wait, the tickets should be first. She scribbled everything out, then reordered the numbers. *Ugh, I need to call Garrett first.* Deep scratches slashed through the notes and she started yet again.

You're alone to handle this, and your mom is useless right now. Let Garrett handle it.

No. She wasn't alone.

"Hello?" a voice finally asked over the line.

"Hi, James." She started, her voice shaky. "I'm sorry, I know it's early, but how soon can you come over? I need you."

||

Robert felt movement again, this time under the draped nylon of a tent, beds all around. His leg jostled sharply, and pain flooded his nervous system in hot shockwaves, shooting up his hip and to the base of his spine. Voices rose around him, loud and frantic. He wanted to shout for them to calm down, but something covered his face, and someone instructed him to take a few deep breaths. Glancing to either side of him, he saw people bent over beds, more noise from afar. He overheard someone describing prep for surgery, stopping bleeding, stabilizing for further evacuation, and shouting numbers and acronyms and initialisms in a quick staccato. But none of it made sense.

Not until hours later, when the sleep and wake cycle sent Robert back to wakefulness. He was being loaded onto a C-130 headed for Germany, someone told him as they settled the gurney onto a rack. He leaned his head to the side to look toward his feet.

His left leg was nothing but a stump, half of it left in Afghanistan.

CHAPTER FIFTEEN

WHEN A FEW WEEKS FEELS LIKE YEARS

DECEMBER 1, 2003

A week is a long time to wait. When Anna was small, she remembered how a week often felt like a year, especially when leading up to Christmas or a much-anticipated birthday. Mom always hid presents at the top of her closet, far out of reach of her curious children. As Anna got older, that week before the end of the school year or a big vacation would drag on endlessly while Anna dreamed about how she'd spend her free time, what her friends would be doing, and the trip her parents spent months planning. Time would lapse slowest of all when Dad was gone. Paper chains to count up the days (because counting down was too unreliable), a special memory tucked inside each one, representing another twenty-four hours not feeling quite like a family. But the phone calls would pass in a blink, with long waits until the next one.

Dad's leaving Shkin involved a helicopter flight to the main hospital in Bagram, a plane to get stabilized in Landstuhl, and then finally arriving in Washington, D.C., at Walter Reed Army Medical Center. There was a rush to process paperwork, get expedited passports, and book flights, but in the end, it was better to wait for him to come to them.

Grams swooped in the day after the phone call, taking on the heavy load of supporting Mom. It was through her that Anna learned the extent of Dad's injuries: one leg lost below the knee, damage to the calf of his other leg, shrapnel wounds to his body, and a likely Traumatic Brain Injury.

With Mom handled, Anna managed everything else. After asking around on post, she processed the Red Cross message for Garrett, sending an emergency notice to his unit, which pulled him from deployment to Iraq. She'd redirected the well-intentioned women of the Family Readiness Group away from Mom and turned them toward vacuuming the floors, washing the dishes, and running errands. Anna had booked the flight to Dulles. She'd emptied the firebox of all necessary paperwork—in case they needed it—sliding social security cards and birth certificates and orders and car titles and wills and POAs into protective plastic sheets inside a thick three-ring binder.

As she watched Mom on the couch, leaning her head on Grams's shoulder as both cried, Anna felt sidelined. She'd called James, and he arrived in less than five minutes. They sat in silence in her bedroom as he held her close, occasionally pulling a tissue from the box on her bedside table and handing it to her while taking the soiled ones.

Yes, she was terrified to see Dad for the first time, but more than that, she was frightened to face him after such tragedy on the heels of their fights and stonewalling. How could she meet his eyes when she'd barely given him a real goodbye? How could she hold his hand knowing she'd walked away when he'd told her he loved her? How could she help care for him when she'd made him feel he mattered so little?

But, as time dragged on, the day finally approached. The family flew to Walter Reed Army Medical Center.

Walking the halls of Ward 57 twisted Anna's stomach, and everywhere she turned, she saw the casualties of war. Wheelchair users scooted around, in many cases, on their own. Only a few amputees. Little did Anna or anyone know that the swell of amputations would come in the years ahead, as high as almost one hundred people in two months as the Iraq surge began. But that was still too far into a future Anna couldn't yet comprehend.

When she saw Dad for the first time, she didn't know where to focus her attention. His body was swollen, responding to the physical trauma he'd endured. Lines ran from him to machines, all beeping or whirring to aid his body in its earliest stages of recovery.

"His body is doing everything it can to save his life. Increasing inflammation helps fight the infection while still preserving blood flow to his most vital organs—his heart and brain," Dr. Rashad, the one responsible for seeing Dad through, explained.

The sheer explanation drove sharp daggers into Anna's chest.

How close had he come to dying?

She couldn't bring herself to ask it.

Anna watched Mom make the first move toward him, pulling a chair beside his bed, taking his large, limp hand in her own. After years of seeing her parents together, Anna knew this was her grounding moment, a way to feel connected.

And didn't everyone feel that way? When grief strikes, don't we all long for that physical touch from someone else, to show their support, their care, their understanding of the tragedy at hand?

I wish James were here.

Mom pressed a kiss to the palm of Dad's hand, the only section not covered with tape or attached to tubes.

The person Anna knew as a mammoth of a man was now helpless, victimized.

How close did we come to losing him?

She shook the words from her head, sitting in a chair beside Mom, averting her eyes from the amputation site she wasn't yet ready to see. To accept this injury as a permanent presence, as a mark of all that happens when things go wrong, meant more beyond that hospital room.

"He's heavily medicated, both to help with his pain and to support the organs that aren't currently receiving the body's attention. There are a few things to watch." Doctor Rashad's dark eyes were kind, and Anna wanted to trust him to help her family. "He has a mild traumatic brain injury, which is to be expected from a blast. When an explosion happens, it moves through the entire body, jarring the internal organs. It can lead to damage, but we haven't found any evidence of that."

Anna's voice was shaky when she asked, "So when he wakes, he'll be aware of everything that's happened?"

Mom held Dad's hand and stayed silent.

"Yes and no," the doctor said. "He likely isn't aware that he lost his left leg in the blast. Right now, we hope to preserve what's left."

"What does that mean?" Anna asked.

"Surgery to the bones, the muscle, the nerves, and the skin can all help in giving him the most use of what he still has and can mitigate any coming pains he may experience. Nerve damage is a big problem in injuries like this. His right leg was also damaged—"

Anna shook her head. "There's more?"

"A blast causes significant injury. Based on the information I've received, I would have thought his injuries would be more extreme. His right leg was wounded at the tibia and calf muscle. He has a few burns as well, but most of his primary surgeries were completed at Landstuhl, so we'll observe those injuries and perform additional surgeries as needed. He'll need skin grafts, which can take time. It's normal for them not to take after the first try, so the tissue will die and we'll have to do it again. All of this will go step by step. Do you have any other questions for me?"

For the first time, Mom focused on something other than Dad's face. "I wouldn't even know what to ask."

"Many family members often ask how long their loved one will be medicated like this. And I can say it should only be for a few more days. After that, we'll cut back slowly. Once we're certain he's stable enough, he could be out of here within two weeks."

"Wait, two weeks? After an amputation?" Anna asked.

"Again, it's a case-by-case determination, but with a single leg amputation, it might only be two weeks. The biggest snag for First Sergeant Pechman is the healing in his right leg. He'll need to have full use of that leg before he can leave the hospital. After that, it's best to stay local for the remainder of his physical therapy and healing, but it isn't required."

Mom nodded absently. "Thank you, Doctor."

"Please let one of the nurses know if you need anything."

Once he left, Anna stared down at Dad, her eyes shiny with tears. "What do we do now?" she whispered.

Mom ruffled her hair, then stared at Dad's face. "We wait for Garrett before we make plans, but I think it's best if you both stay until the New Year. After that, you can go back to New York and your brother can return to his unit."

"But what if Dad isn't ready to leave by then?"

"I'll be here to take care of him."

"Won't you need help?"

"Anna, you have school to worry about. Grams can stay with you until the end of the year. After that, we'll decide if you stay or move down here. You heard the doctor. We have to take it one step at a time. The most important thing is to be here for him in the early days."

What Mom wouldn't say was that she needed the whole family to take this on together in the early days. Who could blame her? No one wants to be left alone to find their footing on the rocky hills of confrontation and recovery. Who would be the one to tell Dad that his Army career was over, that he wouldn't be returning to his unit, that he wouldn't wear the uniform again? While they could all hope that he would wake up glad to be alive, with a want to hold his wife and children close, thankful he wasn't taken from them, that could subside as the revelations of his career and the men left behind crept in.

Already there were subtle changes in Dad: the thick scruff on his cheeks, the hair longer than he would ever allow it. His eyes were closed, a tube was in his throat, and Anna wished he would wake long enough to tell her how much he loved her, that everything would be okay, that they would face it as a family, that things would feel normal again someday, even if that normal were different than before.

I have to hold on to that hope, because hope never stops at all.

DECEMBER 5, 2003

Anna peeked through the gap in the hospital room door, making out the faint outline of Garrett standing in the corner of the room. She'd caught him in the same place every night since he arrived on the second day. His hands were deep in his pockets as he watched the colorful screens mark Dad's heart rate, his pulse, his oxygen levels. Anna eased into the room, staying near the door. Needles were still embedded under Dad's skin and tubes ran to vials and bags. The bloating was still a shock, as were the colors that marred his skin. The red burns had eased into brown. The smudged purple bruises had turned green and marked the places where debris and pieces of whatever fragments were still in his skin. The doctors said his body would eventually work those out, but for the moment, parts of Afghanistan had fused with his body.

"I always thought Dad was such a force." Garrett swayed slightly as his mind worked, and Anna waited, giving him the space to process the tragedy himself.

"I was so excited to follow him as a kid. I'd stick my feet in his boots and flop around the apartment with his patrol cap on my head. It always slid over my eyes and no doubt I'd trip at some point." The corner of his mouth pulled up at the thought. "Even before I understood his job, I loved telling my friends how Dad was off fighting the bad guys, or helping the people nearby, giving food to people who didn't have it, or protecting people so they could vote for a better life." He squeezed his eyes shut as his voice cracked.

"I get it." Anna paused to clear her throat, still raw from hours of quiet tears. "I always loved knowing he was trying to help people. Getting food and supplies to people in Florida after Hurricane Andrew, doing security in the Balkans to help end the genocide there."

Garrett continued as if he hadn't heard her. "I tell anyone who will listen that my dad served as a first sergeant, that he'd already been to Afghanistan twice, that he was part of Operation Anaconda and served in some of the most remote areas of that country. I'd watch their eyes widen when they learned that First Sergeant Robert Pechman was one of the first infantry units in the country at the beginning of the war. But look at him now. It's like he's nothing he used to be."

Anna's skin tingled uncomfortably. "He's still the same person, Garrett."

He sighed, staring at the floor a moment before speaking. "No, I know he is. Right now, it's hard to see him as who I know."

"At least you get to walk away from it."

He said nothing, just moved to the chair in the corner of the room and sat down, leaving plenty of distance between him and Dad. Anna knew the feeling. You step too close and there's the threat of being pulled under like Mom, sucked into the swirl of uncertainty, and crushed under the pressure of all that would come.

The room fell quiet except for the machines.

Anna held up the bag in her hand. "They had some games in the gift shop. I found a chess set. Want to play?"

Garrett stared at her. "Are you kidding? Here? Now?"

She threw a hand out to the side. "What else are we supposed to do? I get it, you want to keep vigil when Mom and I aren't here, but that doesn't mean you need to stare at him and think of a thousand worst-case scenarios." She sat on the floor, opening the mini set and arranging the tiny pieces on the board. "Sit down and take a minute."

He eased himself to the floor across from her, staring at the black and white board, lifting the rook and spinning it between two fingers. "I've never seen Mom so tired." Garrett sighed, then lined up the white pieces in neat rows across from Anna's threatening black army. "Every time she looks at me, it's like her eyes are burning into me. Like she thinks I should end my enlistment and get out, find something else to do."

Anna moved a white pawn forward. "She knows better than that, but I can't blame her."

"I'm not going to change my mind, Anna."

"I'm not asking you to."

"I have to do my time over there eventually."

"And I know you will."

"It's not like I'm going to Iraq now anyway." He scooted a black pawn forward one square.

Who was he trying to convince? "That's not true. They could send you later."

He shook his head. "No, they won't. If it were an injury in a non-military family, then maybe they would. But with Dad being military and Mom having to deal with this, they aren't going to overburden our family. I'll sit on Rear D the whole time. I'm missing the whole damn war."

Anna jumped a knight over her pieces, setting it down roughly and shaking the pawns. "Okay, so you've missed a deployment. Dad mentioned once that you could move to another battalion if that ever happened."

"I've had my bags packed and stacked in the corner of my room for months now, but I don't think I'm ever gonna go. The guys I trained with will go without me, and that sucks. It's like I'm a coward for being left behind."

"That's silly."

"Is it? The dude that's always home and one of the few soldiers without a combat patch? Someone else will take my place now, and what if something happens to that guy?"

"It could just as easily happen to someone else, Garrett."

"Yeah, and what if my being there could stop it? What if I could catch the threat or see the bomb? I got comfortable with whatever would happen to me when I first signed the papers, but I can't deal with someone dying or getting hurt in my place."

Anna stared at the board, only now noticing the pieces Garrett had moved as she was distracted by the conversation. She faked that she was figuring out a move, touching a bishop here, then releasing it in favor of a pawn there. What was it about soldiers and this ridiculous need to be the hero, the one leading others into battle? Did it stem from her family's stupid legacy? But as she glanced at the monitors, recognizing Dad's immobile form, she wondered if it was vengeance, a desire to kill whoever it was that hurt him. Garrett was more likely to go to Iraq than Afghanistan anyway, so it wasn't like he could find the people who did this and take them out. Maybe he'd watched too many movies.

She finally slid a bishop over to capture a pawn.

Garrett stared at the board and asked, "How long will he be like this?"

"They're keeping him sedated, but they should wake him soon."

"How long do you think he'll be here?"

As much as Anna wanted to ask, *where the hell were you when the doctor explained all this?* she chose to ease up. "It can be a few weeks for single-limb amputees."

"That's it?"

"I mean, he won't be leaving Walter Reed any time soon, but he'll be able to leave the hospital."

He shook his head. "I still don't understand how you handled all this. I remember when you cut your hand after we first moved to New York and how you panicked. There was so much blood."

"You explained what I'd need to do, so I did that."

"But you did so much more than that. Paperwork, Anna? That's not like you."

"Well what else was I supposed to do, Garrett? Mom was basically useless." She quickly added, "Not that I blame her."

"You guys came a long way while Dad and I were gone."

She shrugged. "We were all the other had."

"I'm sorry you had to step up like that. I'm sorry I couldn't be there."

Anna rolled her eyes. "You know, Garrett, you were always a big help when I was younger, but I'm older now. I don't need you running for the first aid kit at the first sign of blood. I can walk myself there and deal with it." Heat flooded her face. "Sorry. Just move a damn piece."

Garrett ran a finger over his rook.

So much has changed since he left home eighteen months ago.

"What are you going to do until he's cleared?" Garrett asked, changing the subject.

"I'm gonna try to go back home with Grams, but I'll probably end up back here."

He rolled his eyes. "Yeah right. The chance to stay in place for once?"

Anna stared at him. "Do you think Mom should do this alone? Anyway, we've moved enough times. I'll figure it out like I always do."

"Anna, you won't have a lot of people to support you here. I won't be here. James won't be here."

A white-hot blade slashed her heart as she thought of James. "Would you just play the game, please?" She huffed. "It's not the first time. I'll be fine."

"It shouldn't have been this way for him. It shouldn't have been this way for you and Mom."

Anna shrugged. "We've had a lot of shouldn'ts over the years. What's another few more?"

"I bet Dad will be determined to heal. He'll need help until he passes the shock of what happened. We'll all be here for him. Don't start making plans yet."

Anna glanced at Dad one more time. "Let's just play the game."

She wanted to believe everything would be fine, but it was too soon to tell.

▌▌

DECEMBER 25, 2003

Christmas used to be the time of year when their family was almost suffocatingly close, everyone together to decorate the house and the tree, bake cookies, wrap presents, attend tree lightings and Christmas parties, and play in the snow. Those weeks off school were always family time. While it sometimes sapped her energy and had her aching to return to her room for some silence, every celebration left a warmth in her chest. Whenever Dad was gone, she always reflected on Christmas time, remembering the smell of chocolate chip cookies baking, Ella Fitzgerald's voice scatting over the stereo, Jimmy Stewart smiling at the end of *It's a Wonderful Life* as he hugs his children, and the twinkling of lights against the snowy bushes outside or the warmth they brought to the room inside.

But not this year.

Mom had strung up Dollar Store lights and tinsel garlands around Dad's room, combined with a miniature Christmas tree covered in tiny ornaments on the windowsill. It didn't add much cheer. The lights refracted the tinsel onto the wall, creating red and green reflections that blinked as quickly as Dad's mood swings.

But Mom was trying, and Anna had to give her credit.

The room was like any other in a hospital—white walls, white tile floor, white bed linens. A small table beside the bed. Some machines still connected to Dad beeped and whirred in the background, setting the mood instead of the steady jingle bells in Christmas carols. The decorations were like something out of a horror movie, the thin, twisted wires held up with too many pieces of tape. The lights on the tiny Christmas tree dulled by the fluorescent lights overhead.

Missing most of all was the delight Dad always found in Christmas. He barely smiled. He shoved his few gifts aside and stared at the wall as his children opened their own. And with each interaction he avoided, a little part of her shriveled, decayed, and died. The man who came home wasn't her father. Sure, it would take time for him to get back to himself, she knew that. She knew she would support him through it, but it still hurt.

His silence made her ears bleed, her throat wanting to contract and scream.

This wasn't how it was supposed to be.

He'd been lucid for the first time last week, understanding where he was and all that happened. The first thing he did was take stock of his legs, the right one held in external fixation to heal, metal rods running through it to stabilize the bone, the left one gone from below the knee. Then he dropped his head into his hands and cried.

Local volunteers at the hospital knew that her family would struggle, especially through this holiday season when they weren't at home. D.C. was temporary, but would they move back to Watertown? Either way, the community stepped in, gathering funds to scrounge up gifts for all the families of Walter Reed. Some were simple things—snacks and other consumable treats—but there were gift cards for everyone, a new sweater and some books for Anna, a winter coat and some vinyl albums for Garrett, and a gift basket of bath salts, body lotion, coffee, and tea for Mom. Dad abandoned his packages in the corner.

Conversation was short and stilted, and there were few smiles. His frustration and anger and impatience and pessimism and withdrawal clouded the day. Anna feared how long it would last.

2004

How happy is the little stone
That rambles in the Road alone
And doesn't care about careers –
And Exigencies never – fears
Whose Coat of elemental Brown
A passing Universe put – on
And independent as the sun
Associates – or basks alone –
Fulfilling absolute Decree
In casual simplicity –

—Emily Dickinson, 1891

|| CHAPTER SIXTEEN ||

THE EDGE OF DEATH AND SURVIVAL

FEBRUARY 16, 2004

"I told you before, it's your choice, baby. I don't want you to do anything you don't want to."

Robert twisted off the faucet, listening through the door as Katherine paced the apartment.

"It isn't for you to worry about, Anna. It's been hard for him."

Robert avoided the mirror, propped up on crutches, but how else could he shave the stubble from his face? Last thing he needed was to slip and shave off an eyebrow by mistake. He was already missing a leg—there was no reason to add insult to injury. But when he finally made eye contact with himself, he barely recognized what he saw. When was the last time he'd let his hair go this long? Had he ever had so many months between his daily runs? He noticed the roundness in his face, the additional girth in his middle, and anger flooded his veins, burning hot.

"It has to be your decision, Anna. But I think you should stay in Watertown. Dad and I can work through it together. . . . Okay . . . Okay . . . Then have Grams set things up, and I'll talk to your dad about it."

He shifted a foot as he reached down to rub a sore spot on his thigh, spotting yet another black speck. He worked the skin around it like the nurses had shown him, then finally grasped the end of a splintered piece of metal and pulled it from his skin. The sting was nothing compared to what he felt day after day after day.

"I know, but with all the things that happened over there lately, he's having a hard time."

The months at Walter Reed had been long, and the time slowed for Robert. The hours spent laid up in a bed dragged on, stretching into days that rolled into weeks. While they'd finally moved to an apartment near the medical center, they weren't entirely out of the woods. Every time there was some sense of forward progress—the bone finally healing, the skin grafts finally taking, the incisions finally fading to pink—they had to cut back into him, shave away some more bone, take another section of his leg, finding out that, no, the skin grafts had been rejected. And every time they opened him up, he lost even more of his leg, and he couldn't help but wonder how much would remain when the journey was over.

"It's just . . ."

The door shifted slightly in its frame, and Robert assumed Katherine was ensuring it was closed. He leaned a little closer.

"The bombs, baby. It's hard for him to see those things."

He twisted his fingers into a fist and banged it on the counter once before coming face-to-face with himself again.

The swelling in his body was finally gone, caused by the trauma of the explosion, the jarring of his body, the painkillers, the shrapnel, the infection. Layers of gauze had been reduced to only covering the stub, but as those layers were peeled away, so were bits of himself to reveal how raw he still was.

"Well, I think he blames himself."

That did it. His fist went right into the center of the mirror, sending jagged shards into the sink, the counter, the floor, and fragments into his right hand.

Katherine shrieked from somewhere in the hallway, but a corner of Robert's mouth lifted as he saw only the wall behind the glass. No reflection, no reminder of who he was now, whoever that man was.

The door flew open a foot, straight into the bottom of his crutch. "Robert! What happened?"

"I've got it."

"But your feet—"

"I said I've got it!"

He placed a palm against the door, shoving it back into place, leaving a bloody outline behind.

Jagged hairline cracks ran from the ragged hole to the edges of the mirror. A few slivers had splintered on the counter and smaller pieces littered the floor, a few now lodged in his foot. *Seven years of bad luck—not like I didn't already know that.*

"He broke the mirror . . . Well, I think I can guess. He just . . ." Katherine's voice faded as she moved farther through the apartment.

She watched him each day as if he were a toddler, but only drastic measures would frustrate her enough that she would walk away and leave him in peace.

He slapped down the toilet lid and dropped himself onto it, bringing his foot up as best he could to pick the glass from his heel and toes.

The last two months were a limbo of safe and dead, where he wobbled on that precipice. People applauded a soldier's arrival when he came home safe, walking through the door with all, or else most, of the people he left with, leaving as a unit and returning as one, stepping into the crowd, finding his wife, and taking her home, hugging his kids tightly, grateful for another chance to see them. The trial of separation and duty would have ended in happiness.

The other side was dead, and even then, there would be a homecoming to give his life—his experience—value: the rifle volley, the lone bugler, being buried in his uniform, lying among other war dead in a cemetery, a flag for his family, three spent shell casings for duty, honor, and country. When he first enlisted, he thought about how he would want to die, what it would mean to him, what he wanted his family to know. He'd written the letter in case he never had a chance to say what he felt for Katherine and Garrett and Anna, always taped inside his foot locker, rewriting it as he aged and they did. There would have been closure for them at some point.

People mourned the war dead, sharing memories, visiting the gravesites, leaving coins on headstones, and honoring them every year on Memorial Day, even when that honoring was sometimes an empty gesture. But in their current state of life? No one was checking on them except for the hospital staff and people who knew them well. But Robert was alive, would probably survive, and so the care and support dwindled after two months.

Foot cleared of debris, he wiggled his crutches back under his arms, trying to push himself up, but he still lacked the muscle to do it alone.

Dammit, if there was anything he hated about his situation, it was having to ask Katherine to help him. He didn't want her help, but sometimes, there was no getting around it.

"Katherine!" He paused, listening for a reaction.

"I love you too, honey. I'll call you tonight."

The doorknob twisted, and her face appeared in the crack.

"I need you to help me up. I can't get the crutches right."

She stared at him as he stared back.

He huffed a quick breath. "Katherine, I can't do it myself!"

She straightened a bit, leaning against the frame, still staring at him, still challenging him.

"I don't need you to treat me like a child."

"Then stop acting like one. I'm here every day getting yelled at by you for offering to help, then the next minute you're yelling at me to help you. The least you can do is be nice about it."

"Katherine, would you please help me up."

Her voice morphed into false kindness. "Yes, Robert, why, I'd be glad to help you. But first I'm getting a dustpan and brush. Last thing you need is to slice open your feet."

He bit down hard on the inside of his cheek as she walked away. These slips—they weren't as apparent to her. She never used the singular foot or leg. It was always plural.

He wiped a hand on his sweats and hissed as a sliver of glass dug into his palm, and he welcomed that ache.

Last month, Anna started an online journal that she shared with Robert. "We can share stories of your recovery to keep people in the loop, and they can comment on it to stay in touch with you. See? Some people from Drum already wrote things."

The sentiments wished him quick healing and sent prayers from a distance.

But Robert was caught somewhere in the middle of unscathed and dead. He was the fish flitting around an angler's hook, waiting to discover if he'd get away with the bait or if he'd get tossed on the deck. And while he should be grateful to even reach this stage, to embrace his survival, a part of him wondered if it was worth him surviving. There was no happiness in this. All anyone could question was, will he walk again? Will he keep the other leg? Will he need a wheelchair? What about prosthetics? What about his brain? Constant questions with no answers other than, "It's too early to tell" or "We don't know yet."

Using his thumbnail, he dug at the glass, trying to angle it to pry it loose.

Katherine appeared, then knelt on the floor, silently sweeping the glass into a pile. She'd been with him since the beginning, curling into a chair in the corner of the room while he was in the hospital. One night, she'd even tried to crawl into bed with him and sleep there, but the wires and sensors were knocked loose by drowsy limbs, and they found it was simply too soon for that level of connection and closeness. Instead, she'd hefted the armchair closer to his bed, always staying within reach. Even now, as he yelled and scolded and snapped and tore into her, she would distance herself, then come back to help. Always to help.

Always to her detriment. Exhaustion lined her face, and her hair was limp after days without a shower. Even now that they'd grown more settled in their apartment, she still wasn't focused on her own care—only ever on his.

"Thank you," he forced out, even though part of him wanted to be left alone, to leave the glass, to have it as a reminder that he couldn't be a father who wouldn't upset his daughter's life yet again. How angry would Anna be this time? Their apartment in Rockville, Maryland, had room, but it was even smaller than Watertown. They'd moved some belongings in only two weeks ago, but for how long? Would it be years? Six months? There was no way to know.

One large shard that had yet to fall reflected his face back at him. Robert noticed the dark smudges below his eyes, the lines around his mouth, the flat color of his hair. His gaze followed the length of one leg and the much shorter length of the left. He still had his knee, but for how much longer, he couldn't say. And while he wanted to be thankful for that one bit of mercy (it would be much easier to maneuver with a prosthetic—he'd had plenty of time to consider it), doctors said that his knee could wear out much earlier. Prosthetics had come a long way, but could one move the way he needed it to? His full leg could wear out sooner, particularly in his hip, from attempting to compensate for the unevenness Afghanistan had served him.

He swiped a hand down his face, leaning his elbows on his thighs as Katherine put the dustpan in the sink and swept the pieces on the counter into it. Warm blood still seeped from the cut in his hand and down to his wrist.

"How many more times will you break something?" Katherine's voice was raspy.

He couldn't see her face, but he sensed the judgment.

Why can't you be normal?

"First the tray table in the hospital, then the TV, now the mirror."

The news reports echoed in his head. Last month, a weapons cache explosion in Ghazni had exploded, claiming the lives of nine men from his battalion. Fury had welled in his chest, activated every muscle fiber in his body, and he lifted the tray table and slammed it down on the ground with a strength he hadn't possessed in months. Then, a few days ago, an anti-tank mine had killed a few more of his soldiers. That's when he chucked the remote through the TV. Every one of those names left him reeling, the weight of responsibility settling on his shoulders. Would it still have happened if he were there to lead, direct, propose, adjust? Would he have noticed something the others missed? Had an experience that provided more wisdom to approach the situation differently?

And all the while, the news focused on Iraq. It was as if Afghanistan wasn't a worry anymore. It was all going to shit, and because of that, it didn't need to be the focus. It wasn't worth saving, so why give bad news?

But fine men were dying. Robert wanted to be there with them, to stand alongside them, to hold his rifle to his shoulder and fire at the enemy with the rest of them, to lead them both overseas and back home, his only regard for life being that of the rest of the men in his company. Sure, a replacement would step in for him, prepared to lead, but would he do as well as Robert could have?

"Robert!"

His chin rose to see her facing him, lines across her forehead, arms out to the side in a *what-the-hell, get-it-together* gesture.

"What?"

"I said we need to go to urgent care to get your hand stitched and to make sure you don't have any glass in the cuts. I think I got it all, but why don't you go get your shoes on while I vacuum?"

She got her arms under his armpits, helping to lift him.

"Shoe, Katherine. Singular."

"Whatever, Robert. Go get ready. I want to get started cleaning out the other bedroom. Anna will be down here in a few days, and I want her to feel at home."

Robert planted his foot and got the crutches into position. "She needs to finish the school year."

"She doesn't want to."

"Well, I want her to."

In that apartment bathroom, Robert forced his body straighter, but it felt like he was hunched like an old man. Katherine, on the other hand, was ten feet tall, still not bowing under the pressure of helping him at all hours of the day.

"I don't want her to see me like this," he muttered.

He'd spent decades soldiering, but he would never step back into those combat boots. He was done for. The soldier who led from the front, always stepping in to mentor his soldiers, to prepare them to do their duty, had fizzled out. The father who always made time for his kids now only heard from them through Katherine, both children in different places, continuing on with their lives. The husband who'd always doted on his wife could never fulfill his "one more, then done." Robert had known better than to assure his wife he would be fine, that climbing the ranks would give him a little more distance from the battle.

Robert was—*had been*—an infantryman, and he couldn't be that without being near the enemy. Danger wasn't the only thing that hurt relationships, anyway. Why couldn't he have promised something like that? He'd seen men before him, over the last twenty years of his service, fall apart over financial trouble, over infidelity, over time away, over inconsistency. All those promises made in wedding vows before they understood what this life would be: in the war years when it made life hard, and in the peacetime years when they dreamed of what could be, didn't add up anymore.

Katherine opened the cabinet under the sink and pulled out a box of gauze and antibacterial ointment, setting them on the counter in front of Robert. "Put these on, then we'll go."

Robert accepted the gauze but didn't tear open the wrapping. "Katherine, please."

Katherine sighed, then leaned against the counter. "This isn't our choice."

"It should be. We're her parents."

"Yes, and she's living eight hours away from us with her grandmother in a mostly empty apartment. It's the most unsettled she's probably ever felt. She wants to be with us."

Robert twisted the lid of the ointment and slathered the gel over the cuts.

"You should clean them first."

"I don't think it makes much difference. They'll clean it at the doctor's office." He wrapped the gauze around his fingers and knuckles, no longer able to make a fist. "At least give me until the end of her school year."

"You know, I once asked someone to make a similar choice, and look how that turned out." She immediately bowed her head, rubbing her fingertips along her eyebrows. Robert watched as her shoulders rose, then fell. "I'm sorry—I didn't mean it like that. But Robert, it's her choice. And what's the difference between seeing you or hearing me talk about it? You won't talk to her on the phone."

But how could he? He didn't recognize himself, so how would his kids feel?

He remembered his daughter's averted eyes. He couldn't forget his son's distance. It was as if none of them could see him as *him*, as a person, as their loved one. Instead, he was a victim of another war.

"Has she even thought about this? It's her junior year. It's one more year she can finish with friends—all the people she's known since she started there years ago. She's always wanted stability, and we're giving her that."

"Is it stability when her family isn't there?"

"Your mother's there."

"But *hers* isn't."

"Jesus, Katherine—we don't even know how long we'll be here. What then? What happens when I'm out of here in six months? Where do we go then? Where does *she* go?"

"She'll be in college then."

"Exactly—without us."

"Robert, this isn't some sort of practice run. This is our daughter having her life turned upside down."

"Which we're contributing to by bringing her here. She *hates* the military."

But who was he without it?

Anna always talked about it as his job, something temporary, something he did during the day that could be forgotten once he was home, but it was more than a job. It was dedication, it was something he loved, it was a profession, teaching him skills that he honed over almost two decades of service and changed the world for some people. The military was a part of him now, and no matter how far he stepped away from it in the future, he would always be a soldier.

Katherine dropped the glass shards into the trashcan. "It's up to her. And you'll have to find a way to talk with her. And eventually, you need to call Garrett back. You can't avoid him forever."

His gut twisted at the thought of Garrett. The boy's command had granted him emergency leave to visit Robert in the early days at Walter Reed, but by sending him to Washington, Garrett missed out on the Iraq deployment. During his visit, his son had worn civilians, a pair of jeans, and a Patriots hoodie, and propped himself against a wall. Robert didn't know what Garrett had done the rest of the time, but he was certain it was avoiding the hospital.

When his eyes caught Garrett's short-cropped hair, a streak of envy had cut through Robert's chest, chased by anxiety. Envy that his son would manage to understand brotherhood and courage and patriotism, envy that he would become the leader, envy that he could take out the people who made these bombs. But also anxiety that Garrett would end up like Robert—or worse.

"Now get your shoes on, and let's go."

As Robert watched her walk away, he thought about how sublime it would feel to wrap his arms around his children and pull them close, thankful he was alive to watch them grow, like the years and years and years prior.

But the other part of him hated what he'd become.

He opened the bathroom door and stepped out, worrying, for the first time, about his son carrying on the family's legacy, and he wondered if it would be worth it.

CHAPTER SEVENTEEN

TAKE THE MEMORIES FORWARD

FEBRUARY 17, 2004

Anna shoved her hands into the pockets of her hoodie, relishing the warmth as she surveyed the empty apartment after dropping Grams at the airport. A new year had come and gone since Dad came home, one that should have brought new beginnings—that's what people always said, right? New Year, new me? But Anna, Garrett, hell, the whole family, was starting over yet again. As the saying went in Dad's career, the only consistency was the inconsistency.

This would be the last time Anna would see the place that, more than any other, had felt like home. All that remained were her final boxes, the things she wouldn't dare let the movers—strangers—pack, the few mementos that meant the most to her in an utterly temporary life.

The apartment was now stripped of all the family's belongings. Gone was the nicked wooden furniture, the couch with the tear across the back from when a mover used a sharp knife to open the packaging and cut too close.

She'd promised Grams that she'd make a final circuit through the apartment before leaving all copies of the key in the super's box on the first floor. All that was left was an outline of their lives there, marks of the memories they made, the times that life was good, and they were together rather than falling apart at the seams. Their closeness had been damaged by catastrophe, all going up in smoke in the aftermath of the explosion that devoured half of Dad's leg and a whole lot of his personality.

Good-by to the life I used to live, and the world I used to know; and kiss the hills for me, just once; now I am ready to go.

Emily was doing her best to convince Anna that goodbyes weren't the end of the world, but Anna already knew that.

For the first time, she'd gotten to choose on her own, but what did she do with it? How the hell did she pick moving—again—over the freedom within her grasp in New York?

It doesn't feel like freedom.

Divots were still pressed into the carpet from the weight of the couches and coffee table, marking the spaces where they'd made their living for the last six years. There was the faint pink spot—candle wax from Christmas Eve—when Dad got so excited playing The Game of Life that he bumped the table behind him, sending the luminary to the floor, spilling wax that wouldn't come out. But no flames reflected against the walls now.

She wandered into the kitchen, the room that was always warmest, where she'd most often find Dad when he was home, cooking one of those breakfast sandwiches when he didn't have to be in early, taking care to slow Anna down in her rush to get somewhere, or sitting at the counter with a newspaper in hand. She checked the cabinets, making sure no plates, cups, or pieces of paper were left behind, and peeked inside the dishwasher. She stared at the countertops, trying to ignore all the thoughts of how things would be different, but the cold, silent room was oppressive.

Her fingers played with the mass of keys in her pocket as she walked into the attached dining room. How many meals had they shared around the table, thinking it would continue like that forever?

Her parents' bedroom was next, and Anna opened the door a crack to peek inside, frozen on the threshold. She'd asked Grams to check it before she left, and still, Anna could only stare at it from the hallway, unable to step into her parents' space without them there. She closed the door and backed away. There was no point checking Garrett's room—anything that mattered to him was in Colorado.

Finally, she followed the worn carpet the few steps to her room. The doors to her closet were still taped shut, a way to ensure the movers didn't open it. She ripped it off, taking a small line of the off-white paint with it, crumpling it into a ball, and shoving it into her back pocket.

With every move, Anna carefully packed her books and notebooks, gently wrapping the first editions from Grams or the special editions she'd discovered in bookstores around the country, not trusting any of the movers with the few cherished things she owned. Most of her belongings showed all the signs of a lifetime of moving: deep gouges in her dresser, chunks missing from her bed frame, the rickety nightstand Dad had tried to fix when one of the pieces went missing but was never the same, a paperweight from Ernest Hemingway's house that cracked after she uncovered it at the bottom of a poorly packed box.

She was speechless over the few things that felt like her: some books, a stuffed animal, a paperweight, and Emily Dickinson, her bobbling head now still. James's room was full of things that felt like his. Trophies and medals displayed on shelves, his room painted his favorite shade of blue, the model plane he'd built with his dad when things were still good, a picture of his mom in a silver frame, furniture that matched and fit the space comfortably.

She slid the boxes along the carpet and closed the closet door, not yet ready to leave her room, not wanting to step away knowing all that was ahead.

But she had to.

Dad's most important rule was that family was everything. When he left, Mom, Garrett, and Anna came together. When Mom had the flu a few years ago, Anna and Garrett did all they could around the house so she could rest. When Anna sliced her hand open that time, Mom helped her with buttons and snaps, and Garrett completed her chores for a few days. When Garrett sprained his ankle, Anna reluctantly stepped up for him. Grams had dropped everything to fly to New York to help Mom when Dad got hurt. As much as Anna wanted to stay rooted in place, the fertile soil was with her parents, and their permanence called to her.

The day Dad got hurt was still cemented into the recesses of her brain, sure to remain packed there, time unable to shake it loose. The powers that be took a sledgehammer to her life, knocking down all the walls filled with plans, then rebuilding them in an unfamiliar maze of novelty: new state, new school, new friends in her junior year, new lifestyle, new hurdles to jump in her social and family life.

Excitement had filled Anna when Mom suggested she stay in New York, at least until the end of the school year. Games with Grams, delicious meals, walks to the diner around the corner—it had been special for the first week. But then the novelty dissipated, uncovering the harsh truth.

Mom and Dad are right—home is wherever we're together.

Once she returned to New York last month, Anna had scoured the internet for suggestions about how to support Dad through his recovery, to be there as he learned to walk with a prosthetic, to give Mom a break from the chores and care. To let her get a freaking massage for once and not be focused solely on Dad. While the idea of another limbo sucked the breath from Anna's lungs momentarily, there was more at stake.

Family.

This damn war had done so much already—she couldn't let it break the family.

Three quick raps echoed in the empty apartment, and Anna jumped, quickly spinning to face her bedroom door.

"What are you doing here?" she asked, unable to hide her surprise or keep herself from throwing her arms around him.

James squeezed her tightly before pulling back. "I know you had plans to leave today, but you won't be able to. There's more than two feet of snow on the ground throughout Pennsylvania and Maryland, and it's still coming down. There's a state of emergency—no cars on the road."

Anna's widened. "I have to turn in the keys today." She held them out between them, and immediately, her mind raced with what she would do. "I don't think I can book a hotel."

He wrapped his warm hands around hers. "I've got you. Nana says you can stay with us until it clears up."

She shook her head. *I figured out how to get Mom to D.C., I can damn well figure this out too.* "You don't have to do that."

James stepped back, frowning. "What else are you gonna do? You can't stay here. You can take the guest room. Nana will like seeing you one last time before you leave."

Her heart twisted. "I appreciate that."

He shrugged, then ran his hands over the woodwork in the doorway. "Need help with anything?"

Anna's eyes moved from the nail polish marks on the floor, to the bits of tape on the walls that had held colorful posters about hopes and dreams, to the unadorned window that had let in the morning birdsong. "Here I go again. Another goodbye. Another move," she mumbled to herself.

James swallowed thickly. "I guess so."

"I'm not even sure what I'm doing."

"I don't know if this helps, but I'd do the same thing. It was a hard choice, and it's okay if you're angry that it came to this."

"I hate this fucking war," she whispered. "I can't let it take Dad."

James cleared his throat. "You're doing the right thing."

With a heavy sigh, Anna knelt, trying to lift one of the last boxes until James stepped in.

"You take the smaller one."

Together, they held the last remnants of her life in New York, all managing to fit in two cardboard boxes, and together they inspected the empty space. They stood back-to-back, not leaning on each other but knowing the support was there if they needed it.

"Time to move on," Anna said, her voice soft.

She flipped the light switch using her elbow as she left through the front door for the last time. They wound down the building's stairs, their footsteps echoing in the cavernous opening, making her feel completely and utterly alone—the way it had been for too long, when Mom lost it while Dad was gone, when no one would talk about the separation, when Garrett enlisted and left her to manage all of this alone.

Flurries fell from the sky, the white flakes a stark contrast to Dad's burgundy Chevy. They carefully slid the boxes into the small backseat, Anna's suitcases, supplies, and duffels already arranged in the bed under the protective tarp.

"Hop in and start her up. I'll run these inside, then we can head to your place." As James climbed into the passenger seat, Anna ran through the cold back into the building, dropping the keys into the box inside the door. Her eyes glanced at the old mailbox; the Pechman name already removed from the label.

FEBRUARY 19, 2004

"I'll leave you kids to enjoy the evening yourselves. I'm off to bed. Anna, don't stay up too late. You'll want to be rested for your drive tomorrow."

Anna rose from the thick bearskin rug near the hearth and reached for Nana, holding her tightly. "Thank you for everything."

The older woman gripped Anna's shoulders. "I hope to see you again when things settle down. Don't be a stranger." She smiled slightly before turning toward the stairs, leaving the teens alone.

Anna resumed her spot by the fire, taking a sip of the hot chocolate Nana had made. Rather than choosing from the worn navy couch against the long wall of the room or the recliner nearer the fireplace, James and Anna chose the floor, where they'd toasted marshmallows during Anna's first New York winter six years ago, where they'd sat during the long, cold months to play board games or cards, where they'd eaten Christmas cookies and drank cocoa plenty of holiday seasons past.

Somehow, this house always felt like home to her, even more than her family's apartment. There was something about a lived-in space, where the occupants resided permanently rather than anticipating the next house or building the next home. It was filled with character, from a room full of furniture that fit an overall theme, to walls covered with art or sconces or mirrors. All things that could break too easily during a military move. Pictures covered almost every spare inch of space above the couch in a collage of mismatched frames: James in all stages of life, some of Anna with him, plenty of James and Nana together, as well as an old wedding photo of his parents before everything changed for them.

Anna's heart pinched. Would she one day be a picture on the wall, a mark of a distant memory?

It had been two days since a snowstorm dumped more than two feet of snow in the states to New York's southern border, but crews had finally cleared the highways. It was time to move on, to leave. She had delayed as long as possible.

"You sure you don't want me to come with you?" James asked, breaking the silence. "Nana already said she'd buy me a plane ticket to fly back."

Anna shook her head, staring at the dancing flames. "No. I don't know if there'd be room for you."

"I don't mind sleeping on a couch."

"It's not that. I just . . . my dad isn't himself yet. I should go alone."

"You're doing that thing again."

"What thing?"

"Where you keep people at a distance to make things easier. For you. It doesn't make it easier for everyone else."

She sighed and stared at the fire. "It's not that." *Or is it? First Dad and now James?*

He cleared his throat. "You'll call once you're settled, though, right?"

"I might need some time, James."

Out of the corner of her eye, she saw him shake his head and lean against the recliner behind him. They fell into silence, the crackle of burning wood or the occasional pop of an air pocket the only sound in the background. The light of the fire heated their faces with its flickering glow, capturing their attention as they watched the movement of the flames.

He set his mug aside. "Do you remember when you first moved here?"

She raised an eyebrow. "What about it? It feels so long ago."

He crossed his legs and leaned toward her. "You walked in with two long braids, hugging a book to your chest."

She nudged his foot with hers. "That's what did it for you, huh?"

A far-off look appeared in his eyes. "No, it was how you smiled at everyone that did it for me. You walked into a classroom full of people who'd known each other for years. That would have been scary for most kids. Not you."

"It was my fifth move, and my seventh new school."

"Yeah, but you jumped right in. You found me and eventually fit in with everyone else. Now it's like you've always been here."

Her heart squeezed, but she shrugged. "I learned how to fake it. It isn't that easy—it gets harder the older I get."

"Remember that bully in seventh grade?"

A smile swept across her face, and as much as she didn't want to start laughing, she couldn't help it. "You mean the time I punched him in the nose for pushing you around?"

He barked out a laugh. "I never had to worry about anyone calling me a nerd again."

"Well, getting the braces off and trying out contacts gave them less of a target."

"I don't think I ever would have hit him though."

"I know a lot of boys who would have hated a girl stepping in like that."

He shrugged. "You threw a better punch than I could have."

Both of them burst into laughter, and warmth surged through her body. This was what she'd needed. Instead of talking about everything that was ahead, Anna wanted to revisit the memories full of fun, laughter, and all the things associated with their friendship, to hold onto their connection a little longer.

"Remember my first fair?"

He smiled. "I tried to work my charm and win you a teddy bear."

She laughed. "I still have that bear."

He met her eyes. "I know. I saw it in the box the other day. I was surprised you still had it." Suddenly, his spine snapped straight. "That reminds me." He turned to the side, picking up a book from the recliner and holding it up for her to see the wooden cover.

She'd recognize the slab of dark walnut anywhere. Years ago, the pages inside had been blank, but throughout their friendship, they'd added ticket stubs, photographs, postcards, and other memorabilia of their time together or adventures apart, transforming it into a scrapbook. It was the mark of a lengthy bond, two people sharing so much of their lives for the time they had, willing to memorialize it between two solid covers they could revisit at will.

She lifted it from his hands and ran her fingertips over the relief depicting pine trees, before paging through it. The last entry wasn't even a quarter of the way through the book, and the mass of empty pages was a stark reminder of all they wouldn't experience together. Tears rose in her eyes.

James's face transformed into horror. "Shit, I didn't mean to make you sad. I thought now was a good time to give it to you." He wrapped his arms around her shoulders and pulled her close, running a hand over her hair. "I'm sorry, I thought you'd want it."

She swiped the back of her hand across one eye. "I do want it. I only wish we'd filled it with more."

"You still can." He hugged her tighter. "Fill it with all your adventures."

She pulled back. "But it was always for *us*."

He shrugged. "Send it to me when you're ready. Catch me up on what you're doing."

They inched slightly away from each other, and Anna gripped his hand. There were so many things she wanted to say, to explain why she had to leave, to ensure he understood she *wanted* to stay. With him. Where things were simpler and safer, where comfort would cradle her and peace would possess her.

But she couldn't. Her life was changing, she had a duty to her family, and so she had to leave.

She gently set the book aside.

For a full minute, they simply stared at each other, words and feelings they'd felt and wanted to say tucked away safely to preserve the friendship. But time had taught Anna a lot of things.

"I'm not ready for you to go. It all happened so fast. I get it—we have to say goodbye, but I don't know how," James said softly, interrupting her thoughts. He turned his attention to the fireplace. "You don't have to say anything; I just wanted you to know that."

She was still holding his hand and gave it a squeeze. "There's a saying in the Army: 'There are no goodbyes; only see you laters.' It's a few months to help get my dad through the next year."

"Call when you need to talk. I'll listen."

She smiled sadly. "You always have."

He lifted his hand and rested it against her cheek, sweeping down to the column of her neck as his eyes traveled the span of her face. "It won't be the same without you," he whispered.

She leaned toward him, the few inches between them eaten up in less than a second. "I know."

It was then that he closed the space, pressing his lips to hers ever so softly at first. Somehow, the fire had penetrated her skin, releasing its warmth through her chest and sending tingles to her fingertips and toes. Her head spun with questions about the line they had crossed and where things would go from here, and a small part of her brain screamed to pull back. Instead, she pushed in closer as he shifted to wrap his arms around her. The warmth of his embrace and the security it offered chased away the chill of the future, eliminated the coldness of worry, thawed the ice of the unknown. The fire's crackle, the rug's cushion, the room's walls all fell away until it was the two of them, suspended in the present moment to avoid thinking about the next.

He opened his mouth to deepen the kiss, and she was lost to the light behind her eyes, the flicker of the flames, and the warmth and familiarity of him, all chasing away the darkness of grief and the stillness of pain.

At least for the night.

FEBRUARY 20, 2004

The next morning, Anna rose while the sky was still dark. She hadn't slept long, but it would have to be enough. She gently pulled the covers back and eased herself out of James's bed, then quietly closed the door behind her, stepping carefully down the hallway to avoid any creaks she might encounter. Ignoring the mirror, which would only show how exhausted she was, she washed her face, brushed her teeth, and combed her hair back into a ponytail. She tossed her toiletries into a bag, double-checking she left nothing behind, then entered the guest room to finish packing.

The scrapbook waited on the bedside table, and the lamplight reflecting off the surface caught her eye, freezing her in place. Last night, she told herself she'd let him have it, worried that the pictures and memories would only add to the pain of separation. But as she shouldered her backpack, prepared to turn off the light, she couldn't leave it behind. He would have this place and all the places they'd visited together, and without this book, she'd have nothing. She slipped it carefully into her bag.

She stared at the floor as she descended the stairs and walked through the living room to find her shoes. Then, forcing herself to lean only on the memories, she headed for the truck, closing the front door softly behind her.

She jumped inside the vehicle, starting it up and rubbing her hands together as she waited for it to warm. As she placed her bag on the seat beside her, she noticed her teddy bear buckled into the front seat alongside Emily, a letter tucked underneath them. She lifted the bear, hugging it to her chest as the sky turned gray, that in-between stage of dawn and night. She stared at her name on the envelope, barely visible in the dashboard lights, but she left it on the seat for later.

Emily had always envisioned her escape, and it was something Anna had in common with her. Together they could imagine all that would come after. But for the first time, Anna didn't want to escape. She wanted to stay—in the same old life, in the same old space, forgetting any hope of the beyond.

A stray tear slid down her cheek, and she wiped it away with the rough knit of her mitten as the front light popped on. All she saw was his silhouette leaning against a porch column, unable to make out his face. She fought the urge to race back to him, to hug him one last time and figure out when they would see each other again, but it was time to move on. That's what Dad always said, right? We don't look back; we take the memories forward with us.

She shifted into drive and steered toward her new home, clutching the bear the entire way.

|| CHAPTER EIGHTEEN ||

FLOWER POWER

MARCH 2, 2004

"You sure you don't want any help?"

Anna didn't answer Mom right away, too distracted by the opportunity that the bare white walls of Rockville presented.

"I'll be good."

"I already stowed your clothes in the closet. We are *not* having a repeat of Watertown in there, okay?"

"It wasn't *that* bad," Anna mumbled.

"Baby, you can't leave clothes halfway off hangers or on the floor. They get wrinkled."

"Not like there's anyone here to see it."

"You're starting school on Monday. At least be presentable."

Anna glanced at her flared jeans with patches of peace signs and flowers. "What's wrong with this?"

She rubbed her temples. "I thought I made things clear. Are you trying to poke the bear? I don't mind you dressing that way, protesting—whatever you want to do. But we need to make your dad feel supported. All this staring him in the face right away won't help. You just got here. Ease him into it."

Anna sighed. God help them if the war dove preened in front of the hawk. "It's been two weeks since I got here and a year since that protest."

"But he only came back a few months ago with his life turned upside down."

"*And* ours."

"You're right, and ours. I'm only saying . . . give him time."

Anna slumped. "All right, I'll at least contain it."

Mom squeezed her shoulder before she walked toward the door. "Sure you don't want help?"

Anna stared at the boxes in her new room. "Nah, I'm good. Thanks, though."

Once alone, Anna paused, picturing what her space would become, the most authentic expression of who she was. If Dad didn't want to see the peace signs, he'd have to stay out. With her bedroom in the loft, it would help.

Tradition determined that Emily find a home first, and she now sat in a place of distinction, front and center on the desk, observing as Anna stared at the bare walls as a tingle of anticipation ran from her fingers to her toes. Something about a room filled with cardboard boxes left nothing but opportunity in its wake. Even in the wariness of starting over again, her bedroom was always the same. Sure, this one had a little more room between her desk and her bed, and she'd no longer catch her hip on the corner of her dresser on the way out the door, but once everything was in place, it would be the same it always was. Maybe even better than before.

It was yet another apartment, so there was only one window to let in any light, but the walls were the ideal blank canvas she could fill with her mementos.

Her phone buzzed once, the tiny window on the front lighting up with **JAMES**.

She flipped it open with her thumb, then tapped the circle button to read his response to her picture of the boxes.

So what first? Books? Desk?

She texted back, **Bed first, then bookshelf, then desk. Emily's already out.** She snapped a picture for him, then set her phone aside. Her eyes scanned the scrawled labels, searching for a large box of bed linens. All the book boxes were stacked beside her shelf, her desk items were neatly underneath the keyboard tray, and thanks to Mom and pre-established rules that the closet remain neat in this house, Anna's clothes were already on hangers, safely stowed behind the closed door along with shoes, tote bags, and purses.

Anna shifted a few boxes until she found the one labeled linens and excitedly slit the smooth tape with a boxcutter, lifting the leaves to reveal pillows and blankets. Grams had stuck dryer sheets between the layers of fabric, and they smelled of lavender.

After she removed the bulky pile of linens, piling them on her bed, she turned on her small radio, already tuned to the local NPR station.

"Now onto news from Iraq. More than one hundred Shiite Muslims are dead and three hundred wounded after a series of attacks in Karbala and Baghdad during the Shiite holy day of Ashura. It marks the deadliest day in Iraq since President

Bush declared an end to major combat operations on May 1, 2003. The attacks took place around ten in the morning, local time."

"Turn that off," Dad barked from the stairs. "I don't want to hear it."

She paused, taking a breath and counting to ten, choosing not to engage the disgruntled grouch. She could roll her eyes as much as she wanted behind a closed door, punch a pillow if she got frustrated, stomp her feet in anger, or cry if needed, but when in front of him, she'd stay in control.

Because more than anything, she couldn't lose him to this war.

She shook out the fitted sheet and wrapped it around her mattress, smoothing the wrinkles as she remembered Mom's ground rules. *Don't do anything to rile him or engage his frustration unless necessary. Keep the war talk and debates to a minimum.* As she picked up her flat sheet and pillow case, she nudged the door closed with her foot and continued listening as she tucked the hanging ends of the sheets between the mattress and box spring.

"Three suicide bombers detonated explosives around the al-Kadamiya mosque in Baghdad. According to Ahmed al-Haeliali, a judge in Karbala tasked with investigating the attack there, they believe nine suicide bombers were responsible for the violence in the city. They retrieved ball bearings, nails, and springs from the bombing sites. . . ."

Anna shook her head, removing her pillows from the box and patting them to fluff them up. So much violence directed at their own people. What was the United States doing there? *Maybe Dad's right and I should turn it off.* But as she reached for the dial, further information caught her attention, and she paused in front of the radio.

"On that same day, a gunman opened fire on Shiite worshipers in Pakistan, killing thirty-eight people. This comes just days after one U.S. soldier was killed and another wounded when an improvised explosive device was thrown at their military vehicle."

The news twisted her stomach, and she finally switched it off, lifting the comforter to distract herself. But two families' lives were changed that day, and no one mentioned the soldiers lost—if they even were soldiers and not Marines, sailors, or airmen—who had their lives changed in the split second it took to detonate a bomb. The news treated the dead like nameless, faceless objects.

When Dad was injured last year, the Army called it a mine, but now the military, the government, and reporters used the term improvised explosive devices—IEDs. Weapons of war used to take out as many forces as possible in grotesque ways: buried in the ground or packed into vehicles, blown up from a distance using a cell phone, or up close with suicide bombers. Every few days it was another attack, sending more and more amputees to Walter Reed, if they came back at all.

Anna folded the top of the blanket over just so, then stepped back to survey her work.

The blue and purple peace sign perfectly symbolized her war-dove years. When Grams had taken Anna to a department store to replace the floral sheets of her youth, this one was the first to snag her eye. And as they went from store to store, she found nothing that compared.

Anna lifted the teddy bear from her nightstand and the decorative pillows at the bottom of the box and arranged them in the center of the bed. One pillow said, "Give peace a chance," and the other had white daisies.

Flower power.

Crossing the room to where the mirror packs sat, Anna tilted them forward one by one, searching for the box labeled "Protest." There she found it, quickly slicing the tape and freeing the prints from their cardboard prison.

She spread them out on her bed, each image showcasing protests from the sixties and seventies, hippies and groovy-dressed men and women sticking daisies into the barrels of M-14s or holding chrysanthemums like shields as police or National Guard members closed in. The photos were in black and white, but the flowers were bold reds and oranges and yellows, contrasting sharply against the shades of gray.

No, she wouldn't compare this conflict to Vietnam—didn't want to—but she hoped protesting could be what made the change, no matter how much Dad hated it.

As she lifted her sign from last year in Syracuse, smoothing out the bent corners, someone knocked on the door before opening it.

"Hey, Mom asked for—" Anna watched as his eyes bounced between the images on her bed, the text on the pillows, the pattern of her sheets. "What the hell is this?"

"I'm setting up my room."

"What the hell are peace signs—*that sign*—doing in my house?"

Anna twisted her arms behind her back, staring at his face, sizing up how he'd respond. Last time, he tore the sign in half, so she inched her way to the right to stand between him and peace, between him and who she was, the *real* her, not the version he'd prefer she snuff out.

"Mom told me you wouldn't like it. I promise it will all stay in here."

"Pack it back up."

"I'll keep the door closed," she wagered. Couldn't he leave it alone? Did they have to fight about this after only two weeks of them being back as a family?

"I don't want it here."

"Then don't come in."

"It's *my* house."

"It's *my* room."

She watched as his fingers tightened around the handle of the crutches, but Mom's voice sharply interrupted.

"Robert, can you help me in the kitchen?" Mom squeezed between the doorframe and Dad's broad shoulders.

"Your daughter can help you. I'll be in our room."

"Oh, no she won't. *You* will help me. What has always been the first rule about PCSing?" She waited for him to speak, but he held tightly to his frustration. "We always set up bedrooms first. She needs a place to relax—away from us, in her own space. She can hang up what she wants. No one will see it but her."

Anna and Dad were two hockey players ready to duke it out on the ice, and Mom was the referee stepping between them, ready to lock horns to follow the ground rules, with no space for debate. Her parents were no longer on the same team.

"Katherine, I can't look at this—" His voice grew louder, but Mom cut it off.

"This is not a pity party for you," she said wearily. "Go to the kitchen and we'll talk."

He rolled his eyes and huffed out a breath, the gentle creak of crutches the only sound, fading in the distance.

"Anna, what did we *just* talk about?"

"*He* came in *here*, Mom. I didn't hunt him down and shove it in his face."

Eyes closed, Mom rubbed her temples in small circles. "I can't referee the two of you forever. I will lose my ever-loving mind. Deep breaths, please."

Anna picked up the boxcutter and slit open her first box of books. "He started it."

"I have no doubt. But—"

"Why's he still like this?"

"He needs time, baby. It will get better. He'll be fit for his prosthetic soon, which will change things."

Anna huffed out a breath. "How will that do anything?"

"Hey, I'm on your side too. Don't take it out on me."

Anna swallowed hard, turning her attention to her books. Maybe Mom could bring dinner in here. Anna could sit on the floor, flipping through pages and reminiscing about the old friends she'd made between the covers. Mom didn't deserve Anna's anger, but the strain of constant positivity, the fake smiles, and the false hope would one day shatter her face.

Mom's deep, centering breath broke through the silence. "The prosthetic will make him feel like he's back to normal, give him a sense of independence."

"Yeah, right. This is about a lot more than that."

Mom finally snapped. "You don't know that."

Anna jumped, dropping the books in her hand. As she turned to face Mom, she was shocked by the lines of frustration along Mom's eyes, forehead, and mouth, the way the light caught her pale skin, and how her face was thinner than before.

"Dinner will be in an hour. You can eat wherever you want. Just keep this door closed. Please."

Mom left, a soft click behind her, and Anna sat against the wall beside her bookshelf and stepped into worlds where she didn't have to fake it.

‖

"She's seventeen years old, Robert. You need to let her start on her own path."

The sizzling on the stove had filled the silence since Katherine arrived in the kitchen. Once she'd joined him, she placed a cutting board in front of Robert, who leaned on his crutches as he sliced into peppers and onions for pasta sauce while Katherine broke up sausage in a pan.

"What happened to her?" he whispered.

Katherine laughed, and it made him grit his teeth. "She said the same thing about you."

He slammed the knife against the wooden board. "It's different. Things actually happened *to* me. I'm allowed to be angry."

Katherine added the cut veggies to the meat with a loud hiss as he leaned against the counter to take some pressure off his underarms. "Things happened to her too."

He bit his cheek so he wouldn't have to confess to uprooting his daughter's life again or note that perhaps her anger was rightfully placed. She'd do the last month of her junior year and all of her senior with kids she'd never met. But this—today's fight—was about *her* behavior, not his.

"This isn't how she was raised." What he didn't say was that she wasn't raised to throw away all he and so many others had done in a country where they were easily forgotten.

Katherine set the lid on the pan harder than necessary. "Jesus, Robert, you make her sound like a drug dealer." Her half-laugh had him gritting his teeth. "It's some peace signs and seventies images. What, are you going confiscate the punk rock?"

"It was bad enough when we were in Watertown, all those soldiers I was leading. But here? Where people are trying to find a way to survive? What the hell, Katherine?"

"I already told her to keep it in her room. We've reached an understanding."

"No, it all goes tomorrow."

Katherine slowly turned to face him. "What does that mean?"

"When you take her to register for school, it's all going in the Dumpster."

She crossed the distance between them in one step, putting her face close to his. "Robert, if you do that, she'll never forgive you. Find a way to deal. She'll keep her door closed and you won't have to see it, but don't you dare throw it away. I want my daughter to have a life here, and you need to let her do it her way."

As Katherine turned back to the stove, all Robert could see was Olsen on the ground, Swanson crying over him, a line of body armor and Kevlar hanging on a rack, the helo kicking up dust on that ridge, and the darkness after the explosion.

Peace. What is it good for when we're forgetting they're over there?

After tucking the crutches back under his arms, Robert left the kitchen.

"Where are you going? We're about to sit down to eat."

"Eat without me. I'm not hungry."

His stomach rumbled as he walked away.

|| CHAPTER NINETEEN ||

WHAT IS SACRIFICE?

MARCH 31, 2004

"*Insurgents attacked a convoy Wednesday morning in Iraq that was carrying private security contractors from the civilian firm Blackwater. Four men were killed, and then, in a grotesque measure, their bodies were burned, dragged through the street, and hung from a bridge near Fallujah. This comes only two hours after a roadside bomb killed five American troops near the town of Habbaniya, part of what is known as the Sunni Triangle—*"

Anna leaned her forehead against the cool steering wheel as the NPR station droned on. These stories, the ones that told of the sheer brutality of war, were always the hardest.

"*Brigadier General Mark Kimmitt held a press conference just a few hours ago and had this to say.*"

The broadcast shifted to a recording. "*Fallujah is a Baathist stronghold which profited immensely under Saddam's regime, and a small minority of the people there just don't want it to become a part of the new Iraq.*"

The general talked more about the United States mission there as Anna let the truck run in her parking space outside her family's apartment.

"*In a war unfolding publicly online and on television, the images of this attack have been shocking to many, but none more so than the families who await word from their loved one. Here's the general's words in response.*"

Anna shook her head.

"*Somewhere out there in this world, there are going to be families who are getting knocks on their door from people, telling them what happened to their loved ones,*" the general said. "*It is not pleasant to be on either side of that door, I can tell you.*"

Anna slapped her hands forcefully against the steering wheel before twisting the volume knob with a burning hand, surprised she didn't break it off as
the silence settled.

But as soon as these broadcasts ended, everyone listening would move on
with their lives, the loss of a few Americans having no bearing on their futures,
while the ones closest to the incident would be forever changed.

Deep breaths. Let it go. Get inside. Plaster on a smile. Keep it together.

As she gathered the plastic bag and her backpack, she wondered how those
words became her guide over the last month. Despite three weeks in her new
school, she had no friends. But maybe it was her fault—there was no one like
James. She'd head home, maybe run some errands on the way, then be there to
support her parents. And each day, when she loaded into her truck for that ride
home, she wondered if that day would be when things finally changed.

She shut off the vehicle and prepared herself for coming home. Her phone
buzzed from her purse, and she opened the message from James.

It isn't the same without you here.

She texted back, **Yeah, a lot of things aren't the same.**

She entered the building and chose the stairs over the elevator, offering
more time to think, to breathe, to prepare, to close off so much of herself, to be
what others needed.

You good? Wanna talk?

A lack of signal in the stairwell prevented her from replying, so she shoved
her phone back into her pocket, swallowing hard. If she were still in Watertown,
she'd either be hanging with James, reading a book, or finishing homework on
the average Wednesday. But here? When she was trying to give Mom space from
Dad's repeated assaults, to be the proverbial punching bag for once, she'd be
doing laundry, cleaning up, doing homework, then collapsing into bed.

School should have been a break from being asked to give, a respite from
his raincloud of an attitude, one that could bring a gentle rain followed by a
rainbow or spin up a tornado.

But it wasn't. It was as if she didn't fit anywhere: not in her home, and not
at school.

She slipped her key into the lock, hesitantly searching through the crack
in the door for any signs of his presence. Lately, this was how their interactions
went, her sneaking glances while he stewed on something he wouldn't voice,
everyone tiptoeing around him, careful to rile him too much and face his wrath.
Caring for him, she could handle—and she was glad to do it, ready to be useful,
helpful, seen as independent—but would it kill him to show appreciation once
in a while? Was it so hard to recognize what she and Mom were doing for him?

As she kicked off her shoes, he sat with his legs draped on the recliner, exactly where she expected he would be. And before she attempted to engage, before she opened her mouth and reached for the false positivity, she filled her lungs and exhaled the strain.

For now, she'd hold on to Emily's words. *Hope is a strange invention, a patent of the heart, in unremitting action yet never wearing out.*

She couldn't let her heart wear out—no matter what.

Anna stepped into the living room and held up her shopping bag. "I stopped at the PX after school for a new pair of the sneakers you like."

His eyes flicked toward the bag and narrowed, then returned to the TV.

"Can you try one on, please? If it doesn't fit, I'll exchange them now. I still have to get laundry started before Mom gets back from the commissary."

"Did they at least give you a discount?"

"Not funny. You need both of them anyway for therapy this week, remember?"

He lowered the recliner's footrest and slowly sat forward. "Ah, yes. I'm like Benjamin Button, aging in reverse. Entering middle age but only now learning to walk."

In any other circumstance, she'd appreciate his literary response, had it come from connection rather than spite. She concentrated on calm, refusing to let his tone rile her, and knelt to unpack the shoes, pulling cardboard from inside and paper from deep in the toes.

"Just put the shoe on, Dad."

All movement ceased as his eyes settled on the shoes in front of him and the color drained from his face. "If I can't manage the prosthetic, I'm going to have a closet full of single shoes I can't wear anymore."

Anna swallowed.

"Shame they don't make them fit both feet like in the old days, right?"

She sat back on her heels and watched him. "Enough, all right? You can buy single shoes if you need to, but we aren't there yet."

She huffed out a breath at the use of "we." If you asked Dad, it was him against the world. He didn't see the team he had behind him in the form of his wife and daughter. *No, poor Sergeant Pechman can't get out of his own head.*

"Everything will be fine," she continued. "You'll be using shoes in pairs for years, Dad. We have to get over this hill first. Here, stick your foot out for me."

The shoe slid easily over his sock, and she adjusted the tongue and laces to tie it snugly. "How does that feel? Too tight? Enough room? You don't want them too tight in case your feet swell from the activity."

"Take it off."

She frowned. "Dad, does it fit?"

Louder this time, "I said, take it off."

Anna sighed, then pulled the laces to loosen the shoe. "I'm just trying to help."

As she put the sneaker back in its box, Dad grew silent, staring straight ahead, focusing on nothing. Slowly, he rubbed a thumb underneath his armpit. She remembered how James complained about soreness there when he was on crutches after spraining an ankle in gym class in the fall of eighth grade. He'd spent so much time leaning on them while standing.

"Are the crutches bothering you?" she asked.

"A little sore is all."

Anna lifted herself from the floor and walked down the hall to the tiny linen closet, yanking two hand towels free from the mass crammed onto the shelf. Then she flipped on the light in the bathroom, digging under the sink, past extra toilet paper and boxes of tissues, to find the medical kit. As she tucked the towels under her arm, she unzipped the case on her way to the living room, finding the medical tape. "Here, hand one to me."

He tilted the top of a crutch toward her, and she wrapped the towel around the top and taped it in place.

He swiped a hand down his face. "You don't need to do that."

She focused on her work, gritting her teeth, breathing through the pain that settled in her jaw. *Is a simple thank you that hard?* She held out her other hand—a silent request for the next one—and repeated the process. "It only takes a minute, and you need it."

"I can manage tape, Anna."

"I'm saving you a step." As soon as the words left her mouth, she braced for impact. *Why didn't I think it through before I said it?* His control when she first came home meant it was building, and eventually, that pressure would release in a shocking force of anger.

"Do you think I can't get myself there?"

"No, I think you're incredibly capable, Dad," she said, weariness weaving itself between every word. How many times had she said this over the past month? "Count yourself lucky that I can take your shit." *And give it back when needed.*

"Don't let Mom hear you talking like that," he said, using his old refrain.

"I'm not worried about it." She tore off a piece of tape with her teeth. "And don't think I didn't notice you avoiding my comment."

He placed an elbow on the arm of the chair and leaned on it heavily. "You don't understand how hard this is."

Her hands stilled, and she let the pain of that simple phrase roll down her back. She leaned the second crutch against the wall near his chair before sitting on the couch diagonally from him. "You aren't the only one making sacrifices here."

He swallowed thickly and turned away from her. "It isn't the same."

She shook her head as he slowly withdrew into himself. "Oh, great. That will make Mom and me feel *so* much better."

"I hope that one day, you see it as worthy. Your part in it, too."

Anna hesitated. "I won't, Dad."

This conversation was their nuclear option. It would blow their relationship into pieces they couldn't put back together, knocking them down with the force of the blast, barely able to sit up, the fallout soaking into their bodies, never to leave, a scar on the bond they always had.

A line formed between his eyes. "We all have a responsibility. Mine and Garrett's is to service, yours and your mother's is to be behind us, supporting—"

She threw up her hands and groaned. "God, you sound brainwashed right now."

His lips pulled tight. "Choose your words carefully."

She bit down on her cheek and stared at the floor for a moment as the whistling of the bomb echoed in her ears.

A knock sounded on the door, and Anna released a heavy breath, grateful for the interruption before she started screaming. "I've got it." As she walked to the entrance, she paused, collecting her thoughts and steadying her voice. However, she was surprised to see a woman standing on the other side, who appeared only slightly older than Anna. "Hi, can I help you?"

"I'm here to see Sergeant Pechman. Is this a bad time?"

Is there ever a good time? "Uh, no, this is fine. He's inside. You can come on in."

"Jen? What are you doing here?" Dad called from the chair. "Sorry that I won't be getting up."

"That's fine. You don't need to welcome me."

Gears turned in Anna's memory. "Wait, Jen Jones? Afghanistan reporter Jen Jones?"

"That's me," the other woman responded with a smile.

Jen had remained true to her word and sent every article to Anna, sometimes before publication, and Anna consumed each one, feeling that every line from that country far away connected her to Dad, to help her understand him and find their way back to the relationship they always had.

"It's nice to meet you in person finally."

"You too. As you know, I've heard a lot about you."

Anna smiled, wringing her hands in front of her body, unsure whether to stay or leave them alone. Jen had walked into the living room and sat on the couch angled beside Robert.

"I hope this isn't a bad time to drop in," Jen said. "I thought about bringing a bottle of whiskey, but under the circumstances . . ."

"You're fine. How long have you been back?"

She set her purse by her feet. "I wasn't there much longer after . . . you. Things kept getting worse, so the magazine pulled me back. They said three months is long enough before a reporter needs a break."

Anna followed the conversation back and forth between Jen and Dad, still standing in the foyer. For the past six months, Anna had admired Jen, watching a woman not much older than herself following soldiers around in a combat zone, living in remote outposts with them, and following their stories with a kind heart and understanding, a gentleness in the words she used during a time when war stories were devoid of emotion. Just cold, hard facts that smacked people like Anna in the face.

But as Dad opened up, as his shoulders went slack and his words flowed gently from his mouth, Anna's ribs squeezed tight. What could Jen offer that Anna couldn't? Why could Dad be relaxed with a stranger to the family, yet close up around the people he knew best of all? Why could he welcome Jen into this world but shut out Anna and Mom?

Anna had spent the last month watching the dimness of Dad's eyes. A month of processing the loss of all that could have been and scrutinizing every wince and sigh. Tending to his needs, always before her own. Listening to doctors explain his condition, healing, setbacks, and outlook. Dad's tirades about her actions and how they could be perceived. Waiting for him to stop staring out the window, thinking of all he'd lost, concentrating on what he'd never do. Enduring his snide remarks and self-pity. A month of losing herself to changing bandages and making appointments and pushing a wheelchair.

All those days, all that time . . . And what had Jen done?

"Anna?"

Anna shook her head at the interruption. "Sorry, what?"

"I asked how things are going for you," Jen responded.

How could Anna play this? Was it brutal honesty or the same false positivity most military family members offered after catastrophe? And despite her better judgment, she chose the path her father always favored during interviews. "It's been fine. What brings you here?" *Yes, respond, then redirect.*

"I'm doing a story on the influx of service members. Trying to get to know them, tell their stories."

Anna sat on the arm of the couch across from Jen. "That's good. There are so many people here. Guys not much older than me, probably your age, wounds as bad as Dad's, some even worse. I feel bad for them."

"They don't need pity," Dad responded gruffly, his warmth with Jen suddenly gone.

Anna forced a smile.

Jen's attention swiveled to Dad. "What do they need, Sergeant Pechman?"

"They did an honorable thing."

Anna rolled her eyes. "I bet if you asked them, they wouldn't think it was worth some greater good."

Lines formed on Dad's forehead. "There was a time when this sort of sacrifice *meant* something. When the nation would honor its veterans for their sacrifice, for being willing to answer the call to service. We'd thank them for stepping up so no one else had to. So *some people* could be protesting in the streets."

Jen put herself between them, directing questions at Dad. "When we were in Afghanistan, you mentioned that no one knew what to do about the war there. With that in mind, do you think your injuries, what you've lost, is worth it? The time away, the pain, the healing. Are you proud of what you've sacrificed?"

Anna opened her mouth to interrupt, to protect Dad from the line of questioning, to remind Jen to be gentle, that Dad's mind wasn't where it needed to be. But then she closed it, biting her tongue.

Dad's sigh was weary, exhausted, beaten down. "I'm forty years old. I've lived my life. It could have been an unmarried eighteen-year-old left to find a partner in this shape. It could have been a boy who didn't have anyone to be with him while he healed. It could have been a man who hadn't had the chance to be a father, who wouldn't be able to play with his kids like most dads. My kids are grown. I've had twenty-two years with my wife. I've lived, and I still live."

His voice was flat, devoid of emotion or conviction. It was like he read from a prepared speech rather than feeling it in his soul.

"You were offered a second chance. The blast could have killed you, but it didn't. How are you using that time?" Jen asked.

Robert stared at the floor, rubbing a hand against his knee.

"By doing nothing," Anna said, filling in the silence. *Other than getting mad at everyone.*

Dad gripped the arms of his chair. "I need time, Anna."

Jen glanced back and forth between them. "Perhaps I should go . . ."

Anna rubbed a finger under her nose as tears blurred her vision. "No, you should know this. It's what no one ever talks about. We smile and say all the right things about patriotism and honor and duty, but behind the scenes, we're suffering." She stared at the ceiling, willing the tears to evaporate, to hold them back, but emotion squeezed them. "I mean, Dad never really came back. I may be grown, but I still need my partner-in-crime." Her chest was tight as she pushed the words into the air, and she turned to face Dad. "I mean, Garrett is about to go to Iraq, and he could use some guidance to prep him for how to be a leader—a good one—like you. This war has screwed up *everything* for us. And while it's great that you see this as a worthy sacrifice, you can't expect the rest of us to see it that way." Her voice broke on the last word.

"Anna, you don't understand—"

"No, *you* don't understand. While you're wrapped in all the feelings you won't share, you don't know what it's like to grow up this way. Your life has controlled mine since I was born. It *still* does."

Jen reached for her purse. "Perhaps I should—"

He pinched his nose. "We've been over this, Anna. It's who I am. I was eighteen when I enlisted."

Anna pushed off the couch, standing in front of him with her arms crossed. "No, Dad, it's what you *do*. Who you are is separate from the Army. You can be more, and instead of identifying your talents and abilities, you're focused on not being a soldier. Well, so what, Dad? You can still work for the Army if it's what you want most, but for the first time, *it can be up to you*. You can let Mom and me do the same."

"I had some choices taken away from me, too."

Anna paced the floor in front of the couch, in front of Jen, who slowly stood.

"It's obvious the two of you need time. Please take it. Sergeant, I'll call you for an interview in the next few days."

She quickly crossed to the front door and left.

In the silence of Jen's absence, Anna fought herself to stay silent. Don't poke the bear, right? Don't aggravate him. *Deep breaths. Let it go. Plaster on a smile. Keep it together.* But how could she? How could she keep quiet? That wasn't who she was anymore. She wasn't bearing this life in silence ever again.

She paced over to the window, arms crossed, and stared through it, seeing nothing but the fading light of the day. Her throat was so tight it hurt, and she swore it would split from the roughness of her words. "You know, you and Mom made this choice years ago—together. I didn't. I've never once had a say. And even though I wanted to come here—*to help* you—I was mad too. I wanted to finish school with my friends. I didn't want to leave what felt like home. But what you've said is somehow true—home is wherever we are together. But you're obviously hurting, and you want everyone else to hurt, too. You don't want to sink without pulling others down with you."

"That isn't fair—"

"It *is* fair!" she shouted, turning to face him.

"I didn't have a say in what happened to me!" he yelled back, standing unsteadily. "No one asked if I preferred to lose a leg. Stop breaking this into black and white terms, Anna. It isn't that simple."

"Where's the gray, Dad? We shouldn't be in either war. Do you want Garrett to end up here?"

"Of course not, but dammit, Anna . . . I'm as pissed about this injury as anyone else! I hate knowing I'll never set foot back on the battlefield, that I'll never wear the uniform. It kills me that I wasn't there to protect my soldiers from . . . everything that followed once I left. They needed me there."

Anna finally quieted, the fight slowly seeping through the floor. "We need you *here*," she whispered. Every news story that talked about another death of a service member in *either* country always cut her deeply. She remembered attending memorial services on post—Mom made sure they went to every one that involved a soldier from his company. Anna knew what sacrifice was. But how can someone give, and give, and give, until there's nothing left when there's so much to be grateful for?

And as much as she wanted to throw that in his face, to fight and stomp and wail, she loved Dad more.

As much as she wanted the floor to swallow her whole and transport her elsewhere, she was caught here, trying to find common ground, to show Dad how much she missed him, as tears rolled down her cheeks. "What do you want me to say? You loved and believed in what you did. You're happy to say that in front of people like Jen. You want to be at peace with all that happened, but it's bullshit. You're struggling with all of this, yet you can't even bring yourself to say it out loud. I need you to be honest with yourself."

She dropped into the chair at the table, the emotions too heavy to remain standing. "I need you to be honest with me," she whispered.

"You want me to be honest?" His voice was raw. His face was red. Veins rose on his forehead, in his arms. His hands rolled into fists. "I want to hate myself for what happened. Part of it feels like it was my fault. I'm stuck here when I want nothing more than to be there."

Her tears increased in intensity as she held in the sobs that threatened to escape.

He slammed a fist against the chair. "Had I been there, those soldiers might not have gotten so close to that cache in January. They might have missed that

mine in February. They might have gone home to their families. I. Wasn't.
There. I wasn't there to watch over their shoulders, to mold them into leaders,
to teach them how the fucking war works. But I'm glad I could at least keep one
man from ending up like me, and I'm going to cling to that as best I can when
you aren't plastering pictures of protests and peace in my face."

"It has nothing to do with you, I—"

"You're protesting the war, Annaliese. And what do you think I do in that
war? What job do I have when there isn't war or unrest somewhere in the world?
I can't provide intel in peacetime to watch for the next one. I'm not flying planes
in humanitarian missions. I don't provide health care to service members. I'm
meant to take the fight to the enemy and take them out before they hit one of
my soldiers. My job, as you referred to it, *is* the war. So you might think you're
only protesting war, but it feels a whole lot like you're protesting what I do,
what the people I was *willing to die for* do."

"That wasn't what I—"

"Service members read those signs, Anna, and to many of them, it sure feels
like you aren't standing with them." His shoulders rose as he inhaled, and he
fitted the crutches under his arms. He retreated to the bedroom, leaving Anna
at the table with her mouth hanging open.

॥

Robert closed the door behind him, using every muscle to ensure he didn't
slam it and let his rage pour out yet. Once the latch clicked, he leaned his head
against the door frame, taking deep breaths, using the skills the therapist had
shared with him after the broken television screen and the shattered mirror and
the cracked tray table.

There was just so much anger, so much tension, so much to curse and
scream and yell about.

He'd spoken from the depths of his pain when he told Anna that he struggled with coming home. The cache explosion killed six men in one go. Six men
Robert knew, six men with families, six men with futures, six men who wanted
more out of life than to die in pieces in Afghanistan.

Then there was the ambush followed by another explosion, taking a few
more. And every time the death notices came by or the blip showed up on the
news or someone emailed or called to let him know, the anger increased. The
one flame grew larger, eating away at his insides, burning brighter and threatening to incinerate him and everyone around him.

A tremor settled in his hands, a problem he'd seen more frequently as the
days went by, as he left the hospital and started on his own in an apartment.

He eyed the pills on his bedside table, then glanced at his watch, checking the time. He still had too long until his next pain dose, and he rubbed at his thigh.

It was hard to tell if it was pain at the stump or discomfort in a foot he didn't have, pins and needles stabbing through the nonexistent skin to the invisible bone. Phantom pains, the doctors called it. And he might always experience them. But even worse than that was the nerve pain, like ants squirming under his skin, like his foot falling asleep but unable to stop moving.

He swiped his fingers across his brow, leaning heavily on the door now, knowing he should sit but not wanting his mind to keep racing once he did. But how could he possibly stop it? For the last six months, the hell wasn't being without a limb—the hell was being stateside while the men he trained, the men he led, were left to fight without him. Gaines was a good leader, but it always helped to have the rank *and* the experience, not just one. Maybe Robert's experience would have been enough to do things differently.

Then again, maybe not.

The pain pills caught his attention again, and he stared at the wall, the floor, the window, trying to ignore the thoughts in his head. If he kept reaching for medicine, he would start having problems, and he told himself he didn't want that, didn't want to be his father, didn't want to put Anna or Katherine through what he had experienced.

On the other hand, neither of them understood what he was going through *now*, what he felt: the regret, pain, and grief. He lost a limb one day and lost his future the next. He couldn't be an infantryman with only one leg. The pain was a constant reminder of all he'd lost.

Now he faced medical retirement once his treatment and therapy were finished at Walter Reed. Then what? Another war vet nestled deeply in an armchair, drinking too heavily and missing the man he used to be.

Sweat broke out across his forehead and under his arms, and he swiped at it with his shirt. His good leg—his only leg—grew unsteady from the extended use, so he approached the bed, easing himself down, then swung his only leg up. The relief in his back was instantaneous, and he sighed heavily as some of the tension eased and he sank deeper into the mattress. But his hips—his right hip, more specifically—ached. No amount of adjustment would relieve it. He'd learned that over the last few months. The explosion had jarred something inside, had given his spine a good shake and would likely impede his movement for the rest of his life. In addition, the damn nerve pain made him want to reach for relief.

Thank you, Afghanistan.

The white pill bottle stood in stark contrast to the dark finish of the bedside table, and the blue line of the label taunted him. It was only a few extra pills.

He'd already been adding an additional tablet here and there when the pain was at its worst. After all, he'd been blown up, for God's sake. This wasn't some paper cut or broken bone. The bone had been *cut away*. What would a few extra hurt? It would ease the pain, maybe let him rest or even fall asleep for an hour, then wake up feeling more in control.

The temptation won out, and he shook out five pills instead of two.

Anna crept up the stairs to her room, thankful she didn't have to wander in front of Dad's door.

We never know how high we are till we are asked to rise, and then if we are true to plan our statures touch the skies.

That's what Dad was asking, wasn't it? What Mom was asking? Step up, do your best, and all the good on the other end will have been worth it. But if Dad came back from this and returned to his old self, would it make all this worthwhile? Their differences and arguments?

As much as she wanted to turn on some music and sulk in silence, there was work to do. Laundry and homework and helping Mom with dinner. She picked up her pajamas from earlier in the morning and a few stray socks from under her desk, shoving them into her already stuffed hamper. After peeking over the handrail to ensure Dad's door was still closed, she tiptoed down the stairs toward the washing machine in the hallway and dumped a load in. Mom would cringe at seeing the mixed darks and lights, sure it would ruin Anna's clothes, but who had the time?

As the washer swished, Anna returned to her room and opened her laptop, signing in to her email and waiting for it to load. Finally, a new message appeared, and Anna clicked to open it.

> Hi, Anna:
>
> I apologize for being there as you and your dad had a disagreement. As much as I wanted to hear your concerns, it wouldn't be right to witness it. That said, I think you have a story to tell, and I'd be honored if you would sit for an interview with me at a time and place of your choosing.
>
> Stories like yours—struggles like yours—need to be out there. What you're facing is something few understand. Your dad is thankful to be alive but grieving what happened to others. I should know. I made it out of that truck without an issue, yet your dad's life changed.
>
> But you showed me something I don't often see—the experience of those at home. I can't tell you how many families put on a brave face

and show they're determined to power through, but you weren't afraid to speak your mind. Even to someone like me. If you'll let me, I'd like to show the experience of those at home. The American people need to know that these events don't just affect the service member.

If you need it to be anonymous to protect your relationship, I will do that.

Let me know.

All the best,
Jen Jones

Anna immediately clicked the reply button, and her fingers hovered over the keyboard. Jen was offering a place for Anna to speak freely, share the darker side of this experience, and use her *voice*, with protections that could preserve her relationship with her father. Any other chores could wait.

Hi, Jen:

Thanks for emailing me. I'm sorry things got so awkward so fast. I'm sure you wanted some time to talk with Dad. I hope you can set up another time soon.

As for my take on everything that's happened, before I say anything, I want you to know I love my dad. I've never hated his job, but I have hated how it's upturned my life at times. He was gone a lot, but it was always to help people. And no matter how much I hate these wars, all our goodbyes, how his life has ended up, the way he treats me in his anger, I will always love my dad more.

If you want my opinion, here it goes . . .

|| CHAPTER TWENTY ||

FIRST STEPS, MIXED FEELINGS

MAY 8, 2004

Robert sat in a chair as his physical therapist slipped a silicone liner over his stump, adding two white sock-type sleeves, then the socket for his first prosthetic. His wound was still healing, but the doctors said it didn't matter—it was time to get up and get moving. This prosthetic wouldn't be the fancier version he would use in his day-to-day life in the future, but it would be the one that would teach him how to walk again.

Here he was, forty years old and learning to walk again.

He averted his eyes from Katherine and Anna, staring at the floor instead of facing them.

"All right, Sergeant Pechman, you ready to give it a go?"

Robert nodded, using the crutches to rise to his feet, swinging his way toward the parallel bars that would help him remain upright until he got a feel for his new leg. Susan, his physical therapist, wrapped the safety belt around his waist and fastened it. Then, she grasped the prosthetic leaning against the wall and attached it to Robert's stump, explaining to him how to do it himself.

He could only stare at the clear plastic opening that encased his leg up to mid-thigh, and the pole topped with a sneaker—the one that had short-circuited his brain when he thought he might never use a pair of sneakers again.

"I'll be right behind you the whole time," Sue said. "When you're ready, hold tight to the bars and take a small step—only a few inches—and feel free to take it slow."

He filled his lungs with a fortifying breath, forcing the worries from his head.

"Come on, Dad. You can do it. Take that first step."

When he glanced ahead, he saw Anna waiting at the end of the bars, and he flashed back to a time when their roles were reversed.

She'd been ten months old then, a tiny thing with full cheeks and eyes that took up half her face, only a thin wisp of hair atop her head. He'd walked in the front door of their home on Fort Carson, only to catch Garrett, who had raced to the door to give him a bear hug. Curious to see what all the fuss was about, Anna crawled from the kitchen toward the living room. Robert clapped his hands gently and called for her, and a mostly toothless grin spread across her face as her tiny voice called out, "Dada!" Slowly, she squatted with her hands on the floor before rising next to the wall, placing a hand against it as she wobbled. Then, focused only on her excitement of reaching him, she took her first step. And then another, her stance wide, her limbs slightly bow-legged.

"Katherine, she's doing it! She's walking!" he called, not wanting her to miss those first steps while she cooked dinner.

Anna's shoulders jumped a bit at his call, and she fell forward on the carpet, shooting out her hands to catch herself, then resolutely pushed up to stand again, her lips pursed in determination. Garrett had run over to her, bending down to match her, then standing straight. "Like this, Nana."

Robert had moved toward her then, grasping her pudgy hand in his own, running a thumb against the dimples at her knuckles, her skin smooth and delicate compared to his rough and weathered one.

"You can do it, sweetheart. C'mon, let me help you."

He'd never forget how small she was, an inch or two past his knee, but she held his finger loosely, walking with him to the kitchen, around the dining table, and back toward the door; her giggles echoed off the bare walls as drool dribbled from the toothless border of her mouth.

He left her at the edge of the kitchen and resumed his place at the door. "Come on, baby girl. You can do it." She gave him a slight frown, calling for Dada, but he remained by the door. "Take that first step, baby."

And then she did. One after another after another until she wrapped her tiny arms around his neck and squealed in delight as he blew raspberries against her cheek.

He shook his head, remembering that his daughter was now almost an adult and waiting expectantly at the end of the line. He wanted to please her, to show her he was still the same dad she'd always had, but he couldn't help but admit that it wasn't true.

He wasn't the same person anymore.

He breathed deeply, gripping the parallel bars tightly, then reluctantly stepped forward. He wobbled like a toddler as he took that first tentative step, still regaining his strength despite his weeks of physical therapy. He moved toward Anna, avoiding her eyes, avoiding the fake leg, avoiding his hands on the bars.

Nothing about it was empowering. Three sets of eyes—Katherine's, Anna's, and the therapist's—were all on him, and he felt like a polar bear in a southern zoo, passersby gawking at the poor animal in its cage in a place it wasn't meant to be, the mighty beast weak from the strength of the sun and heat.

"That's it, Dad!" Anna called, tears forming in her eyes. "You're doing it."

His knuckles were white, and he swore he was bending the metal like clay beneath his hands, but it held sturdy.

"You're doing great, Sergeant."

Three steps later, the exhaustion hit him. Sweat was thick on his forehead, a drop or two sliding down the back of his neck, and his heart pumped as if he'd run rather than walked. No longer could he lift the prosthetic enough to move forward, only able to shuffle it ahead.

"I don't think I can go any farther."

Anna gripped the crutches that rested against the wall, and he accepted them without a word.

"You did great for the first time," Sue reassured him. "Right now, it feels unsteady, kind of like riding a bicycle. You think you're going to fall, but eventually, you'll be walking with ease. It'll get easier the more you do it."

"Easy for you to say," Robert growled. "You have the same two working legs God gave you when you were born."

Anna gasped and Katherine tsked, but Sue was unfazed.

"Don't think you're the first person to tell me that," she said as he got the crutches under his arms. "Have a seat so I can remove the prosthetic, and you can take a break. We'll get back to physical therapy tomorrow."

He settled back into the chair against the wall as his heart slowed.

Anna handed him a cold bottle of water and smiled. "Those are just the first ones. You should be proud."

He sipped some water so he wouldn't have to say anything. The false positivity, overly kind words, and gentleness with which his daughter spoke to him were too much.

This wasn't how it was supposed to be.

II

Anna didn't miss how Dad turned away from her or how he guzzled water so he wouldn't have to speak. His lips were white from squeezing them together, holding every word inside, and his temple pulsed in a quick beat.

"You need to give him some space," Mom whispered. "You're on a collision course with his temper."

"But didn't you see? He took his first steps. Every day, he'll get better. He should know that." Every step was a sign of his healing, an inch passed on the mile-long road to recovery, another notch of progress, another notation for success.

"And each one will be a lot for him to process," she reminded Anna. "There is such a thing as overdoing the encouragement."

While watching him grasp the bars, Anna's fingers itched to cover his, to encourage him, but she knew he'd only grow frustrated. Instead, she'd bitten the inside of her cheek and still felt the ridges her teeth had dug.

"He doesn't always have to get so frustrated, Mom."

"He's getting better. Give him time."

"I'm proud of him," Anna mumbled. *But how much love and care can you put into another person who refuses to appreciate it?* She shook her head and told herself, *No, it's what I have to do.*

Mom placed a hand on Anna's shoulder. "You're doing so much, and you're doing great. I don't know what I'd do without you here."

Anna had mentioned it to a therapist who had checked in on the family two weeks ago.

You keep showing up.

So Anna continued to show up, smiling when Dad needed it most, even when it threatened to split her face in half. The first year would be hard—but didn't everyone know that? Eventually, they'd identify a new normal, not keep trying to revert to the old. That was the part Dad struggled with—he wanted the old. He didn't want to figure out how to move forward, so he sat in his pain, letting it course through his veins rather than working to flush it from his system.

Back in the therapy room, Anna glanced at Dad, then whispered to Mom, "We're struggling right now because it's new, right? It's no different than wanting to hate the newest duty station or avoid the new people we meet."

"Eventually we'll find where we fit," Mom responded. "We don't know what that means right now."

But her family didn't fit together. Mom had no place to plant her feet. Anna had been encouraging her to get back to school, finish the credits, and finally get her degree. Mom kept saying, "Now isn't the time."

But at this rate, when would the right time come?

"I'm ready to go back," Dad grumbled.

Anna wasn't yet ready. "I'm going for a walk and then I'll get the bus home."

Robert's head snapped to hers. "I don't know if that's safe."

"It'll be fine, Dad. I've done it before. Besides, you both could use some time for yourselves. I'll be home by dinner."

She watched as Dad went out the door, and Mom followed, always within arm's reach.

Wedding vows almost always include the phrase "for better or worse, in sickness and health," and while Anna knew her parents had said those same words, they'd never been tested to this extent. They'd never struggled with illness, and while "worse" had meant money was tight for a time, barely one hundred dollars left over after all the bills were paid, her parents were still happy. They'd lit candles in the evenings to save on electricity costs. They'd rented homes with fireplaces to cut back on heating costs. They'd gotten creative with the menu to ease the grocery bill. Anna and Garrett received school lunches paid for by the government. And while the kids knew the money struggles, Anna couldn't remember them threatening her parents' relationship.

Years ago, when Anna was fed up with James's bully, Grams had told her, "You tell that boy to leave your friend alone. A good southern woman can cuss the hair off the back of your neck if you refuse to listen," she'd said.

"But I'm not southern. I'm from nowhere," Anna had responded.

"But you've been raised by strong southern women. Now, don't you go off swearing, but you tell that bully how it is."

Anna had never forgotten those words, but Mom knew them, too. Watching her shrug off Dad's anger and frustration in preparation for another day squeezed Anna's heart.

All Anna knew was that she wanted something different, and it created a struggle between those hopes and dreams of her heart stored between two leather covers and the duty to family etched on her brain. And each time her heart fluttered at the thought of her future, only a year away, she was ashamed. She came to Ward 57 because she wanted to help—because she swore she wouldn't let the war win—but every day she watched Dad curl deeper and deeper into himself, the war was winning. But until she could change her circumstances, until she started applying to colleges, this was her mission.

As she walked the halls of Walter Reed, headed for the exit, she thought about how much she'd grasped her caregiver role. School understood her family's situation and excused her to attend Dad's appointments, whether with doctors or physical therapists. She jotted down notes, responded with questions about recovery, and attended every therapy session to note his progress. She didn't gnaw her lips raw like Mom. She didn't fold her hands into fists. She watched with narrowed eyes, unwilling to miss the slightest sign of progress or stagnancy. She wanted nothing more than to be back in New York, spending her summer with James and other friends, going to Fort Drum teen programs, enjoying nights at the movies, getting ice cream, or visiting a restaurant, but for now, she would continue cooking in their small apartment kitchen, watching whatever movies came on TV, and pouring her energy into Dad. Because that was where she was needed most.

Finally, the front doors were in sight, and Anna's heart raced as they grew closer. She was ready to escape the sterile smell of the hospital and avoid the apartment that crammed them all together. Being outside provided her with the respite she needed. In those moments, she would step outside, chilling her lungs with the cool, crisp air of the winter wind, squishing the damp ground of the spring thaw under her boots, or warming her skin with the summer sun. It was then that she was finally alone, able to open the box and set her emotions free, mourning the choices taken from her family and cursing the blooming resentment deposited in its place.

"You should have seen him, Garrett. He took three steps!" Anna paced the kitchen after her parents had gone to bed, tangling the phone cord between her fingers.

"How is he?"

"Better. It's a long road, but the doctors say the worst is over. No more worries of infection or additional surgeries. The most he'll need is adjustments to his prosthetic as his stump changes."

"Can we not call it a stump?" Garrett said, his voice edgy.

She paused her pacing. "What else do you call it?"

"I don't know, Anna. Something that doesn't make it sound like it's all that's left of him."

"Well, it's part of all that's left of him. If you don't like the word, you can take it up with the doctors."

He sighed. "How's his head?"

She batted a tiny crumb around on the counter. "He's still . . . difficult. Adjusting. The company gets home in June, so he should finally turn off the news. He keeps telling Mom that he wants to go up to New York for their redeployment. She doesn't think it's a good idea, but no one will tell him that." *Gotta be careful with his feelings and all.*

"They've followed up with TBI stuff, right? He would have been rattled pretty hard."

"It's been months now, Garrett. Any signs would have shown by now, but when they evaluated him that first month, it was all minor stuff that would heal on its own."

A long pause extended between them, though she heard him breathing over the line, and her hand stilled.

"What's up with you, Garrett?"

"Nothing."

She turned away from the counter, shifting a toe along the tile floor. "Seriously. Talk to me."

"I don't know. I'm worried about him."

Anna sagged against the kitchen wall. "He has Mom and me. You should worry more about yourself."

"You think that's the problem?"

"I think this is hard on you. Dad's injury threw you off track. It didn't just happen to me."

He sniffed.

"Garrett?"

"I . . . This is the second time I've missed deploying. People are coming back hurt, replacements go over, and I'm still sitting here on rear detachment."

Anna was relieved to hear it. As long as he was on U.S. soil, working on day-to-day stuff at home, she didn't have to worry about him. "They still can send you. Maybe they think you need time."

"Maybe."

The ticking of the clock on the wall was loud in the breaks in conversation. "Please talk to me."

He cleared his throat. "Ever since I saw Dad in that hospital bed, I can't get it out of my head. At first, it was this . . . nagging anger. I wanted to get over there and take out the people who did it. But eventually, it got worse."

"How?"

"Sometimes, I still hear Mom crying. Instead of Dad in a bed, it's him in a coffin. Sometimes, it's . . ." He sniffed and exhaled loudly, and Anna pictured him centering himself, staring at a spot on the wall as words rolled in his head and he caught the right ones. "I have nightmares now. I wake up, covered in sweat, sure that half my leg is gone."

"You're thinking about it too much. You need to start focusing on other things."

"One keeps coming back," he continued as if he didn't hear her. "An explosion dissolves my leg into a pulpy mass below the knee, bone fragments and sinew hanging free, blood oozing from the wound. I watch my foot fly over my shoulder."

Anna covered her mouth as a sob attempted to escape. She sniffed back the emotion, listening to the reassuring hum of the fridge, stilling the quiver of her voice. "Have you talked to anyone?" Her voice cracked.

"They'll think I'm afraid to go, trying to find a way out. I still believe in what I signed up for, Anna. Dad's injury is a reality check that it isn't a video game or a movie—it's real. There are real consequences for me, for other people, *my friends.*"

"You've always said that more people come home safe than are injured."

"There are lots of other ways for the war to follow people home than being injured."

Anna slid along the wall to the floor, and the cool tile felt refreshing against her bare legs. "I know."

"I mean, what if something happens to me? What if I have a girlfriend? Some have walked away when things get hard. And if I don't have a girlfriend, how can I expect someone to be with me and deal with all that?"

"Listen, Garrett. Even though Dad can be an asshole, that doesn't mean it would be the same for you if—and that's a giant if—something *did* happen."

"But what if it did? I can't ask a woman to hold my hand when I learn to walk again, to feed me if I can't, to dress me, put me on the toilet . . . I already see the strain it puts on you. When was the last time you finished a book? When did you last think about your own appointments or your future? You're putting your life on hold for him. What if that leads to resentment?"

"I'm here because they need me." *Because I need to know everything will be fine like you always said.*

"I know you are, but that's the problem. They're adults—you're still a kid. You should be doing kid things, Anna. You should be out with friends on the weekend, buying cheap shit at the mall and sitting in a food court for hours. Do you even know what movies are in theaters right now? What music everyone is listening to?"

"You don't understand it. You're fifteen hundred miles away, so none of this affects you. If I don't keep the family together, who will?"

"That isn't your responsibility, Anna!"

"I need you to trust my judgment. I've got it."

Silence stretched over the phone line until Garrett broke the quiet.

"I worry about bringing this on my own family someday. Kids I can't toss a ball with or chase around the yard and throw over my shoulder. Wrestling on the floor like Dad did with us . . . What if I have teens that have to be in your position? I'd hate it. I'd hate myself for it. Just . . . don't forget about you. Get the college brochures, think about what you want to do. I don't want you worrying about anyone else right now except yourself."

That part of her she tried to keep restrained in the dark corners of her mind was stepping into the bright light of the North Star, guiding her toward the future she'd always wished for, but she was finding it harder and harder to turn away from it. There was a comfort in stepping away from this role of caring for grown adults.

Hope is the thing with feathers that perches in the soul and sings the tune without the words and never stops at all.

Never stops at all.

"I don't need you to worry about me, Garrett. I need you to worry about *you*. Seriously, think about seeing someone." *And if it keeps you from deploying, who the hell cares?!*

"Since when are you the one watching out for me?"

"Since I grew up. I'll talk to you next week. Same time?"

"You bet. Take care, Anna."

"You too."

And as she hung up the phone, she couldn't help but see him inside his barracks room, surrounded by packed bags and completely alone.

|| CHAPTER TWENTY-ONE ||

THE REUNION THAT ISN'T YOURS

JUNE 3, 2004

Robert stared at his face in the hotel bathroom mirror longer than necessary. The lines at his eyes and mouth created hairline cracks in the valleys of his face. His uniform sat in a balled-up camouflage bunch in the corner of the bathroom, too tight to button around his waist, the blouse pulling across his belly and slack at the chest when the opposite used to be true. He gripped the cold counter, wondering how he would make it through the day, how he would handle soldiers stepping off buses and hugging their families, ready to return to their lives as normal.

He glanced at the empty pill bottle on the counter. One call to his doctor would get it refilled at any pharmacy even though it wasn't due to be filled. The pain constantly plagued him, and each day, he'd put down six or seven whenever he felt like it. And when that didn't work, he was happy to wash them down with a couple of beers. And when that didn't work, he could fall into a dreamless sleep.

Picking up the bottle, he turned it over and checked the refill date. His hands shook when he calculated how long he'd have to wait. He leaned on the counter, dipping his head and digging his fingers into his scalp. "No, no, no, I can't make it through today like this," he whispered. He stared at the label as if a new number would click down like an old-fashioned alarm clock. *Just kidding! It was an illusion. Everything is good here. Go get that refill.*

Now what would he do? How could he wait that week? How could he get through today? He had nothing.

He dropped the toilet lid and sat, holding his head in his hands. He couldn't jump in the car and drive to the drugstore. He couldn't go to another doctor, faking some sort of ailment the doctor might not notice.

Suddenly, an idea hit him. He pushed himself up and turned on the water to brush his teeth for the second time that morning. As he brushed, he allowed his crutch to slide, then swore out loud as he knocked the unopened bottle into the sink, easing himself onto the floor as best as he could but hitting the surface harder than intended, sending waves of pain from his hip and down his leg, making it hurt for real.

The door handle rattled, then a knock sounded when it wouldn't open. "Robert? Are you all right?"

He took two heavy breaths and made some extra noise like he couldn't get himself upright. "The crutch slipped in some water I spilled on the floor. I knocked my damn pills into the sink, and they all went down."

"Okay, can you reach to unlock the door? I'll help get you up."

Normally, he'd fight against her help, tell her he wasn't a child, that he could stand up on his own, that she needed to give him a minute. But this time, he leaned into the help, let it wrap its arms around him, knowing it would lead to relief.

Robert inched toward the door and twisted the lock, pushing himself backward as Katherine eased it open. Her face contorted into pity, and it sent waves of anger through his head. He fought against it and averted his eyes. It wasn't difficult—it's how he'd spent the last six months.

"Tell me how best to help you get up."

He shook his head. "I can do it. Give me a minute."

Over the months, Robert's arms had strengthened, and he could lift himself onto the toilet lid and get his crutches back under his arms to push to standing. Katherine pulled the hand towel from the counter and wiped up the puddle on the floor, then turned off the sink and pulled the pill bottle from near the drain.

"Why would you have this open next to the sink anyway?"

"I was going to take one, but I wanted to brush my teeth first. I figured I could wash it down after I rinsed my mouth."

She stared at him a second longer, then put the lid on the container. "You have an appointment first thing Monday morning, so we can ask the doctor to refill your prescription then."

Robert's stomach felt like he was falling from an airplane without a parachute. "I think we should call today. I went down on my hip, and it's sore. It'll be a long weekend."

A line formed between her eyebrows. "You need to be more careful."

He shrugged. "I want to feel independent sometimes, and I forget that I'm a little off-balance."

"Well, I'm standing right out there, ready to help when you need it. You don't have to fight to do it alone."

"Can you call the doctor now?" It would be easier if she handled the interaction instead. It would sound more honest.

"All right. You finish getting ready and I'll call. Just . . . be careful, please. You're lucky you didn't hit your head on anything." Then she left to get her phone.

Part of him thought about how they might decrease his dosage if he called, but if she could explain the pain she saw in him—unintentional—then maybe they'd be more willing to write the script early and maintain the dosage. That methodical plan, that deeper thinking, should have shocked him, and years later, he would remember this moment, but at the time, it was a logical way to get what he needed.

But *why* did he need it?

His hands shook as he counted the seconds Katherine was on the phone, her voice barely loud enough to be heard over the bathroom fan. Already, thoughts flowed through his head, all the questions he had about his own actions, all the worries about his men overseas, all the concerns about how they'd judge him, all his fears for the future, for Katherine, for Anna, for Garrett. Even for himself.

He stared at the sink, but he knew there were no pills somehow caught inside—the bottle was empty. He'd simply have to wait.

Katherine knocked on the door again and pushed it open, this time without resistance. "He said we can pick up a full bottle at the post pharmacy. You need to be more careful. They won't refill it early again. They're making an exception this time, Robert."

"Why do you have to say it like that?"

"The doctor reminded me that you need to be careful of your dosage." He could hear how she wanted to say more, wanted to launch down her long path of lecture and chastising but wouldn't because it would only drive the wedge between them deeper.

"It was an accident, Katherine." The lie spilled through his lips so easily. He expected it to burn his mouth, building up and spreading to his throat, but instead, it was like honey. It was sweet and thick, a subterfuge that caused no harm nor hinted at the bigger problem forming beneath the surface. It wouldn't go on forever—he just needed a little help to numb himself right now, a chance to forget the horrors of Afghanistan and cope with the judgment of his fellow soldiers.

Katherine crossed her arms, creating yet another barrier between them. At least she was still willing to help him. It meant he hadn't lost her yet.

"I'm worried about you," she said, her voice barely loud enough to rise above the racket of the bathroom fan.

"What do you mean?"

He watched her chest rise as she inhaled. "When I look at you, I don't see Robert anymore. You haven't been Robert since you came back."

He pinched the bridge of his nose. "I'm trying, Kay."

"Do you realize you yelled at me for the first time ever after you got back? And you've done it repeatedly? You never raised your voice to me before—not once—in all the years we've been married. Until you got back."

"I said I'm trying," he responded tersely. "I came home, lost a leg, and found out my entire life changed that day."

"It changed for us, too, you know."

"Why does everyone keep telling me that? It isn't the same, and you know it."

She ignored his barb and plowed ahead. "Sometimes it's like you died that day."

"Maybe a part of me did," he snapped, and even with the howl of the fan, his voice echoed off the tiled walls.

She sucked in her cheeks and her eyes rose to the ceiling as she blinked a few times. "Well, soon you have to pick yourself up. We're about to see a bunch of boys who've been through the wringer over there, and your self-pity won't help them." She held up the empty pill bottle. "I will never make a call like that again, so don't ask me to lie for you anymore." She slammed the container down and left the bathroom.

The honey quickly turned to vinegar.

For the first time in months, Anna had a weekend to herself. At first, she stood in the center of the apartment, relishing the silence. The television that usually blasted from the corner sat silent and dark. The armchair where her father brooded sat empty. No washing machine running in the background, or dishes clanging in the kitchen. It was pure, unaltered silence, the kind that rang in her ears, buzzing and whirring like bees, mingling with the thoughts in her head. Her mother had kissed her earlier on Friday morning before the sun even rose, then left for the return of I-87. Anna spent the day in school before returning home, ordering some food for delivery, and settling in with a book for the evening. But now, she wanted something more, something just for her, a way to feel like who she was before someone else's life blew her future to pieces.

A list of Anna's old haunts ran through her head. The secondhand bookstore around the corner from her house in Watertown, the diner she'd visit with any willing meal partner, the park where she'd happily shoot hoops. Part of her brain nagged at her over her lack of involvement in her family's new town, the phone numbers on scraps of paper piled on her dresser and covered in dust, the offered plans she brushed off using Dad as an excuse.

Enough moping. I've got to get out of here.

She'd found a spa within walking distance of their apartment, having always wanted to sit in one of those saunas with the heat and steam and cedar scent, sweating from every pore before running out of the tiny shack and jumping into a cool, refreshing pool, rinsing the salty deposits from her skin. There was something about the transition from the heat to the chill, the perspiration to the rinsing, a way of cleansing the body of all the weight she'd carried, sweating out the negativity and washing it away.

So that's what she would do.

"Wait, you're actually taking a weekend to yourself?" James had asked during their weekly phone call the previous Wednesday night.

Anna had rolled her eyes, thankful they were talking over the phone so he couldn't see. "I think I need a break."

"Good," he'd responded. "You should do it more often. You find a place nearby?"

"Yeah, some place called Lavender Forest. I expect it to make me fall into relaxation through smell alone. I wanted to try their sauna."

"Only a sauna? Why not go all out? It'll be good for you."

That was her hope, but anything more would eat up the small allowance Mom gave her each month.

Now, Anna stopped in front of the glass doors, the business name etched on the window in a calligraphy-style script. She pushed her way inside.

"Welcome to Lavender Forest. Can I help you?" the receptionist asked from behind a desk. The entrance was small. Only a thin bench in front of a window with the trickle of a fountain from the corner and some sort of chime music playing softly through speakers.

"I'm Annaliese Pechman. I booked a visit to the sauna for today."

The receptionist's eyes flicked back and forth across the screen. "Oh, here you are. You've booked the relaxation package. You can follow me." The receptionist stepped away from the desk before Anna's voice pulled her back.

"I'm sorry, there's a mistake. I only booked the sauna for today."

The woman smiled gently. "Let me double-check." She clicked the mouse on her computer a few more times but repeated the same news: "It says relaxation package right here."

"Could we maybe drop the package and just do the sauna?" Anna quickly glanced around the small entrance and saw she was still alone. She dropped her voice to barely above a whisper. "I can't afford it."

The receptionist's smile grew. "But it's already been paid for, honey."

"What? How?"

"Well, even if it's a mistake, I would take it if I were you. Someone else covering your salt water soak, facial, massage, and sauna? Sounds like the perfect gift for a day at the spa. Follow me and we'll get you settled in."

The woman led her through a narrow hallway and into a wide waiting room filled with plush chairs. Bottles of water, wrapped sandwiches, and individual salads were stacked in a small refrigerator on a table along the wall. An arched doorway on either side of the room led to lockers and showers. "You'll find your name on one of the lockers. Change into the robe and slippers and put your belongings inside. I'll have Leslie, your therapist and technician, meet you out here."

Anna went through the arch the receptionist had gestured toward, searching the doors for her name. She finally spotted it and opened the door to remove the robe and slippers but spotted a folded card in front of them.

Hope you can fall into relaxation with more than just the smell and sauna. Enjoy it!
—James

Tears rose in her eyes as she rubbed the pads of her fingers against the card. It was easy to picture his face, imagining the sly smile he'd get whenever he knew he was right and she was wrong but didn't want to boast about it. She tucked the card inside the book in her purse. This was the greatest gift he could have given her.

As she slipped her arms inside the robe, the plush fibers rubbed softly against her skin. She tucked a foot in each slipper, then pulled the sash tight around her waist. A corner of her book peeked out of her purse, and she hesitated to leave it behind. What could be more relaxing than sitting in a sauna and reading? She cradled it in her arms before locking up and finding a vacant armchair in the waiting area. It wasn't a difficult search—the place was mostly empty, or else other clients were in the midst of self-pampering. Anna had just opened her book when a dark-haired woman entered the room with her arms crossed behind her back.

"You must be Anna," her deep, soothing voice said. Anna nodded in response. "I'm Leslie, and I'll be working with you today. Do you know where you'd like to start?"

Anna froze. So many options yet no idea what most of them even meant. "Do you have a recommendation?"

"I would suggest the massage, then the sauna and salt water soak, then ending with a facial."

"Let's do that."

"You can follow me."

She followed Leslie down the dark gray hallway, dimly lit with sconces spaced evenly the length of the wall, into a small room painted a soothing purple. A dark massage chair was in the center, another fountain flowed from a tabletop filled with tools for the massage therapist, and the room smelled of lavender. Anna felt her body slacken as she stepped inside.

"You left your massage preference blank. Do you know what you'd like?"

"I don't know much about massage."

Leslie smiled kindly, as if she'd heard that response a hundred times. "That's okay. Why don't you tell me what brought you here?"

Anna hated when people asked her questions like this. Even during her first day of school in D.C., someone asked why she'd shown up in the middle of the year. She struggled to explain that it wasn't her choice, that her dad was injured and she was helping him through it, that she had to uproot so she wasn't stuck alone during a time when she needed her parents. But today was for her, and she wanted the most from it, to have the attention lavished on her, to have someone care about her needs.

"Well, I moved down here when my dad was injured, and I've been helping take care of him."

Immediately, she saw the shift in Leslie's face as she processed what Anna had said. It was the one of pity. Something about seeing it on an adult's face made it even worse, something that said, *that poor child*. Anna averted her eyes.

"That must be a lot for you," Leslie responded. Her voice was soft and the words heartfelt.

Anna shrugged. It was easier than expanding.

"Do you find that you're stressed?"

"I don't know. It's a lot sometimes, but I'm not sure if it's stress or not."

"Does your body feel tired? Do you find your shoulders pulling up throughout the day? Any pain at the base of your neck?"

"Yes to all three? I guess my body feels sore more often now, but I'm not doing anything to pick him up or anything."

"You can still strain your muscles from stress even when you aren't lifting anything. All that adds up. I would recommend Swedish. It's a great way to ease the muscles that are sore from stress rather than strain. It's one of those massages that'll leave your whole body relaxed, and the heat in the sauna will help more. I think it'll soothe you for the entire visit."

Anna held onto the tie of her robe and nodded.

"I'll leave the room and you can hang the robe on the hook on the back of the door and slip under the sheet there. We'll have sixty minutes. Did you have any questions?"

"No, thank you."

Leslie smiled a final time before gently closing the door behind her.

As Anna stretched out on the soft massage table and settled her face into the hole at the top, she felt confident that she had made the right choice.

And she'd get Mom a gift certificate for her own after she returned.

||

Robert's hands shook as he approached the gym. Cars were parked in the lot in neat, orderly lines, and military police guided others into the grass across the street. Already, the energy crackled in the air. The squeals of young children dressed in red, white, and blue, holding American flags or wearing patriotic bows in their hair, raced alongside mothers in flowy dresses, their hair and makeup done to perfection.

Robert remembered those moments.

Everyone moved as one, a mass of ants ready to devour a picnic, picking up what they needed most and taking it home to savor it. The buses would arrive any minute, packed full of soldiers finally ending their long battle overseas. How long the war would go on—overseas and at home—remained to be seen.

Robert had decided to wear his prosthetic, a chance to get used to it and appear "normal," a word he struggled to use but felt he had to accept. What was normal anyway when a prosthetic was attached to you and you had to use another support to walk, all in clear sight of the public? The doctors said he would soon graduate to a cane, and that was almost as frustrating to Robert as learning to walk again. He would skip from pediatrics to geriatrics.

As he inched closer to the entrance, his mind kept returning to the contrast between this homecoming and his own. The redeploying soldiers would walk into the warm embraces of their families, receive pats on the back for a job well done and appreciative remarks from a colonel or general, then go home for a rest, knowing they could return to work in a few weeks to prepare to do it all again. It's what Robert had done when he came home in 2002, and all of the homecomings of years prior. But coming home injured, he missed out on the hugs and pats and remarks—he didn't know where he was for five days and suddenly woke up in a hospital bed with his leg gone, floating in and out of consciousness for days.

"Are you ready?" Katherine asked softly.

"I'm fine." He swallowed hard and gripped his crutches tightly with sweaty hands, carefully setting them against the ground so they wouldn't slide from under him. He'd worn shorts, not because he wanted the attention of the families in attendance, but because it was hot, the socket sometimes made him feel sweaty, especially if he was nervous, and he didn't want to risk his leg loosening. But as he walked through the open double doors of the gymnasium, eyes, heads, and bodies turned his way. And as usual, they'd see the crutches, notice both hands gripping the handles, then slide down the line of support to his bionic leg.

Robert had met amputees at Walter Reed, and the hospital anticipated seeing more of them in the months and years ahead, but for the average person, even a military family member, they weren't yet used to the sight. And because his uniform didn't fit, no one could have known if he were a veteran from this war or another, a serviceman or a civilian, the victim of a tragic accident or that of the brutality of war.

Katherine placed a hand on his shoulder, the same thing she'd done at the rest stop they'd hit at the Pennsylvania/New York border, but like that time, he shrugged it off under the guise of readjusting his crutches. He didn't need her help or support to face it. This was a future he might never escape. Instead, he walked toward the first empty spot in the corner and sat.

An array of people surrounded him: wives excitedly talking with their children, parents pacing the floor. Those who'd done reunion plenty of times sat on the bleachers and waited. A few faces were tense, either due to secrets, or reintegration, or of all the things their loved one had experienced overseas.

"Well, look what the cat dragged in," a familiar voice said. Robert turned, not sure he believed it, and saw Sergeant Morton, with the same calm, detached exterior Robert appreciated when the squad leader took control at Shkin. Morton sat with his back to the wall, picking at his raw cuticles. His eyes flicked from place to place in the room as he continued talking. "How are things, man?"

Robert shook his hand. "Good to see you, Morton. You get home in one of the early parties?"

He hesitated for a minute, then shook his head. "Nah, man. I brought myself back."

"What do you mean?"

He shrugged, still observing the room, only glancing at Robert from time to time. "I started having trouble in February. I reported it to Captain Gaines, and he recommended I come back. I've had a lot of appointments at the VA clinic ever since."

"I'm sorry to hear that."

"It's all right. It isn't all that different than you, is it?"

Robert glanced at his leg, then focused on Morton, whose head swiveled with sharpness in his eyes and rigidity in his shoulders. Many would say he faked it to get home, that he simply didn't want to be an infantryman anymore. But Robert knew the man's character, had seen him cry after Olsen's death, had listened to him encourage and grieve with the members of his team. After months of always making sure everyone was taken care of, did he have anyone who could do the same for him? Was there someone checking on Morton's well-being?

The first returning soldier marched through the door, then the room erupted with noise. Applause built around them and people stood on the bleachers, stomping their feet, cheering, yelling, laughing, smiling. Robert's ears closed off from the sheer noise echoing in the room, and the hair on his neck stood in anticipation, that familiar feeling of coming home. He rose along with everyone else, clapping as his company entered the gym, Captain Gaines leading the soldiers along with a man Robert didn't know.

That should be me, he thought. *I should have led them over there and led them back home, made sure every one of them made it.*

Morton clapped, a corner of his mouth tilting up as he watched his buddies return.

The post commander stepped up to a podium to give his brief remarks, and Robert's eyes moved from face to face. Swanson's eyes were hard now, no longer twinkling with the mirth of inviting cheerleaders to Shkin, remembering his best friend and bunkmate who should have been standing beside him in formation. Instead of the smile that always sat in the corner of Bryant's mouth, he clenched his jaw, any hint of a smile gone. Doc stared into a far-off place, likely still seeing the people he couldn't save. At that moment, Robert knew they all had a long road ahead of them, not just him. It wasn't him versus the world anymore. He had people here, people who needed the support and connection.

The problem wasn't that he lost his leg, or had crutches, or had to learn how to walk, or lived in constant pain—his problem was that no one understood him. Not Katherine, not Anna, and not even Garrett, who hadn't yet deployed. None of them could understand the effects of war, and how, no matter what happens in the end, you carry it with you, every loss, every victory, every face, and every relationship. In that room, Robert finally felt the most alive he'd been in almost a year.

The soldiers were released, and the families drove from the bleachers to the court as if a team had landed a game-winning shot in overtime. Some ran into each other, others tried to skirt the people who'd already found the person they'd missed for a year.

"Who do you want to see first?" Katherine asked.

"Wait a minute." Robert knew that some of his men—no, *the* men—might not have anyone here to welcome them home. Dates were always subject to change, even when the arrival was only a few hours away. Flights could be diverted, there could be mechanical issues with planes. Yes, even the civilian wrenches in plans could affect military homecomings. It sometimes meant that soldiers wouldn't have any loved ones to welcome them back to American soil until days later.

In moments like those, the military family stepped in. Leaders would attend every redeployment ceremony, and rear detachment teams would make arrangements to arrive. Military families would seek out donations and set up the barracks rooms for soldiers so they would have a comfortable space to come home to, a freshly made bed to fall into, and some snacks to stave off any hunger until the DFAC opened in the morning or they had time to get their own things from storage.

In times of need, they'd come together.

Robert noticed that Bryant and Swanson stepped off to the side, away from the crowds pouring onto the basketball court. Bryant rubbed a hand along the back of his neck, watching the people embracing only feet from him, and then stepped away. Gripping his crutches tightly and taking a deep breath, Robert walked over to them.

Both of the young men noticed his approach and quickly stood straighter. "Welcome home, boys," Robert said, clapping each of them on the back.

"Thank you, Sergeant," they responded in unison.

Swanson noticed Robert's new leg. "How are things going for you, Sergeant? We gonna be calling you the bionic man?"

"Ha, not yet." He forced brightness into his voice. "Things are going well enough regardless."

"How does it feel to be home?" Katherine asked. Inwardly, Robert cringed.

Both boys were kind about it. "It's great, ma'am. Thank you."

Robert tilted his head, letting her know to walk away. Thankfully, she did so without another word.

"You boys get comfortable in the barracks tonight and be there for each other in the coming days, all right?"

"Did I see Sergeant Morton when we came in?" Swanson asked.

"You did." Robert glanced at the bleachers, but Morton was already gone. "He's either talking with someone else or he left."

"I'm surprised he came at all."

"Why do you say that?"

"He was in bad shape, Sergeant. There was a weapons cache that exploded. He was close to it, saw what happened to the guys, had to help pick up . . . pieces . . . He wasn't the same after that. Got aggressive with the locals. He was high-speed whenever we were out and sort of shut down when we weren't. The CO talked to him, and a few days later, he was on a bird out and a replacement came in."

Robert stared at them as he pieced together Morton's presence in the bleachers, how his eyes constantly shifted, how his back was always to a wall, how the exit was nearby on his left. "I thought I was the only one."

"Nah, Sergeant. I don't think we'll ever be the same," Bryant said. "It doesn't feel right coming home without Olsen, or Wallace, or Hawthorne, or Houser."

"Houser?"

Swanson stared at his feet before focusing on Robert. "IED. Back in February."

Robert swallowed hard. "I didn't know."

"I'm sorry I had to be the one to tell you."

Robert flexed his fingers and scrunched his toes in his shoe, grounding himself in the moment like his therapists had said. He needed to be here for his boys now.

"You fellas have support coming in?"

"Yeah, Sarge. My folks are on their way," Swanson said. "I called them to say I was in New York."

"Mine come next week," Bryant added.

"Well, you be there for each other until your families get here. Keep that connection going in the barracks, during meals, and on the weekends."

"Sure thing, Sergeant."

Robert patted them each on the shoulder before moving on, his shoulders weighed down by the heaviness of these young men so changed by their service. Stepping back into a normal that wasn't their own would take time, but if they didn't have the chance to feel alone, it might make the transition the tiniest bit easier.

Robert continued through the crowd, patting men on their shoulders as they departed with their wives or children or both. He wouldn't hold any of them up, wouldn't ask them to stop to chat, knowing they were eager to see their family members and return to a normal life.

But "normal" didn't mean anything to anyone anymore.

॥

JUNE 4, 2004

Katherine had been silent for the first three hours of the drive, but in fairness, so had Robert. What was there to talk about after the reminder of those who would never come home alive? After seeing how hard things would be for anyone coming home, not just the injured?

Finally, she let the sounds of Queen fade with the turn of the dial, and her voice was raspy as she spoke.

"I did some research when you went to bed last night, then made some calls this morning. It sounds like you would be eligible for COAD."

"What the hell is COAD?"

"Continuation of Active Duty. Injuries don't mean you have to leave the Army. As long as you can move into another job, you could stay in."

He stared at her for a moment to ensure she was serious. "Kay, I'd be nondeployable. Forever."

She shrugged, not even glancing at him. "You'd be around soldiers every day, other infantrymen. Yes, you'd probably have to be the rear detachment first sergeant, but there are worse things. You could still lead and work with soldiers every day."

The window button snapped as he repeatedly flicked it with his fingers. "But I wouldn't really be a soldier."

"You'd wear the uniform every day, still do PT, be required to meet your most basic obligations, and you'd still get rated. Just like you always have. Sounds like a soldier to me."

He shook his head while she sighed.

"Don't think I didn't notice you relax there," she continued. "For as hung up as you were about everyone seeing you again, you were right at home going from person to person. It's like you never left. You returned to yourself then more than I've ever seen it since—"

"They understand me."

"And we don't?" she asked weakly.

Robert stared at the passing trees while raindrops raced toward the back of the car.

"I know you always say 'it isn't the same,'" she continued, "but I'm telling you, if you want to get back to it, there's opportunity. But you need to clean yourself up a little."

His head snapped toward her. "What the hell does that mean?"

"The pills, Robert. You've been taking too many for too long. You won't ever pass a piss test that way, and you know a drug test is one of the first things they'll do."

"If you've got it all figured out, then why didn't you say anything before?"

"I told myself I'd wait for the right time. This is the right time." She flicked on the turn signal and pulled into the shoulder, pressing the hazard lights after putting the vehicle in park. She turned in her seat to face him. "I finally saw some life in you yesterday. If that's what you need to feel like you're still living, then go do that. All we have to do is get doctor signatures and fill out an application. You'll go before a board and then be back to work."

"I thought you didn't want that?"

"I didn't want you to deploy. COAD isn't the same thing."

"Anna won't like it either."

"Anna will graduate soon and move on with her life. She'll be glad you're doing the same. Think about it. The application information is in my bag." Then she put the car in gear and edged back onto the highway. "I'm going to resume my classes next month, so getting back into the swing of things will be good for you."

Robert watched as the trees passed by slowly, then all in a rush as he considered the option of staying in. Could he let go of deploying again, not building that camaraderie with other soldiers, that special brotherhood that develops only in a hostile environment, when the person to your left or your right can help assure your survival?

On the other hand, how would it feel to never again don the uniform? To hang it up permanently in its dark garment bag in the back of the closet like his father's. To stow the medals and certificates denoting years of labor, time, and separation in a simple shadowbox on the wall. To enter the real world and do . . . what, exactly?

Perhaps stretching out another year or two would give him time to find a landing place.

"But I mean it, Robert. You'll need to find a way through this without the pills."

That wouldn't be a problem. He had a mission now, a targeted objective to reach, and that was something he knew how to do.

|| CHAPTER TWENTY-TWO ||

TO FIGHT ALOUD IS BRAVE

AUGUST 30, 2004

Anna wove through the aisles in the small convenience store, searching out the long line of periodicals on the back wall while Mom pumped gas outside. Each glossy cover captured her eyes as she searched for the one with the red border, already knowing she'd find it. A part of her wanted to rush forward, flicking her fingers through the faced-out stacks, but she also wanted to savor the moment.

Somewhere in those magazines were her words.

Finally, her eyes caught the cover she'd been avoiding as long as possible. And there it was: A child holding a red, white, and blue balloon on a string standing in front of a brick wall emblazoned with "Stop the War."

Of all the days to see the visual . . .

She delicately lifted a magazine from the back of the pile despite knowing she'd have one at home waiting for her in the mailbox. But she wanted a special one with crisp pages, not yet opened or consumed by another nor bent to fit inside a mailbox. One that was hers. She hugged it against her chest like a tiny newborn baby, then turned toward the checkout counter.

From above the attendant's head, a television mounted on the wall called out a story she knew all too well, and she didn't need to watch the B-roll film to know what was on screen.

"*The protest in Madison Square Garden yesterday, hosted by United for Justice and Peace, is being called one of the largest protests in U.S. history, with more than eight hundred thousand demonstrators assembling on the streets of New York City.*"

"This everything?" the attendant asked gruffly. A thick beard hid the lower portion of his face.

"Yeah, and the gas on pump three."

He typed in a few keys. "That'll be $25.76."

Anna paused as she reached for Mom's credit card. "Are you serious?"

"Record highs, kid." He jutted his thumb toward the screen as he tore off her receipt. "Those folks got somethin' right. The damn war is driving up prices."

"*During the march yesterday, New York Police report that some eighteen hundred protestors were arrested. The demonstration captured attention due to some of the imagery on the streets, including the group One Thousand Coffins—*"

"Yeah, maybe. You have a good one." She carefully lifted her magazine and the receipt and headed to the car.

When she stepped into view, Mom's smile filled her face as she rolled down the passenger-side window. "Did you get it?"

A corner of Anna's mouth tilted up as she opened the door and got in. "Hot off the press."

"Well go on. Open it!"

"I'd kind of like to wait, Mom. Take it all in myself. I haven't even seen the final version."

Mom put the car in drive. "All right. If you say so."

"I hope we can get to the mail before Dad does."

She wished for a crystal ball she could consult, a way to conjure his mood from a distance, to gauge his response, to see what her future held. Not only had Anna and Mom spent the weekend in New York City to take part in the demonstration she'd heard about on TV, but Jen Jones's magazine published, and Anna knew there was no way Dad would miss it. He only subscribed to the monthly periodical to read Jen's stories.

"Take a minute, breathe, and get yourself together before we get there."

The corner store was only a five-minute walk from the apartment, their last stop on the way home from New York City to Rockville, so Anna knew there was no time to breathe or calm down or consider how he'd respond. As they approached the one traffic light between them and home, Anna hoped it'd turn red. It was the longest light in the city, for God's sake, and couldn't it give her a few minutes?

But no. It stayed green, and Mom sailed right through the intersection.

"He's gonna lose it, Mom. He'll know it was me."

"So you go in and own it."

"Can't we just not tell him? Let him assume but not confirm it?"

Mom huffed out a breath. "No, that isn't an option. This is the double-edged sword of finding your voice. Not everyone will like it, but you can't cower from it either. People won't always agree with you."

"It's a little different when you have to live with the person."

Mom pulled into the parking lot and parked near the front doors.

Nothing like forcing me to face it.

"If he gets mad, he gets mad. You have the choice whether to stand behind what you believe in—something you think more people need to understand—or hiding behind the anonymity. You already know what you can expect, but he could also surprise you. You don't have to justify yourself to him, but you do have to be honest with him."

"He's already gonna be mad at us because of this weekend." She couldn't bring herself to say *protest* aloud.

She shrugged. "He might be, but at least he knew we were going. *But*," she stressed, "we don't have to remind him of that."

Anna begrudged her that point, unbuckling her seatbelt and pulling herself out of the car. Her feet were sore from hours of standing and her voice was scratchy from shouting with the crowd. The news was right about it being an anti-war protest, and the march—an estimated eight hundred thousand people—went right in front of the Republican National Convention. When Anna had asked Mom to go along, she'd quickly agreed, calling a family friend who lived in the city and asking to use her apartment as their home base for the weekend.

But the lightness of that first time in Syracuse wasn't with Anna this time. Instead, she came home feeling drained.

Upon entering the building, Anna slipped her key into the skinny mailbox inside the main door, finding it empty. *There's a crystal ball, after all—a shame it can't show me his face.* Her stomach dropped to her feet. "Dad already got it."

"He would have read it one way or the other. Come on—let's walk into the lion's den with your head held high."

Perhaps Emily had said it best: *To fight aloud, is very brave.* But Mom had always said that being brave didn't mean being fearless.

They rode the elevator up to the third floor and Anna let Mom open the door, stepping into her shadow, using her body as a shield. Anna peeked over her shoulder and saw Dad in his armchair, the magazine open to the center—the feature story, *her* story. His eyebrows pulled together as his eyes moved line by line across the page. The prosthetic he was finally used to wearing was fit to his leg, and the crutches were gone for good.

Anna slipped off her shoes, stepping lightly across the living room floor, her eyes never leaving his face while Mom strode into the apartment like it was any other day, making her way toward the kitchen.

The pressure in Anna's chest mounted as she sat in the furthest corner of the couch as Dad flipped the page with a snap, not acknowledging her presence.

The aftermath of that protest years ago had scarred her skin, pulling it tightly in a moment like this, making it itch. That had been bad enough, but how would a national magazine airing their dirty laundry feel? Hadn't Dad always said that the problems in the family stayed within the family? Wasn't that why he'd asked her to delete the blog about his healing journey? She tucked her hands between her knees and squeezed her legs together to keep the jitters in check.

From the kitchen came the sound of ice against glass, and Anna wished she was old enough to have a swig of something that would burn the entire way to her stomach. She twisted her wrist to hide the phone number written there in permanent marker, the "in case of emergency" number Mom's friend had insisted on. As Anna waited in the silence, she recalled the sounds of the raised voices, the heat of the sun in the cloudless sky of deep blue, and the brush of bodies on her left and right.

She heard a sniffle and faced Dad. Tears leaked from his eyes and down his cheeks, dripping onto the magazine in his lap. He paused for only a second to wipe them away with the heel of his hand as he continued reading.

Mom appeared at the entrance to the kitchen holding a low-ball glass containing an amber liquid, the imprint of lipstick on the rim. She leaned against the wall as she watched her husband, and the silence lingered.

Finally, after what felt like decades, thousands of heartbeats, tense muscles shooting cortisol through her body, Dad closed the magazine and sat it on the end table beside him. He gazed at Anna, the tears making his eyes glassy, his eyelids a dam attempting to hold them in. Slowly he leaned forward, holding out his hand to her.

She stared for a moment, then slid across the couch toward him, taking his right hand with her left, the dark marker facing up in contrast to her pale skin. But his eyes remained on her face as he sniffed again and squeezed her fingers.

Anna swallowed hard, unsure how to proceed, not wanting to break the silence with words when wrinkles on foreheads and around mouths, and tears, and physical touch said so much more.

"I'm proud of you," he whispered. "Proud of your voice. Proud of your conviction. Proud of your bravery. You don't need to tell me this was you—I can hear your voice in every word. I'm proud of you. Emily would be proud of you."

Anna wanted to bask in Dad's praise, but she had to know. "How did you know it was me?"

"I heard the same words you used when we fought that night in Watertown before I left. Back then, I couldn't see what you were saying. I was so focused on the personal offense I felt that I wouldn't listen to anything I thought went against that. You had said 'One is enough.' I see that now."

Anna's eyes welled with tears she tried to blink back, but she was grateful that the overwhelming weight she'd carried for so long had suddenly lifted from her shoulders. He was proud of her, for speaking her mind and standing by her convictions, even when they didn't match his own.

"I never meant to upset you," she said. "I care about you and Garrett—but you wouldn't listen to me."

He squeezed her fingers again. "I'm listening now."

Anna turned to Mom to confirm she heard the same words. She was still leaning against the entrance to the kitchen, a small smile scrunching the corners of her eyes, which were as wet as everyone else's.

Dad tapped the magazine's cover. "You made it clear that you care so much because you don't want anyone to feel how you have for the last four years. But I don't want you to feel this way either. Mom and I talked back in June, and I'm going to make things better."

Anna glanced between her parents. "What does that mean?"

"There's a chance I can stay in. I'm going to file the paperwork and work on getting my life together."

Anna pulled her hand free. "Stay in? Why?"

Dad glanced at Mom but sat up straighter in the armchair, leaning toward her. "I need to stay around soldiers, Anna. Being completely removed from what I did before isn't working. When we went up to Drum for the redeployment ceremony, I felt like me again." He held up a hand as her mouth opened. "Before you get upset, I wouldn't be deployable, but they could find me steady work in garrison."

"But we'd still move."

"Not you. You'll be off to college next year. Mom and I will get you settled no matter what."

"But what about Mom? She still has two years of school to get her degree." Anna turned her attention to Mom, who finally joined the family in the living room.

She stopped behind Dad's chair. "After your dad and I talked, I found a distance learning program. All my credits will transfer, and there's a two-week seminar I have to attend before graduation. I wanted something that wouldn't force me into a classroom in case I needed to be here for Dad. I might even finish my degree work earlier."

Anna watched as Mom placed a hand on Dad's shoulder. "So that's it, huh? We try to go back to what we were doing . . . before?"

"We don't know yet," Dad said. "I still have a whole process to go through, so it'll take time. It might even be a year until it's all said and done."

"But we'll always have a home for you, Anna," Mom said. "No matter where you choose to go to school, we'll do everything we can to get you settled there and have a space for you wherever we are."

She glanced between the two of them. They were back in tune again, Dad healthy, Mom happy. Anna didn't know what to feel, but her gut response was to be grateful for this epiphany and trust it would be good for everyone. But something still felt off. "I guess that's it?"

For the first time in almost a year, she watched as Dad smiled. "That's it, kiddo."

Anna smiled back, and hope took flight in her chest.

She gestured to the magazine. "Can you share that with Mom?"

Dad stood. "It's all hers. I'm gonna head out and pick up a copy of my own." He grabbed his wallet and keys from the table and headed for the door.

"Thanks, Dad. For what you said. It means a lot."

He paused before turning around to face her. "I love you, sweetheart."

"Love you too."

Anna carefully picked up her own copy, not wanting to crease the pages or mar the corners, and headed to her room. Mom rubbed her shoulder as she passed by.

Once safely in her own space, Anna opened the magazine to the two-page spread. Her fingers grazed the lines down the page as she reassured herself that this entire afternoon was, in fact, real.

She'd never be able to use the article in a portfolio—there was no proof it was her, after all, but she knew, Dad knew, and everything felt right. In place of the anonymous byline, she could imagine the serifs and curves that made up "Annaliese Pechman." But it was hers, and that was enough.

What It Means to Serve: A Military Child's Perspective
By A Military Child Living Near Walter Reed

Editor's note: This feature is written by a military child in her own words but under the condition of anonymity to protect her family.

My dad's life changed in a split second in 2003. It was a roadside bomb, something you hear about every day in the news now. But what you don't hear every day is that when their life changes, so does the family's.

Walter Reed is made up of so many people like my dad, with more arriving every day, starting their journeys at the beginning while mine is coming to its end. Soon, my dad will be starting a new stage of his life, my mom will be wrapping up her degree, and I'll be off to college, but other families are caught at the beginning, not knowing what's to come.

The days of worry about how much worse their loved one will get before he gets better. Processing how they barely recognize their loved one in the hospital bed amid the layers of gauze and mass of wires. The hours of frustration, the days of sadness, the regret and worry that ebbs and flows over weeks and months. The times they're told to "be strong" or hear their loved one called "brave" when all they want is for him to be whole.

Then comes learning who the newest version of that person is. What makes them angry, frustrated, tense, and learning the ways to avoid those triggers. Turning off the news so they don't hear about the most recent attack in Kabul or Kandahar, Baghdad or Al Hillah.

That's how it went for me. And even months after that explosion, once the smoke dissipated and the mess was cleaned up, I'm still not sure if my dad ever came home.

Yeah, he's here. I see him every day, but things aren't how they once were. And while I miss who my dad was, I miss seeing him smile even more. It happens so rarely now.

When people talk about sacrifice and troop deaths and honor, when they do interviews with the recovering wounded and everyone has on a brave face, there are people who are hurting, forever changed by a single moment in time.

My dad was injured in an explosion in Afghanistan, and no one talks about that war anymore. My brother is supposed to go to Iraq, and everyone is talking about that war.

Whenever I think about my brother, I fear this could be his future, too. That in following in my dad's footsteps of service, he'll follow them all the way to Walter Reed or Sam Houston, or worse, to Arlington.

On March 20, 2003, I was in a city an hour from where I lived, carrying a protest sign against the war in Iraq. My sign said, "One is enough," and I never knew how true it would be.

One war is enough.

One family member in service is enough.

One ending in tragedy is enough.

But every day, it happens to more than one person.

It happens to an entire family, and no one is talking about that sacrifice . . .

The words that had formed as she poured her heart into that article didn't feel as true now that Dad had read it, now that they'd had that conversation in the living room, now that they shared that understanding.

Because when she'd written that article, Anna had been searching for hope, digging into the corners of rooms and under beds and behind couches hoping to one day find it, harness it, and use it. But now she'd found it.

She slid open the top desk drawer she'd failed to open for four months. At the top, still in a prominent position, was her leather journal. It was time for it to be out in the open, to breathe in the hopes and dreams, to absorb the ink from Anna's pen as she shared them. She moved it to the center of her desk, right in front of Emily's watchful eyes.

|| CHAPTER TWENTY-THREE ||

HOPE TURNS TO DUST

OCTOBER 12, 2004

Katherine pulled up to the front of the building, putting their sedan in park as Robert inhaled deeply.

"You're going to do great. I know it."

He stared at her for a moment, the size of her smile, the light behind her eyes, the sheer joy in him doing something for himself. Even though she'd wanted him to get out all that time ago—was it only two years ago?—knocking them out of each other's orbits, they were now back in sync. And for all her cursing of the Army, they both knew it was right for him.

But it couldn't stop his hands from shaking or ease the pressure in his chest. "Do I look okay?"

She rolled her eyes—*Is it a wonder who Anna gets it from?* "We went over every square inch of that uniform at home. Everything is shined up, in line, exactly how it's supposed to be."

"It's been a while since we put a uniform together."

"It looks great on you." She reached between them and straightened his tie. "There. Now you're ready. Go get 'em, Sergeant."

He kissed her briefly even though the touch of her warm mouth made him want to go slowly, to linger in the heaven that had existed between them for the past month. "Thanks for everything, baby."

He left the vehicle, and she pulled away to find a parking space while he walked through the glass doors of Walter Reed. The only thing between him and continued service was a panel of three medical officers and a simple piece of paper that would soon bear their signatures.

As his heart raged in his chest, Robert turned right into the bathroom. He peeked under the stalls, searching for any sign of another's presence. As his footsteps echoed in the empty room, he twisted the knob to turn on the water and pulled out the bottle he never left home without. Only a few white pills rested at the bottom, but he knew he needed them now rather than later. He dumped the remaining capsules into his mouth, then cupped his hands, filling them with water to wash them down. The water spun above the drain, forming a small tornado.

How many had it been today? He'd already lost count. There were the few when he first got up and more when he left the house, but still the pressure raged in his chest and left his hands unsteady. The last four months had been full of sweaty sessions with his personal trainer at the gym, extensive food prep in the kitchen to create more nutritious meals, and hours of physical therapy to get comfortable with his prosthetic, all to prepare him for this moment.

The time had paid off.

As he dried his hands with a rough paper towel, he scrutinized himself in the mirror. His white collar lay flat against his shoulders, the crossed rifles and "U.S." discs angled perfectly in line with the olive-drab lapels. The blue cord wrapped under his arm and over his shoulder, and he thought back to his basic training days at Fort Benning.

Why is the sky blue?

Because God loves the infantry.

His ribbon rack was a horizontal line of color, his metal marksmanship badges and Airborne wings in the exact middle. He'd measured three times and had Katherine check his work.

Like she'd said in the car, he was ready.

He threw the paper towel into the trashcan on his way out, inhaling a centering breath. *No turning back. There's only forward.*

This wasn't the first board he'd faced in his career. Every few years he went before one to gain points toward his next promotion. He knew the ins and outs, the questions about his abilities, demonstrating the knowledge of his profession, and identifying specific examples of his leadership.

But he'd never been before a Medical Evaluation Board.

He stopped before their table, back perfectly straight, hands curled into fists at his thighs, thumbs along the seam of his pants. "Master Sergeant Robert Pechman reporting for the COAD medical review."

"Have a seat, Sergeant." None of them smiled back as he sat in the chair across from them. *That's okay. They have to do so many of these.*

"Sergeant, while I appreciate your interest in continuing to serve your country, I'm not entirely clear why you're here," a tan, balding man began.

Robert frowned. "Sir?"

"We went over your paperwork," the man said, flipping through Robert's application packet, "and you don't appear to be an appropriate applicant."

"Sir, I only lost the one leg—below the knee. My doctors submitted notes that express my ability to serve."

"We don't have any questions about your ability or desire from a fitness aspect, Sergeant," a woman said. "But you don't meet the minimum requirements."

The balding man picked up the conversation. "You checked the block that you have between fifteen and twenty years of service, but your service record shows you reached twenty years back in June."

Robert swallowed the lump forming in his throat and stilled the hand instinctively moving toward his pocket. "Sir, while I enlisted in the Army back in June 1984, I wasn't actively serving while here at Walter Reed."

"But you were, Sergeant. You continued drawing your usual paycheck and additional benefits, and your time on active duty continued," the woman said.

"And beside that point, your drug test showed you're still using oxycodone."

"Yes, sir, I do still have issues with pain here and there."

"The amount you tested for is much higher than we would allow, even accounting for your injury. That said, Sergeant, we cannot approve your request to continue on active duty. While I would usually offer to write a letter for transition to the National Guard, your substance abuse is a problem."

"Substance abuse . . . but—"

"The Army would pay for thirty days of treatment, but your years of service still wouldn't allow you to remain on active duty and your medication abuse would preclude you from serving in the National Guard or Reserve forces."

"Because of that, we have no choice but to refer your case to the VA for the preliminary rating board."

"Medical retirement?"

One board member, an African American man with glasses, cleared his throat and propped his elbows on the table, linking his fingers together. "Sergeant, we thank you for all you've given your country and how you've served for so many years with honor and distinction. You have skills you can offer the Army in a civilian capacity, but your substance abuse poses a problem no matter what career you decide to move into. I strongly urge you to use the VA's program to get the care you need. We wish you well, Sergeant."

The finality with which he spoke, the kindness in his voice—it was all an attempt to smooth things over. The hope turned to dust before his eyes, and all the dreams for his future drifted out the door.

Robert cleared his throat. "Thank you for your time." He rose from his chair, his vision blurring, unable to discern anything in the room except the scuffed tile floor.

He caught his toe as he walked away, stumbling a bit, and he knew— *he knew*—they were assuming it was his prosthetic or the pills or something else, reassuring them that they made the right decision. But no amount of well wishes, kindness, or reassurance could make this better.

Each breath caught in Robert's throat as he left the hospital, and he yanked at his tie, loosening it while searching for Katherine.

She was seated on a bench near the doors and jumped up when she saw him. "Done already?"

"Let's go home." He walked away as if the building were on fire, and his insides burned.

"But how did it go?"

"I don't want to talk about it!"

She shrank back from his anger, but he didn't care. She'd go back to her studies, Anna would move on to college in a year, and he'd be the one left behind. Again.

"Let's go home."

Keys rattled against the door, and Anna put her newspaper aside. She smiled brightly as the door opened, the words bursting from her mouth before she could pull them back. "How'd it go?!"

Mom caught her eye first, shaking her head quickly and motioning for Anna to leave the room.

But she had to know. She had to understand what was ahead. Things had been so good for the past few months, and Anna was certain they were on the mend, but the lines on Dad's face were deeper than they'd been before.

He grasped the closure of his uniform top and ripped, sending a button clattering to the floor and skittering under the couch. Anna's mouth dropped open as he ignored it, stomping his way back toward his bedroom.

Anna turned to face Mom. "What happened?"

Mom interlaced her fingers, twisting back and forth, and Anna worried she'd soon snap them off.

"I made a mistake," Mom whispered as she dropped onto the couch, staring at the floor. "I swear I read every line on those papers and there wasn't anything about years of service." Finally, she turned to Anna. "He has to medically retire."

"What? Why?"

Mom shrugged. "They won't let anyone who has served for twenty years or longer stay in. He'll have a meeting with the VA to determine his retirement and disability coverage."

"And then what? He can't sit around here—he needs something to distract him."

"I can't make those choices for him, Anna. And give him some time before you ask."

Anna leaned forward, placing her elbows on her knees, pressing the heels of her hands against her eyes as if it would somehow erase Dad's face from her memory. The devastation was palpable—for everyone. "Mom, I can't go backward again. I *can't*."

Mom's hand rubbed her back in gentle circles. "It won't, baby. He needs a few days, then we'll figure out a path forward."

Anna lifted her gaze and observed Mom's face, wishing a meter would show above her head to gauge how truthful she was being. Was this honesty or a distraction? The reality or a pipe dream?

Mom sighed before kneeling on the floor, stretching under the couch to retrieve the forgotten button. "I'm going to gather his uniform before he destroys it."

But rather than walking down the hallway, she retraced her steps back to the entryway, reaching into her purse and removing an orange pill bottle. Based on the sound of the rattle, one Anna had learned to interpret, this was freshly refilled.

Anna's eyes locked on the container. "What are you doing?"

Mom stared at the floor as she walked by. "I'm going to hang everything up and stitch this button back on."

Her footsteps echoed down the narrow hallway, fading away, and Anna stared at a dust bunny that skittered across the floor in her wake.

Those damn pills wouldn't help him understand anything.

2005

I can wade Grief -
Whole Pools of it -
I'm used to that -
But the least push of Joy
Breaks up my feet -
And I tip - drunken -
Let no Pebble - smile -
'Twas the New Liquor -
That was all!

Power is only Pain -
Stranded - thro' Discipline,
Till Weights - will hang -
Give Balm - to Giants -
And they'll wilt, like Men -
Give Himmaleh -
They'll carry - Him!

—Emily Dickinson, 1891

CHAPTER TWENTY-FOUR

LYING FOR TWO

FEBRUARY 11, 2005

Anna stepped off the bus and followed the sidewalk, skipping over patches of ice and piles of snow. She shoved her gloved hands deeper into her coat pockets, snuggling further into the thick layers of her scarf to protect against the gusts of wind cutting between buildings.

Her phone buzzed with a grainy image of vast piles of snow back in Watertown. She smiled, then snapped a picture of the few inches in the grass along the sidewalk with the message, **Yeah, ours doesn't compare.**

She'd been in Maryland almost a year now, and she loved that it still brought snow, sleet, and ice, frigid temperatures, blizzards, and wind chill. It was a reminder of home, or the closest thing to it. The difference between New York and Maryland was that here, spring wasn't far. Come the end of March, the warmth would creep into the ground, the leaves of flowers would push their first stalks of green through the dirt, and the trees would bud, leaving a green dusting on everything.

Already, it was less than four months until graduation. She'd been accepted to a few colleges, in Maryland and elsewhere, but her future was still largely undecided. Ever since the MEB, when Dad discovered his military service was over, she'd shuffled that future into the distance. Until she knew he was steady, what other choice did she have?

Somehow, they'd gone ten steps forward only to have five major leaps backward.

Anna pulled open the doors to the apartment building, unwinding her scarf and removing her gloves. She shook out the moisture from her coat before heading to the stairwell, hoping that taking the steps would warm her. When she reached her floor, she waved to Mrs. Waters, who lived closest to the elevators. Anna stopped to say hello to Mr. Stearn and his dog, a Scottish terrier named Winchester, wrapped in a thick red and green plaid coat. Finally, she reached the door to her apartment and let herself in, carefully setting her wet boots on the tray inside the door.

Mom's bag was gone, off to the library to study, only a few months out from her own graduation. Anna noticed Dad's chair was empty, and the TV was dark and silent. His wallet was on the coffee table in its usual spot, so he was definitely home. She turned the corner into the kitchen, expecting to see him there, but the room was vacant.

"Dad?" she called.

There was no response.

She frowned and pulled out her phone, texting Mom. Her breathing increased, but she tamped down the worry.

Just got home from school. Do you know where Dad might be?

She closed her phone and tucked it back in her pocket, but once in place, it chirped with an incoming message.

He should be home. Maybe he's napping?

Her response shattered the silence, and Anna's ears buzzed with activity, piecing together all the possibilities, the butterflies in her stomach crashing into each other and landing in a heavy heap that made her nauseous. She dropped her phone to the floor.

The hallway leading to the bedrooms was dark, and she trailed her fingers along the wall as she approached her parents' door. She knocked. "Dad? Dad!" She twisted the doorknob, but it wouldn't budge. She knocked again, harder, the force of her hand shaking the barrier on its hinges. "Dad!"

Standing on her tiptoes, she ran her fingers along the top of the doorframe, finding the key to the knob and pushing it in until she heard the lock pop. Then she flung the door open to see Dad on the bed, eyes closed, mouth open, two bottles of beer on the table beside him along with those damn pills.

"Jesus, Dad." She put a hand on his shoulder, shaking him roughly. His head lolled to the side, and his eyes partially opened. "Thank God." The exhale of relief dropped her shoulders by inches and eased the weight in her stomach.

He mumbled something unintelligible.

"We need to get to a doctor. Come on."

"Umfine," he responded, his speech slurred.

"You aren't fine. I thought you were dead, Dad."

Reaching his hands behind himself, he tried to push to sitting, but he was unsteady. "Whatimeissit?"

"It's a little after three. I just got home from school."

"Gimme a li'l an' I'll be fine."

Anna stepped back and stared at him. "This isn't 'fine,' Dad."

He waved his hand, trying to shoo her out of the room.

"You seriously expect me to walk out the door? What the hell?" With every word, her voice rose by a few decibels.

"I jus' woke up. I needuh minute."

She swallowed thickly. "No, you need more than a minute." Her voice broke. "You need help."

He shook his head.

Grabbing the beer bottles between the fingers of one hand, Anna swiped the pill bottle with the other and walked out of the room. She tossed the glass in the recycling bin, then read the pharmacy label.

She frowned at the prescribing doctor's name. It was a civilian doctor from in town. She retrieved her phone from the living room floor before taking a picture of the bottle and sending it to Mom. **We have a problem.**

How had he convinced a doctor to give him pain medication? When would he even have gone? He refused to drive himself anywhere. Mom made a lot of excuses for him, but she couldn't be helping him, could she?

Then Anna remembered how the fighting had eased off between them last summer. And while he'd been furious after the MEB, the two of them were still okay. They'd started date nights again, at restaurants in the shopping center across the street so they could walk. Even though their relationship wasn't as Anna always remembered, the semblance of that closeness was returning. And at least the apartment became a little quieter, giving Anna some space.

Could Mom have grasped a minuscule glimmer and excused the leaden burden that came with it?

While Anna had suspected something was up with the pills, had she ignored it in favor of the positive changes in him? Had she let herself drift too far toward the dreaming that she had neglected the habits that had formed?

Anna's phone beeped and she flipped it open to check Mom's response. **Don't worry. His doctor couldn't fit him in so he referred us to a civilian dr.**

She wasn't sure how long she stared at the words before texting back, but they grew blurry as tears leaked down her cheeks. **They've never been that busy to see him.**

Her response was almost immediate. **Lots of injuries coming in now.**

Oh, how easy it was for her to lie, to make excuses, to use the other injured as an excuse for Dad's poor habits and behaviors. After all they had been through, when would someone in this family acknowledge what it really was?

For the first time since Anna moved to Maryland, she felt like she was standing alone. No Garrett, a disconnect from Mom, and practically nothing from Dad.

She threw her phone onto the counter, the back popping off and the battery coming loose, scattering across the butcher block surface. As she leaned heavily against the cabinets, all the fight left her, and she slid to the floor. She fought every tear that threatened to escape, telling herself that she wouldn't cry, she wouldn't break down, she wouldn't fall apart, but no amount of willpower would stop them.

As if growing up with Dad coming and going wasn't bad enough, now that he was here, he still wasn't here. Oh, they had that breath of fresh air last summer when hope was on the horizon, warming their skin like the rising sun, but cold hands had snatched it away, the light disappearing as quickly as it had arrived. A flash of brilliance, then silent darkness. She remembered how proud he was of her article, how he had carefully pried up the staples that bound the magazine, gently removing the pages so he could frame and display them.

That man was gone.

That man never came home from Afghanistan, and while she'd hoped with all her heart that he could, she worried he never would.

Finally, he landed back among the living and crept toward the kitchen, grabbing a glass from the cabinet above her head. Ice cubes smacked the glass with every beat of Anna's heart against her ribs. Water ran as he filled his cup, then he leaned against the counter to take a sip.

She finally studied him, the discolored bags under his eyes, the way he still couldn't stand straight. Anger sharpened its blade inside her, ready to fight. She gathered her strength and picked herself up off the floor, crossing her arms against her chest.

"So you're seeing civilian doctors now? Letting Mom lie for you?"

"It's none of your business, Anna."

She huffed out a humorless laugh, cocking her head to the side. "I walked in to see my dad passed out in his bed. How am I supposed to take that?"

"You should know by now that pain medication can cause drowsiness."

"That was *drowsiness?* I don't think so."

"Anna, don't assume you know what this is like."

His dismissiveness strengthened her resolve, and she pushed herself back onto her feet. "Are you forgetting that I've been here almost as long as you have? That I've watched you go from what you came home as and turn into whatever this is? I don't get it, Dad. You have a whole life ahead of you, but you're settling by drawing the little bit of retirement pay you get and hiding out in this apartment each day, surrounded by beer bottles and pill bottles. Is that all there is for you? Is there nothing else you can do? You can't tell me this is it."

"I'll get it figured out."

Anna laughed humorlessly. "It's been over a year."

"I got blown up and—"

"We all know that," she shouted, tired of hearing the recycled line over and over again. "You were ready to stay in the Army, so it couldn't have been that bad."

"I need time," he forced out.

"Time won't bring you back home. I wish it would, but we both know it won't."

He slammed his hand flat against the counter. "Enough, Anna!"

In the past, she would have jumped at his outburst. She would have trembled at the anger rising on his face. She would have worried whether he was okay. To his credit, he would have immediately apologized. He would have given her space before approaching her later on, hugging her and saying he was wrong, maybe explaining his feelings in the moment. He would have sworn to do better next time, and she would have noticed his efforts.

But that was in the before.

She tilted her head to the side and calmly walked away, and he refused to follow.

FEBRUARY 24, 2005

An overdose came two weeks later, and Anna was unprepared for it. She'd found Dad in his chair, the same place he frequented, his prosthetic off, face pale, breathing labored. Beside him was an empty pill bottle and a few empty beer cans. Her stomach had dropped and chills flowed down her back, the hair on her neck standing on end. She'd hesitated to get closer, worried how bad it could be, but the signs were there. She'd tried to nudge his shoulder.

"Dad? Dad, wake up. Can you hear me?"

His chest had risen and fallen unevenly, but other than that, she didn't know what symptoms to look for, how to measure if he was conscious, if his heart rate was too slow, if his pulse was dropping.

Her hands shook as she gently patted his shoulders, assuring him she was only stepping away for a moment as she raced for her phone. And now she sat in a firm chair in the frigid waiting room alone, her hands tucked up in her sleeves as she replayed the images of the previous two hours. The blue of his lips was reflected in the flash of the ambulance lights outside. The voices of the hospital merged with the urgent sounds of the paramedics. The gurneys rolling through the hallway were just like the stretcher wheeled out of the apartment, Dad's still body lying atop it. She still felt every jostle from the ambulance ride over, but the harshest jolt of all came when she realized she needed to leave, to walk away from all of it, to step back from the unhealthy connections forming between her parents. It was time to be done with all of it and walk away.

For good.

"Anna?"

She raised her eyes to see Mom standing on the other side of the swinging double doors, but Anna refused to reassure Mom or ask how Dad was. The doctors must have pumped him full of whatever to save his life, after they'd cracked his chest with the force of CPR and shocked his body with jolts of electricity to get his heart going again. All for what? To bring him back so he could continue existing as the shell of himself?

"Why don't you come back and see him?" Mom asked softly.

Anna shook her head slowly, then stared at the floor.

"If you're worried, they've stabilized him. He'll be okay."

She laughed humorlessly. "You think that's what I'm worried about? That he's going to die?"

Mom moved closer and sat in the chair beside Anna, who leaned away. "I know this is a lot—"

Anna rose quickly from her chair. "I don't need you to explain anything to me. I know what's going on. I know what I saw. How could you lie to me all this time? How could you constantly cover for him?"

"It's not like that—"

"It's exactly like that. Who's been driving him to all these appointments or pharmacies to get more? He sure isn't driving himself. And in all of that, did you ever once think that I would be the one to find him someday?"

"Keep your voice down," Mom hissed as her eyes flicked around the room.

"Are you worried someone will think you're enabling him? Because that's exactly what you're doing. How many questions did they ask you because Dad couldn't answer them? Did you know they asked me the same thing? I hope you know I was honest."

"I told them everything they needed to know."

Anna laughed. "And do you think he's suicidal or made a mistake?"

"Oh, Anna . . ."

"It doesn't matter because they're the same thing. Either way, he's the same shell of himself and you're helping him stay that way."

Mom's hand shot out and squeezed Anna's arm, trying to pull her back down to a chair. "Remember that I'm still your mother. Sit down. Now."

Anna shook her off instead, stepping back, lowering her voice. "Do *you* remember that you're still my mom? The parents I remember from before this all started would never have made choices that ended up at this moment. They'd have thought about the kids, a stable life, *doing* something. Instead, you make excuses. You let him take whatever he wants as long as he's nice to you. But Mom, that doesn't help anything."

"No matter what you think, Anna, you should see your father. He could have died."

It was the one thing Anna dreaded hearing anyone say aloud. How many times can a kid hear that their father almost died? Tears welled in her eyes, and her face contorted into despair. "Maybe we'd be better off!"

As soon as the words slipped through her lips, she wanted to pull them back. It was her greatest fear and the one thought that circled her head whenever she saw that orange bottle or heard Dad slur his speech. *Maybe we'd be better off if he did himself in, shook out one too many, and fell asleep, never having to wake up again.* And then she'd hate herself for even considering it. But this time, while the urgent voices of paramedics echoed in her head, she recognized it as the harsh truth it was.

Mom stared at her for more heartbeats than Anna could count before finally standing and pushing back through the double doors to return to her husband, leaving Anna alone.

Again.

She forcefully wiped her eyes with her fists before finding a seat in the far corner, well away from others waiting in the middle of the night. She gripped her hair at its roots as she leaned forward in her chair. All her thoughts collided, creating sparks that fed the tiny ember of anger she'd carried for too many months.

He didn't need more pills. He didn't need more well wishes or healthy eating or exercise. He didn't need perspective shifts and mindset adjustment. No more surface support. He needed therapy. But people have to *want* help to receive it.

As she pulled her sweater tighter across her body, she shivered at all that could have been. She didn't want her father dead. More than anything, she wanted him healed—*fully* healed—but the road was a marathon of hills and curves, one she wasn't suited to run alongside him.

He was simply drifting, hitting the big highs of the wave but knowing it would bottom out quickly. She simply couldn't ebb and flow with it anymore. It was time to find calmer waters to anchor in, stabilize herself, and find a new future.

She'd watched Mom make excuses for him, time and time again, and it all led to this moment, this understanding that Anna would no longer wade through the darkness. She was finished with the denial, the lies, the enabling . . .

The next step would be for her.

‖ CHAPTER TWENTY-FIVE ‖

WHAT COMES NEXT

JUNE 6, 2005

"Congratulations, Class of 2005!"

The mass of students launched an eruption of voices and graduation caps into the sky. The sun was beginning to set, and a hazy halo encircled the stadium lights. Excitement crackled in the air. Graduates moved through the crowd to hug friends and hunt down caps that floated too far. Voices chattered as the applause in the stands faded into a buzz of voices as family members gathered their things and returned to their vehicles, off to prepare for the after-party, showering the grads with cards, checks, and cake.

But Anna gripped her cap as she watched the people around her. Girls posed for pictures with flip phones and digital cameras. Boys looped arms around each other's shoulders, shouting to one another. A sharp pain buried itself in her chest and spread to the fingers gripping the flimsy cardboard hat. For a moment, she allowed herself to think of the friends she could have made had she attended the same school all her life, to have watched her classmates through their Ninja Turtle and Barney phases, through awkward years of braces and glasses, when limbs were too long and features misplaced, then blossoming into young adulthood and preparing for college. Her ears burned with the thrill of learning a friend's secret and holding it in her heart for years, knowing it probably no longer mattered but remained a source of connection. Her fingers ached to write her email on a piece of paper to stay in touch as they moved off to universities around the country.

What would it be like to graduate with the same people you've always known? What kind of friendship does a bond like that produce? Will they stay connected even after they split off like hairs to attend college? A group of girls looped their arms as they raced toward the parking lot. A few boys gave back-slapping hugs as they spoke loudly about their plans for the evening.

The night was warm but chilling quickly as the sun dipped lower. The field was mostly bare, employees stacking chairs onto rolling carts, pulling the school colors from the stage, and packing up the podium and microphone. Still, Anna's feet were firmly planted in the AstroTurf. A girl stopped a staff member to ask him to take a picture of her and her friends, and he happily obliged. Anna clutched her arms close to her body as she turned away from the scene toward her truck.

Her phone chimed, and she pulled it from the pocket of her graduation gown to see a message from Mom.

Just got back. See you soon!

Like most of the parents, hers left for the apartment once the graduation was finished, but unlike the other graduates, Anna's gathering was bound to be filled with awkwardness and discomfort. Ever since that fight at the hospital, Anna was either at school, the local library, or shut up in her room. In her stomach, she felt the emptiness of attachment, the absence of real, true friendship, of depending on someone and knowing they'd always be there.

Her phone vibrated in her hand, and she smiled when she saw it was from James: **Congrats! C u soon.**

She tapped a message back: **Thanks. Headed home to get stuff ready for you.**

At least there was one good thing ahead—the chance to connect with James.

Other than the letters they'd written for the past year, the texting and the phone calls, they hadn't seen each other since she left. He'd invited her to prom, but straddling two worlds, that of her former life and the one now, everything that was to everything that is, she realized she couldn't go backward.

Besides, James didn't know her parents like this—*her* like this—and how would he understand it? If he had squeezed into their tiny apartment, he would have seen everything. How would James have processed seeing Mom and Dad this way? To see Dad either drunk or doped up on pills, to witness her parents' disconnect. It would be as unfamiliar to him as it was to Anna.

But after all the time she'd been gone, she had to see James. He'd arrive tomorrow, and Anna had spent the last two weeks planning every hour of their day. They'd tour the city together, go to Baltimore to visit Inner Harbor and Fort McHenry, go a bit farther to see Gettysburg or Fredericksburg. Maybe even the Frank Lloyd Wright design in Alexandria—*he'd probably like that.*

"Hey, Anna! Do you have plans for tonight?" a voice interrupted.

Anna turned to see Jessica and some other girls smoking cigarettes at the edge of the school grounds. "Yeah, I have this thing with my parents."

"You could come with us if you want. We're going bowling, then to a party with one of the guys from the football team."

Anna smiled. Even though she wouldn't accept, it was nice to be offered, to be recognized, to be *seen*. "Thanks for the offer, but I'm good. Hope you guys have fun!"

She turned toward her truck and saw someone leaning against the driver's side door. Based on the height, it was a boy wearing shorts and a hoodie. She squinted as if it would clear the image, but she saw the hands tucked into the pockets, the wide-legged stance, and she knew.

She ran toward James and wrapped her arms around his shoulders. "What are you doing here?"

"Surprise!"

She pulled back but held his forearms tightly. "I thought you weren't getting in until tomorrow."

He smiled as his eyes moved over her face. "Your mom and dad called Nana, so I changed my plans. I watched with your parents, then they helped me find your truck before they left to get stuff ready."

"Aw, well, thank you for coming. It's great to see you. Go ahead and hop in." She opened the back door to place her cap on the narrow seat, then draped the nylon gown over top before climbing into the front. "All set?"

They fastened their seatbelts, and Anna backed the truck out and steered it toward the apartment as the weight of time settled between them.

"So . . . how are things? You haven't talked much lately."

She let out a long breath. How much could she tell? "I haven't had much to say, you know? Things have been so busy with Dad, then helping him get back on his feet."

His penetrating gaze cut through the fog of their separation.

"What?" she asked, glancing at him as they passed under a streetlight. "You've never held back before, so don't start now."

"I don't know. It isn't my place, and I don't know the situation anymore."

She slowed as the traffic light turned from yellow to red, and she used the break to eye him.

"It's just . . . You left New York over a year ago to care for your dad. He's retired now, your mom is about to graduate, too. You haven't told me anything about your plans, and you haven't asked about mine either."

Now it was her turn to deflect. The truck lit with a green glow, and she pressed the accelerator, thankful for her chance to focus on the road. "I've been accepted to a few colleges."

"Yeah, but where did you choose?"

"I . . . haven't yet."

"Anna, c'mon. This matters a little more than your dad. I should know."

Anna glanced at him as she flicked on her turn signal. "You're right—I know you are. Garrett already told me the same."

"All right then, let's talk college. Which schools made the shortlist?"

"I got into the University of Maryland, Towson, and a little school called Lancaster University in Pennsylvania. That's the furthest one."

His head fell back against the seat. "So you didn't apply to Syracuse?"

"I did, and I got in, but I don't think I'll accept." *I can't go back there.*

"Anna . . ."

"I know you're bleeding orange, but I don't know if it's best for me. Level with me."

"I am leveling with you, but I want you to decide what's best for you. And *only* you."

"I've got it." To soften her words, she reached toward him and ruffled his hair. "How was prom?"

"I wish you would have gone with me when I invited you."

She didn't say that she wished she'd gone, too.

"I always figured we'd go together. You know, if you had still lived there."

"Don't be so sure. Mike Rawlings might have asked me."

James blew a raspberry. "Yeah right. That stuck-up jock? He only ever noticed the cheerleaders, and I'm sure that in every dimension where Annaliese Pechman exists, in *none* of them are you a cheerleader."

Anna swatted his arm. "Be nice."

"I didn't go. I didn't see the point. I guess everyone kind of feels that way, sort of stretching things out knowing everything is about to change."

"How was graduation? You at least went to that, right?"

"I wanted to skip walking, but Nana wouldn't have it. She wanted the whole thing, so I said I'd go, but I didn't want a party or anything. She agreed to that."

"How is Nana?"

"The same as always. I swear, she reached a certain age and then time froze. She started skiing this past winter."

Anna chuckled. "Why am I not surprised."

"I believe her exact words were, 'no regrets.'"

A laugh burst out of Anna, and the world filled with color as the fog of the last few years finally faded away. For the rest of the drive, they talked about home—her *old* home, the only place that ever felt like home, but the one place she couldn't return to. It wouldn't be the same. So she held on to his every word, moving through the school in her mind, seeing the teachers he referenced, being back in the classrooms. She could picture the snow falling onto the pavement, turning it from deep black to gray, to white, the hills in the distance covered in a thick layer of powder. She could see the birds in the trees in the mild summer, the people flocking to the lakes to cool off in the heat, the kids racing outside to get ice cream or snow cones.

Home. Such a strange word to a person who lived her whole life as a nomad, a few years here, another there, the fabrics of her life pieced together like a quilt to tell the story of where she'd been. A little piece of each place living forever in her heart. For the longest time, none of it felt like home. But here, talking with James, the person she'd known the longest, the friend who had been with her and continued to stick with her despite the distance, he recognized every stitch, every scrap of fabric, and every seam.

Perhaps she had found a slice of home.

⚏

The day after graduation, Anna led James around Washington, D.C. Their plans were simple: walk the city, see the memorials, go to the Smithsonian museums, and find meals and snacks along the way. What they missed the first day, they'd see the second day. But the whole time they spent together.

The first day was warm and clear, the sun shining brightly, reflecting off the tidal basin near the cherry trees, the Jefferson Memorial, and the Lincoln Memorial. They packed turkey sandwiches, bottled water, a bag of Doritos, and a slice of graduation cake and had a picnic right there by the reflecting pool, watching the birds and tourists, talking about what was next.

"It was nice of you to stick it out with your parents last night, even though you'd rather be anywhere else," James commented, taking a bite of an apple.

"Was it that obvious?" she asked around a mouthful of sandwich.

"For me, yeah. You don't smile as much now."

She frowned, staring at the remainder of her sandwich. "Things aren't anywhere close to what they used to be."

He folded the apple core into the paper wrappings of his sandwich. "So tell me." Clasping his hands around his knees, he faced her and waited patiently.

The sandwich froze halfway to her mouth, and she sat it on the blanket, hoping the ants would keep their distance. She gazed across the water to keep from seeing James's reaction. "Dad overdosed. Back in February. I'm the one who found him." She shook her head. "I don't know when I figured it out. I didn't want to think there was something bigger. I ignored it, I guess. But he never went anywhere without that bottle of pills, and every refill, it was filled to the top."

While most people would have reached for her then, pulling her close and trying to soothe that memory away, James knew her better. "Jesus, I'm sorry, Anna." His voice was heartfelt. "Is he an addict?"

"I don't know. Mom lets it go because when he's doped up, he's easier to be around. I can't do it anymore. I hate being at home. I hate seeing Mom do whatever she can to deal with his anger or give in to whatever he says he needs. It'll ruin them both one day."

"What are you going to do now? Head to college, study journalism, and then what?"

Anna crumpled up the parchment paper around her forgotten sandwich and tossed it into her backpack. "I don't know. I guess find a job somewhere."

"I'm guessing you wouldn't want to come back here afterward."

The statement about stopped her heart, and she frowned at her realization. "This is the first time I've had to think so far into the future, when it's been up to me. I'm used to thinking in two- or three-year increments, knowing I don't have control over where it goes. This time I get to make the choices. It's weird."

"It'll be good for you. For once, it's all yours."

"It's also kind of scary. I'm excited for college, but I'm also locked in once I decide. I'll have four years in *one place*. I'll start and end college with the same people. It'll be a new experience for everyone."

"Have you decided?"

"You mean since yesterday?"

"You got to sleep on it."

Anna watched the small waves travel close to the bank. "I think Pennsylvania. You helped. Thank you."

He shrugged. "You'll do great."

The corner of her mouth tipped up. "What about you—still taking a year off?"

He rubbed his hands together slowly. "About that . . . There's something you should know."

Anna turned to face him.

"I wanted to get out of Watertown—out of New York, even—and I found something that sounded exciting."

"Which is . . . ?"

"I'm going to work up to becoming a helicopter pilot."

"Wow, good for you! That's a big change, though."

"I guess I wanted to do more? I still love architecture and I could still get out of Watertown doing it, but it would take a lot more to establish myself and I'd be in an office all the time. I tried to think of community service-type stuff. I'm also not sure I want to do the whole city thing. I've lived in a small town too long."

"How do you get started doing something like that?"

"Well . . . it's . . . with . . . the Army."

Anna turned back toward the tidal basin, stretching her legs out in front of her and leaning back on the heels of her hands. She stared across the water, listening to it splashing against the bank in front of her and watching the people out in kayaks and paddleboats. The silence stretched on as the wind stirred up the trees, rustling the leaves above them, the shadows dancing on the ground.

"Would you please say something?"

"I don't have much to say. You have a plan, you want to do it, you've already done it, so what is there for me to say?"

He bent his legs and leaned forward, placing his forearms on his knees and clasping his hands. "I wish you'd say something," he muttered.

She breathed deeply. "Why this? Why the Army?"

"Well, I *did* grow up in a military town. But it's the best way to get out, get paid, take time, and learn something I can do in other places. I can take the skills I learn there and fly life flights or something afterward. I don't have to stay in as long as your dad. I'd still like to get a degree just in case, but I want to do more than be an architect."

She was determined to halt the smile that dared to creep across her face. It was so James. Nothing would be spur-of-the-moment. He'd have a plan, contingencies, and still meet the goals he always held close. "If you're happy, then I'm happy."

A line formed between his eyebrows. "I expected a lecture."

She shrugged. "You told me to do what made me happy. The same goes for you."

He picked a piece of grass and rolled it between his fingers. "Still fighting against the war?"

She huffed out a breath. "Still hate the war, yes. I'm not protesting. It . . . wasn't for me anymore. I spent a lot of time with the people at Walter Reed, getting to know them. I think I want to focus on them."

"More like your magazine article."

Anna smiled. "Exactly like that. I want to share their stories. I want people to know the names of the service members they see in papers or on the news."

"You'll be great at it. I read your article and so did Nana. When she finished, she sent me out to buy three more copies."

"Thank you. That means a lot. And as much as I hate to admit it, you'll be great at whatever you choose, too."

He nodded, but she watched as he clenched his jaw for a moment, tearing the blade of grass into small pieces. His shoulders rose as he breathed deeply before he spoke again. "I was hoping you'd write to me this summer."

She smiled. "Haven't I already been doing that?"

"I mean through Basic and stuff. Maybe go with Nana to my graduation and help her find her way."

Anna chuckled. "I doubt she needs any guidance."

"I'd like for you to be there."

"Sure I will."

The column of his throat moved as he swallowed hard. "I'd like to see you when I can after that. Meet you at school or find a middle point during your breaks."

Anna's eyes narrowed slightly. "Meaning . . . ?"

"We've known each other a long time—been friends a long time. I'd like to go away knowing I have someone." She opened her mouth to respond, but he cut her off. "I don't mean as a friend, Anna. I've thought a lot about our last night in New York, and we definitely weren't just friends that night."

She ran her fingers through her hair. How could she explain that she'd dipped her toes into what could be because she knew it wouldn't? A few steps well beyond friendship that distance would soften over time as their lives continued separately. "James, nothing has changed. Between us."

His head jerked back. "What do you mean 'nothing has changed?' *Everything* has changed. We're adults now. We have the freedom, the space, to make big choices. We aren't stuck in the vacuum of Watertown. I think a lot of things changed that night in New York, too."

"Not for me."

"How can you say that?"

A half-truth would have to do. "I guess I saw it as a one-time thing, you know?"

Silence wrapped around them. Would he one day discover that she wasn't the girl he once knew? That too many earth-shattering things had happened in a year that she couldn't trust herself to make life decisions? And while she knew James wouldn't judge her for it, she would judge herself.

He picked at his fingers as he worked out the problem in his head. "Is that why you didn't want me to come see you? Why you haven't visited me?"

"No, I—"

"You didn't want to keep anything going?"

"It had nothing to do with that. My life here . . . it's . . . *different*. *I* didn't even want to be here—why would I want *you* to be?"

"But that night, the letters since, the phone calls and texts . . ."

Her heart stirred at his earnestness, but she pushed it away. "I want to stay in touch, I want to know what you're doing and where you are, but I don't want anything more than friendship."

"With me, you mean."

"With anyone!" She rubbed her fingertips across her forehead. "If I've learned anything over the last year, it's that I need to figure my own shit out. I need to make some decisions for myself, I need to understand what my goals are." She huffed out a breath, lowering her frustration. "When I was little, I remember thinking that when I was older, I'd have ice cream for breakfast and cookies for dinner and watch whatever I wanted on TV for as long as I wanted. Then, the first time my parents let me stay home alone in high school, I warmed up leftovers and read in my room until they came home. It's the same thing with planning what's next. I've been dreaming of this moment forever, but now that I have it, I'm freezing up and struggling to make decisions because I don't want to screw it up."

James wrapped his fingers around her hand. "All of these are things we could figure out together. I'm not asking you to give up *anything*, to *change* anything. I'm asking you to be with me in whatever way works best right now."

She shook her head. "I can't do it, James. I do care about you. I'll write to you. I'll be at your graduation and get together when it works. But that's all I can plan right now."

He pushed himself off the ground, tucking his hands in his pockets and walking to the edge of the tidal basin, staring into the water. Then, he glanced at her over his shoulder. "Is this because I enlisted? Is that scaring you?"

She stared at the blanket, unable to meet his eyes. "I don't know. Maybe," she said softly.

He huffed out a breath and shuffled his foot along the rough sidewalk, gravel and dirt crunching under his shoe. "I don't get it. It's me, Anna. I'm still me."

As much as she wanted to swallow her honesty, this time she couldn't force it down. "But I don't know if *I* am. These last few years I've been trying to figure out who I am. Is it the girl who protests and stands up for what she believes? Is it the girl who drops everything for her family? Do I believe in *anything* anymore?"

"I don't think you're different—"

"And being with you, stepping back into a life I didn't choose . . . I'm not ready for that, and I wouldn't make you happy. I wouldn't give you the support you need."

"But you would. You already do. You'll write to me and visit me—"

"Everything would be tainted by the Army. I wouldn't be like my mom, James. I wouldn't want every break from school to be flying to wherever you are, or to constantly say goodbye and count down to the next time, or never know when you're leaving or when you're coming home, and for me to mean *nothing* in the grand scheme of things because I'd be a lowly girlfriend and not a wife. I'd be miserable and I wouldn't make you happy. I'd drag you down with me."

I will not be my mother.

He sighed and watched the peaked water. "I thought after all we've been through, the years we've spent together, you'd see this as an opportunity, not something to be afraid of." He turned to face her. "Don't you think I'd work with what you need from me? Encourage you, comfort you, do everything I possibly could to make this easy on you? I would never ask you to do it on your own."

"I love that you want to promise me that, but being with you *would mean* doing it on my own. You could support from afar, but I'd have to make my own happiness, and I can't do that for another four years. Not after everything with my parents. I *can't*."

She pushed the words out of her throat, and they burned a line up from her gut. Hadn't she entertained the idea once upon a time? That someday, when she was older, established in a career, ready to intertwine her life with someone else's, hadn't she hoped it would be James? And if it couldn't be him, someone like him? Wasn't his comfort and care one reason she valued his friendship? Hadn't he proven his capabilities?

But imagining him in that uniform, picturing how the Army would turn him into something else, the possibility that he would come home a different person, those were the parts she couldn't witness. To one day learn James had forever disappeared, much like how Dad had ceased to be Dad, would be more painful than she could say.

"I'm sorry, James. I can't." She blinked back the tears as she said it, the burn spreading through her body and threatening to scorch the earth around them.

"I was so sure of a different answer," he whispered, more to himself than to her.

Her arm twitched, the urge to comfort him so instinctual, but she forced herself to stay in place, the muscles in her arms strung taut.

"I'm sorry," she whispered back.

They remained silent for a while. The squeals from the boats on the water, the rustle of the leaves in the breeze, and the tourists wandering the walkway behind them filled the void, an ambient noise driving them each deeper into their thoughts.

James finally cleared his throat, a nod signaling his acceptance. "Well, where to now?"

She swallowed hard, knowing there was no way to predict exactly where they'd go from here.

|| CHAPTER TWENTY-SIX ||

STEPPING OUT ALONE

AUGUST 15, 2005

The door's slam echoed in the early morning, and Anna walked into the apartment for the final time, grabbing her purse from its usual spot by the door. Mom was waiting, her bathrobe cinched around her waist, her hair in a rough bun.

"You didn't need to get up this early. Five in the morning isn't your thing."

Mom twisted her hands together. "I wanted to see you off."

Anna controlled her eye roll and swooped her purse strap over her head. "I could have managed."

"Please don't be cold with me."

Damming up the sigh before it could sneak out, Anna sucked in her cheeks instead, pausing to face her mother. "I'll see you at winter break."

Mom frowned. "You won't be home for fall break? Or Thanksgiving—"

"I already applied to stay. It's only a couple of days off school anyway."

"It might be nice for your dad—"

"I'll see you in December, okay?" She turned toward the door when Mom's soft voice stopped her.

"It's going to be quiet here without you. Garrett's been gone for a while, but I've always had you."

"Yeah, well, I can't be your buffer anymore, Mom. Dad's all your problem now."

She shook her head. "I never meant for things to go this way."

"The last few months kind of did me in. I guess I'm a little bitter about that."

"That isn't fair, Anna. You don't know the pressure I've—"

"Listen, I'm glad you've found something for yourself that makes you happy. But it'll never be enough when you have him holding you back."

"What would you have me do?"

Anna shrugged. "An ultimatum sounds like the best option."

"With you and Garrett both gone, he doesn't have anyone—"

Anna nodded, already able to finish the sentence. "Yeah, I know. But what does it matter when he accidentally kills himself one day? I can't be here for that. I've seen enough."

Reaching for the door handle, Anna was ready to walk, but the images of Dad's last deployment sendoff ran through her head. Instead, she reached for her mother, wrapping her arms tightly around her. "Take care of yourself, Mom, and stop making excuses for him," she whispered. "I'll call you when I'm settled."

Then she stepped out the door, shoulders pulled back by confidence, letting the door slam behind her. But once the lock clicked into place, a firm barrier between them, Anna sagged against the wall. *What is wrong with me?*

Her coldness had chilled the apartment, and icicles had grown across the foyer, dividing mother and daughter, distorting their views of the other but hopefully not permanently. Eventually, the ice would melt as the hurt ebbed and the healing began, but the scars would always remain. And even though Anna's inner child screamed to turn back, to reassure her mother that everything would be okay, Garrett and James had told her it wasn't her responsibility. This time, she would embrace that. Enough excuses. Enough empty apologies. Enough fights that never resolved anything.

Now she turned to face her independence, the call of it luring her toward freedom. It should have been what she always wanted, finally taking control of herself and her choices.

Hope is the thing with feathers that perches in the soul and sings the tune without the words and never stops at all.

Perhaps Emily still had it right.

Anna pushed off the wall, adjusted her purse, then headed for her truck. Ever since 2001, she'd been in darkness. The scraggly fingers of branches had scratched at the window, the thumps in the night kept her awake, and nightmares haunted her when she finally found sleep. But through it all, hope was what had carried her. It had perched in her soul, singing a song only she could hear, and never stopped at all.

The last two months had felt long, a slow countdown to finally leaving, and as she stepped outside of the building, she felt light for the first time in years. The air was fresher, and she filled her lungs and flooded her body with rejuvenating oxygen. She thought of all the things ahead as the bird stretched inside her, shaking loose the feathers of pain and sorrow and opening its beak to sing the first two notes of its song.

And every one—every one was for Anna.

||

Robert pulled the slats apart and watched through the blinds as Anna backed the truck out of her parking space and turned toward the exit.

He watched as she pulled onto the street and as the taillights got smaller and smaller until they disappeared from view.

He stayed by the window, recounting the last two years of her life and his own, memories that swirled in his mind like the water going down the drain, all wrapping around itself, undistinguishable and fading away slowly. Even if he reached out to stop the flood from leaving his mind, his hands wouldn't be enough to stanch the flow. It would slip through his fingers all the same.

He should have been hefting heavy boxes into the back of the truck while Anna and Katherine went inside, leaving him to hulk everything up the steps once they arrived at her college. Instead, Robert didn't know the name of the dorm or her roommate. *This isn't what a father should be.*

Robert flashed back to the first time Anna went to school, her hair in pigtail braids, the neon-colored jumper she'd worn with a striped T-shirt underneath, the bright pink jelly sandals, and the backpack too large to be worn on her shoulders. Robert's unit had offered a late work call so Robert could be there with Katherine to drop Anna off at the front of the school for her first day. Their daughter had paused before walking inside the doors, turning to wave back, blowing a kiss from her tiny hand. Katherine had watched then, tears rising in her eyes as their last baby shuffled into school, the first full day without both of her parents, the first school of what would be many. Robert had wondered who Anna would meet, what her new friends would be like, the lessons her teacher would plan, what sorts of stories she would come home to tell.

But now, he watched the wind pick up outside as the tree branches swayed, and his vision blurred until he blinked a few times. In the dark room, he rose unsteadily to his feet, then glanced at the bottles of booze on the bedside table, illuminated by the red numbers of the alarm clock glowing through them, the pill bottles silhouetted. The streetlights in the parking lot below cast a glow through the blind slats, creating horizontal bars on the walls around the room.

Somewhere over the years, he'd stopped caring, about himself, about his family. He'd leaned on medications to take away the pain and embraced the haze that followed, usually with the help of a few beers. If he could find his place in this world, he'd be fine. If he could find some sort of purpose, he'd be fine. Then he'd stop the booze and stop the pills and stop the feeling sorry for himself and eventually rise up.

Katherine sometimes referred to it as wallowing in pity, *you have to stop wallowing, Robert,* but she'd been happier, hadn't she? The pills, the booze . . . it kept him calmer, eased the fighting, led them back to some sort of balance in their relationship, and he worried what would happen when he was finally ready to not lean on the crutches anymore. Would it be like learning to walk again?

He sighed heavily and reached for the phone charging on his bedside table. The bright screen illuminated something he'd overlooked. He turned on the lamp to reveal a cloth-bound copy of the collected works of Thoreau. Anna had been carrying the book around for the last few months, usually with a pen in her hand, scratching every so often against the page. As he ran his hand over the dark blue cover, he noticed a neon pink sticky note peeking out the top of the pages. He stuck his fingers in front of it, and the well-loved book fell open to an underlined passage.

"I went to the woods because I wished to live deliberately, to front only the essential facts of life, and see if I could not learn what it had to teach, and not, when I came to die, discover that I had not lived. I did not wish to live what was not life, living is so dear; nor did I wish to practice resignation, unless it was quite necessary. I want to live deep and suck out all the marrow of life."

In the narrow margin to the left of the text, Anna had scrawled, "I love you." He closed the book around his thumb and pressed his other hand to his eyes. It was as if this were her final attempt to save him, for no one's sake but his own.

He'd joined the Army out of responsibility—a way to build a good life out of a difficult situation—and he slowly sucked out all the marrow of life. He'd built a family with deep bonds, one that endured numerous moves and clung to each other when life got hard. But somewhere along the way they stopped doing that, and it all started with the damn war. That was when the ropes connecting them all began to fray, and without anyone to hold them together, they were hanging by a thread.

One thing Robert always believed he was good at was leading. Put him in front of a platoon or company of soldiers, and he'd figure out one-on-one counselings to mentor soldiers, nip and tuck his COs and LTs to nurture them into good officers and better leaders, and step into the shit when they were in it and steer everyone to safety. Couldn't he do the same thing now? Step back into the leadership role?

Sitting on the edge of the bed, he stared out the window, seeing nothing, squeezing the book to his chest until the sky lightened to gray and the street-lights outside finally clicked off in favor of the morning sun.

⚓

Swiping a tear from her eyes, Anna was surprised to notice she was *still* cry-ing. She'd thought that driving up alone would be exciting as she considered all that was ahead for her. But instead, she felt alone, wishing Mom and Dad were in the passenger seat. Deciding on the next best thing, she dialed a number on her phone, switching to speaker.

"What up, little sis?"

A loud static filled the line. "Hey, Garrett. I wanted to let you know I left this morning. I'm almost to campus."

"You shouldn't be on the phone and driving."

"I'll be fine. Low speed limit and plenty of traffic lights."

"Still, you—"

She huffed out a breath. "While you're right, I . . . wanted to talk to someone."

"I'm sorry I couldn't be there. Being this close to deployment, I can't take leave, and—"

"Garrett, it's fine. How are things for you anyway?"

"Well, I've filled every possible area of space in my rucks and foot locker, even squeezing out the air in my clothes to fit even more."

Anna laughed. "I remember how funny we thought it was when Dad did it. What did we call it?"

"Pancaking."

"Yes! That's it." Her smile deepened as telephone poles passed on the side of the road. "So what's next for you?"

"My stuff goes to storage in a few weeks, then we're off to Fort Polk, Loui-siana, for rotational training."

"What does that mean?"

"They mimic Iraq in a training area. Explosions, real Iraqi people acting as inhabitants of the city. They say it's supposed to get us ready for the real thing. We'll see. Anyway, I'll be in the Green Zone for a year or so."

"Damn. I know it isn't like Fallujah, or Al Anbar, or Sadr City, but . . . damn."

"Some of the guys in my company have talked about the bombs and what it's like fighting in cities, but risk is always there, right?"

"If you say so . . ."

"*Anyway*, how was the drive?"

"Garrett, the traffic was *insane*. I didn't realize 695 would be so crowded so early in the morning. But I made it. The area is as pretty as the pictures, though."

"Wishing you'd made that college visit like I told you to?"

Anna pushed down her turn signal as she stopped at a traffic light in southern Pennsylvania. "Shut up. It's fine. The brochure was nice enough and Google showed me the rest. What more is there to see? All their statistics were laid out in the packet."

"I don't know. What if the dorms suck?"

"Don't all dorms suck? I thought that was half the fun."

"Hopefully they're better than barracks," he responded.

She laughed. "Aren't most things?"

"You're not wrong. What's up first when you get there?"

"I guess unload the truck and get my room set up. There's a welcome lunch, and then some tours. I guess I should get the layout of campus down."

"Ask for a map," he commented to his directionally challenged sister.

She scoffed as she turned the corner. "I'll be fine, but—Holy *shit*, that's a lot of people." She pressed the brakes to slow down as large groups crossed in the crosswalk.

"Yeah, hundreds of coeds *and* their parents. Lots of out-of-towners—"

"I'm an out-of-towner."

"Yeah, but they'll be leaving. You'll become a local."

"I should go. I should use both hands while driving so I don't accidentally run over someone's . . . *gigantic stuffed animal*." She couldn't contain her glee. "Who brings a teddy bear that size?"

"Hopefully not your roommate. All right, I'll let you go before all the shiny things start catching your attention."

"Probably a good idea." She paused for a beat. "But thanks for distracting me, Garrett. I love you. Wish you were here."

"Call me once you're settled. Tell me all about the shitty dorms that are supposed to be shitty."

"But not as shitty as barracks. Bye, Garrett."

"Later, Anna."

Anna ended the call before the road cleared as much as her mood had, ready to park her truck and unpack at her new home.

|||

The dial tone echoed in Robert's ear, and his finger hovered over the end call button, but Garrett answered before he could press it.

"Wow, you either really miss me, or you're the fastest unpacker ever."

He cleared his throat before speaking. "Uh, it's Dad."

Garrett stammered, "Oh, hey, Dad. I was just talking to Anna. What's up?"

Envy spiraled up his spine. "Your sister called you?"

"Uh, yeah. She's moving in this morning. She got to campus okay."

Robert was relieved to hear she'd arrived safely. "That's good. Glad to hear it." He cleared his throat again. "I wanted to check in. See how you're doing. You said you were leaving in a couple of months."

"Yeah, I'm actually packing for JRTC."

Robert faltered. "They're sending you there already?"

"Yep, then we should be back for a few weeks.

"Well, that's a good idea. I'm glad you can get that prep in before you go. That will take you far when you get over there." When Garrett didn't respond, Robert kept going to fill the silence. "I'm sure it will help your unit, too. Keep everyone safe."

"I gotta head to work soon, Dad . . ."

Robert sniffed. "I don't want to hold you up."

Garrett sighed. "What did you want to talk about?"

"You're leaving soon."

"Yeah, they finally got me with a deploying unit. I'll be with 1-12 under the Fourth Infantry Division. Headed to Baghdad."

"The Fourth Infantry at Hood? I thought they were at Carson."

"They stood up a brigade combat team here, kind of like how 10th Mountain has a BCT at Polk."

"Ah, got it. Well, I'm glad you could finally get on a deployment." He bit the inside of his cheek. *Did you have to say it like that?*

"I didn't sign up for Iraq."

"No, but it's where the mission is. You have work to do there that's just as important. Your platoon is counting on you to fulfill your mission, to watch their backs, and they'll do the same for you. They're your family while you're gone. And you'll get to help people—show them their former leader was a dictator and better things are ahead."

Robert pinched the bridge of his nose. "Your contract will be up next year, so if this isn't what you want it to be, you can leave and use your benefits to go to college and find something new. You can switch from infantry to another branch, try the officer track. But if the Army isn't for you, that's okay, too."

"Yeah, but you stuck it out."

"I didn't have the options you have. No matter what, you'll do fine, son."

"I'm not worried about it, Dad."

"Well, your mom and I are. But I know the man you are, and I know you'll do fine. Whatever happens. You're smart, driven, and you pack a hell of a lot of integrity."

"I didn't think you paid any attention to what I've been doing."

There it was—the hurt Robert couldn't ignore anymore. "I always am. It doesn't mean it isn't a little hard to hear sometimes, all the things you're doing while your old man can't, but I'm proud of you, son. You wanted to fight for your country, and I'm damn proud of that. But hell, I'd be just as proud if you did something else. The Army isn't the only answer."

"I'm surprised to hear you say that."

"It's something I'm working on. I have some things lined up in the next few weeks. It's time I take my own advice."

"Mom's starting a new job, Anna's off to college, you're finding a new career path, and I'm going to war."

"We're all stepping into something new."

But we're all stepping out alone.

|| CHAPTER TWENTY-SEVEN ||

NEW BEGINNINGS

AUGUST 15, 2005

Anna inhaled deeply as she put the truck in park, watching as the chaos unfolded around her. While it wasn't an extra-long moving truck and a crew of movers unloading boxes and furniture into the house, it was its own disorganized jumble. Cars parked beside her and lined up along the sidewalk in front of the buildings. Trunks threatened to fly open despite the bungee cords determined to hold them closed. Boxes filled the rear windows of minivans, small items shoved into every crevice to maximize space.

As Anna rolled back the tarp of the truck, she took inventory of the items she'd brought with her. Everything was labeled and color-coded: desk items in red, bed items in yellow, clothing in green, and small appliances in blue. All her life she'd packed as much as possible into as few packages as possible, but for some of her peers, this was their first-ever move.

"Welcome to the University of Lancaster. Are you moving in?" a volunteer asked her. The girl wore a bright yellow polo that verged on fluorescent, with "Monica" embroidered in black.

"Uh, yes. Stevens Hall. Can you point me where to go?"

Monica smiled. "You're one of the lucky ones. Your building is just at the other end of the parking lot. Here's a cart you can have. If you get lost or have any questions, wave at someone in one of these shirts." She moved on to a family a few spaces down, who were unloading boxes, large trash bags, and plastic bins.

Anna stacked the red and yellow items onto the cart first, knowing that her desk and bed were furthest into the room. Only a few boxes were left in the bed of the truck.

Images swirled in her mind—Georgia, North Carolina, Louisiana, Hawaii, New York, Maryland—move after move after move with her family. Her memories were full of overloaded vehicles, pets riding in the footwells with Anna's feet on top of the crates, the fast-food detritus that accumulated in the car after days of crossing the country. Every move was like a baptism, the chance to start over. But somewhere along the way, the novelty wore off, especially when weaving her way into tightly bonded friendships that had been forming for years before Anna's arrival.

She rolled the cart along the smooth parking lot, side-stepping as another cart spilled the contents of a box across the asphalt. The coed's parents frantically picked up the scattered items and pieces of paper as the wind threatened to lift and steal them into the late summer morning.

While rolling her cart into an elevator, Anna double-checked the university paperwork mailed to her over the summer. She found the dorm information, checked the floor and room number, then pressed the button for level twelve. It only took a moment to get high enough, and then she made her way down the hall, excusing herself frequently as she cut through groups of cackling girls, weepy mothers, and stoic fathers. She turned into her room, surprised by how much space she would have after the suffocating quarters of Maryland.

When she opened the door to reveal a small room that would only feel smaller once she unpacked, butterflies stirred to life, but this time it wasn't the nerves of the new place or the fitting in. It was the excitement to make it her own. The weight of textbooks and notebooks and her laptop would soon strain the desk. Maps and art and pictures and letters would cover a good deal of the concrete block walls. Her clothes would soon fill the closets that flanked the entrance to the room. And all of it would be hers until *she* chose to move off campus.

Already, the bed to the left was made up neatly. Linens in a bright blue and pale green paisley pattern smoothly covered the mattress, the comforter almost to the floor where Anna spied running shoes, a pair of high heels, and snow boots tucked underneath. Her roommate had stacked her drawers atop each other and placed them behind the partial wall in the closet space. A glare caught her eye, and Anna realized it was the reflective strip of a PT jacket. She'd know it anywhere. *Great . . . Still stuck with the Army thing . . .*

There weren't many things on her roommate's walls yet. A flag Anna didn't recognize hung high on the long wall beside the bed. A blue, four-pointed star with a yellow circle in the middle stood on a white field, and pairs of red and blue waves stretched between each point to the corners of the flag. A red design was stamped above the star and looked like an eagle with a man's head.

A thin piece of pale lace fabric hung below it. Two layers of strings crisscrossed above the bed's headboard with a series of colorful photos clipped on with small clothespins.

Anna pulled the boxes off her cart, wanting to bring everything up before unpacking. It's what Mom always said—figure out what you have before you decide where you'll put it. It had guided her well over the years of various kitchens and dishes, reminding herself what all they had before determining where each piece would go. Anna paused as she reached for the first box, preparing herself for the memories contained within them. She shoved the red boxes under her desk and placed the yellow boxes in the small space between headboard and desk, neatly lining up the corners. As she grabbed the cart and headed for the door, it opened.

The girl who entered had a big smile on her face. "Hi, I'm Zahra. You must be Anna."

Anna and Zahra Bashir had exchanged brief emails after getting their room assignments. Anna already knew she was from Michigan, her parents were originally from Iraq, and that she would major in nursing. She didn't have any pets but always wanted a big dog. She enjoyed running, reading nonfiction, and gorging herself on carbs of any kind. She was a neat-freak and promised Anna would never have to remind her of the mess. She *hadn't* mentioned joining ROTC. Then again, Anna didn't want to share anything about her dad's Army experience either. For once, she wanted to be just Anna.

"Hey, it's nice to meet you in person," Anna said.

"You want any help with your stuff?"

"I just have to run down for the last of it."

Zahra's eyes followed the lines of the room. "Aren't your parents grabbing the rest?"

"Oh, no. I came by myself."

Her dark eyebrows rose. "Wow, I wish I could have done that. The whole gang is here: my mom and dad and even my grandmother. I appreciate their help—I mean, look at all they did!—but it was a little tight with all of them in here. I sent them for a walk around the pond to see the swans."

"Smart."

"You want a hand?"

Anna shrugged as a smile pulled at the corners of her mouth. "Sure, if you want to."

❚❚

Boxes quickly filled the little bit of floor space, and Anna and Zahra squeezed through as they unpacked the yellow boxes marked "Bed." As Zahra talked about her summer and her hometown, Anna listened silently, nodding along as if she truly understood those experiences. But what could she say? She was from nowhere, had no idea what "hometown" even meant, and her life had been hell for two years. All she could do was rely on memories from what felt like a lifetime ago.

From the bottom of the cardboard box, Anna removed her teddy bear, smelling the funnel cake in the air as she looked at it. Then, she removed the newest addition from the box—another teddy bear wearing a T-shirt that said "Mother Rucker," which she and James bought together when she attended his graduation.

"You got a boyfriend?"

Anna shook her head as she stared at the bear. "It's not like that."

Zahra raised an eyebrow. "If you say so."

While James was finishing up his training, Anna knew it wouldn't be long until he was joining a unit somewhere in the United States in preparation to deploy. It seemed like everyone was deploying nowadays. Garrett wasn't far behind. James and Anna continued to share letters, and she'd written him one for every day he was in basic training (having heard plenty of stories from Dad about how mail was appreciated). She hadn't heard back often, but he'd managed to call her once. He'd told her about the girlfriends who sent their soldier cookies or treats and how the soldiers got into trouble for some of them.

Her thoughts and unpacking were interrupted by a trio speaking loudly among each other in a language Anna didn't know. The shiny dark hair of the woman and the sparkling brown eyes of the man were Zahra's. An older woman draped her head with a scarf much like the one attached to the wall above her roommate's bed. All three continued to speak quickly until Zahra raised both hands and shouted over them. "Can we please speak English?"

All three instantly quieted and faced Zahra.

"Anna, this is my mother, Noura, and my grandmother, Shera. Back there is my father, Tavi."

The older woman, Shera, turned her eyes toward Anna and a smile crinkled the corners. "Ah, we get to meet the room sharer."

"Room*mate*, *Sabta*."

She waved Zahra's words away as if they were a pesky fly. "Same thing, my *sahra*." The woman approached Anna, standing in front of her. Lines were carved around her mouth and eyes, a few on her forehead. Her hair was tied back and hidden under her scarf, which was tied loosely under her chin. The woman took Anna's face in her hands. "You will bring out the best in each other and give each other belonging. I am sure of it. I am sad to leave her, but I am delighted to give her to you." The woman patted Anna's cheek then stepped back, looking around the room. "Let us make this space yours."

Yours.

Anna paused, looking at the bare walls.

"By 'us,' she means you, too," Zahra said with a smile.

And with that, a family that wasn't Anna's helped her unpack her room, just as had happened in all the places she'd lived before, strangers entering the home to help, then leaving as friends.

Zahra removed bubble wrap from a desk lamp. "You have to be the only person in this building who packed like they were moving to a new house."

Anna looked at her color-coded boxes and the growing mound of packing paper and bubble wrap. "Really? I think I packed well."

"That's what I mean. Too well."

"Zahra, leave her be," Noura said.

"I've moved a lot," Anna muttered.

"Really? How many times?"

Anna took a moment to count them in her head. "I think this is number seven."

A pencil rolled off the desk as Shera's head turned. A strip of paper fluttered to the floor as Zahra stared.

"You've moved seven times in eighteen years?" Noura asked.

Anna shrugged. "I know people who moved more." She busied herself with unpacking shoes and placing them neatly under her bed, trying to avoid the look of motherly care that Noura gave her.

Tavi, Zahra's father, was the only person who didn't speak much. He hung back from the women, but Anna didn't miss how he watched his daughter. As Noura put Anna's clothing on hangers, Tavi hung them in the closet according to his wife's instructions, but he swallowed hard as the pile grew smaller, knowing his time with Zahra was winding down.

His subtle care touched Anna. For a moment, she wished she'd invited her parents to help her move in, to let Mom dote on her and to let Dad show how he'd changed. What would it be like for them to see her off in this moment? To say goodbye knowing that their touch helped set Anna on the right path for another first day of school? Instead, she shook her head, packing the memories into a cardboard box and shoving them under the bed. It wouldn't make a difference though as sadness wrapped around her heart.

Zahra and her grandmother organized Anna's desk. Shera straightened the lamp and carefully lined up the edges of the books while Zahra placed extra paper, pens, and pencils into the top drawer.

"I'm curious about your flag," Anna said. "I've never seen it before."

The corner of Zahra's mouth tilted up as she turned and looked at the wall, folding her arms against her chest and leaning against the desk. "It's the Assyrian flag."

"I thought your family came from Iraq."

"No, not Syrian. Assyrian," Noura said. "Our people span areas in Iraq, Iran, Turkey, and Syria. Over the past century, many Assyrians and other ethnic minorities have been plagued by genocides in the Middle East. We were fortunate enough to come to the United States."

"Dearborn has a huge population of people from all over the Middle East, so in some ways, we always felt at home," Zahra added.

"And the head scarf?"

"It is a *yalkhta*. I wear mine always, but Zahra does not," Shera said, focused on her task at the desk.

"I used to wear it daily," Zahra argued.

"And now you save it only for church."

"We discussed that it's her choice, *Yemmah*. She's a woman now," Noura interrupted.

Zahra tore the tape from another box as she whispered, "We can talk about it later." She pulled out a book with a wooden cover and ran her fingertips over the relief. "Wow, this is beautiful. What is it?"

Anna snatched it away. "It's nothing." She slid the book under her pillow.

"First a bear, now a book. Hmm . . ."

Anna reached for another box and Zahra joined her. "Let's finish up before dinner."

II

After dinner at a local pizza place, they walked back together, Tavi and Noura walking with their arms around each other, while Zahra looped her arm through Shera's, Anna trailing behind. The time was winding down, and Anna could see that Zahra's family was struggling with the goodbye. As they hugged in the hallway, Anna sat at her desk and looked out the window.

"It was wonderful to meet you, Anna," Noura said, as she entered the room a final time. "We won't forget you either." The older woman folded Anna into the kind of hug only a mother can give, arms wrapped around, so much love exchanged in the simple gesture. "Take care of our girl." Then they waved goodbye.

"It's crazy to think this is it," Zahra said as she closed the door. "They're just walking away and we stay here."

"There's something my mom always used to say when I left for school in the morning. 'Do good and be good.' We won't always make good choices, but hopefully we can do some good."

"I don't feel like I'm old enough to be here," Zahra said with a laugh. "Do you?"

Anna stared at the ceiling as she considered it. After two years of taking on the role of caregiver, she no longer felt like a child. She knew bone-deep exhaustion, the twitching muscle of false positivity, the chest-tightening tension of the unexpected, and those weren't things most people her age felt. But was she prepared to be completely on her own?

The burn of tears began, but Anna blinked them away. "In some ways I do, but then I think about life after college, this great big unknown. It's scary." Anna pulled at a loose thread on her bedspread.

"Well, the good thing is, you don't have to figure it out today or on your own." Zahra dropped onto Anna's bed, and then nudged her with an elbow. "You have me. Anything we need to figure out, we can do it together."

And that was it, wasn't it? Anna could make choices that concerned *her*. Not pleasing her parents. Not pasting on a smile when Dad announced he had new orders. Not grinning and bearing it when the vacation they'd been planning had been canceled due to another deployment somewhere in the world. Not being careful where she stepped in case she set off one of Dad's tripwires with protests or unwanted opinions. Now she could step fully into herself.

And after all this time, it was exactly what she needed.

‖ BIBLIOGRAPHY OF KEY RESOURCES ‖

Associated Press. "Afghan Blast: Accident or Attack?" *CBS News*, February 14, 2004. https://www.cbsnews.com/news/afghan-blast-accident-or-attack/.

"Behind the Battle." *Florida Sun Sentinel*, April 7, 2002. https://www.sun-sentinel .com/news/fl-xpm-2002-04-07-0204040755-story.html.

CNBC Television. "Last American plane flies out of Afghanistan." August 30, 2021. https://www.youtube.com/watch?v=4fWDjcAPDCM.

CNN. "President Bush Speaks at VMI, Addresses Middle East Conflict." April 17, 2002. https://transcripts.cnn.com/show/se/date/2002-04-17/segment/02.

Dickinson, Emily. *Emily Dickinson's Poems As She Preserved Them.* Edited by Christanne Miller. Cambridge, Massachusetts: The Belknap Press of Harvard University Press, 2016.

Finnerty, Ryan. "How Fort Drum was changed by 9/11 and 20 years of war." *WRVO Public Media*, September 9, 2021. https://www.wrvo.org/regional-news/2021-09-09 /how-fort-drum-was-changed-by-9-11-and-20-years-of-war.

Geibel, Adam. "Operation Anaconda, Shah-i-Khot Valley, Afghanistan, 2-10 March 2002." *Military Review* (May-June 2002): 72-77. https://www.armyupress.army.mil /Portals/7/Army-Press-Online-Journal/documents/Geibel-v2.pdf (accessed October 15, 2021).

Marquis, Christopher. "The World; How Powerful Can 16 Words Be?" *The New York Times*, July 20, 2003. https://www.nytimes.com/2003/07/20/weekinreview/the-world-how-powerful-can-16-words-be.html. McGirk, Tim. "Battle in 'the Evilest Place.'" *Time*, October 27, 2003. https://web.archive.org/web/20061125015259 /http://www.time.com/time/magazine/article/0,9171,526466,00.html.

NBC News. "America's Longest War Ends As Final Flight Leaves Kabul." August 31, 2021. https://www.youtube.com/watch?v=4b3gVocEopY.

NBC News. "The Today Show." September 11, 2001. https://www.youtube.com/watch ?v=0uiSq0jfVpM.

Nuthall, John. "Syracus hosts forum on war in Iraq." The Daily Orange, March 20, 2003. https://dailyorange.com/2003/03/syracuse-hosts-forum-on-war-in-iraq/.

Rivera, Geraldo. "At Large with Geraldo Rivera." Fox News. November 23, 2003. https://www.youtube.com/watch?v=ylz13t8L7mM.

‖ GLOSSARY ‖

ACS   Army Community Service; enhances community readiness and resiliency through free programs and assistance.

BCT   Brigade Combat Team

BDUs   Battle Dress Uniform, the green, black, and brown duty uniform of the time. These were phased out in support of ACUs, or Army Combat Uniform, which utilized a digital pattern.

Butterbar   Perjorative term for a second lieutenant.

CIB   Combat Infantry Badge; bestowed upon infantrymen who engage in combat. It's similar to the CAB, or Combat Action Badge.

CQ duty   Charge of Quarters, a type of guard duty.

CO   Company Commander

DCUs   Desert Combat Uniform, the tan and brown uniform worn during deployment during the early years in Afghanistan.

FOB   Forward Operating Base

Fobbit   A pejorative term for someone deployed to a combat zone but who doesn't leave the FOB.

IED   Improvised Explosive Device. These were often referred to as "mines" during the early years of the war.

JAG   Judge Advocate General; military lawyers.

JRTC   The Joint Readiness Training Center, a training location located at Fort Polk, Louisiana (now known as Fort Johnson).

K2   Karshi-Khanabad Airfield

Klick   A military word for "kilometer."

MEB   Medical Evaluation Board

MEDEVAC   Medical evacuation, usually by helicopter.

The net   The company's forum for radio communications.

PCS   Permanent Change of Station; also known as a military move.

POA   Power of Attorney

PT   Physical training; scheduled exercise first thing in the morning, usually with the unit.

QRF   Quick Reaction Force; a group of soldiers meant to be on standby and able to respond within moments.

ROTC   Reserve Officers' Training Corps; associated with colleges and universities. Cadets take military science courses and will commission as second lieutenants in their service branch of choice upon graduation. Cadets are nondeployable while enrolled in ROTC, but can serve in the National Guard or Reserve components while in school.

RPG   Rocket Propelled Grenade

SITREP   Situation Report; a quick rundown that offers all the information needed to understand a specific situation.

TBI   Traumatic Brain Injury

TF   Task Force

TOC   Tactical Operations Center; the command post and hub of all communication.

UXO   Unexploded Ordnance

WMDs   Weapons of Mass Destruction

‖ ACKNOWLEDGMENTS ‖

When I first decided to write this book, I never knew it would take me more than five years to produce. I spent that time researching, drafting, editing, more researching, more editing, adding passages, deleting passages, and writing a whole 130,000-word book. Which I then chucked out to start from scratch. But it was worth it. I finally have a finished product I'm proud of, and it's thanks to a village of people.

I'd like to thank the Combat Studies Institute out of Fort Leavenworth's Operational Leadership Experience for all the work they do recording and cataloging various service member experiences to record a history of the War on Terror. The interviews and records available online helped shape Robert's narrative for a more authentic story. I'd also like to thank Douglas Schmidt, historian for the 10th Mountain Division, for his insight on the early days of Fort Drum, New York, in the aftermath of the 9/11 terrorist attacks.

The experiences of Robert post-injury would not be what they are without the support of Kat and Brandy, who dipped into their own painful histories to share details of PTSD, adjustment disorders, and life after injury. Both have done amazing things since for the wounded and PTSD communities.

Joanna Guldin-Noll, thank you for your time and efforts in reading an unknown number of terrible drafts but believing I could be better (and never telling me how bad they actually were). Thank you for pushing me to keep going after repeated rejections and for always challenging me to do more, think more, make this story more. My thank-yous will never be enough for all the help, friendship, and confidence you bestowed upon me.

I owe loads of appreciation to my various critique partners for their cheerleading, coaching, and critiquing that injected more color and life into this story: S.L. Astor, Amanda Krieger, and Krysann Sedberry. None of you could possibly know how much you shaped this story, but having your creative minds working in the background made it better. Your emotional support was the icing on the cake, and your gentleness with my vulnerability was welcome.

I would never have ended up here without the urging of Ania Ray, who kindly invited me to my first prickle with Quill & Cup, a community of female writers. The Hedgie House opened its doors to me in November 2021, when I was on my second version of this story. Once they showed me to my room, I knew I'd never leave. I'd especially like to thank Allison, AKA, Bestie, Danni, Elizabeth, Elzevera, Feya, Lilian, Jamie, Jenn, Katy J., Mandi, Nicole, and Sam C., who I spent countless hours writing with. You all are destined for great things, and I can't wait to follow you on that ride.

To my beta readers, Amanda K., AKA, and KP Palmer: Your encouragement and affirming feedback gave me the courage to say, "I can do this!" Thank you for being so supportive and for being a part of my life.

Alan Foster taught me the basics of journalism when I spent a year in his classroom. Even when I left campus to start my career, he followed my journey. Thank you for the nudge to write a book and to grasp my potential. I hope I didn't fuck it up. And to my rockin' newspaper editor and journalism mentor, Chuck Cannon: I miss you always. You taught me more than you'll ever know.

None of this would have been possible without the Sunbury Press team, who also happen to be my coworkers. Lawrence Knorr accepted my submission quickly, and as my trusted boss, I knew this book would be in good hands. Thank you to my editor, Gabrielle Kirk, for her thoughtful feedback and suggestions and guiding this story to the best version of itself. It wouldn't be what it is without her. Thank you also Crystal Devine for her design of the interior of this book and Caitlin Audrey for her work on the cover.

To my mom and dad: Thank you for taking the time to read all the silly stories written on that old Compaq computer when I was growing up. You supported my writing when I was so young and nurtured the idea of doing something with it. You never tried to direct me toward a career path you felt was "more worthwhile" and always supported my love of all things creative. That support made me want to follow my dreams as I got older. I hope to do the same for my children.

To my children: You made me want to do something that makes me proud, to show you that you should follow your dreams, no matter the criticism or the fear. I hope that whatever you choose to do when you grow up, you choose something that truly makes you happy. I promise to support your endeavors as my parents did for me. Remember: I don't care what path you choose in life, just be kind and love what you do.

To my loving husband, Frank: Words cannot express how grateful I am to have you in my life, to be my partner, to walk with me on our journey. You knew how long I dreamed about publishing a book. During my moments of self-doubt—and there were many—you consistently urged me to keep going when the doubt closed in suffocatingly close. Thank you for offering your rare free hours to read pages, to correct inconsistencies and historical errors, and to listen to me fret about people who only existed in my own mind. So much of our experience is wrapped up in this story, little bits sprinkled throughout, and I'm grateful to you for allowing me to lean on what I know and for your thoughtful input from the service member perspective. But mostly, thank you for wiping away the tears after my numerous rejections and celebrating with me when I finally did it. I love you always.

And finally, to the military families: You live a life that's often hidden from view, and even what we present to the public isn't always the whole story. Thank you for your strength. Thank you for your love. Thank you for turning unfamiliar communities into homes. Thank you for being the guiding hand for your service members and your children. Thank you for being bold.

‖ CONTENT WARNINGS ‖

This book contains offensive language, descriptions of graphic violence, descriptive combat engagement, substance abuse on the page, and references to disability that some may find offensive. These come from the mindset of the characters in the story and are not condoned by me.

SARAH is an editor and award-winning journalist originally from Lancaster, Pennsylvania. She has written for *The Fort Polk Guardian*, an Army installation newspaper, winning three state awards for her work. Her work has appeared on Mission: Milspouse, MilSpouseFest, Military.com, The Homefront United Network, We Are The Mighty, SpouseBUZZ, and Army News Service. She formerly consulted for MilitaryOneClick (now MilSpouseFest) and devoted five years to content editing for Army Wife Network (now Mission: Milspouse). A five-time Pillar Deployment Retreat speaker, she has a heart for military spouses and frequently volunteers in her military community.

When she isn't busy writing novels, she works as a book editor for Sunbury Press, specializing in military fiction and nonfiction across multiple imprints. She loves to read, stitch, or play the piano. You can find her on Instagram @keepitpeachey, where she shares about military life, books, writing, and editing, or on her website, keepitpeachey.com. She's from southern Pennsylvania currently moving around the world with her active-duty Army husband and their three military kids.

The Whispers of War is her debut novel. Two more novels will complete the *Scars of War* trilogy.

www.ingramcontent.com/pod-product-compliance
Lightning Source LLC
Chambersburg PA
CBHW011404010726
47495CB00009B/2778